I0728260

TOUCH: A TRILOGY

Touch: A Trilogy

A.G. Carpenter

Falstaff Books

Touch: A Trilogy Copyright © 2017 A.G. Carpenter

All Rights Reserved.

Cover Design - www.RockingBookCovers.com

Print Book Design - Susan H. Roddey, Clicking Keys
www.ClickingKeys.com

This is a work of fiction. All characters and events portrayed in the contained works are fictitious or used fictitiously. All rights reserved, including the right to reproduce this book, or portions thereof, in any form.

ISBN: 978-1-946926-13-5

For more information on this or other Falstaff Books publications, visit www.FalstaffBooks.com.

Published by Falstaff Books
Charlotte, North Carolina
Printed in U.S.A

CONTENTS

For those who are haunted, for those who carry scars.
For those who struggle with monsters, within and without.

OF LIPS AND TONGUE

PROLOGUE

On a hot July day Mama went cracked, locked my sisters and me in the tool shed, and lit us up like a Christmas tree.

Addie, being the eldest, tore apart every shelf looking for something to break down or pry open the door, but Mama was cleverer than that; all that was left was the jars of turpentine and cans of old paint and the stacks of paper meant for the church fundraiser. Smoke curled in around the edges and every board was lined in shimmering red. I knew right then we weren't getting out.

But Addie was determined and she pounded on that door 'til her knees and elbows and hands were bloody and raw. She looked at me and sighed, her strength all used up. "Sorry, Del."

Then she melted like a birthday candle in the summer sun.

The baby went quiet. She was small, just brought back from the hospital on Tuesday, and thin 'cause Mama didn't want anything to do with her. The smoke and the stink from the burning paint were just too much. She coughed once or twice, put her fist in her mouth, and got real heavy in my arms.

The tin roof screamed as the heat curled it up off the nails. Or maybe that was Mama still mouthin' off about how she was saving our souls from the fire that burns without ceasing. With both my sisters dead and the tool shed in flames, I lay down on the dirt floor and waited to die.

I should have known I wouldn't. With seven generations of witch on Mama's side and rumors of unnatural behavior in Daddy's family, more than a few relatives had the Touch. A shame it couldn't have laid as heavy on Addie and the baby as it did on me.

The roof peeled back far enough I could see sky and the smoldering branches of the hickory tree overhead. My clothes drifted away like leaves, the blackening fabric glittering with fire on every edge. Voices drifted in over the heavy breath of the flames. I wondered if the neighbors had come to see what was going on.

One of the roof beams gave way and a length of chain Daddy used sometimes to pull Cousin Larry's car out of the ditch tumbled onto my arm—

red hot iron laying imperfect circles all down my neck and shoulder. Jesus save me, it hurt. I screeched bloody murder and the door shook, like someone was throwing themselves against it.

I'd sucked in another breath to scream when the door busted in and two men stomped through. The wet burlap bags over their heads steamed as the fire sucked at them. One of them kicked the chain away from me, yanked me up, and crashed out into the yard.

Bouncing over one broad shoulder, I could see it wasn't just the neighbors who had come to see what was going on. The fire volunteers had their truck pulled up in the middle of the vegetable garden, loops of canvas hose spilling everywhere. Sheriff Mains and his deputies had their white and black cars with the gold star on the door parked in a glittering string down the driveway. All of 'em trudged back and forth across the mangled remains of the tomato plants and squash vines.

My rescuer plopped me down on the grass, hard.

"Ow."

Beneath the sooty edge of his sack, Mr. Feller's eyes got round as saucers. "Fuck me blue." He snatched his makeshift firecoat off and ducked his head. "Beg pardon, Del. I... uh..." His face reddened, sweatier than usual.

The crowd around the edge of the yard stirred. Maybe they realized something unexpected was happening. Or maybe they were just hoping for a glimpse of my charred body.

I sat up and pulled my hair forward to cover as much skin as possible. I wasn't charred except for that one arm, but I sure was naked. My cheeks burned with embarrassment. The fire hadn't killed me, but the thought of sitting out here with all my private bits exposed for God and everyone to see came close.

Sheriff Mains shoved a few of the volunteers aside. "What's going on?" He stopped, face going white and stiff as a new painted fence as he laid eyes on me. "Delaney." His mouth worked for a moment. "You hurt?"

"My arm," I said. Lumpy with blisters, it had split open, leaking yellow and blood.

"Jesus." He snatched one of the volunteers by the arm. "Get the antiseptic cream and some gauze."

"And a blanket," I said.

The man just stood there, his mouth flapped open like a catfish on the dock.

"Antiseptic cream and gauze," Sheriff Mains bellowed. "And a blanket." He waved a hand at the rest of them. "You. Keep the crowd back."

The volunteers scattered and Mains dropped to one knee beside me. Pulled his hat off and rubbed the sweat from his face with his sleeve. "Delaney."

"Yes, sir."

"Your mother..." He paused, eyes buzzing like a fly in a jar. "She came at us with a shotgun. Blew a hole the size of my head in the side of my car." Annoyance cut a hard edge through his words. "We didn't have a choice."

I rested my hand on his knee to show there were no hard feelings. "I expect you didn't."

His mouth crinkled up. "I'm sorry, Delaney. Real sorry."

They all were.

The doctor at the hospital and the nurses who changed the bandages on my arm 'til the skin finally closed back up said so every day. "How you doing, Delaney? So sorry about what happened." The neighbors who came to the burial service when we put the baby in the ground just looked sorry—standing around in their church clothes, hot and awkward.

The psychiatrist who met with me every day used different words, aiming to sound like he wasn't pitying me. Or scared. But even if they sounded different, his words meant the same thing.

"Real sorry about what happened, Del."

It didn't stop them from declaring I should be put in an institution for observation. For my own safety, they said. Special needs, they said. Just until I was old enough to live on my own, they said. But I knew they didn't ever mean to let me out. Folk that don't burn can't be let loose in society.

In case they turn like Mama did.

Magic and madness don't always run hand in hand, but there's a reason they call it the Touch. No one wanted to see what would happen if I went cracked. So I stayed in the asylum like they told me to and figured on never seeing the world beyond the gate with my own eyes again.

Then one day The Salesman woke up.

CHAPTER 1

Mrs. Hayney's dog finds the bodies.

Fella worries a shoe off with a bit of foot still melded to it and brings it back to the yard. She ain't happy about it, not when she thinks it's a piece of trash he's dragged up on her porch. And then she sees those little bones that make up a person's toes. Five chalky shards and a couple of burned toenails poking out between the charred rubber sole and flaky vinyl upper, and she goes all hysterical.

Screams like she was the one been burned up, staggering 'round and flapping her hands. "Jesus. Sweet Jesus." She pauses, takes another look at the shoe, just to assure herself that it ain't full of mud and sticks.

It isn't.

She pats the sweat off her upper lip. "Jesus," she says again.

Bored with all the screamin' and takin' the Lord's name in vain, Fella snatches that shoe back up with a wag of his tail.

"You give that back." Mrs. Hayney picks up her broom and whacks at him, but he scampers out of the way. Running back and forth across her yard and around the old pickup truck with the weeds growing through the fenders. Him bouncing and wagging his tail and enjoying the chase, and her sweating and beating the hell out of him with her tongue. "Just you wait 'til I get ahold of your flea-bitten ass. Give it. Give it!"

She gets him cornered against the fence next to the propane tank and wallops him good. He drops the shoe with a yelp.

"That's a good Fella." She motions him back toward the trailer. "Go sit. Go on, now." And he might be interested in that shoe, but he don't like the thought of the broom slapping him again so he slinks off.

Mrs. Hayney stares at the remains, her round face dimpled with thought. Sure as hellfire she doesn't want to touch it, but leaving it there will only bring the dog back for more mischief. She unties her apron, lays it over the top, then adds an upturned bucket and a couple of bricks to weigh it down. A nudge with her foot and it don't tip over so she trudges back to the trailer.

There's a leftover biscuit on the stove and she gives that to Fella. Eyes the beer in the fridge, but gets a glass of water instead before picking up the phone and dialing the nine one one dispatch. Better to not be sipping on a Koors if she's going to be telling stories about body parts lying in her yard.

"Nine one one. What's the nature of your emergency?"

"My dog's gone and brought part of a body into my yard."

"When you say part of a body..."

"It's a foot." She's breathing heavy into the phone.

There's a momentary pause on the other end. "Give me your address and we'll send a deputy out right away."

"Thirty two oh six Grisham Road. And he'd better bring some gloves. It's all burnt-like."

The deputy is a young man by the name of Collins—thin as a rail, with a head that seems just a touch too big. He takes one look at the ashy shoe and the splintery toe-bones inside and starts sweating harder than Mrs. Hayney. "Do you know where he found it?"

"Probably back in those woods." She waves her hand at the trees and underbrush that squeeze up against her fence.

"Okay." He coughs and wipes his mouth on the back of his hand. "We'd better go take a look."

"Nuh-uh." Mrs. Hayney crosses her arms over her chest, firm. "If I wanted to scare myself green, I'd already a gone."

Collins glances at the woods, touches his sidearm nervously. "But..." He takes another look at her, eyes like ice chips under her lowered brows. "Yes, ma'am."

It's clear he ain't happy, clambering over the rusty chain-link and pushing and picking his way through the pokeweed and brambles. But he's the one with the badge on and somewhere the rest of that body is waiting for him.

He swallows hard, rethinking his choice of words. Human dead are still just dead. Not really any different than finding a possum splatted in the road. Aside from size and such, that is. But whatever is waiting back here is just dead.

The carpet of old leaf on the ground is thick; his boots raise the sour-sweet dust of rotten beech and oak and maple. All prickly as hell and there's brush snagging at his ankles and the backs of his hands.

He stops and wipes his head and neck to dispel the tickle of sweat creeping across his skin. Wonders if he should just go back and call the dispatch for a proper search party. He glances back the way he's come, toward the brighter green edge of the woods. Maybe just a little farther.

He ducks under a low branch and pushes on. It doesn't take a dog to catch the scent of the corpses. Blood and burned and rotting.

It takes a moment longer to spot the hand, crusted fingers curling up through the leaf mold under an elderly beech like a diseased coral fungus.

"Oh," Collins says. "Damn." He tiptoes closer, pulls his hat off and takes a few deep whiffs of the hot felt and sweat. It's a damn sight better than the stink rising in the woods.

'Cause it ain't just the one body.

There must be at least a dozen.

CHAPTER 2

Twice a week, I go down to the psychiatrist's office and read some of this books for an hour. It ain't much. I mean, it isn't much, but it helps me find new words and remember ones that aren't the small magic of the many tongues around here.

This is the first thing my Daddy taught me.

Words are thoughts and everyone has them. Has the power to set them loose in the world like raindrops on a field. Small magic and easy to ignore from them... from those who don't have the Touch. But words seep in and take root, and with them, thoughts. You take in the words of others and you take in their thoughts and let them shape you.

The words aren't always bad. Some say witch and maybe I can see that's just a name that means those whose words come like a storm. But some say it and they mean one who hurts or steals things that shouldn't be taken or loses all sense of right in the world. If I slip and let that word take root, I let that thought take root, too.

The small magic of many tongues. Because the power is in the repeating.

So twice a week for the past ten years I've come down to the psychiatrist's office to read and teach myself new words and new thoughts. Reshape myself and my world into something that ain't... that isn't fearful or hurtful.

I start by copying down another line of a poem to take back and memorize. The medication makes it hard. Both the writin' and the memorizin'. Magiprex they call it. Not very clever, but I suppose that makes it easy to know it's not for blood pressure or seizures or something. It's supposed to keep the Touch asleep and me and everyone else safe. Mostly everyone else.

I can't say for sure if it do or don't.

Does or doesn't.

Small magic spoken by many tongues.

What the Magiprex does do is make it hard to write. I can still walk and sit okay. There's only a little slur when I talk, but getting my fingers to hold the pencil and make letters I can read again later is slow business.

So, I start by copying another line of a poem. Maybe two if they is short.

Maybe two if they are short.

Then spend the rest of my time reading. The days in between I work to memorize what I've written down so far.

I got one done and repeated enough I haven't forgotten yet. "Going Blind" it's called. Written in German, but there's a book here with it translated because I can barely hold the words I learned when I was small, let alone grasp the power of a second tongue. The poet has a girl's name in the middle, but the psychiatrist says that's because he weren't Baptist like most folks around here so he was named after the mother of God. Still makes me laugh, though maybe I shouldn't. One of the attendants tells me that Delaney is supposed to be a boy's name.

But Rilke's poem is good, especially the last verse.

She followed slowly, taking a long time,
as though there were some obstacle in the way;
and yet: as though, once it was overcome,
she would be beyond all walking, and would fly.

It took me weeks to get it all written out and twice as long to get the words tucked away in my head and my heart where they could take root. Now I can say it every hour if I want.

The psychiatrist likes to ask me why I pick the ones I do. Sometimes I tell him I like the way they sound or maybe because it made me cry the first time I read it. We both know I see myself in the Bohemian's verses. Waiting for the moment when I, too, will fly.

Today I'm copying a piece of Wallace Stevens. The title is in French, but it's about a woman named Ursula and a garden. I've got the first lines done. Just two more to finish the first verse.

Ursula, in a garden, found
a bed of radishes.
She kneeled upon the ground
and gathered them,
with flowers around,
blue, gold, pink, and green.

I smooth the paper flat and stick my tongue out, concentrating. Blue. Gold. Pink. And. Green.

Fold the paper up carefully and put it in my sweater pocket. I'll work to memorize it later.

There's another stack of books on the table. History and poetry mostly. The psychiatrist has his hobbies, and his books are usually of one kind or the other. One I started last week is about movies and has lots of pictures of women with big eyes and short hair, and men with mustaches and neat suits.

There's a scuffle of feet in the hall outside and voices sharp with curiosity and fear.

"How many have they found?"

"First reporter said a dozen, but now they're sayin' undetermined."

"You think that means more or less?"

"It don't matter how many. It's the how that's creepy. Burned up."

"And hid."

The words get indistinct as they move down the hall. Not that it matters. I've already seen what they're whispering about. Probably know more in that seeing than they do. More than they ever will.

I glance at the clock. There's still a half hour left for me to read, but the scars on my arm are prickling. Something is happening—something more important than finding new words.

So I get up and walk to the door, covering my hand with my sweater sleeve out of habit before I touch the knob. Ain't much in the institution that's made out of iron, but I've been stung by it enough to take precautions now. Of course, it makes it hard to turn the knob, but after a few tries, I get it far enough that the door swings open.

The nurses are all gathered around the TV at the end of the hall, eyes wide as they listen to the nasal cadence of the reporter.

"The bodies were found this morning in a wooded area off Grisham Road. It is uncertain at this time how many were discovered and a larger search is being conducted as we speak. It has been confirmed that the bodies appear to have been burned, though the coroner can't tell us if that was the cause of death. Sheriff Tolbert says they do not have any suspects in mind at this time. He did confirm a team from the FBI is being sent in to assist in the investigation."

"It's the Salesman," Lettie says breathlessly. "It's got to be."

"That's just a folk tale." Mrs. Pratt starts nudging them away from the TV. "And you know better than to start bringing that up in here."

"That's right." Malcom grins. "*She* might hear you."

Too late I realize I would have been better off staying in the office. *She*, with that tone and leer, means something I don't need to hear. *She* means The One That Don't Burn. *She* means me.

Too late I start to back down the hall.

Lucia turns and sees me. "Ah, mi dios." Her hand flutters from forehead to heart, marking herself against evil.

They all shuffle and mutter. The small magic of many tongues falling like raindrops on thirsty ground.

I let my hair fall forward around my face and stare at my shoes. Cling tight to words that are not as dark or fearful and remember that my voice is a storm.

As though, once it was overcome,
she would be beyond all walking, and would fly.

Mrs. Pratt is the first to move. She puts her arm around my shoulders gentle and firm, walking me back down the hall toward the office. "Del. Aren't you supposed to be reading?" She holds her arm out, the little gold watch clasped around her solid wrist sparkling even under the fluorescent light. "Only quarter 'til one. Why don't you come back in and sit? What are you reading about today?"

"The silent era of film."

"Sounds fascinating," she says in a tone that is false as her smile. She guides me back to the chair in the office. "Now you go ahead and read for a while longer. I'll come get you when it's time to go back to your room."

"Yes, ma'am." I nod and bend my head over my book, pretending to look at the words until she closes the door behind her.

The scars on my arm are prickling worse than ever, and I rub at them through the sweater sleeve. Something bad is awake. Something that burns and though I know this has been coming, my heart beats faster.

I close my eyes trying to catch a glimpse of the thing the nurses called The Salesman, but I can't see anything except the black-red insides of my eyelids.

I feel it though, laying my hands flat on the table and touching the trembling little threads that lead away across the hours and minutes. Seeing the thing that waits as surely as I saw Mrs. Hayney peering into her fridge and wishing for a beer. Feeling it in my skin intimately as Collins' puffing and sweating as he crept through the underbrush looking for the dead girls.

Distant. Quiet. And hungry.

It's evil in way that cannot be ignored.

"Just you wait," I whisper. "Just you wait."

CHAPTER 3

They've only uncovered the first few corpses, marking the others with little flags at either end so they remain undisturbed.

Percival stands with his arms crossed on his chest, looking for a pattern in the placement of the dead. Five of them form a loose ring, but without the proper spacing needed for the points of a pentagram. The other seven are scattered farther away and to no discernible purpose.

He settles on his heels next to one of those they've uncovered. The smell is intense—like roadkill that's been tossed in a fire pit. Decay and ash meld into a sick-and-sweet stink. He coughs and stares at the shifting leaves overhead until his stomach calms.

His ears are ringing. An echo of screams raises the hair on his arms despite the sweltering heat, voices pleading or cursing or threatening. None of them went easy or quiet. All the soft and thin bits have burned away completely, leaving cheekbones and teeth exposed, while the arms and legs are still a mass of flesh. A hot fire, but not sustained.

He licks his fingertips and holds his hand out over the corpse, fingers spread wide as though trying to catch hold of something.

The roar of fire fills his head. Flames. Flames in the rough shape of a man. And an iron box, red hot and unforgiving. Fingertips torn open to the bone. Heat pouring into lungs as thick and deadly as water.

"Agent Cox." The voice, and the hand on his shoulder, are firm, dragging him back to a reality that is less terminal, if not markedly more pleasant. Martinez, jacketless, and sleeves rolled up as a defense against the smothering heat, tucks his sunglasses into his shirt pocket. "Pretty grim out here."

"Oh." Percival jerks up onto his feet. Staggers for a moment until he rests hands on knees and gulps a few breaths paying no mind to the stink. His tongue is gritty, the taste in his mouth not unlike having licked an ashtray. "Yeah."

Martinez looks at him, eyes narrowed in a way that might be concern. "You all right, Cox?" He sounds irritated, but Percival has learned that Martinez doesn't say anything he doesn't mean, even if his tone seems to say different.

"Yes. Mostly." He coughs, spits out a mouthful of bile, only just remembering to turn toward the middle of the clearing so he doesn't splatter it all over the body.

"You saw something." Martinez may not be easy to read, but there's a tremor in his voice. If it's some unnatural thing that has resulted in the dozen bodies, he'd rather not know. All the same, he cannot help but ask.

"Flames. And a big metal box with handles on the end. Like a steamer trunk. Or a sort of casket."

"Huh." He nods, shoulders relaxing. "That makes sense."

"It does?" Percival wipes his mouth on his hand.

"Turns out these woods are part of piece of property that used to be a crematory."

"Used to be?"

"The facility's still there, but closed down. Apparently they'd been taking money for services and burying the bodies in a pit. Gave the families back urns filled with cement and wood ash."

Percival frowns, rubs fingertips against his palm, the skin still unnaturally warm. "I don't think it was a person that did this."

"Maybe not. Can't hurt to check them out." Martinez looks at him again. "You sure you're all right?"

"Just the heat. And this." He waves a hand at the corpses. "This is a little over my head."

"Yeah." He claps Percival on the shoulder. "Don't worry. You'll get used to it."

"You think so?"

"Or you'll go nuts and blow your brains out like Harold did." Martinez touches the gun holstered on his belt, reflexive. "I'd suggest talking to someone if it gets that bad. Harold didn't."

Percival nods. The others on the team won't even talk about their previous teammate. Aside from some veiled references to new talent. But Martinez mentions him with clockwork efficiency. And invariably as some kind of cautionary tale.

"I'm sorry," he says. "About Harold. That's a difficult thing. Finding a friend dead like that." He looks at Martinez hesitantly. Might be he's overstepping his bounds. But he ain't a Sensitive for nothing.

For a moment the hardness leaves Martinez, the practiced disinterest fading into grief. And gratitude. The relief that someone knows how raw he feels inside. He rubs his forehead. "Sometimes, I think..." He clears his throat and puts the sadness back inside, like folding a handkerchief and tucking it into a pocket. "We should go."

Percival licks his lips. "Sure." The back of his neck prickles. The sense that someone is watching him comes so strong he glances over his shoulder. He sees nothing but the silver beech trunks and green leaves.

He stuffs his hands in his trouser pockets. "Sure."

CHAPTER 4

Hannah Gartner and her daughter, Tammy, stare through the screen door sullenly. "If you from the papers, we ain't got nothin' to say."

Martinez holds up his badge. "FBI, ma'am. We just want to ask you a few questions."

"If I say no?"

"We can go down to the sheriff's office instead."

"Huh." Her lip curls back from her teeth, but she shoves the door open anyway. "Our show's on in a few minutes so better make it quick."

"Yes, ma'am." Martinez squeezes past without hesitation.

Percival follows more slowly, nodding to Mrs. Gartner and Tammy as he passes between them. He resists the urge to straighten his vest, smooth the hair curling across his forehead, and go wait by the car. The back of his neck is prickling with more than the sullen glare of the women, righteous in their anger. *There is something important here.*

The interior of the house is rank with the smell of yesterday's breakfast and fifty years of cigarette smoke. Mrs. Gartner plops back down on the faux leather couch, crosses her arms over her chest, and glares at them. "Well?"

Percival hesitates. He's still wobbly at the knees, but asking for a chair seems to be pushing their luck. He looks around the room, trying not to stare. Trying not to judge, though it's hard with the piles of newspaper, clothes hanging from a piece of rope strung up behind the couch, the TV mumbling incoherently at his back.

"We heard the sirens." Tammy settles on the other end of the couch. A younger, paler version of Mrs. Gartner—equally large, but somehow lacking the solidity of her mother, if not the spite.

"That's right." Martinez pulls his notebook out of his shirt pocket. "A number of bodies have been found. Local authorities tell us the property is yours."

"Those woods are big," Mrs. Gartner says.

"Yes, ma'am. But this would be the area near Grisham Road and the Hayney property."

Her eyes get narrow, but she nods. "That's ours all right."

"Have you seen or heard anything unusual out that way?"

She shrugs. "Can't say that I have." Pokes her daughter with a hard finger. "What about you? Seen anything, Tammy?"

Tammy purses her lips, shakes her head so hard she jiggles from head to toe. "Don't leave the house much."

Martinez makes a note. Or pretends to. "You mind if we look around outside?"

"Go ahead. Ain't much out there." Mrs. Gartner's lips get thin. "Most of it been sold to pay for court fees and such."

Martinez glances at Percival. "You want to come?"

"I'll wait here." The house is stifling, but the back of his neck hasn't stopped itching. A sure sign there is something else to be learned here.

"All right." He looks at the two women as he tucks his notebook away. "I'll be outside if you need anything."

Percival shoves his hands in his pockets and does his best to look awkward. "Could I get a glass of water?"

For a moment it seems as if they won't relent, but Mrs. Gartner lets her breath out in a huff and pokes her daughter again. "Get him a glass of water, Tammy."

"I don't—"

"Did you hear me?"

"Yes'm." Tammy shuffles through a doorway hung with strings of wooden beads, and there is a rattle of glass, the thump of a cabinet door. After a moment, she returns with a glass of water. "Here."

"That clean?" Mrs. Gartner asks, sharp-like.

Her daughter squinches up her face 'til her eyes are hid and her nostrils are flared wide, but she goes back into the kitchen without a word. This time there's more noise and a few words that make Percival's ears get hot.

"Why don't you take a chair while we wait?" Mrs. Gartner motions to a battered recliner nearly hidden under a drift of newspaper inserts.

"Thank you." He moves some of the paper off the seat and sits down gingerly.

"How'd they die?"

"I'm sorry?"

She waves a thick hand toward the door and the sun-covered yard beyond. "You said there were bodies found out there near Hayney's place. How'd they die?"

"I really can't..."

"They was burned, wasn't they?" Tammy shuffles back in from the kitchen. "Here." She hands him a new glass of water. "No spit in that one."

"Thank you." He takes a quick sip, then rests it on his knee.

"Were they burned?" Mrs. Gartner leans forward, eyes keen under the flabby slope of her forehead.

"Yes, ma'am."

"I knew it." Tammy grins triumphantly, and there's a brief hint of her mother's strength in her wide shoulders. "Always seem to forget that John-John went to prison for not burnin' nobody."

Percival nods. "Once people get an idea about you... it's hard to change their mind." He takes another sip of water, then a deep breath while he waits for the anxious tremble to fade.

Mrs. Gartner looks at him like she's weighing him with her eyes, tallying up each word he's said and putting it into one column or another to find his worth. Finally, she nods. "That's the truth."

A cockroach skitters out of the pile of paper he just moved, running back and forth. Tammy raises one broad foot and brings it down hard. "Hah." She rubs her shoe on a greasy patch of carpet. "Got 'em."

Percival takes another swallow of water. "I'm not sure..." He pauses. It's against protocol to discuss the details of the case with civilians, but that itch won't go away. "I think it may be something other than human behind these bodies."

Tammy sucks in a breath. "The Salesman."

He fidgets as the itch turns to an outright sting. "Salesman?"

"That's just a town legend," Mrs. Gartner says, but there's a thoughtful tilt to her head.

"Maybe someone is trying to imitate it. What sort of story is it?"

"A love story," Tammy says quickly.

"A ghost story," her mother says a breath behind.

"Like *Romeo and Juliet.*" Tammy drops onto the couch. "Only not everyone dies."

"Can I hear it?" Percival wedges his free hand under his leg to keep from scratching the back of his neck raw.

"I'll tell it." Mrs. Gartner settles back against the couch cushions with a nod. "The Salesman. Story is he came to town after the war."

Percival frowns. "The war?"

"Between the States." Her lip curls up in a way that says *Yankee*.

"Of course. So, this was over a century ago."

"That's right." She smooths the front of her dress, fingers circling the floral pattern like she's tracing a map. "He came to town after the war, and the menfolk all disliked him for bein' a Yankee. And because he was handsome. But the women, the young ones anyway, they liked him plenty because he had a big metal trunk full of ribbons and glass brooches that looked almost like real gemstones. And because he was handsome."

"But there were only one girl that caught his eye." Tammy has one hand pressed over her heart. "That was the mayor's daughter, Emily."

Her mother fixes her with a stare as sharp as needles. "You goin' to let me tell this or not?"

"Yes'm." She presses her fingers to her mouth to keep any further words trapped inside.

Mrs. Gartner turns her attention back to Percival and smiles apologetically. "There was only one girl that caught Jack Green's eye. The mayor's daughter, Emily. She was fairer than most with a gentle disposition, and when she turned her affection on Green, the other young men in town were... unhappy.

"But Emily and Jack were in love and you know how that is. When you love someone down to the soles of your feet and out to the tips of your fingernails, love them with every breath and in each heartbeat... when you love someone like that, it's all you see.

"They would meet at the edge of town and walk through the woods. It was said if you followed them, you might see them dancing. Or hear laughter bloomin' under the spreading limbs of the beech trees." Mrs. Gartner licks her lips and fumbles with the pack of cigarettes on the arm of the couch. Lights one and sucks at it 'til the stale air in the house is gray with smoke.

"Jack Green asked for Emily's hand, but her daddy would have none of it. Told him he'd be damned before he let his daughter marry a Yankee. And Jack, some say he swore to have Emily any way he could, and some say he didn't say anything. But everyone agrees those two young folks eloped. I guess maybe they thought once the thing was done Mayor Decker would have to go along with it.

"But that wasn't how it went." She takes another drag at the cigarette. "They came back to town, and Decker dragged his daughter back to his house and locked her up in the cellar. And a mob of menfolk grabbed Jack Green and shut him up in the trunk he used to carry his goods around in."

Percival swallows hard. "The box."

"That's right. They pulled it out to the edge of town and stacked it all around with wood and lit it up." She stubs out the butt of the cigarette and smooths her skirt across her knees. "He screamed and begged them to let him out, but even if they'd wanted to, the flames had hold of that iron trunk and there weren't no getting it back.

"So then he cursed them. Swore they would pay for what they had done. No matter how they might hide their daughters, he would find them and pull them into his heart of flames and ash. One hundred brides to replace the one they had stolen from him. And having uttered that curse, Jack Green died."

Silence fills the room. Percival has seen things that would turn many a head white with fear, and heard plenty more that are even worse. But this story has a weight to it. A heft in the words that says more of them are true than aren't.

He takes a drink of water. "Who else knows this... story?"

"Everyone," Mrs. Gartner says. "They say if you walk out in certain parts of the woods late at night you can see him standing out there under the trees. Waiting."

"Waiting for what?"

She shrugs, arms folded tight across her chest and a distant look in her eye.

There's a knock at the door and Martinez steps back inside. "I'm all done out here."

"You find anything?" Tammy smiles, hard and satisfied and knowing that whatever he might have expected to find, it wasn't there.

"No. Like you said, there's not much left." He looks at Percival with a curious lift in his eyebrows. "You ready to go?"

"I think so." He stands up, sets the empty glass on the edge of the cluttered coffee table. "Thank you for the water. And the story."

Mrs. Gartner nods, reaching for her cigarettes. "You be careful now." Hard to say if she means it, already pointing the remote at the TV on the opposite wall.

As Percival steps onto the front porch, the belligerent tones of a daily exploitation talk show rumble through the house. He takes a deep breath, waiting for some deeper signal. His stomach quivers, but the nausea isn't supernatural.

"Are you all right?" Martinez is waiting at the bottom of the stairs, eyes hidden behind his sunglasses.

"Thinking."

"Yeah. You've got that look."

"Look?"

"Like you're about to figure something out."

He waits, hoping Martinez is right, but all he feels is confused. "She told me a story. A ghost story about a town legend. It sounds right. A man murdered for marrying the wrong woman."

"Swore revenge in some terrible way?"

"Yes." Percy rubs his fingers through his hair. "But she said it happened after the war."

"That's more than a century past." Martinez unlocks the SUV. "It happens though."

He's unsettled by the seriousness of it. "Maybe. But this... if it were true, wouldn't there be others? Before now?"

"There might be records. I'll put in a request to the sheriff's department. See if anything turns up."

"Okay." Percy slides into the passenger seat. "Like *Romeo and Juliet*, only not everyone dies."

"What?" Martinez pauses, one hand on the gearshift.

"Nothing." He slouches down in the seat and covers his eyes with his fingers. The itch on the back of his neck is gone, but his head is pounding. "Not everyone dies," he mutters.

What happened to Jack Green's true love?

CHAPTER 5

The squat brick building that houses the sheriff's department cannot handle the influx of new investigators, and the FBI team has been shuffled into the basement of the old library on the other side of the parking lot.

Percival huddles on a folding chair, nursing a cup of coffee, and waiting for the aspirin to kick in. The musty air isn't helping, thick with the smell of old cardboard and older books, which is just cool enough to make him clammy in the humidity. He tried walking around outside, but the heat is stifling and the glare off the cars makes his vision blur.

He knows this pain. The growing warning that there is big magic near. The knowing doesn't make it any easier.

"Here." Martinez sits down next to him and holds out a Styrofoam bowl. "You'd better eat something."

Percival's stomach clenches at the thought, but food will help if he can keep it down. He digs the spoon down to the bottom of the bowl and scoops a bite of noodles into his mouth. It's better than expected, and he takes a few more bites as the nausea lessens.

"I asked for the files on any similar murders. Burned corpses dumped in the woods." A pause while Martinez takes a bite of sandwich. "A few came back, but none like these. Mostly exploded drug labs. One that was an attempt to cover up a shooting."

"What about less recently?"

"The sheriff's calling in his predecessor, Bill Mains. Apparently he's more familiar with the older stuff. Bit of a history buff, too." He stands up. "I'm going to grab a Coke. You want something?"

"No, thanks."

"Okay. The machine's down the hall to the right if you change your mind."

Percival nods. He's more concerned with finding out what happened to Jack Green's wife and unborn child.

There's a rustle of conversation near the door and an older man approaches, sits down in an empty chair without being asked. "Bill Mains." He sticks out his hand and Percival shakes it.

"Agent Percival Cox."

"Percival." Mains laughs. "That's a mouthful."

"Yes, sir." They both sit back in their chairs, sizing each other up. Mains is a broad shouldered man with a broader belly. Square features and light hair that's turned white over the years, and blue eyes that tend to shudder when he's nervous, rolling left, then right under the deep overhang of his forehead. They're shifting back and forth as he studies Percival.

Where Mains is squared off and blunt, Percival Cox is tall and thin with strong features that hint at cultural roots that are something other than white. Strong enough for Mains to forget to act like he ain't a bigot.

"Cox," he says. "That Jewish?"

Percival shrugs. "Maybe. Did they tell you why I wanted to talk to you?"

"Tolbert said you had some questions about older cases."

"About Jack Green. About The Salesman."

Mains lets out a hard breath. "The Salesman is just a legend."

"But Jack Green and Emily Decker are not."

Mains' eyes flit back and forth while he squares his shoulders, like a dog posturing at the gate. "Those names are long dead and best left that way."

But Percival leans forward intently. "Emily Decker. Emily Green, I suppose. She was carrying a child when her new husband was murdered, wasn't she?"

"Twins." Mains wilts at his answer. "About nine months after Green disappeared, she had two boys. Then up and moved out of town with them."

"So any descendants live elsewhere?"

"Sort of." He glances over his shoulder, then leans forward. "One of the many-great grandsons came back and married a local girl, Lydia Stiles."

"And they had children?"

"Three daughters. But Lydia... she had the Touch, you know? And maybe there was something in Green's blood. But their girls were strange. And Lydia, she had always been off. They fought about everything seemed like. Then one winter he just disappeared. Got tired of it all maybe." There's a twist to his mouth that says that ain't likely the truth, but he doesn't dare guess what is.

"Anyway. That next summer Lydia just went wild. Locked her three girls up in the shed outside the house and set the damn thing on fire."

"So they're dead."

"The eldest one. And the baby." He licks his lips and his eyes stutter back and forth again. "But Delaney... She came out naked as a baby bird, but untouched. Save where a bit of hot iron fell on her arm."

Percival blinks as his headache stabs at the back of his eyes. "She didn't burn?"

"Not a hair on her head." He shakes his own. "Kind of a shame, too. She ain't got no family left. And losing all of 'em like that left her queer in the head."

"Then she still lives around here?"

"They keep her over at the institution. Greenhaven. Better for everybody. She don't have to worry about food or anything and that way..." He pauses. It is one thing to question a man about his heritage and blame it on curiosity if offense is caused, but only a fool will voice a slur about those with the Touch or the Sense. "Better for everybody."

"And the curse?"

"You mean that nonsense about Jack Green swearing to claim a hundred young women? That's just superstition."

"But the bodies they've found do seem to mimic the story. Could be a copy-cat thing." Percival stirs the last few swallows of soup around the bottom of the bowl. "Could be there's some unnatural thing out there that's been called up by someone with a grudge."

Mains looks at him hard. "Delaney, you mean."

"You said she was queer in the head."

"Not the killing kind of queer though." He smooths his hair across his forehead. "Not the kind to hold a grudge like that. She's a sweet girl. Strange but kind, you know?"

Percival hesitates, but the ache in his head is insistent. "I still think I should talk to her."

"Sure." Mains shrugs. "Be careful though."

"I thought you said she was harmless."

"I said she were kind. But she don't burn, boy. You don't take a thing like that lightly."

"The Touch, you mean."

"That's right. And Delaney, she's got a way about her. Magic of the tongue they used to call it. You keep your questions in mind when you talk to her or you'll find yourself answerin' hers. Smilin' at her just because she's smilin' at you."

Percival nods. "I'll be careful." He stands up, holds out his hand. "Thank you for your help."

"Certainly. You need anything else, you folks know where to reach me."

"Yes, sir." Percival tosses the last of the soup in the trash and goes out to the hall to look for Martinez.

He's standing at the far end of the hall with the other two members of their team—Elliot, tall, pale and cool, and MacKenzie, dark and intense. From the way Elliot is slicing the air with her hand, they have new information. And with MacKenzie standing with her hand resting on her gun, it isn't good.

Percival hesitates, but this is his team. Avoiding them only aggravates the situation. He slips his hands into his pockets and walks down the hall, trying not to hunch his shoulders as the tension pushes against him like a physical thing.

Martinez, who has blessedly embraced the role of sledgehammer, nods his head. "Mains tell you anything useful?"

"He said the story about Jack Green and Emily Decker was true enough, but maybe not the curse part. And they have a descendant. Delaney Green."

"She seem like a source for all this?"

"Hard to say without talking to her. Mains said she was crazy, possesses the Touch, but is too kind to be murdering anyone."

Agent Elliot makes a sour face and taps her fingernails on her belt buckle. "Does Miss Green own a pickup truck?"

Percival shakes his head. "I doubt she owns much of anything. She's been staying at some sort of mental institution since her mother tried to kill her when she was young."

Elliot props her hands on her hips and looks at MacKenzie. "We've had a couple of witnesses down on Grisham Road say they saw a truck out there. A couple of guys carrying something back into the woods." She raises an eyebrow and glances at Percival, daring him to challenge her on it.

"Descriptions? Or any idea who they might be?"

"A general description and a few possibilities based on those." She frowns. "I thought you were dead set on this being unnatural."

"I'm certain it's connected to the murder of Jack Green. But that doesn't mean it can't be two guys with a sick sense of the world and a pickup truck trying to make a name for themselves." He forces his shoulders to relax. "We've seen that happen before. Someone trying to make some legend come to life. Or seem like it has."

"True." MacKenzie sounds grudging, but she nods. "I take it you want to talk to Miss Green?"

"Yes. Just to be certain." Percival tosses his hair out of his eyes trying to seem casual.

"All right." MacKenzie nudges Martinez. "Why don't you go with Cox? Agent Elliot and I will go run down this list of names."

Percival looks at Martinez. "Are you ready to go?"

"Just need to get my jacket and the file on the bodies." He strides back toward the makeshift office space.

Elliot fidgets. "We should probably be going, too."

"Be careful." Percival tries to smile, but his head is still screaming big magic.

Her lips twist, finally producing something like a grin. "Of course, Agent Cox. You too."

He waits until they've left before leaning against the wall of the corridor. The enameled bricks are cool to the touch and he presses his forehead against them, trying to ease the ache.

"You're still in pain?" Martinez sounds irritated, only thinly veiling his concern. He has his jacket slung over one shoulder, two file folders tucked under his other arm.

"It's getting better." Percival straightens. "The soup helped and I think the aspirin…"

"But your head is still sounding a warning."

He nods. "Like a damn bell."

"For us or them?" A twitch of his head indicates the already departed Elliot and MacKenzie.

"Us, I think. But that's not unusual. Running into someone with the Touch."

Martinez looks doubtful. "And you're certain you're up for this?"

"It won't get better with waiting." He pries himself away from the stability of the wall. "What's that?"

Martinez hands him the second folder. "File on Green's mother and the dead sisters. Thought you might want to look through it. Maybe give you some insight into this woman before you're sitting nose to nose with her."

Percival balances the folder on one arm and flips through the reports. The words sting his fingertips. Two young females, age 14 years, and 12 days. Burned alive. Evidence of prior neglect.

He closes the folder gently and forces himself to smile at Martinez. "Thank you. I'm sure this will help." Despite his best effort, his voice trembles.

Martinez hesitates, knuckles showing white as he clutches his jacket—like he wants to hit something. "You let me know if this gets too big for you. We can call in backup."

"Sure." Percy follows him down the hall. Mains' words are whispering 'round the inside of his head.

She don't burn, boy. You don't take a thing like that lightly.

CHAPTER 6

The operational director at Greenhaven, a spindly woman with the unfortunate name of Drowner, is displeased about the request to speak with Delaney Green.

And curious.

She purses her lips, tinted with a lipstick that is too harsh for her bland coloring, and paces around the office, pausing to straighten a book on the shelves and return a folder to the organizer on her desk—reasserting the severity of the room.

Percival does his best not to draw away from her as she moves closer. His sensitivity is running high, and the combination of her disapproval and curiosity is both cold and sharp.

"This is a murder investigation," Martinez says.

"I appreciate that, Agent Martinez. But you must understand that Miss Green is not an ordinary patient. Exposing her to outside elements..." Her gaze slides across Percival. "I don't know how she will react to the presence of other magic. Even the paltry energy of a Sensitive could trigger an adverse reaction."

"She's medicated, yes?" Percival lets some of his irritation bleed out, the immovable quality he showed with Mains rising to the surface.

"Yes." Ms. Drowner looks back and forth between the two of them. "But this is a young woman with the Touch. When we first tested her, the results indicated she was likely a Power, not just aware of the flow of the world around her but capable of influencing it. Of changing it."

Martinez shrugs. "Most with the Touch test that way."

"It's not unusual, but since then... her tests bring back zero results."

"The medication is effective."

"Or there is no way to calculate how strong she is." She says it with a little smile.

Martinez raises an eyebrow, his face so carefully controlled that Percival knows he wants to call the whole thing off. But also acknowledging he isn't the one who will be sitting face to face with Delaney Green.

Percival rubs his forehead. "Is she difficult to handle?"

"Not at all." Ms. Drowner says it automatically.

"Unstable?"

This time she's slower to answer, reluctant to concede any point that will let him press his request to see Green. "She's odd, if that's what you mean. Always writing down these little bits of poetry and trying to memorize them. Or sitting out in the garden and staring at the sun."

"I need to talk to her."

"Why?" Ms. Drowner leans forward, eyes wide in a face that seems too small for the rest of her head. "I can't see how she can tell you anything of use. Not about these… murders."

Percival straightens, like a cat stretching—languid, but dangerous. "I'm afraid I can't discuss the particular details of our investigation."

Martinez coughs. "That's correct. We can ask to speak with her and we don't have to tell you why."

She blinks at them, pulls her carefully tailored sweater tighter across sharp shoulders. "Fine. I'll have the orderlies bring her down to one of the front rooms. You may have to wait a few minutes while our psychiatrist finishes up his afternoon session."

"Psychiatrist?"

"He'll want to supervise the interview."

"No." Percival shakes his head. "I'll speak with her alone."

"It would be better…"

"Alone," he says firmly.

"We will have to observe the conversation."

"From outside the room."

Her lips grow thin, but her curiosity is strong. "All right." She stands up, twitches her skirt to settle the folds. "Wait here."

Martinez waits until the door shuts behind her. "I hope you know what you're doing."

"Even if the medication hasn't dulled her, I don't pose a threat."

"That you know of."

"True." He stretches, easing the tension in his neck and shoulders. "Better to know now, than later. And better me than you."

"Yes." Martinez nods. "But you'll be careful."

"And you'll be right outside." He says it not just as a reassurance, but because it is reassuring. Martinez's concern, although smothering, is better than the distance and unsubtle whispers from his previous assignment. Even Elliot and MacKenzie show more concern, albeit in a backhanded fashion by making it clear they considered their previous Sensitive partner an integral part of the team.

Before he can get any more sentimental, Ms. Drowner returns. "We're ready." She motions toward the door. "If you'll follow me."

Percival clutches the folder with his notes on the investigation and the initial photos of the corpses to his chest as they walk down the hall. It doesn't seem to be a horrible place, as far as institutions go. This part of the building has lots of open rooms, and the patients are all dressed in real clothes. But there are still crisp tiled floors in neutral colors and blank walls that stretch out like a tunnel. And they have to pass through a locked door as they enter the next wing.

An orderly and a man in a worn suit wait outside one of the doors. Ms. Drowner flops her hands back and forth as she makes introductions. "Agent Cox. Agent Martinez. Dr. Everley."

Percival nods, certain his palms are too sweaty to shake hands.

Everley reaches out and flicks his fingers against the folder. "Do you intend to show Miss Green something in there?"

"Only if it becomes necessary."

"May I see?" Everley's curiosity is duller than Ms. Drowner's. He is concerned more with Miss Green's health and less with finding out about the investigation.

Percival hands him the file and waits while the psychiatrist glances through the photos.

"You are either naïve or clever, Agent Cox." He passes the folder back with a dry grin.

"You think these will upset her?" He has already mulled over the wisdom of showing charred bodies to a young woman whose sisters were burned alive.

"No. But if that's what you're here to talk to her about..." He pauses.

Ms. Drowner is canted over, trying to catch a glimpse of the photos and a snatch of the conversation. She straightens back up, smooths wispy hair back from her face. "You acknowledge that we bear no responsibility for anything that might happen in there?"

"Yes, ma'am." Percival drawls the words, touching his forehead in mock sincerity.

She scowls, but waves her hand. "All right."

Dr. Everley nods. "Good. We will be in the next room. There is a two-way mirror, but we won't be able to hear you. The orderly will stay outside the door. In case you should need assistance."

"Thank you." Percy walks a few steps down the hall as they file into a different room. Then back. Breathing slow and putting his memories to rest.

The orderly watches him with a twist in his mouth that might be amusement. "Ready, sir?"

"Yes." Percy tucks the folder under his arm and opens the door before he can change his mind.

CHAPTER 7

The moment what I see in my head and what I'm seeing with my eyes come crashing together is always disorienting. Things that were distant and spirit-like take on solid shapes and real smells and sounds. I blink and press my fingers against my cheeks as they grow warm.

I've seen Percival Cox enough over the years to have gotten familiar with the shape of his mouth and the strong curve of his nose. I know that his skin has more color than mine and his hair has thick waves that curl into his eyes.

But it's different seeing him in the flesh, so to speak. It's not just because I'm fond of him. If it were Martinez closing the door behind him, I would still be nervous with the adrenaline pushing hard with every thump of my heart.

The dream is real, and encountering it as real is difficult. Sorting it out is difficult too—the things I know because they're in my head and those I know because I can actually see them. The things I feel with my own hands. The things I feel with Percy's hands. For a giddy moment I'm wearing my own skin like an oversized shirt, staring out through my eyes like slits in a mask. But I pull back up to the surface and lower my hands to my lap. This is real. This is now.

If Percy notices, he doesn't let on. He takes a moment to look around the room, making special note of the two-way mirror, then settling into the empty chair on the other side of the metal table in such a way that he sits squarely between me and those watching us. "Miss Green?"

"Yes, sir."

"I'm Agent Percival Cox."

I smile at him as friendly as I can manage. "Nice to finally meet you."

"I just have a few questions and then..." He pauses. "Finally?"

"I've seen you before. In dreams." I look at him intently, hoping for a flicker of recognition. "Don't suppose you remember that, though."

"Well." He stops again. Does he?

"They're pretty much all the same. You. Walking in the woods. Sometimes it's daylight, but most times it's night out. You come down the deer path between the trees, and I'm standing there, waiting for you. And I'd swear you were lookin' for something, but you never see me. You just pass on by." My throat gets tight just thinking about it.

"Yes." He fidgets, picking at a tear on the corner of the file folder lying between us. "I remember those dreams. I don't remember you."

"Because you never see me." Another smile tempers the impatience in my voice. "But this is different. Not a dream where I can only stand and watch you and wish."

"Wish?"

"Wish to be a tree so that I could brush your hand as you pass. Wish to be the breeze so I could whisper in your ear. Wish to be moonlight so I could lay softly against your lips."

His heart beats fast and a knot forms between his eyebrows. Is this some sort of test? Sheriff Tolbert and ex-Sheriff Mains have both warned him I'm tricky. Seductive, Mains said. For certain he notices I'm watching him close, still smiling like a fool. "Are you teasing me, Miss Green?"

"Maybe." I toss my hair back over my shoulder. "I don't get many visitors, you know."

"I know." The surge of sympathy is genuine enough. He hopes it is, anyway. Surely I haven't twisted his future already. I haven't even touched him. He clears his throat. "Do you know why I'm here, Miss Green?"

I sigh, but it's no surprise he's straight to business. "They say The Salesman has come to claim his revenge."

"A dozen bodies in the woods," he says firmly. "Burned in such a way that folks around here are telling me stories of some long gone carpetbagger who tried to marry the wrong woman."

Energy flickers through me and I lower my gaze, knowing otherwise he'll see the change in my eyes—the brown one turning dark as midnight, the green one bright as spring grass. "He weren't no carpetbagger, Mr. Cox."

"No?"

"He worked an honest trade and didn't take advantage."

"I suppose you'll tell me next he isn't gone either."

That makes me laugh and I lean forward across the table. "You don't have to play games, Mr. Cox. I'll answer your questions plain."

"I can't be sure of that."

"Fair enough. But I'd guess you have to ask me anyway. So why don't you, and stop trying to lead me around to telling you what you want to hear."

Percy licks his lips, flustered and not knowing exactly why. Except for maybe they've told him I'm a witch. And in spite of himself, he thinks I'm pretty.

The thought makes my cheeks get hot again. In spite of my teasing, I was not expecting him to see anything other than my plain cotton dress and fraying sweater or the vague twitch in my hands that is the ever-present shadow of the Magiprex.

He thinks I'm pretty.

I tuck my arms against my chest and rock gently to dispel the rush of emotion.

He clears his throat. "Is there any truth to the stories?"

"True that my somethin'-great granddad was a salesman from parts north of here. Not a real Yankee like yourself, but close enough for those that were angry about the way the war turned out. True that he fell in love with the Mayor's daughter, Emily Decker, and they eloped against her father's wishes and their better judgment." My scars are itching and I rub them slowly. "True too that when they came back to town my somethin'-great granddaddy was snatched up by a mob and burned alive in the metal chest he used as a sample case."

"And the rest? The oath of revenge?"

"That's just fear. Rumor. Guilt."

"Guilt." He frowns.

"You know how when you do somethin' wrong? Not the accidental things, but somethin' you know is wrong but you done it anyway?"

His hand, still resting on that file folder, trembles. "Yes."

"That eats at you. Makes you try and find ways to make it seem like it was right." I touch my scars, thinking about all the time I wasted trying to find a reason for what Mama did. "Those folk that murdered Jack Green knew they'd done somethin' awful. So the first thing they did was make it seem like their jealousy and murderin' was somethin' good. So they told that story 'bout Jack's revenge. Made it seem like he was hateful. Like he was dangerous."

"Then the stories about the ghost?"

"Now that's true. But he ain't never tried to hurt anyone." I pause, cheeks flushed and trying to find my words again. The ones that ain't... that aren't so simple.

Percy digs his thumb into his temple, feeling the headache slipping back in behind his eyes. "Jack Green is a ghost."

"Yes."

"But he or it..."

"He."

"He isn't murdering young women."

"No."

"But someone is."

"Some one." I break the words apart with my tongue, drawing attention to them. "Some thing."

"Thing?"

A shrug and a half-truth, because I can feel that evil out there, but I can't say one way or another what it is. "Someone, I'd guess. Heard the stories. Knew the folks around here would be quick to point the finger at unnatural causes."

"Okay." He glances over his shoulder toward the two-way mirror, wondering if maybe the sheriff is right and he won't get anything but roundabout words from me. Answers that leave him more twisted up than before. But he remembers the itch on his hands, the taste of heat and blood. "Thing is, I thought there was a trace of magic out there in the woods."

He opens the folder and lays the photos out gently. "This is what is left of Lily Blackwell and Charlotte Camstock."

I lean in close, looking at each one carefully like I haven't seen them before. My hair slithers out from behind my ears, and I push it back from my eyes impatiently. Slap both hands down on the pictures as though I can push myself right into them.

"Huh." I sit back in my chair and tuck my hands in my lap. Going to need to wash. "I won't be able to tell from these."

"Tell?"

"If it were magic that burned them up like that. Someone or something." I turn so I can look at him square with my green eye because it's always kinder than the brown one. "I think, maybe, you need to find someone with the Touch. Before you find yourself in deep."

"What do you mean?"

"I can't tell you nothin' more than that. Not from those. Not from here." A shrug of my shoulders takes in the blank room with its scuffed metal furniture.

Percy scowls. *There's the hook.* "You want me to take you out there to see for yourself."

"Did I say so?" I shake my head. "But you had best be thinkin' hard on what sort of power can put fire to those with the Touch."

Even he can feel the twitch of energy from the other side of the mirror. "These women were witches? Like you?"

"Ain't many like me, Agent Cox. There's a difference between them that don't burn and them that is hard to burn. But some fool with a can of kerosene and a lighter would have had a hard time doing either of them like this." The Touch ripples under my skin again, and I lay my fingers against the nearest photo careful-like. "This is something dangerous."

He frowns, rubs his thumb across his forehead. The lines around his eyes are stitched with pain. That's the toll of his gift, this time in response to the Touch sleeping inside me. He shivers as though a bell has been struck as his sense tries to plumb the depths of the magic under my skin.

I lay my hand over his and the room peels away. The table and chairs remain, but there is grass under our feet and sunlight pressing hot on our heads. This is a field I used to play in when I was small. Addie and I would lie out in the sun after lunch or run through the weeds in the cooler evening in the never ending attempt to fill a mason jar with fireflies. It has been years since I was here, even in my head, but there is no forgetting the sweet smell of the grass.

Percy's eyes get wide. "Stop it."

I lift my hand away quick and the walls crash down around us. The clock on the wall hums as the second hand chases its tail around and around and around, the minute hand pacing slowly after it.

Click. Tock.

Percy touches his forehead again, but the pain is gone, the alarm his body had sounded in his nerves no longer necessary. I have shown the power in my bones. Now he must decide what to do with that knowledge.

Click. Tock.

Slowly he slides his hand back across the table 'til his fingertips just touch mine. His lips move silently so Ms. Drowner and Dr. Everley on the other side of the mirror cannot catch his intent.

Again, he mouths.

The room melts away, and this time the table and chairs go too, leaving us standing in that endless field.

He looks around, reaches down, and crushes the seedy head of a stalk of grass in his fingers. "Is this place real, Delaney?"

"The place is real, but your solid self, and mine, are sitting at a table in Greenhaven."

"And this?"

I tap my temple. "In my head."

Most men would be all wobble-kneed with terror by now, but Percival Cox is braver than he looks. His fingers tighten around mine, and he takes a few steps, stops to look around again. "Do you come here to get away from the... institution?"

A shrug. "I go elsewhere. But this is a place I haven't seen in a long time."

"Oh?" He looks at me. "Why?"

I lick my lips. "The places I normally go are private. Or crowded."

"Crowded." There is a momentary tremor of fear in his hands. Struck by the thought that I have dragged others into this place and trapped them so they are subject to my will.

The idea is amusing, if impractical, but I need him to trust me. That means showing him the truth.

The ground shivers, walls thrusting up through the grass, shedding dirt as rafters curl over us like hands closing up around a lightning bug. For a moment it's dark, then sunlight creeps through the ragged curtains over the windows. Every detail familiar as my own skin—worn carpet in a shade that hasn't been popular in forty years, the floorboard halfway across the room that cries like a cat when you step on it, the floral patterned couch and not-matching armchair.

The TV cackles in the corner of the room, and Mama stomps back and forth between the kitchen and the living room, pointing at Daddy—sometimes with her finger and sometimes with the butcher knife. She ain't the only one.

There's another one of her sitting on the couch smoking a cigarette. Upstairs screaming about somethin', too.

And outside shutting the door on the tool shed and throwing kerosene against the walls like she's tossing out the dishpan.

I step out on the porch, past Addie playing with her knock-off Barbie on the steps and swingin' on the tire in the oak in front of the house.

Percy looks down at me. "These are memories."

"That's right." I tap the side of my head again. "Some days it's downright busy in here."

He turns, fingers ticking against his leg as though counting. "I don't see you."

That makes me grin. "Of course not. Because I'm here."

The flames lick at the tool shed and the door shudders as Addie tries to break it down, but I know she is not strong enough. She never is.

The sheriff and his deputies pull up in the yard, blue lights twirling and sirens wailing. Mama runs past us into the house, hair pouring loose across her shoulders, and that wildness in her eyes that said she has come undone.

She comes back out a moment later with the shotgun in her hands as Mains and his deputies pile out of their cars and spread out across the yard.

He pauses, one hand dropping to his sidearm, the other held out as if he can stop her with the gesture. "Easy, Lydia. We don't want to hurt anybody."

She snugs the shotgun against her shoulder. "Ain't nobody left to be hurt."

His eyes get hard, even though he's still got that one hand outstretched. "Lydia. Where are your girls?"

"Go to hell."

Percy flinches at the thump of the shotgun, puts his arms around me as bullets sing past in response and Mama goes headfirst down the steps.

I squeeze his hand, reassuring. "Those won't hurt us."

The firetruck rumbles to a stop, half the tomato plants crushed under the front tires. The volunteers spill out. They ain't had time to dress in their special overcoats, so a couple of 'em just grab up a wet piece of burlap to cover their heads and take off toward the shed. They bust it down with their shoulders in spite of the flames tickling at their arms and legs.

I've seen it a hundred times. Mr. Feller and Mr. Barnsley go in through that doorway with the steam curling up off them. Barnsley, a big man with a bigger smile, comes back out with the baby in his arms. She's so still and small, tiny fingers untouched by the fire, but her mouth all lavender from the smoke stealing her breath.

Barnsley sits down on the ground and cries, rockin' back and forth and smoothing the dark wisps of hair on the baby's head. We had a cat once and her kittens got sick and she done the same thing when they died. Fussin' and lickin' them over and over as if that love could put some spark back in them.

I've seen it a hundred times. Still makes my throat get tight and hot, and the tears that wouldn't come that day slip out and curl across my cheeks. Usually I just stand here and cry 'til I'm all emptied out, but today is different because Percy is here.

His arms get so tight around me I wonder that he doesn't crush the air right out of me. He looks down at me and his eyes are a reflection of the storm around my heart.

I'm used to the pity. Everyone's always real sorry about what happened to my family. But it don't change the fact that no matter how terrible they think it all is, they're still scared of me.

But Percy don't look scared. And the sorrow on his face is something more than pity.

There's a crash in the house and raised voices. Mama and Daddy yelling at each other while Addie comes scooting out the front door and takes off across the yard. Headed for the sunny field where we started.

The screen door bangs shut behind her and Percy takes a deep breath. "This is where you spend your time, Delaney?"

I shake my head. "Not anymore."

The house breaks apart, twisting into the tall columns of oaks and beeches. A carpet of moss and the dark mould of last year's leaves washes out across the yard and buries the squalling and blinking cars. The silence that follows is dizzying.

Then a mockingbird sings in the distance, the leaves overhead shimmer in a thousand shades of green, and the tension melts away. "This is the place I come to think."

He loosens his arms around me, reaches out to touch the rough bark of the nearest oak. "This place is real, too?"

"Real enough." I've looked at plenty of pictures to make this one in my head, but the details are of my own making. "But it's quiet here. And there is no one to look at me. Or whisper."

He nods. "Do they know?"

I shake my head. Watch him careful-like. If he tells them what has happened, they will do something about it. More drugs. The unhappy kind that make me limp and weak. The kind that break my focus so that I cannot come here where it's quiet and no one can look at me.

If he tells them what I've shown him, what I've done, I will be at the mercy of the dreams, unable to wake as the world flows through my poor head.

"And now?" His mouth curls with concern. "We have been... gone for some time."

"It is different here. Our solid selves have only been quiet for a few heartbeats."

"We should go back." He drops my hand, but the woods remain. "Delaney. Please." Fear touches his voice. Not for himself.

For me.

"You aren't going to tell them." I can't keep the relief bottled up.

"No. Now take us back."

"Why?"

"Because I know what they will do if they know you still have the Touch. More drugs to put it to sleep. Or you. And if they are not certain about the drugs..."

A shiver creeps down my spine. I'd made the mistake of letting the Touch show once before.

There had been a terrible storm coming. A bridge would wash out and Mrs. Pratt and her grumbling pickup truck would be swept away and she would drown—a slow and miserable death as the river rose without mercy. I'd had seen it as sure as anything and told Mrs. Pratt not to go home. When she didn't listen, I made the mistake of pulling every thread I could find to keep her from leaving.

I saved her life, and for that she's always made the effort to be kind to me in spite of her fear, but the others—Dr. Everley and Ms. Drowner—said I had to be controlled.

They answered the Touch with electricity. Even now my hands shake at the memory.

"They will try and scramble it out of me."

"I don't want that to happen to you." His voice is flat. He wants me to think he is compassionate enough to not wish such an ill on anyone. And that is not a lie. But the flicker in his eyes tells me it is not the whole truth either.

"All right." I take a breath and the woods peel away like sheets of paper caught in the wind.

Click. Tock.

He moves his hand to collect the photos. "I appreciate your help, Miss Green." He closes the folder. "If I have any further questions…" A pause as the ridiculousness of it sinks in on him.

I smile. "I will be here, Agent Percival Cox."

He nods and stands. "Thank you." His lips tremble, but we are both aware that others are watching us. So he just nods again. "Thank you."

I tuck my hands inside my sweater sleeves and wait for the orderly to come and take me back to my room where the dinner tray will be waiting since I've missed the regular supper time.

My fingers tingle with the memory of Percy's hand holding mine. I stare at the tabletop, letting my hair hide me from Dr. Everley, still watching from behind the mirror, before I let the smile touch my lips again.

Oh, Percival Cox. You'll be the death of me.

CHAPTER 8

The sun is sinking behind the horizon as Percy and Martinez walk to the SUV. Still hot, but the light is soft and soothing.

Martinez stops to pull his keys from his pocket. "You all right?"

Percy frowns. "Fine."

"I saw her touch you."

He rubs his lower lip remembering the woods and the madhouse full of memories. Touch was right, but no word of that would come from his tongue.

Percy had spent a few years in an institution, in the care of folks that were less understanding. Three years of electro-shock therapy and heavy doses of the magic-suppressing drugs before they'd realized those with the Sense didn't have the power to change anything and would be better put to use finding those who could. He still remembers how much worse it had all been on the meds. The magic is always there but no longer controlled. He still remembers the shock therapy burning new holes in his mind 'til he almost laughed when they tried to tell him he had magic of any sort. Almost.

"Cox." Martinez gets up in his face.

Percy manages to coax his lips into a smile. "I'm fine. She's just lonely. Flirting, I think."

"Why?"

"Why not? She is young and has little else to do."

"I don't like it. How do I know she hasn't tweaked something in you?"

"You don't. Except that I'm telling you she hasn't." Percy tries to keep hold of his inner calm.

Martinez is skilled at provoking a response. "And you're certain she's not manipulating you?"

"Yes." He smiles more broadly to assure him of the lie. There is little he is certain about with Delaney, but he clings to the idea that Mains told him the girl would not cause deliberate harm. "Perhaps we should make an agreement that you will stop asking me if I'm all right and if I'm not, I'll tell you."

Martinez crosses his arms, considering. "I don't know, Cox."

"It would be easier."

"Yes. But will you do it? Harold..."

"I'm not Harold." He says it as gently as he can, but Martinez still flinches. Percy sighs. "If I need help, I will ask for it."

"Right." Martinez nods reluctantly. "Don't forget that."

"I won't."

"And the girl?"

Percy struggles to keep his voice casual. "What about her?"

"She said she didn't know what was murdering those other women."

"Yes." Percy glances back at Greenhaven. "It seems true enough. I think she might have a better sense of it than I do, but she can't see it clearly enough to add anything useful."

Martinez opens his mouth then shuts it again.

Percy grins. "I'm sure of it."

"Then we'll have to hope Elliot and MacKenzie have turned up something concrete."

"They will. Or we will."

"How do you know?"

He taps his fingers against the folder in his hands. "She said these women had the Touch. But in a small way."

Martinez raises an eyebrow. "All twelve?"

"I only showed her two. Lily Blackwell and Charlotte Camstock. But if they had the Touch, there's a good chance the others did too."

"We can check on that. Get a list of other women in the area who might be the next target." Martinez is buzzing with purpose. This is what makes him happy, the work that leads to a break in the investigation. He pulls his phone out. "I'll call Elliot and let her know."

"All right." Percy rolls his shoulders. "I'll be there in a minute."

His head is no longer throbbing, but there's a twist in his chest, subtle but slowly growing. A catch when he breathes too deep, a deeper ache like a bruise. He stretches, shakes one hand and then the other to get the blood flowing.

Remembers Delaney's warning.

This is something dangerous.

He glances over his shoulder as if he can catch a glimpse of her, but there is only the sprawling building and the tall iron fence.

"Hey, Cox." Martinez is waiting by the SUV. "You coming?"

"Be right there." Percy takes another deep breath and pushes the thoughts and concerns for Miss Green to the back of his mind. Something wicked is waiting for them.

CHAPTER 9

The funny thing about the future is once you see it, you can change it.

This is the second thing my daddy taught me.

Most folks think it's the other way around. That seeing what will happen means it has to be. But it ain't so.

I never saw the tool shed and the fire. Never saw Addie melting in the heat nor the baby getting so quiet in my arms.

I did burn more dinners than you can count on three hands 'cause Mama had put something in the meat. Slept cold and huddled up with Addie because it was better to turn the heater off than breathe in the fumes from a damaged vent. Locked us in a closet rather than get in the car to go run errands and maybe wind up at the bottom of the lake.

Lots of things I saw. Lots of things I changed.

But I never saw the tool shed and the fire.

The trickiest part is knowing what is still to happen, what is happening, and what has already happened. The visions don't always say.

I saw Daddy die a hundred different ways before he disappeared, and a few times after. I still don't know if it was poison or the shotgun Mama got him with. Only that he never was found.

The terrible thing about the future is if you see it, you can change it.

But the past... you can't change that no matter how much you try.

CHAPTER 10

Neeny Johnson lives about three miles outside town. Her house is old, perched on top of a hand-stacked stone foundation that boasts a Civil War cannon ball on one corner. A tired little building with floors that groan in protest as Neeny trudges back and forth.

She has a little sign hung from the front porch. Painted it herself—a crystal ball and a couple of tarot cards, and *Fortunes Read* block lettered underneath. The money isn't much, but it keeps the lights on and pays for a bottle of wine now and again. A few years back she was offered a job telling fortunes over the phone. Pay was a lot more steady, but there was a lot of guesswork involved. Neeny don't like to guess when it comes to folk's futures.

So she keeps on doing things her way, laying out cards, peering into the glass orb, and reading tea leaves or coffee grounds for the older women that like to have a proper visit and chit-chat while they have their fortune told. She pays attention to the details and she ain't never steered no one far wrong.

She creaks around the little house and sets it right for the evening. Puts the tarot cards back in their wooden box, polishes the glass ball, and wraps it up before putting it in its case, too. She had one she used to leave out on the table, but the cats got to rubbin' on it one night and it cracked clean in half when it hit the floor.

She brushes a few crumbs off the tablecloth and plants her hands on her hips. "There." All neat and ready for the morning.

The cats are sitting near the back door. When she turns on the light in the kitchen, they sing a little chorus, reminding her that it's dinner time and they have not eaten in oh-so-long.

"Hold on now. Don't get your tails in a knot." Neeny lets them in, then opens the bucket with the cat biscuits and portions some out into the row of saucers along the wall beside the fridge. Touches each of the furry heads and murmurs their names. "Marble. Black Spot. Chester. Magnolia."

It's Wednesday night and that means tomato soup and crackers for dinner. She empties the can into a saucepan, adds water, and sets it on the burner to heat up.

Out the front there's a thump. Sounds like a car door, but it's too late for any clients to be dropping in.

Neeny frowns. Trudges into the front room and peers out the window.

It's dark as dirt outside, but there's a truck parked in her driveway—engine running and the headlights shining right on her porch.

She squints through the window. Two men stand out there, one on either side of the truck. Not moving. Just watching her house. She pauses, glances toward the yellow-lit kitchen where the phone is. Maybe she should call down to the Tanners and ask their mister to bring his shotgun up to check things out.

But it's Wednesday and she knows they won't likely be back from church yet. "Probably just looking for directions." She runs her hand across her hair and opens the front door. "Can I help you?"

The men come a few steps closer. The headlights illuminate them in halves, but their faces are still unfamiliar. The one on the left clears his throat. "We're lookin' for Miss Johnson."

"You've found her." Normally she gets a flush from that. A wave of satisfaction from helping someone out, even in something so small. But something about this just don't seem right. Neeny puts her hand back on the doorknob, reassuring herself that she can go back inside and shut the door behind her. "If you're wantin' your fortunes told, you'll have to come back tomorrow. I'm done for the day."

The one on the right shakes his head. "We ain't here for no fortune telling." And somethin' in his voice—flat and desperate—makes the hair on her arms stand straight up in alarm.

She yanks the door open and scurries back into the house. Just gets the bolt across as they start pushing on it. The old frame creaks under the stress, and she turns and runs for the back door. Ain't got time to pick up the phone. The windows are all open. Another minute and they'll be climbing through the screens.

Neeny busts out the kitchen door, the cats swarming her all bristle-tailed and trying to figure out what the hell is goin' on. She don't have much time to think. Her feet already running and running across the back yard toward the trail that leads behind the cornfields over to the Tanner's place. Certain that if she can just get there, she'll be safe.

The trail is dark and she doesn't get very far before her foot catches on the ground and she goes down. Panting and struggling to get back to her feet.

Something slips over her head, cloth sticking to her face, but it don't keep her from screamin'. Loud. Always did have a big voice. For a moment the men let go, and she stumbles a little farther, trying to run and pull the pillowcase off at the same time. Still screaming like the devil in church.

They grab her again, push her down on the ground. One of them tries to push more of the pillowcase into her mouth, and she bites down on his fingers like they're celery, producing a screech to rival her cats. Something hits the side of her head real hard and it all gets fuzzy.

One of the men is jumping around, clutching his hand to his chest and cussing a blue streak. "Bitch bit me."

"Shut up, Merv. Help me with her hands." The other fellow has a piece of rope, twisting it around Neeny's wrists a few times before knotting it.

"I think she broke 'em." Merv pulls his foot back to kick her again.

"Stop it. Can't use her if she's already dead."

They look at each other nervous-like. Merv swallows hard and pokes her.

Neeny groans.

"She's all right, Luke."

"Better be." He touches his arm, wrapped up with bandages and smellin' of antiseptic. "Help me now."

They roll her up in a tarp, then twist more rope around the ends so she's wrapped up like a fat blue sausage.

"Good. Wait here while I get the truck," Luke says.

Neeny tries to move, but her arms are pinned in front of her, the pillowcase pushed against her face. She sucks a breath and puts everything she's got into her voice. "Help."

Merv kicks her, catching her in the shoulder.

She ain't one for cryin' much, but tears come out anyway. "What do you want?" The tarp crinkles and something taps her face. Merv, petting her head like he's soothing a dog.

"Please." She struggles harder, but the tarp doesn't give.

And he kicks her again. "Be quiet. We got somethin' special in store for you."

She's scared, but a little whisper in the back of her head says things will only get worse from here. She's shaking too hard to form words, so she screams.

"Shut up, bitch." Merv kicks and stomps 'til finally she gets quiet.

The truck rattles up the dirt trail and Luke jumps out. "What the hell are you doing?"

Merv rubs his fingers, still aching where they were bit. "She was screamin'. Even out here someone would have heard."

They both pause and listen, but there's no sound but the distant buzz saw of a cicada.

Luke bends down and jostles the tarp-swaddled woman. "Shit." He unties the rope around the outside. "Help me unroll it."

They each grab a corner and lift up. The body rolls out on the dirt trail and stops, belly down. Face bloodied, her eyes staring back at them, cool and empty as glass.

"Damn it, Merv. I told you."

"She was shriekin' too loud." Merv kicks her again, his mouth twisted up sullen-like. "I had to get her to shut up."

"Now we'll have to find another one."

They stare at each other for a moment, angry. Afraid.

The kitchen door of the house is a yellow splot in the darkness, but it twitters. And again. The phone ringing insistently.

Merv nudges Luke. "Come on. Let's get out of here."

Luke twitches. "Yeah." He grabs up the tarp and throws it in the back of the truck, flips the spare tire over on top of it so it won't blow out.

The doors slam and the truck backs around, kicks up dirt as they drive back down to the road, past the little house with the phone ringing and ringing and ringing. The tires squeal on the blacktop, and Luke and Merv disappear down the dark road.

CHAPTER 11

Percy is tired. They've been on the road most of the day, and the rest of it has been crowded with death and magic that has left him drained. He sits down at a table in their makeshift office, rests his head on his arms. Just for a minute or two while Martinez starts the search for names of women with the Touch who live within the county.

The noises of the room—phones ringing, the growl of voices, the nearly inaudible but bone-piercing whine of the florescent lights overhead—swirl past him and grow more distorted as his breathing slows and he sinks into a fitful sleep.

The dream is waiting for him. The one she told him about. He remembers it well enough now that he's standing in it, but this time it is eerier than normal. The woods seem darker and more familiar. Familiar because he realizes they look like Del's woods. Darker because this time he feels the pull of something down the path.

He walks forward, looking to see if he can see her. She told him she was here.

Somewhere.

She told him he never seemed to see her and passed her by. Knowing it, looking more intently doesn't seem to change that. There's not even a whisper of movement to be seen in the deeper shadows that fall off on either side of the path. No flicker that might be moonlight touching pale skin.

Something calls to him from the end of the path. Not with words. Not with sound even. This summons churns in his guts, drawing him forward even as every step raises the hair on his arms.

He remembers this too. Normally he pulls himself awake, avoiding whatever lies in wait. Not this time. He pulls his sidearm free of the holster on the last few steps, watching for any threat.

The clearing is broad and bright with moonlight. A house sits on the other side, lopsided with the years, kudzu slowly dismantling the rest. Near the middle is a large box, the metal scarred and split at the corners. Standing in it is something in the shape of a man, the height of a man, but made of stuff other than flesh. Ash and coals and fire. So much fire.

He knows this is The Salesman.

Not a ghost.

This entity is beyond human.

There's a woman too. Not Delaney. Someone else. Someone his brain doesn't know and presents only as female. Scared. Screaming.

Percival tries to grab her and pull her back to the edge of the woods where his frantic mind tells him they will be safe. He fires his gun at The Salesman. The bullets send up sparks, but the thing—guilt and fear shaped by the repetition of many tongues into coals and anger—reaches out and grabs hold of him.

Jacket and shirt catch fire. Flames wrap around him, burning. Smothering. Inescapable.

"Huh." Percy lurches upright, out of the clutches of the dream and The Salesman.

Overhead the lights hum and buzz. Martinez is still on the phone, busy scribbling something on a sticky note.

Percy touches his arms, but his clothes are unmarked. A dream, not a manifestation. But a dream of what? Delaney said she'd seen him before in that dream. Does she know what waits for him at the end of the path?

As soon as he thinks it, he knows the answer.

"Looks like we've caught a break." Martinez leans on the edge of the table.

Percy rubs his eyes and focuses on the present. "Oh?"

"Sheriff Tolbert put together a list of names to start with. Women rumored to have some measure of magic. We started calling and one of 'em isn't answering." He checks the piece of paper in his hand. "Neeny Johnson. She runs a fortune telling gig out of her house."

"Maybe she's out."

"Could be, but apparently she's not one to leave the house much. Has her groceries delivered by one of the neighbors and doesn't own a car. I'm heading out there with a deputy right now to check things out."

"If she's only just been taken, there's a chance to keep her from winding up dead."

"And a chance to catch whoever is doing this."

"You've talked to Elliot and MacKenzie?"

"They're checking the last couple of names on their list. Hopefully they'll find something."

Percy nods. "I need to talk to Delaney Green again."

"Why?"

"I didn't ask her enough questions."

Martinez glares at him. "You think she's got something to do with this after all."

"I think she knows more about it than she first told me."

"Then she lied to you." Martinez crosses his arms as though he will get between Percy and danger.

"Yes."

"And you think you can get the truth out of her this time?"

Not if she doesn't want to tell me. Percy shrugs. "Seems like things have changed."

"Well, I'm headed out to Neeny Johnson's place." He says it as if that settles everything.

"Good. I'll take a car and go talk to Miss Green."

Martinez looks at him in alarm. "You should..."

"I'll be fine," Percy says, pushing his chair back with more confidence than he feels. "Call me when you get to Miss Johnson's house. All right?"

Martinez hesitates, but this is the stuff he's good at, and they are all eager for a break in the case. "Okay."

"Be careful," Percy says, offering his hand.

"Hah." Martinez shakes it. "All right. Take an officer with you."

"Sure." He rolls the kinks out of his shoulders and heads down the hallway, emerging from the dry, cool air of the library basement into the humid night. Walks across the muggy parking lot to the sheriff's department to get a cup of coffee and find a deputy willing to drive him out to Greenhaven.

The latter proves more difficult than anticipated. A nervous young man by the name of Collins shuffles through a list on a clipboard, shaking his head the entire time. "Looks like everyone's on assignment, sir." He licks his lips. "If you want to wait, someone might be available in an hour or two. Maybe."

Percy frowns. "I need to go out to Greenhaven."

"Yes, sir. I understand. But..." He pauses, cheeks flushed with the effort of thinking of a valid excuse.

Sheriff Tolbert and ex-Sheriff Mains come out of Tolbert's office. "Is there a problem, Agent Cox?"

"He wants someone to go with him to see Miss Green again." Collins blurts it out before Percy can say anything. "But we're... busy."

"Ah." Tolbert frowns. Clearly he's not keen to send anyone out to Greenhaven either.

Mains chuckles. "I'll drive you out there."

The sheriff nods. "Good idea." He looks at Percy. "You don't mind, do you?"

"I guess not."

"That's done, then." Tolbert nods, satisfied. "Give 'em the keys to 39."

"Yes, sir." Collins opens a cabinet on the wall and retrieves a pair of keys. "Here you go."

"Thanks." Mains looks at Percival. "You ready to go?"

"Yes. The sooner, the better."

The parking lot is still radiating waves of heat, but little wafts of cooler air trickle across. Percy frowns. "Is it always this warm?"

"In summertime, yeah." Mains pauses to look for car 39. "You must not have been down here long."

"A few weeks. And most of that's been in the office." Percy tilts his head back, watching the stars blinking through the brown and violet dusk overhead. "Can't see the sky like you can here."

"Naw." He shakes his head and unlocks the door on the cruiser. "That's the problem with the big cities. You lose yourself in 'em. Couldn't pay me enough to move away from the stars."

Percy slides into the car, careful not to slosh his coffee. Then buckles his seat belt as they pull out of the parking lot. "You don't seem afraid of Miss Green."

He laughs. "Are you?"

"Not yet." He looks at the ex-sheriff steadily. "But everyone else..."

"It's not that I ain't scared of her. There's lots of things in the world that should scare us. Disease. Critters. Freak accidents. I could stay at home, lock myself up in a room, and hope death wouldn't find me, but a smart man knows it don't work that way. If a bullet's got your name on it, it'll find you."

Percy takes another sip of coffee. "She's seen your death, too."

"Not sure what you mean."

"She told me about a dream that I'd had. Said she'd seen me in it. Only this evening, I stayed there—despite a feeling of creeping dread—and it ended... I ended in the arms of The Salesman." He touches his arm again, still feeling the flames eating through his skin. "I figure she must have told you something similar. That's why you aren't afraid of her."

"Ah." Mains works his lips together for a few minutes. "I first met Del when she was small. She'd run out in the woods to hide from her mother and gotten a little turned around. Eventually her father called us to help look for her. I found her about a mile away, sitting on a fallen tree as calm as could be, even though it was full-dark by then. Waiting for me.

"Just a little thing with a milk-white face and eyes that don't match. Like the Maker ran out of parts." He chuckles. "But there she was and I said, 'It's okay honey. You don't need to be scared.' And she looks at me, ever so solemn. 'I ain't scared. I knew you'd come.' And something in the way she said it, I knew she didn't mean she knew someone would come lookin' for her. She knew it would be me.

"So I say, 'How'd you know that, little girl?'

"'Oh. I know lots of things. And my name's Delaney, but I suppose you can call me Del.'

"And I said, 'Lots of things? Like why the sky is blue?'

"'Oh, no. Like how you'll die, Mr. Mains.'" He stops. His hands knotted so tight on the steering wheel the bones show through his skin. "Such a little thing. She reached up and took my hand and asked me if I wanted to know how it would happen."

"And you said yes."

"Of course, I did. By then she had her tongue in me. Bending my ear. Bending my future, too, I expect. Like she's doin' with you."

"Then you think she has a hand in what's happening here? With The Salesman?"

"Not in raising him. Or it. That one of her inevitables, I reckon."

"Inevitables?"

"Things she can't change." Mains grins, dry and humorless. "Just 'cause she has the Touch don't mean she can do whatever she likes."

"But…"

"If it is her that's brought you here, and given that look in your eye I'd say it is, then she's trying to do somethin' good."

Percy raises an eyebrow. "In my dream I died."

"I do, too."

"And that doesn't frighten you?"

"Hell, yes. But it's been eight years now since I went into that barn lookin' for a meth lab. And eight years since I didn't turn my back on the hay loft." His grin turns sly. "Once you know the future, you can change it, boy."

Percy looks at him, breathless. "She's trying to save my life?"

"You have that dream before?"

"Before I met Miss Green? Yes."

"Bet you always woke up before you got to the end though. Because you were afraid."

"That's right." He's staring at Mains hard. Does the old sheriff have a bit of the Touch too? "She wanted me to see how it ends."

He shrugs. "Well. I can't say what Delaney wants. But if I were to guess, it'd be that she's taken a liking to you."

Percy rubs his fingers through his hair and hopes that's a good thing. Remembers the way she looked at him when they first met and the strength of her fingers twined though his. "Yes." He nods. "I think she has."

"Hah." Mains pulls the car into the lot at Greenhaven. "Don't worry about it, boy. Better to look the devil in the eye, yes?"

Before Percy can think of a response, Mains is already stepping out of the car. "Come on. They'll just be getting her into bed for the night."

Percy swallows hard. "I think I want to take her with me."

"Out of Greenhaven?"

"Yes."

Mains rubs his chin. "If you say so. I don't suppose it will make any difference."

"She'll get what she wants."

"That's right. Whatever it is."

Percy starts down the sidewalk to the main doors. *Whatever it is.*

CHAPTER 12

No matter how much you try to change things, some things are meant to happen.

This is the third thing Daddy taught me.

I've been dreaming of The Salesman's awakening since I was a little thing. And I've pulled and twisted the threads that led up to it as hard as I could. None of it made a difference. The magic in that haunted tale, repeated countless times over the century and a half since poor Jack Green was murdered, the fear that shaped every telling, these are too much to be undone even by my hands.

But though there are some things can't be changed, what happens next is less fixed. For every bottleneck, for every terrible event that cannot be moved, there are countless ways to resolve it.

This is how I first saw Percival Cox. A single thread that ended with him burning in the arms of The Salesman. I can't say I didn't think he was handsome, but I didn't mean to keep him far from that brutal magic because I loved him. Not at first.

But Percy was a thread that led toward the end of the burned girls, toward me stepping outside the grounds of Greenhaven for the first time since I was thirteen. And I clung to it.

CHAPTER 13

I sit on the bed, the piece of paper with the Stevens poem smoothed out on one knee. The memorizing is not so hard, even with the meds making things slow and strange. The hard part is finding a part of my brain the Magiprex hasn't curtained off. The hard part is finding a place I'll be able to find again.

The first few lines are where I left them.

Ursula, in a garden, found
A bed of radishes.
She kneeled upon the ground
And gathered them,

I squint at the paper and add the last two.

With flowers around,
Blue, gold, pink, and green.

The door opens and the orderly, Malcolm, sticks his head into the room. "Put your shoes on, Del."

"It's almost time for bed."

"Not tonight." His hand is trembling on the door knob. "That agent that were here earlier is taking you out."

I catch my lip between my teeth to keep the smile hidden away. "Out?"

"He says you're a witness or something and he wants you in his custody."

"But Ms. Drowner..."

"Just about split herself in two." He leans against the doorframe with a grin, his nervousness gone for a moment. "But she ain't got a good reason to keep you here. And it could be..." He pauses.

I don't need him to tell me that some of the paperwork regarding my extended stay is the result of some behind-the-scenes bargaining. A local judge who ain't comfortable with meeting me on the street taking a thinly-justified recommendation that I be kept under continued observation. The lack of an outside assessment once I reached a legal age. And the forged signature on the documents that give my consent to be kept at Greenhaven.

But he doesn't know that I know, and he sure don't want to be the one to tell me. He gets all twitchy-like again and slides over so the door covers everything but his head.

"Put your shoes on. The fellow's waiting."

I fold the paper up and tuck it safely in my sweater pocket. Then tuck my feet into my shoes and stick the Velcro straps down carefully. "I'm ready."

Malcolm leads the way, walking fast to keep some distance between him and me. One of the florescent lights is out of sync; as we walk underneath it, the hallway flickers past, matching the rhythm of my heart. I pull the cuffs of my sweater up into my fingers to hide the shake in my hands.

I know that the air outside the gate will not be any different and I will see the same stars I can see from the window of my room, but I have dreamed for so long of being outside the walls of Greenhaven. Now that the moment is here, I'm dizzy with anticipation.

Ms. Drowner is waiting at the front desk. Her hair stands up over her head in a lopsided halo, her lips pale where she has chewed her lipstick off. The pen in her fingers rattles against the edge of the clipboard in her other hand. "Are you certain you feel well enough to leave, Miss Green?"

I tilt my head to look at her square with my brown eye. "Why would I not?"

The shadows under her eyes darken. "Of course." She holds the clipboard out. "Sign here. It waives any liability the institution might have for releasing you early."

That makes me smile. Early. As if I haven't spent more years here than I have anywhere else. I take the pen and scrawl my name on the appropriate line. "Is that all?"

"Your things will be left where they are. Should you decide not to return..." The clipboard slips from her trembling fingers. "If you do not return, you will need to make arrangements to collect them."

I nod. My things are four cotton dresses, two pairs of sneakers, the sweater I'm wearing, and a small drawerful of socks and underwear. None of it particularly valuable or personal. Besides, I don't think I'll need more clothes, the road I'm taking.

The silence stretches out like a taffy thread. All eyes fixed on me, as though they can keep me here with the looking. Lips trembling with the silent plea for me to stay. But their small magic has no power in this moment.

I push my hair back from my face. "Where is Agent Cox?"

"Outside." Ms. Drowner tiptoes toward the door. "This way."

The air outside is warm, and stars glitter like salt overhead. The walkway is illuminated by a string of small lights on either side; larger lamps form a deeper pool of light near the gate. And in that pool, two men are waiting.

I've been expecting Percy, but the presence of Gil Mains is a surprise. I don't see how he moves much anymore. Not since I kept his thread from breaking. That's the way it goes. Once you see the future, you can change it, but only for so long. Eventually the threads turn pale, like a spider's web, and can't be altered. I can see the last few steps in Main's journey, but we aren't there yet. Not yet.

I stop at the end of the walkway, touching the air with my fingertips in an attempt to discern Mains' purpose here, but his thread cannot be felt either. Not yet.

He touches his forehead. "Evening, Delaney."

"Mister Mains. I was not expecting you."

"No." He glances at Percy, a thoughtful twist to his mouth. "I expect not. But Agent Cox wanted someone familiar with the area to drive him around."

Percy nods. "Yes." His eyes are darker than before, a restless hitch to his movements. Trying to behave casually in the presence of Ms. Drowner, but I can see the questions burning on the back of his tongue.

"I am ready to go." I cannot hide the tremor in my voice. More than ready, I am eager. To see the stars without the thick glass of the institution's windows between me and them. To breathe air that has not cut itself on the barbed wire at the top of the fence that surrounds the building and grounds.

He steps forward and takes my hand. Palm to palm. His fingers twining through mine— warm and strong. "Come on."

I glance over my shoulder as we walk toward the car. Ms. Drowner stands where we left her. The light turns her hair so pale and thin she looks as though she has none, her eyes dark hollows in her face. I shiver, seeing the shortness of her thread. "Wait." I pull my hand loose from Percy's and run back.

She draws away from me when I try and put my hands on her shoulders, mouth tightening up in a nervous little knot. "Miss Green?"

"You be careful. On the drive home tonight. All right?"

"Hush." She turns her head and spits between her fingers. "You hush now, hear?" Claps her hands over her ears and runs back up the sidewalk, her shoes clack-clack-clacking all the way.

She'll go inside, put the new paperwork on her desk. Maybe she should go ahead and file it, but she's agitated now. Afraid that I've seen something true and mad at herself for being afraid. Grabbing her purse and getting in the car. She won't be paying attention when she gets to the crossroad with Highway 39. Won't see the semi-truck trying to make the last leg of the haul from Chicago to Atlanta.

"Delaney." Mains is looking at me.

I brush my hand across the threads, trying to find one doesn't end with poor Ms. Drowner tumbling ass over head with her car breakin' to bits around her. But they're all short, even the ones that don't end in glass and blood on the interstate.

Percy touches my arm, careful-like. "What is it?"

I shake my head. If I'd had more time... the *best* I can do is to set one of these short threads thrumming. The cell phone will slide onto the floor. Ms. Drowner will unfasten her seatbelt so she can reach it, then start the turn out onto the highway before she buckles it back. When the truck hits her, the impact will throw her out of the car and her neck will snap.

"It'll be quick." Better than being trapped while the car burns around her or crushed so tight against the steering wheel she suffocates before the emergency response can cut her free

"Delaney." Percy's clutching my hand again, but tight this time. "Tell me what to do." He's so earnest. Innocent despite the terrible things he's seen. As if he can attempt the things I cannot.

I try to look at him gently. "Take me away from here, Percival."

He leads the way to the car and opens the door for me like a gentleman, never mind that I'm climbing into the backseat and there's protective mesh between it and the front.

His phone rings.

I suppose it doesn't sound any different than any other day, but a chill touches me. Knowing what's waiting at the other end. Neeny all flopped out dead. The Trainer boys prowling somewhere in the night, looking for another woman with the Touch. All of it marking the last few turns on this long road. All of it leading toward The Salesman.

I push my hair back from my eyes and look at Mains. "You need to take us out to Neeny Johnson's place."

CHAPTER 14

By the time we reach the house, it's not just Martinez waiting. The coroner's wagon sits on the little dirt track that leads past the house. The coroner himself sits on the rear bumper between the outstretched doors, a cigarette clinging desperately to his lower lip. A couple of sheriff's cars sit farther along, blue lights flickering off the overhanging branches and headlights fixed on the large and empty remains of Neeny Johnson.

Mains pulls the car up by the mailbox and turns the engine off. Percy looks back at me with a frown. "Stay here with Mains, all right?"

I nod. Not like I can get out of the car unless they let me out. And I've already seen what's happened to poor Neeny.

"Okay." He looks at Mains. "Okay?"

"Sure."

"I'll be back in a minute." Percy gets out, slams the door behind him, and strides across the yard toward the coroner and Martinez.

I rub my face on my sleeve and turn sideways on the seat so I can put my feet up. It's quiet, save for the half-hearted buzz of a cicada in the tree across the road.

Mains is watching me in the rearview mirror. The weight of his gaze slides across my face like ice in a hot skillet. He clears his throat. Rolls down the window and spits into the yard. "I hope you know what you're doing, Del."

"I wouldn't be here if I didn't."

"Maybe. But this Cox is smart and stronger in your ways than he lets on. You twist him the wrong way and you'll pay for it."

"I ain't... I'm not twisting him at all." I look at him stern. "I didn't twist you, did I?"

He frowns, still not looking at me direct. "I figure you're more interested in Cox than you ever were in me."

That brings a flush to my cheeks, but there's no point in lying about it. "I'm grown now."

"Yes." The seat cushion creaks as he turns to look me. "You plan to grow old with him, Delaney? Marry him and have children like…" He stops. Even in the dark, with the blue glare of the police lights skipping across the side of his face, I can see the emotion in his eyes. Anger and sorrow over what happened to my family. And a share of guilt that with all the calls about fighting and the trips out into the woods to find me or Addie when we'd run off from Mama he hadn't seen how bad things were. That he wasn't able to stop it.

I shake my head. "I can't say what I expect. But you know I don't ever mean to hurt anyone deliberate-like."

Mains can't hide the shiver, but he doesn't look away. "I know, Del."

I touch my fingers to my chest, trying to soothe the ache in my heart. Mains is the only one who didn't have to come visit but did anyway. The only one who hasn't let his fear keep him away. Maybe he's just smart enough to know that physical distance is a small obstacle. Maybe he can feel the pull of destiny, bringing us back around to the thing Mama started that day when she tried to burn me off the earth and took my poor sisters instead.

I take a deep breath, swing my feet back off the seat. "It's stuffy back here. Can we get out for a few minutes?"

He shrugs. "I guess. No lookin' at the body though."

"Already seen it."

A sigh. "Of course you have." He gets out, opens the back door. "Stay close."

"Yes, sir." I don't have much interest in seeing Neeny in the flesh, but I didn't leave Greenhaven behind just to spend my time sitting in the back seat of police cruiser.

The summer air touches my face like silk. Or what I imagine silk feels like—softer and less artificial than the bright blue stuff my nightgown is made out of. I shrug my sweater down my shoulders 'til it only covers my hands, arms bare to the night.

Sometimes when I'm wound deep in the threads of the future, I don't just see what happens, I feel it, too. Usually when the feelings get strong. Collins finding the bodies in the woods. Neeny running through the dark with the Trainer boys on her heels. So it ain't like I've not felt the crunch of dry leaves underfoot or the caress of the evening breeze, but it weren't like this.

This is seductive and melancholy—living in my own skin. For a moment I let loose of the threads that lead away from here, let loose of what's coming and just breathe under the stars.

A cricket chirps in the weeds beside the road. Then something rustles, quiet. I click my tongue and yellow eyes glint in the shadows. One of Neeny's cats, prowling away from the commotion behind the house.

"Here, kit." I settle on my heels to make myself small. Hold my hand out and wiggle my fingers in invitation. "Come on."

He edges out of the grass, flicks one battered ear forward and back.

"Come here, tom. I won't hurt you."

He's a tabby, a little fat thanks to Neeny's affection, but with the grace and reflexes of a bird killer. I figure he'll show the others how to hunt now that they're on their own.

"Here, pretty boy." I make more noises with my tongue. "Come on."

He flicks his tail back and forth sharp, but edges forward to allow his head to be scratched. Then a little closer to rub his cheek against my leg.

Mains shifts his weight, the gravel at the edge of the road crunching underfoot.

The tom hisses and lunges back into the undergrowth. A moment later the cricket's cree-sqree stops mid-chirp.

I stand up and tilt my head back to look at the stars. Not like I could have kept him anyway and he's needed here. But I've almost forgotten what it's like to be touched affectionately.

Mains looks at me, forehead wrinkled up with worry. "You all right, Del?"

"Just breathing."

"You sure?"

"Yes." I pull my sweater back on as Percy comes back with Martinez.

"Looks like someone tried to grab Miss Johnson and something happened. She's dead." Percy looks at me with a frown. "I thought you said this was something supernatural."

"I might have."

"Something that drives a pickup truck?" Martinez sounds annoyed.

I fold my arms across my chest. "Is she burned up?"

"No. Looks like someone stomped her to death."

"Then whatever has been doing the burning weren't here." I don't feel like spelling it all out because that's a sure way to make them start looking at me suspicious-like, but for a moment I think I might have to.

Percy looks at Martinez. "Maybe we've got multiple suspects. Someone who is kidnapping the women, and someone or something elsewhere that's burning them up."

Martinez nods. "Okay. So the guys in the truck come here. Try to kidnap Miss Johnson, but she winds up dead. They leave. But whatever the plan was…"

"They'll have to find someone else," Percy says.

"I'll tell Tolbert and his men we need to get in touch with the other names on his list. Put word out on the TV if we can." He glances at me. "What about her?"

"I'm taking her back to the motel. We'll talk there." Percy smiles at me, faint but reassuring.

"Keep your phone on." Martinez is already hurrying back toward the other cars.

Mains takes a deep breath. "I guess you want me to drive you back into town then."

"Yes, sir." Percy opens the back door for me. "If you don't mind."

"Not at all." He pauses as though he might say something else, then closes his mouth with a little bob of his head. "Not at all."

CHAPTER 15

The heart always wins.

This was the final thing my daddy taught me.

He said it by way of explanation on one of those days when Mama was at her worst. Love is the one constant and powerful thing in this world. The only true answer to all the ills of the world. If there were more love, there would be less of all the bad things.

He said it by way of apology when Addie had begged him to take us and leave Mama behind. Love was the reason he had chosen to be with her in the first place, even when others had warned him against it. Love was the thing that wouldn't let him leave her in the darkness that crept out of her head.

He said it by way of a promise when I had told him the shape and bloodiness of the threads in my future. Love was the thing that would shed light on the difficult decisions. It was the wisdom that is felt, not learned.

This was the final thing my daddy taught me. A week later he was gone for good.

I didn't mean to fall in love with Percival Cox. He and I together were the means to the best end. I never meant him harm, but I didn't much care at first what hurt he went through before his path would cross with mine. I just knew that his future lay with mine. He was my one chance to be free of the chlorine-soured walls of Greenhaven, and I was his chance to avoid the fire and hate of The Salesman's embrace. That's how it was at first, anyway.

A means to an end.

But there was a patience with which he endured the twists and turns of his road, a compassion and gentleness he practiced when confronted with the worst of the things one human does to another that gave me hope that it was not too late to save him. It drew my heart to his as surely as I was drawing our physical selves together. I fell in love with him, not for the way he smiled at me, but for the way he smiled at others. Not for the loving words he whispered in my ear, but for who he was on his best days and his worst.

I didn't mean to fall in love with Percival Cox, but in the end, the heart always wins.

CHAPTER 16

The motel is faded like an old Polaroid, all the colors in the wallpaper and bedspread and carpet turned to yellows and oranges. I sit down on the edge of the bed as Percy turns the knobs on the A/C unit. He was quiet on the way back from Neeny's house, apparently choosing not to talk in front of Mains.

Now it's just me and him, and the tension is so thick I am dizzy with it.

He takes off his jacket and tosses it on the chair. "You mind if I wash up? It's been a long day."

I shrug. "We have some time."

A frown touches his mouth, but he goes into the bathroom and pushes the door shut.

I pull the piece of notebook paper from my pocket and look at the words again. A few more times and they will begin to stick. I doubt I'll have the time to learn the rest, but at least I will have the first verse tucked away.

With flowers around,
Blue, gold, pink, and green.

I close my eyes so I can write them more clearly in my head. With flowers around, blue, gold, pink, and green.

"Delaney?" His hair is damp, shirt unbuttoned and the towel still hanging from one shoulder. He pads barefoot across the carpet and settles on the edge of the bed next to me. "What's this?"

"Just memory practice." I let my hair fall forward around my face to hide the embarrassed flush in my cheeks. "It's helps me manage the fuzziness caused by the meds."

"Ah." He looks at the paper more closely. "Is this Stevens? Cy est Pourtraicte, Madame Ste Ursule, et les Unze Mille Vierges, right?"

"Yes."

His eyes are deep and curious. "An interesting choice."

"I like the part about the garden. And..." The flush in my cheeks grows hotter. "The end is a little naughty."

"Hah. Yes." Percy stands up and crosses the room to rummage through the suitcase sitting next to the TV. "Do you think he was right? Does God have a desire for intimate companionship?"

I lick my lips, watching out of the corner of my eye as he takes off his shirt and puts on a t-shirt. "I think we all have desire for companionship. Though some, I guess, don't desire physical intimacy."

Maybe he hears the question in my voice, though I do my best not to phrase it so. In all the years I've watched him, I have never seen him in more than a casual relationship with anyone. Intimate sometimes, but not lasting. I do not expect the same level of affection from him as I have for him; he has only known me for a brief time. But there is a fear, deep in my gut, that even if we did have years ahead of us, he would never grow to love me.

He looks at me, a knot between his eyebrows as though tryin' to figure somethin' out. Me, maybe. His fingers tick against his pants leg. Trying to figure out his words, then.

"Why didn't you tell me you had seen me die?" There is no anger in his words, but I feel guilty nonetheless.

"Folks are not usually so fond of being told the when and how and wherefore of their end. Especially not when it's violent."

"But you told Gil Mains."

I nod. "I was young still. And the good he would do if..." I hesitate. One thing you learn real quick when you mess with the future is that the dream of a better future is just that. You can pull on those threads and change the numbers, change the timing, but some things you can't prevent, and in the end, everyone dies.

"If he didn't die when he was supposed to."

"Everyone dies when they're supposed to, Mr. Cox. Just depends on what they do while they're alive."

"And some you give a little helping hand." Percy sits down next to me.

It is a simple answer to a question that is fraught with complication and complicity, but I nod. "Yes."

"Then there's a way for me to avoid death in the arms of that thing called The Salesman."

"Once you know the future, you can change it."

He considers that for a little while. "And your future?"

"Uncertain. But I am more... interested in the present. In this moment." I lean forward and touch my mouth to his. Not a kiss, but an invitation. My lips and breath brushing against his while my heart thuds hard in my chest, before I sit back.

His eyes widen, looking at me differently, though he doesn't move away. "Delaney."

"Percival." I don't dare to breathe or move or even wish, unwilling to touch any of these threads. Whatever happens next, he must do it on his own, even if it means he walks away.

He takes my hand, folds both of his around it. Trying to use his Sensitivity to read the situation. The pain that nearly crippled him earlier is gone, replaced by the electricity we both feel.

"Explain this to me, Delaney. We have only just met." A pause, remembering I have seen him before. "I have only just met you, but I feel... is this your doing?"

"You and me being here in this place. That is my doing. But not how you feel. Not even how I feel." I clutch his hands tight. "I did not mean to fall in love with you, Percival Cox. But I would never use you so poorly as to make you feel the same for me."

He frowns. "Not deliberately."

My breath sticks in my throat, knowing his words are true. It is possible I have Touched something in him without realizing it. "Never deliberately, Percy." It is just a whisper, but I look him square in the eye despite feeling naked and ugly and cruel.

This time he is the one who leans forward to press his lips against mine. At first we only touch, an uneven reflection of each other—palm to palm and mouth to mouth. Touching. Waiting. Growing comfortable in this moment.

The sense of electricity builds 'til I am shaking with it. Percy too.

He is the first to move. One hand tangles in my hair. His other arm wraps around me, his hand moving under my sweater and the heat of his skin soaking through the thin cotton of my dress.

And this thing which should be strange and awkward because we are new to each other—the caress of tongue and gentle tease and pull of lips, our breath coming and leaving together—it is as easy and natural as the beat of my heart. Of our hearts.

By the time he pulls away I am full to overflowing with feelings so unfamiliar, I barely recognize them. Joy. Contentment. Excitement and anticipation. Desire. All making my heart heavy and raw and about to explode if I don't run or scream or hit something, and, since I can do none of those here, I cry instead. Not delicate tears like the lady actors cry in the shows on TV, but big, hot ones that make my face sticky and my nose run.

"Shhhh." Percy pulls me into his lap. "It's all right."

"I'm sorry." I try to dry my face on my sleeve. "It's just..."

"You have been alone for a long time." He says it quiet and with his cheek pressed against mine.

More tears spill over, and all I can do is hold on while my heart pours out in big hiccupping sobs. "S-silly," I stammer after a while.

"No." He smooths the hair back from my face and looks at me. "No, Delaney. Not silly. Or stupid," he adds before I can open my mouth again. "I have walked a little distance in your shoes. Cried these same tears, though it was years ago."

I shake my head. He is referencing something from the years before I knew him. "I don't understand."

"When I was younger, I was in an institution for a while," he says, and the lines around his mouth tell a story I feel in my bones. "Only a couple of years, but the memory is still sharp. The static in my head from the meds. And the... the shocks. The way no one wanted to touch me or talk to me. How no one would even look me in the eye because they were afraid that somehow I would do something to hurt them. I remember how even when I wasn't locked up alone, I might as well have been."

His arms are like stone around me. I touch his face and feel the anger still burning under his skin despite the calm facade he presents. "But you are out now."

"As you are. As you should have been."

"Then we might not have found ourselves here."

"Not here, but somewhere. If we are meant to be together, there will always be a road leading me to you."

"Ah." For a moment I want to tell him the truth, but it is not time for that. Not yet.

I kiss him again before I can change my mind. Lose myself for a while in the taste of him and the heat of his body between my legs, until we have both put some distance between us and the memory of isolation.

He sighs. "Are you certain you want to do this now?"

"Yes." The pinch of worry returns. Despite the kissing, perhaps he has no desire for physical intimacy. "Don't you?"

"I do. But your first time..." He hesitates and a flush touches his cheeks.

"We will take it slow and you will be gentle with me, Percy."

He relaxes. "Yes."

"Good." I comb his hair back off his forehead. "It will be all right."

He murmurs in agreement and tugs at the edge of my sweater. "Can we take this off?"

I shrug it off reluctantly, nervous about showing him my scars, but knowing I cannot keep them hidden forever.

His eyes flicker and he touches the rough skin. "How did..." He stops as I tuck my arm against my chest and attempt to cover them with my other hand. "I'm sorry. That was rude of me."

"No." I shake my head. "You are right. They're ugly." I let my hair shield my face again. I'm ugly because of them. It's why I wear a sweater even in the hot months. To keep them hidden. So there is one less reason for folks to flinch away from me.

"Hush." He reaches down and snags the edge of his shirt, pulling it off over his head in a single motion. "Here." He takes my hand and presses it against the scar on his shoulder. "Does this make me ugly?"

"N-no." I'm stammering again. My heart beats fast and all of me tingles with the need to touch him.

"And this one?" He lays my other hand over the longer scar that wraps around the bottom edge of his ribs.

"No."

Slowly he unbuttons the front of my dress and slips it off my shoulders. Then the thin strap of the worn bra underneath. Brushes his fingers across the lumpy ovals on my shoulder. "And these?"

I shake my head. "No." It's just a whisper. I cannot manage anything else past the lump in my throat. I had not thought it was possible to love him more than I already did. Even knowing that there is some measure of pity in his feelings for me, I am breathless with the sense of fullness that comes from holding him. From him holding me.

I stand up and let my dress slide down my hips to fall to the floor. Pry my shoes off. Fiddle the hooks on my bra apart. The cool air raises gooseflesh as I slip my underwear off. The carpet is rough under my feet, and I shuffle back and forth for a moment 'til I find a patch that's less worn.

Percy sits on the edge of the bed. His hands are on his knees and his gaze fixed tight on me—sliding hot across my body. "So that's it?"

"It's just skin."

"Hah." He unbuckles his belt, stands up, and lets his pants drop. "I forgot you are not as shy as you seem." His boxers follow his pants and it is my turn to look at him.

"You are not so shy as you seem either."

He shrugs and there is an uneasy slant to his mouth, smoothed away a moment later. "There is something about you that makes me comfortable where I am not with anyone else."

I am afraid that is my doing. But I cannot know for certain, and there is no undoing it now. These threads are set.

I take a step closer. Take his hands in mine. "Percival."

"Delaney." He tilts his head down to kiss me, as deep and honest as anyone has ever been with me.

I close my eyes. I had hoped that once I reached this moment, I would find a different road. I want there to be new threads that do not require the magic and blood I have poured into the ones that have led us here.

But these threads are the ones I have twisted and pulled since I first saw Percy. Worn thin to the point where all might break away and leave me drifting without direction or control and faded 'til I must use all my skill to discern where one ends and another one does not.

I had hoped once I reached this moment, I would find another road, but this is the only way. Neither of us will survive without the other, no matter how much I might have twisted the roads that lead away from here.

I wrap my arms around him, breathless and warm. "Now?"

"Yes." He pulls me back onto the bed so that we lie next to each other.

I smooth the scar on his shoulder with my thumb. These things do not make us ugly. "Gently then. But not too slow."

CHAPTER 17

Afterward we lie together, legs still intertwined and hands laying claim on each other. His hair curls around his ears, damp with sweat, skin glowing against mine. I rest my head on his shoulder and wish this moment never ends. I know it will. I know it must.

"I wish it didn't," I whisper.

Percy murmurs and opens his eyes. There is a moment of confusion, soon replaced with worry. "What's wrong?"

"It's nothing."

He touches the corner of my mouth. "You look upset."

"I'm just tired."

"Then sleep."

"In a minute." I comb the hair off his forehead. "I want to remember this."

Percy lies quietly for a little while, watching me. One hand moving across my body, drawing little circles on my skin as his fingers drift across the hollows and hills of my belly and breasts. "Are you afraid?"

I lick my lips. "A little." I look at him more closely. "Are you?"

"Yes."

"Why?"

"Because I cannot see the future, Delaney." He says it crossly. "I cannot even fathom what sort of... thing this Salesman must be. How can I tell my team how to stop it? How can I fight something I know will kill me if it touches me?"

"I will not let that happen."

He shivers. "You do not..."

"Listen to me." I lean my forehead against his. "It is the story that has given birth to this thing. Small magic from many tongues. The repetition of fear and hate collecting like drops of rain forming a puddle. Growing larger over the years as more tongues whispered revenge. Larger, but without form. And without form, it had no power."

A moment while he thinks about it. "Then something has changed."

"Yes."

"Do you know... I mean, have you seen it?"

"Maybe." I shrug. The threads are numerous; I do not see them all nor remember every one that I see. "I think that... pool has found a way to take on a form. It has attached itself to something ordinary."

"Ordinary?"

"Something physical. Something that can be destroyed."

"How?" He clutches at me, desperate.

"You will know once you see it." I touch his cheek reassuringly. "Everything physical can be destroyed."

Percy nods, though the pinch of worry remains. "You'll help me?"

My lips tremble as I force a smile. He can't know how his words cut to the bone. "Yes. I'll help you."

"Good." He pulls me into the circle of his arms, lets his breath out slow. "We should rest now." Already his eyes are sliding closed again, a sleepy burr to his voice.

I rest my head on his shoulder. His heart beats slow and steady under my hand. This is a moment I wish could last, but I know it won't.

Everything physical can be destroyed. Even them that don't burn.

CHAPTER 18

Six good years.

Gil Mains stares at the coffee in his cup. A thread of steam creeps across the surface, but he doesn't have the gift to see any meaning in it. He sighs and takes a sip.

Six good years with his wife he got because of Delaney. And one year of pain and beauty after the cancer got hold of her liver. He takes another swallow of coffee.

The doctors had talked about new treatments and options for drawing the last few months of her life out. But the numbers were still so small. Odds that no fool would take if it weren't a question of watching someone you love eaten up from the inside.

He'd gone to visit Del. Offered her whatever she wanted that he had to give. Begged her to do something to save his wife. Had cursed her when she said she could do nothing more.

It was the only time he ever saw her cry.

He stands up and takes the empty mug to the sink. Washes it out and wipes it dry with a towel. Some weeks he lets it all pile up in the sink. There's more than enough dishes for just one man and no one coming to visit, so it's more trouble than it's worth to wash each plate when he's done with it. Let them pile up for a bit as long as the flies don't find 'em.

Same with the rest of the house. He don't let it get too bad. Not filthy-like, anyway. Just dirty sometimes. No one's there to fuss if the bed ain't made up every morning or the clothes folded and put back in their drawers.

But today Gil's thinking of his wife and he's put it all straight. Today he's thinking of Delaney and The Salesman and feeling tight and strange in his chest like he's going to walk out that door and never come back.

Six good years. And one hard one.

Del told him she couldn't do nothing more than what she already had. There weren't no changing the fact that his wife was dying or how she was dying. But she wouldn't be facing the pain and fear alone.

Six good years and the chance to hold Lettie's hand when she passed. It wasn't the future he would have picked, but he wasn't the one with the Touch and as much as Del scared him...

She's more kind than not. If she said it was the best way, he had to accept it.

But today, with the sky so washed out by the sun it don't have no color and the feeling of electricity in the air that says a storm is coming, he wonders what else she has in store for him.

Not that he won't do it.

He'd promised her whatever she wanted that he had the power to grant and he meant it, even if it seemed at first that he was getting the short end of the stick. Because Lettie was dying and there was no stopping it.

She fought the best way she knew how. Not the way the doctors wanted with their offers of experimental treatments and promises of better odds that were measured in fractions of a percent. Not the way he wanted with his desperate bargaining with the only Power he knew for sure.

Lettie had lived fiercely in the twelve months she had left. Cramming twenty years of living into one and dragging him along with her. And eventually he realized that six good years was enough if it meant having the one.

So Gil Mains stands on his front porch watching the heat boil up off the road and the horizon getting grayer with every passing minute and he knows that he has a promise to keep.

He rubs his head, thoughtful-like.

Inside the phone rings and he nods.

"Huh. I figure that's about to come due."

CHAPTER 19

I don't spend much time around normal folks. Even at Greenhaven I'm usually alone for most of the day and night. Not left to myself, but alone nonetheless.

I'd forgotten how deep the whispers cut, just how heavy the looks get. Even with my hair combed and pulled back neatly on the back of my neck and the scars that run down my arm hidden under the thick weave of my sweater, even with trying to stand straight and smile and not stare at anyone too hard with my brown eye, I still stand out like a sinner on Sunday.

Percival is in Sheriff Tolbert's office along with the rest of his team and a handful of senior deputies. Since I'm here only because Percy insisted I not be left behind at the motel, I'm balanced on the edge of a hard bench in the reception area doing my best not to fidget. A task made more difficult by the ornery nature of the bench—too tall to let my feet touch the ground unless I sit on the front edge where the wood is cut in a clean corner instead of rounded like a sane piece of furniture.

I rub my forehead and stare at my hands again. Try and organize things in my head.

By now Ms. Drowner is unfortunately dead. I figure that's the source of most of the hot looks and cold words flying my direction. But there's also Luke and Merv. MacKenzie and Elliot didn't find them at home and their truck was spotted abandoned this morning.

Tolbert ain't stupid, so he's guessed the boys have stolen a different truck or maybe a car and are out looking for another woman with the Touch. Truth be told, there aren't that many. Half the names he put on that list last night are no more special than a cow turd, but most folk will seize on any difference as a sign of supernatural powers. I figure Luke and Merv aren't any different.

By now Tolbert's also figured out they aren't going to intercept them before they snatch another woman. The only way to stop someone else from gettin' burned up like yesterday's dinner is to find the place they're taking her.

The place where Jack Green's bones were buried. A place where the good folk didn't have to see a headstone or even the yellowed grass over the big metal box they'd murdered him in.

"Afternoon, Delaney." Mains' voice brings the hard bench and the worn vinyl tile floor back into focus.

I look up at him, careful-like. "Hello."

"I thought you'd be stuck to young Cox." His mouth twists, adding an obscene and knowing emphasis to the words.

"He's meetin' with the sheriff."

"And you aren't invited."

I shake my head. "Not yet."

"Not yet." He sits down beside me on the bench. "I got a call said they were puttin' together some kind of search party."

"They want to find The Salesman." I say it too loud because I'm nervous.

The skinny fellow on the other side of the counter that separates the reception area, with its artificial plants and the uncomfortable bench, from the rest of the office area twitches and flaps his hand around—a Southern Baptist doing his damnedest to cross himself.

Mains grins, dry as a drought. "Easy, Del. They'll put you outside if you ain't careful."

"Might be better that way. Nobody lookin' at me. Hot though."

"Storm's comin' in soon enough."

I glance at the doors, the blacktop all washed out in the glare outside. "Dark is coming early tonight."

The door to Sheriff Tolbert's office slams open and he stomps out and across the long room toward us. Percy's right behind him, eyebrows pulled down low. He's been arguing, no doubt. Trying to lift the blame from me for all that's happened.

Tolbert hooks his thumbs in his belt and glares down at me. "You know where the Trainer boys have been taking those women?"

I shrug. "I can guess."

He ain't like Gil Mains who only got cleverer when he was afraid. Grabs me by both shoulders and yanks me up onto my feet, pushes his face up close, all red and sweaty. "Don't play games with me, girl. You might have the city boy fooled, but I know you've had a hand in this. You tell me where they're headed or by God I'll make Greenhaven look like a resort."

He's pinching me so hard my fingers hurt, but I look at him square and cool with my green eye. "They'll be wherever Jack Green's bones were hid."

"Where?"

"Somewhere in the woods out west of town."

"That's a big place. Where exactly?" He shakes me like I'm a kid he caught throwing shit on his porch.

"That's enough." Percy has a hand on Tolbert's shoulder, dragging him back a step.

Martinez steps into the intervening space, nearly trampling my feet as he gets between me and Tolbert and pushes him farther back. "Leave her alone." He's cool as always, but solid as a wall.

The lobby crackles with tension—the deputies clustering behind the main desk, ready to swarm out to assist Tolbert, and Percy and his team lookin' ready to throw down themselves.

Mains clears his throat, staring hard at Tolbert. "Stupid," he says.

Tolbert looks at me again and the color fades from his cheeks. He licks his lips and gives a hitch at his belt. "If she knows—"

"I don't know." That part, at least, is true as the day is long. I know there's a clearing out there and an old house, but the woods are big and I've only been out there once in my physical self. "If we search for it, we'll find it."

Maybe Tolbert feels the weight in those words, the knowledge that this will come to pass. For sure he remembers who he'd got hold of. He takes another few steps back, wiping his hands on the front of his shirt as though he can rub away bad luck. He looks at Percy. "Well?"

"She'll stay with me," Percy says. "And Mains."

Mains nods. "Sure."

Tolbert licks his lips. "What are we looking for?"

"A clearing." Percy looks at me for confirmation. "With an old house, half-covered by vine."

"All right." Tolbert scowls. "We'll start on Stringer's Road and move west." He waves a hand at the deputy behind the counter. "Get the rest of the men in the cars. We don't have a lot of time and there's a storm comin'."

CHAPTER 20

The woods are dark and I put my hand on Percy's arm as we look for the path through the trees. To the left Mains is also searching, his light flashing now and then as he scans the ground for some sign of the track. Martinez is to the right, moving more heavily, his light fixed on the ground in front of him. I know that farther out are the other members of Percival's team—Elliot and MacKenzie—but the undergrowth is too thick for me to make them out or catch the flicker of their flashlights.

I tuck my hand more snugly into the crook of Percy's elbow. This is the trickiest part. I have studied the details of these woods for years—the types of trees and underbrush, the way the land rolls, the build-up of leaves. The individual parts are all tucked away for reference, but I have not been able to walk here in this specific place.

Finding the threads of the folk that pass through here has been a challenge. Men cooking meth in the underbrush, the occasional young couple looking for a private spot to grope and kiss—all of 'em making me blush and fret, but in the end, I've learned the shape of these woods nearly end to end.

Walking in them now I'm pleased to note the overall similarity to the place I took Percy before, but the transition must be seamless, or I may lose my grip on him.

The darkness helps. I only need to add the large oak just in front of us, the half-lit beeches on either side. The rest is hidden.

As I have hoped and planned, Percy doesn't notice at first. We tramp along in the darkness. At least it seems that way. In reality, our physical selves are standing in the woods just beneath the edge of a great old oak. But our real selves, the undying parts, are here. In my woods.

Percy stops and shines the flashlight around. "Are you certain this is the right direction?" He squints into the darkness. "Mains." There is no answer.

"Maybe he's fallen behind."

"Maybe." He scans the ground with the light again, and this time there is something other than dead leaves and soft-rotten sprawl of fallen beech limbs. "What's this?" He picks it up, brushes the leaves from the pale blue cover.

"It looks like a book."

"I meant..." He shakes his head and looks at the spine. "Saint Joan."

"George Bernard Shaw," I whisper. It was one of the first things I memorized. One of the first things I lost behind the walls the meds have built in my head— chemically rearranging my brain as Dr. Everley tries to hide me from the magic in my bones.

Percy flips through the book. "These pages are blank." A pause. He turns his light back toward the woods. "Mains. Martinez." Yelling now, but there is no response. "Where are we, Delaney?" His flashlight is blinding.

I put my hand up to shield my eyes. "You know the answer to that, Percival."

"Your woods. Your head." He turns around, the leaves whispering underfoot, but nothing changes. "Why?"

"Because this is the only way. If we find that path and you reach the end of it..." I pause, searching for words to explain what I have seen will happen if he comes into contact with The Salesman.

I want more than anything to tell him that I do not fear losing him to death because it is only a temporary separation. The thing that shakes me to my soul is the other futures I have seen. The countless times he faces The Salesman and it wakens something dark and hideous in his soul. The things that he has forgotten. But even that I cannot tell him without risk.

He takes my hesitance as confirmation of his own fear. "I will die."

I nod, willing to leave it at that. "Yes. You would die. But I told you I wouldn't let that happen."

"We have discussed this. We are all taking precautions."

I look at him silently.

"Aren't we?"

"I followed every thread, Percy. Hundreds of them. And down every road more people died. And the more blood spilled the stronger The Salesman grew." I lick my lips. "And you died."

"You told me once you know the future you can change it."

"Yes. And there was one thread that put an end to the terror. But only if I kept you from stopping me."

"Stopping you." He grabs my arm, hard. "Delaney. Whatever it is you're thinking of doing, it isn't necessary."

I smile, wishing he was right. "Yes, it is."

"No. We'll find another way." He leans his forehead against mine. "If you are doing this because of me..."

I touch the book tucked in the crook of his arm. "You are part of it. But there is more to it."

"I will not let you risk yourself. This is unnatural fire. It might kill you."

"I am not afraid of death, Percy."

He shakes his head. "No, Delaney."

I can barely breathe around the weight of my heart. It smolders like the flames I know are waiting. I close my eyes and dig deep and desperate for the words that are still buried in my head, still buried in the book Percy found.

"Yes: they told me you were fools, and that I was not to listen to your fine words nor trust to your charity. You promised me my life; but you lied."

"Ah, Delaney." Percy sucks in a deep breath. He understands now. The idea of being forever shut up in Greenhaven is the only thing I truly fear. But the fire in his eyes tells me he will not let go of me easily.

I put my arms around him, finding strength in the words I hid away so many years ago. "You think that life is nothing but not being stone dead. It is not the bread and water I fear: I can live on bread. When have I asked for more? It is no hardship to drink water if the water be clean. Bread has no sorrow for me, and water no affliction. But to shut me from the light of the sky and the sight of the fields and the flowers..." My throat aches and I lay my head against his chest as tears break free.

He murmurs in my hair. Wordless at first. His voice a deep and soothing vibration. Then, quiet-like. "Ursula, in a garden, found a bed of radishes. She kneeled upon the ground and gathered them, with flowers around, blue, gold, pink, and green. She dressed in red and gold brocade and in the grass an offering made of radishes and flowers."

The flashlight has fallen to the ground, leaving his face in darkness. I bite my lip, reaching out to touch the world I have built here. Overhead the clouds peel back and the moon pours through as big and full as it is possible for the moon to be. So I can look at him. So he can look at me.

He tilts his head down and kisses me. Desperate. His hands on my face. Warm and tender. "I will not let you go, Delaney Green."

"Ah." I smile in spite of everything. "You must, Percy."

"Then all of this..." He stops, eyes wide and dark. Considering for the first time that Martinez and the others might be right. That I may have raised The Salesman.

I reach up and take his hands in mine. "I want to be free, Percy. But not like that."

"Then how? You told me something changed that brought the nightmare to life. Something that turned the small magic of many tongues into something real and hungry and evil."

"But it weren't me." I toss my hair back over my shoulder and the woods around us shake and resolve into a rough clearing. Overhead the moon grows hot and bright, and the gentle trill of tree frogs changes into the distant call of the mockingbird. On the far side an old house slowly withering with age.

Percy sucks in a hard breath and steps closer. "This is the place in my dream."

"For good reason." I slip my arm around his waist. "Now watch."

Luke and Merv Trainer were never good for much. And may be that weren't their fault. Their daddy and his daddy and his daddy before him had all believed that the only education a man needed was the one he gave himself, that it was better to survive by one's wits than to work a long day in the service of another man. Of course, what they meant by surviving by their wits was taking whatever they could from any who was kind enough or foolish enough to offer them the opportunity.

The boys had come out here to this run down house in the middle of the hot summer woods because there was a rumor that the old lady who used to live there had buried some of her money somewhere in the clearing. They were smart enough to know to look for spots in the ground that were sunk in, but impatient too, digging little holes all over the clearing and finding nothing.

'Til one of 'em hits the corner of the box. The shovel thunks, metal-on-metal, and the energy shoots right through them. They dig fast now and steady, working around the edge and down the sides, scooping the dirt off the top until they have the whole thing uncovered. It ain't no coffee can like they'd been expecting to find. This is big and square, and it looks old, too.

Luke looks at Merv, a big greedy smile on his face. "What do you 'spect is in it?"

Merv shrugs. "Could be nothing. Ladies clothes or somethin'. Books." He grabs the handle on one end. "Help me get it out of the hole."

It takes a minute, sweat pushing out through their skin and slicking their shirts down, not to mention swearing in two voices with a fair amount of racial and sexual invective directed at the son-of-a-bitch who buried the damn thing in the first place. But they get it free of the dirt and stagger a few steps before setting it down. Straighten their backs and shake the sweat out of their eyes.

"It's heavy enough," Luke says, hopeful-like.

"Made of iron or somethin'." Merv works the edge of the shovel under the corner of the lid and pries up with it. The metal groans, but the rust flakes and breaks loose. "Get that other side."

Luke sticks his fingers under the lip and pulls up. "Damn." The lid flops open in a waft of dust and damp. He steps back, clutching one hand tight against his chest, little threads of blood leaking out between his fingers. "If I get lockjaw over a pair of old ladies' bloomers..." He trails off.

Merv is staring into the chest, face as white and green as the wood ears that grow on dead trees. "Jesus."

Luke edges closer. The chest is filled with ash and bones. Human bones. He knows because the skull is there, jaw gaping wide in a grisly jeer. "Fuck." He grabs the shovel from Merv and digs around in the trunk, but there ain't nothing of value in there. The pins and ribbons Jack Green used to sell have long since turned to dust and ash.

"Nothin'." Luke glares at Merv. "We done spent all this time diggin' that up and there ain't nothin' in it but a bunch of bones."

He flicks his hand, angry, and little drops of blood glide off his fingertips and land on the bones and ash. Even the blood of an idiot and an ass like Luke Trainer has a fair amount of magic in it. It calls out to the waiting magic of lips and tongue, and all the fear and hate and make-believin' about The Salesman comes straight to life.

The bones shiver, one against another, and the ash clots up around them in the imitation of flesh.

And Luke and Merv should be running like hell, but they just stand there, mouths open while The Salesman stands up. It flexes as if takin' a breath, but a thing like that don't breathe, and fire licks out of every joint and covers it like skin.

"Ah." The Salesman sighs and looks at the Trainer boys with eyes that are nothin' but flame.

Luke swallows hard. "Wh-what you want?"

The Salesman tilts its head to one side. Its desires and needs are simple. Shaped by a century and a half of tongues telling a story that weren't true. "Revenge." The fire covering its body licks out to turn the muggy summer afternoon even hotter.

He shakes his head. "Naw. You just get back in that damn chest, you hear?"

The Salesman reaches out faster than anyone can blink and grabs Luke by the arm. Just for a moment, but it leaves a blister the size of a hand on his skin.

Luke shrieks, doubling over on the ground while the Salesman stands over him. It's still got one foot in the iron trunk, but I figure Luke don't know that it can't step any farther because he looks up, his eyes all wet and bloodshot. "What do you want me to do?"

"Women," The Salesman says. "Bring me women and I will take my revenge."

The clearing shivers and my woods return, with cool moonlight to soothe away the fear and fire we just witnessed. I take a deep breath. "That was how. And it weren't me."

Percy looks at me, still suspicious. "You could have kept those two from finding the trunk."

"Someone else would have. Later, when I was too old to do anything about it. Or when I had no way to get out." I catch my lip between my teeth. "I was tempted there. But those roads... more people die. Not just the thirteen girls that died this way, but hundreds. And the story changed, let The Salesman walk free of his coffin and then more died." I shake my head. "I couldn't let that happen."

"Then let me go with you."

"No. You'll be brave even though you don't mean to and I'll lose you. And my freedom. I cannot even say for sure which would hurt me more. But you cannot come with me."

He shivers, holding on to me as though I'm the only thing keeping his legs from shaking right out from under him. "Delaney, I'm afraid."

"I know." I stretch up on tiptoe to kiss the tears from his cheeks, kiss his mouth with as much love as my lonely soul can muster. "It will be all right." I touch my fingers to his forehead and will him to sleep. "When you wake up, it will be all right."

He gets heavy in my arms and we sink toward the ground. "Delaney." His tongue is blurry with sleep.

"Yes, Percival."

"Promise me that I'll hold you again safe before the sun comes up."

I smile. "I promise, Percy."

He sighs and falls dead asleep and we drop back into the solid world.

Up ahead Martinez and the others are still picking their way through the trees, leaves scuffling underfoot despite their efforts to be quiet. There is no moon nor stars here, just the storm clouds as dark as the inside of a fist overhead and thunder grumbling on the horizon. The rain will be here soon.

I shove the flashlight into the pocket of my sweater and drag Percy into the shelter of the oak and make him as comfortable as I can in the hard pillows of its roots. He'll wake soon, but by then I will be too far ahead for him to catch up.

I kiss his mouth again. Whisper in his ear when he murmurs in his sleep. "I promise you will hold me again soon."

It is the biggest lie I've told yet.

CHAPTER 21

I know the bones of Jack Green were buried somewhere in these woods. Know too that The Salesman lurks somewhere in a clearing, but there is a lot of ground to be covered, and I don't have the time to search it all.

There is a game that high school girls play sometimes, staring in a mirror and saying a name until a death's head appears behind them. Some versions you say the name of some boogey man and some you say your own name. What those that play don't realize is this is the surest way to summon a ghost.

I don't have a mirror, but blood will reflect my call just as well. I stab my finger on one of the plentiful brambles and blow the welling drops of blood into the air. "Jack Green, Jack Green. Come to me. Jack Green, Jack Green. Come and see."

A cool wind slithers past my knees and a shadow rises from the ground, thin as breath in winter. It's hard to make out his face and the flashlight don't help, but there somethin' in the shape of his eyes and the strength of his mouth that reminds me a little of the face that stares back at me from the windows at Greenhaven.

I push my hair back over my shoulder and bob a little curtsy. "Hello, many-great granddaddy."

The ghost drifts close enough the skin on my arms prickles with the sudden chill. *What do you want?*

"Show me where your bones lie, Granddaddy Green."

Mine no longer. For a moment his teeth flash, surprisingly white and horrible in the winter-mist of his face. *Something evil has taken them.*

"I know. And I plan to fix that. If you'll kindly show me where they and it be."

He points off into the trees. *This way.* He moves like a thing in a dream—legs and feet going through the motions of walking but drifting over far more ground than each step should.

I have to run to keep up, the flashlight clutched in one hand, the other one shielding my face from the slap and scratch of branches. Falling once as my foot skids on a root hidden in the leaf mould and scrambling back upright and running on, despite the hot trickle of blood creeping down my shin.

Behind me I hear the voices of the rest of the search party. No doubt they have heard the noise and are following. Or looking for Percy. I still need to reach the clearing before they do, but I doubt any of them will interfere with what I mean to do.

Granddaddy Green slows and turns to look at me, then points again. *There.*

A bright spot in the trees leads me out into the clearing where everything is just as I have dreamed it.

Luke and Merv are carrying something big and wiggling between them. I don't have to see the worn blue plastic of the tarp to know they've got a woman wrapped up in it.

And toward the other side of the clearing is the sooty bulk of the iron chest and the thing named The Salesman standing in it, more terrible than anything I can imagine.

It is shaped like a man, but misshapen too—lumps of ash that mimic muscles but don't move, and skin that flickers bright and dark like the spots that come from staring at the sun. There is something else about it, hard to pin down in any fashion, but it is inhuman. Not a man with a broken mind or soul, or a ghost that was once flesh and blood. The Salesman is the sum of everything dark in the human spirit—envy, fear, guilt, spite—all stuck together with the bitter magic of unkind tongues.

My gut hurts like I've been eatin' glass, but I know that girl that Luke and Merv are dragging across the clearing will die if I don't do something.

My feet move, following the road I have laid for myself.

I run straight across the clearing, past Luke and Merv who react too slow to do anything but drop the woman they got between them. Straight to stand in front of the fury and flame that is The Salesman.

It looks at me, fire pooling in the big dark hollows of its skull. "Foolish." One knobby hand grabs my arm, and my sweater smokes and flames ripple up the sleeve and down and around my body. The thinner fabric of the dress flares up fast, but my skin remains unbroken.

Not that it don't hurt, 'cause it stings like I stepped in a shower turned too hot or too cold, but it don't burn. I don't burn. I raise my arm, pull against its grip and a couple of pieces of smoldering bone break off and fall to the ground. A thread of smoke rises from the tall grass, then the bits disintegrate into dust.

The Salesman may not be human, may not even be sentient in the way we tend to think of things that move and kill in the name of revenge, but conscious or not, it wants to survive. It lets go of me, shuffles back in the iron chest, but the words of the story that brought it to life also bind it to the box.

I step into the chest and grab its other hand, twisting it around 'til more fingers break off and dissolve in my hand. I slip my arms tight around its waist as it tries to hit me. "That ain't doin' you no good."

It puts its arm against my throat and tries to choke me, but its strength lies in its flames—the ash and bone underneath are fragile.

It screams at me. "Let me go."

"Oh, no." I grin the best I can with my heart playing Skip to My Lou in my chest. "I'm gonna break you into little bits and scatter you far and wide across these woods 'til you can't ever put yourself back together."

It pushes harder against my throat and I cough under the pressure, but one of its wrist bones snaps like a green twig. The flames lick higher, the last threads of my sweater curling off and away. "Let me go."

"You know I won't do that. Deep in your borrowed bones you know I'll hold on 'til I ain't nothin' but bones myself."

The flames wrap around us, hot and hotter, and the iron chest starts to glow. Hot iron. That what burned me before and will do again, just like it did Jack Green. It wasn't the flames but the trunk that was his undoing, and his bones are in the middle of The Salesman. His bones are mortal against the touch of fire and iron.

A thin layer of ash still covers the bottom of the chest, providing me with a fleeting protection from the red hot metal as I push The Salesman back against the edge of the box.

It screams again and I'm certain I hear the voices of the thirteen girls it murdered in the sound. Glowing white hot now in an attempt to burn me up and I glow too, my bones soaking up the heat and magic pouring out of The Salesman.

Its legs crumble away at the knees as the iron pressed against the back of its legs takes a toll.

I turn and drop The Salesman into the chest and stagger out of it. Grab the edge of the lid and throw it closed even though it burns my hands—skin peeling back like paper to leave the bones all naked underneath. But I'm not the only one hurt.

The iron is glowing too hot now for the thing named The Salesman to survive. For a moment or two it thumps and screeches against the red hot metal, beating itself to pieces as Jack Green's bones finally and permanently crumble into dust.

The chest itself breaks apart, unable to stand the supernatural force that has been exerted upon it. The sides crumble outward in a shower of sparks and the lid falls in with a whumph that sends fine black ash curling like fog.

It should be quiet in the clearing now, but someone is still screamin'.

Me.

My hands and feet all burned to blood and bone and the rest of me glowing white hot and fearsome as The Salesman itself.

Luke and Merv are still standing there, mouths open like their jaws are broke. Stupid bastards.

Lightning slices overhead and the thunder hits the clearing hard as a kick to the head. Sparks fly off me like dust off a rug, and I reach toward the Trainer boys with my burning hands.

They take off for the edge of the clearing, hoping to reach the dark and shelter of the trees. But I ain't The Salesman bound to Jack Green's chest or any other place, and my magic is different.

I lay my glowing bones against their threads and burn their future into nothing. They drop headlong into the grass where their bodies crackle and spit like bacon in a frying pan.

They don't suffer 'cause I ain't cruel. Just angry.

More lightning crackles overhead and I scream at the clouds. Where is the rain? The first heavy drops sizzle on my skin making dark marks that fade as quick as I see 'em. More drops follow, slap-slap-slap against the ground, and they temper the flames but cannot quench the magic burning in me.

There are more voices. I can barely hear them above the screech of my own voice, which just goes on and on and on because the pain doesn't stop. Neither do the flames. I shuffle around, guided by these threads I have been laying into place for years.

Mains tucks the shotgun up against his shoulder. His cheeks are wet and maybe that's just 'cause of the rain, but I'll bet it's not.

To the left are Martinez and Percy. They have their guns out, yelling at Mains to put the damn shotgun down. They don't want to shoot him. They might even know that he's got the right idea, but years of training say they can't let him put two barrels full of buckshot in my chest.

But Mains ain't afraid of death. Just like I ain't. Though I figure neither one of us can muster the strength to pull the trigger ourselves.

I hold my arms out wide so he can see that this is what I planned and swallow the pain for long enough to let my voice die out. Look at Percy who is yelling, not just at Mains, but at me. Begging me for something.

"Please," he says, over and over. "Please, Delaney."

Even that won't cool the fire.

I smile, and my lips crack away. "I will wish to be moonlight."

There is thunder, but no lightning, and the buckshot splinters me into a thousand pieces. The world breaking apart, leaves and dirt swirling up around me as I fall. Everything is so bright.

Grass tickles my skin and I lay quiet for a moment. Wind whispers across me from head to toe, and the air is sweet with the smell of warm-gold grass and honeysuckle.

A shadow touches me, and I open my eyes and squint up at the face looking down at me.

"You gonna lie there all day?" Addie says. She's got the baby hitched up on one hip, her fist planted on the other.

I sit up and brush bits of dry grass out of my hair. The field stretches out to the horizon, save for the western edge where there's a darker line of trees marking where the woods begin.

Addie moves so she stands between me and them. "Took you long enough."

"Yeah." I stand up and stretch. My feet are all right and my hands, too. Not even scarred. Maybe 'cause whatever I have left, it ain't my physical self. Least not the one that don't burn.

"Yeah," I say again. "I came as fast as I could."

CHAPTER 22

Percy sits on the steps of the abandoned house and watches as Sheriff Tolbert directs the collection of the bodies and supervises the interview with Martinez.

It turns out there was a road that led back here. Small and close to overgrown, they were able to follow it back out to the main road and bring the coroner's van and a couple of cruisers back, plus an ambulance for the woman who'd been tied up in the tarp. She was mostly unhurt, although hysterical. The emergency folks gave her a sedative and packed her off to the hospital to rest.

Percy rubs his hands together, trying to feel something other than cold. The storm has blown over and the moon peeks through the ragged clouds. Somehow the cold light does nothing to soften the burned ground or the memory of what happened here.

Martinez sits down next to him and holds out a Styrofoam cup. "MacKenzie thought you could use coffee."

"Thanks."

"It tastes like shit, but it's hot." Martinez forces a smile.

Percy can't summon the energy to smile back so he takes a sip from the cup. Watches as the coroner and his assistant roll one of the Trainer brothers up in a piece of plastic, then shimmy the corpse into a body bag.

Martinez fidgets, uncomfortable with the silence. "I've seen some pretty bad stuff before." He shakes his head. "But this was messed up."

Percy cradles the cup in his hands. "Yeah."

"You think..." Martinez stops for a moment, fiddling with his own cup. "It was like she knew what was going to happen."

"She did."

"But why?"

He rubs his fingers together, remembering the book in Del's woods. "She wanted to be free."

"By dying. Horribly. And taking Mains with her. Because if she knew what was going to happen to her, she must have known..."

"She did." His shoulders ache and he stretches. "So did he, though not as clearly."

Martinez looks at him sharply. "And you? Did you know?"

"Not enough. Not in time." She'd planned it that way. Dangerous and seductive, just like they'd warned him. And now he's sitting here all in one piece and she's gone. Percy can't complain about being alive, though the grief is strong enough to turn him cold straight through. But there's a nagging feeling that this ain't over.

Mains told him Delaney averted a death by violence and saved his life. Gave him eight years more than he might have had. Then took him all the same when it worked best to her purpose.

Now he's sitting here on the steps of the porch instead of being scooped up off the burned grass and shoveled into a bag, and Delaney's gone. Maybe he's already paid whatever is owed.

Maybe she'll come back to claim that debt.

Percy's hands shake. He ain't sure if it's relief or fear. *Maybe she'll come back.*

"Cox?" Martinez is looking at him. "You okay?"

He swallows hard. "Maybe."

"You should get some sleep. You'll feel better in the morning." Martinez has him by the arm, guiding him toward one of the cruisers.

"Sure." He nods as Martinez mutters on about staying with him, making sure he talks to the psychiatrist right away. Slides into the car and leans back against the seat without protest. He could use some sleep. And time to think.

Percy leans his forehead against the window once the car pulls away. The deputies are shoveling dirt onto the flames that still burn where Del was standing. Persistently and desperately smothering the supernatural.

He sighs and closes his eyes.

Maybe she'll come back.

EPILOGUE

Summer never ends here.

Addie and the baby play in the grass all day while the sun winds back and forth—not standing still, but never falling below the horizon. An eternity of perfect days.

The baby doesn't move like an infant, walking with her feet wide to balance her head—still too big for her tiny limbs. I suspect she can talk, too, but she doesn't. At least not to me, but sometimes I see her snuggled up on Addie's shoulder, and it seems they might be whispering to each other.

Every now and then the baby pulls an acorn out of the pocket on her tiny dress and stuffs it into the ground before she wishes it into a tree. The shade underneath is cool and still, and they lie down underneath and sleep. Not because they need to. None of us need to eat or sleep or drink nothin'. But I figure they get bored with running in the warm grass and weaving necklaces of daisies and bluebonnets.

An eternity of perfect summer days but never any nights.

They never go into the woods either.

I can see the trees on the western horizon, dark as storm clouds in the distance. But every time I try and walk there, Addie drags me off to play some other game.

I'm taller now and older if you count years spent in flesh and blood, but she's still the eldest of the three of us. I know I don't have to do what she tells me if I don't want to, and there's not much she could do to stop me, but it's hard not to think of her as the one in charge. Or maybe it's guilt. She's been here all this time with no one but the baby for company. Even though neither of us says it, we both know I'm not intending to stay.

An eternity of perfect summer days but never any nights.

It's not a bad way to pass the time. I run and sing, even though my voice wobbles on the high notes and Addie's is clear as glass. Tickle the baby who chuckles and clutches at me with her little hands, and make a chain of daisies that winds from my head down to my bare toes. Lay under the ceaseless sun and sprawl in the shade of the baby's oak tree as if I ain't ever going anywhere else.

But sometimes I catch the scent of the trees—the sweetness of old leaves and rain—and long for the shelter of the woods instead of the wide open field that lays everything bare. Sometimes I dream of fire and moonlight.

We have an eternity of perfect days, me and Addie and the baby, but sometimes I long for the night.

That's where I'll find my way back to Percy. In the murmur of beech leaves and the spreading arms of old trees. That's where I'll find him.

Addie's yelling for me to come and help her swing the baby back and forth. A smile on her face and long gold-brown hair flying out in the breeze, but there's a wrinkle above her nose like she used to get when Mama would start yelling. She waves her arm, beckoning me to come back, and the baby claps her hands together and chuckles. Begging me to stay in every way except actually sayin' it.

And I will stay. For now, anyway.

The woods will be waiting.

OF SHADE AND SOUL

PROLOGUE

The car rolled up beside Percy almost silently. "Hey, son." The driver leaned across the passenger seat. "Is there a place to get a cup of coffee around here?"

Percy stopped, thumbs hooked through the straps on his backpack. "There's a diner on Oak Street."

The guy behind the wheel grinned, sheepish. "I'm just traveling through. I don't know…"

Percy pointed up the street. "Turn left up there. Then four blocks and turn right."

"Left, four blocks, then right." He nodded. "Thanks." He looked at Percy curiously. "Can I give you a lift somewhere?"

"No thanks." He squinched his eyes shut as his head throbbed more fiercely. *This one's a creep.*

"You sure? Maybe just up the block?" His mouth smiled, but his eyes were hungry. "Most kids would die for a chance to ride in a car like this."

Percy paused, looking at the car. Flat black with big wheels and a racing stripe over one side. He shrugged. "Yeah. I guess."

"Come on. Here." The creep put the car in park and turned the ignition off. "Why don't you sit in the driver's seat? I'll sit over here." He stepped out of the car and came around to the passenger side. "Just for a minute."

Percy looked up and down the block, but it was empty. The old folks who lived on that street were already inside eating dinner. "Okay. But just for a minute."

He walked around the car, slid into the driver's seat. The leather was soft and smooth against the back of his knees. Even sitting up straight he could barely see over the dashboard, clinging to the steering wheel in a sudden rush of fear that the car was about to swallow him whole.

"Hey." The creep reached out and laid his hand over Percy's. "You okay?"

The magic was subtle, comforting—like sunlight in early spring. Percy blinked, sleepy. "You shouldn't touch me like that."

The creep smiled again. It was as dark as his eyes. "It's okay. Just relax."

Percy shivered as the magic grew colder, his heart slowing with every passing second. He twitched, tried to move his legs, his arms, his head, but the soft leather seat of the car held him fast.

His throat hurt, a scream building in his chest. A whimper at first, it grew as his fear did, and the hot, dark thing in his gut woke up.

It was not afraid. It was angry. And it was hungry.

Percy screamed. The thing inside him roared and sank deep claws into the creep, tearing the life right out of him.

The weight holding Percy in the car lifted, and he scrambled out into the street, skinning his knee on the blacktop as his feet tangled with each other. The scream faded into hiccups as his heart started to beat again, and the hiccups faded into silence.

He licked his palm and wiped it across his bloodied knee, then stood up and straightened his backpack.

The creep in the car sprawled across the seats, dead. His eyes were bloodshot and glassy, skin pulled tight across his cheekbones.

Percy leaned forward and poked his outstretched hand, but he remained dead. The thing in his gut grumbled as it went back to sleep. "You shouldn't have touched me," Percy whispered.

He brushed at his knee again and then turned back up the street. He was late and Mom would be getting worried.

CHAPTER 1

Time moves different when you're dead.

Maybe because of the crazy sun Addie's dreamed up. It never sets, just dips down to kiss the horizon, then plods back the way it came. Back and forth with barely a pause for breath at each end.

I try to keep track, but it ain't easy. I've got no pencil or paper. Not even a stick to make marks on. Just my head, and it's never been so good at holding onto thin things like facts or numbers. Nonetheless, I count how many times I've seen my shadow growing long across the rippling grass. Count and then divide by two.

Seven.

I think.

Addie don't plan on letting me go again. Her shoulders get real square every time she sees me looking at the dark line at the edge of her sunny field, and her eyes start to look like Momma's. Maybe remembering how she learned too late that all my talk about the Touch weren't imaginary, and Daddy and I weren't just plain crazy.

But the field and the sun are not of my making. If I want to reach the woods, I'll have to wait 'til Addie's sleeping.

Twice I've waited for Baby to grow an oak tree and the two of them to lay down in the deep shade and sleep. Twice I've run as far and as fast as I could and come up short. Close enough to smell the sick-sweet moulder of old leaves and feel the damp air under spreading branches. Close enough to see the smooth grey bark of the beeches and hear the insistent peep and chirp of the tree frogs. Running 'til I can't stand any longer and never crossing the last stretch of grass between me and the dark edge of the woods.

It's not 'til the third time I see Baby pulling an acorn out of her pocket to grow another oak tree that I realize the woods are not of Addie's making. She is not keeping me here; Baby is keeping me out.

I wait until they are both asleep—Addie curled up like a kitten, knobby knees almost touching her nose; Baby flat on her back, arms thrown over her head.

I take off my sweater and roll Baby up in it real careful-like. She smacks her lips, but settles in my arms, content. I smooth her hair across the top of her head and start walking.

It doesn't take long to reach the point where I can go no farther. I hold my breath and keep walking, hoping that having Baby with me will be enough to cross the last stretch. My feet move on the ground, step after step, but the woods remain stubbornly out of reach.

I plop down in the grass with a scowl. My arms are tired. Despite her tiny size, Baby is heavy.

The woods breathe out, fluttering the edge of my dress. I blink back tears, desperate for the company of trees and the silver light of the moon. Desperate to find Percy.

In my lap, Baby sighs and stretches. She pushes my sweater aside and stands up. "Tears, Delaney? That's not like you." Her voice is strange and small.

"I need to find Percy."

She squints at me. "That boy is nothing but trouble."

I shrug. "They all are, one way or another."

"Huu." She flexes tiny fingers. "Addie's bound and determined to keep you here. Said she ain't letting you back to do nothin' that will get you burned up."

My cheeks get hot. "I haven't hurt anyone recently," I say, indignant. "I mean, maybe the Trainer boys. But after all the killing they did, I figure they deserve what they got."

Baby is silent, watching.

"Gil Mains made a bargain and got the better end of the deal, if you ask me."

But she isn't.

"Ms. Drowner weren't my responsibility. All I did there was make sure she went a little easier. And Percy…" I shake my head. "He only stays hurt if I don't get back to him. So that's on you and Addie if you keep me here." I smooth my dress across my knees. "You know what would have happened if I hadn't done what I did."

"Same thing as will happen if you go back." She looks at me stern. Unsettling with her oversize head and big eyes. Maybe she's seen something I haven't.

I flex my fingers, instinctive, trying to find the threads. Trying to get a feel for the future she sees. "You know there aren't many who can stop Percy once he remembers he's strong."

"I ain't worried about who will stop him." She leans up on tiptoe. "Who's going to stop you?"

"Me?" I blink and sputter. I've seen that too, a few times. Little threads on the edge of things that lead to a place where I go wild and hurt folks deliberate-like. "I haven't hurt much of anyone recently, and I don't intend to start."

Baby steps up in my lap and presses one tiny hand to each of my cheeks. Stares deep into my eyes 'til my head starts to ache with the strain. "Ah." She hops back into the grass. "You always forget, Delaney. Your own future is the hardest to see."

"You cannot keep me here. I will find a way out." The ground beneath us trembles, the grass blurring with the strength of my words.

She frowns. "I don't aim to keep you. But first there is something you must see."

I turn and look back across the field—dusky where we sit, but bright under the distant track of the sun. Aside from the oak tree there is nothing but grass from one horizon to the other. "Here?"

"In the woods." She holds up her hands. "Up."

I stand up and reach down for her, reluctant. "My arms are tired."

"Then put me on your shoulders. But my legs are too short for this journey."

"Just how far are we going?"

"Far enough." She settles herself on my shoulders, little arms wrapped around my head. "Mind the branches."

I take a breath and a step forward. This time the ground doesn't go all squirrely. Another couple of strides and dry leaves crackle under my shoes. "What about Addie?" I glance back over my shoulder toward the solitary oak tree.

"If you tell her you are leaving, she will try and fight you."

"You will tell her I said goodbye?"

"Yes."

It will have to be enough. *I cannot stay.*

I turn my back on the field. "Which way?"

Baby's hands tighten against my forehead. The leaf mold creeps back, slow, to reveal the dark earth underneath. "Follow the path."

Something in her voice makes the hair on my arms stand up. But whatever she wants to show me can't be worse than what I've already faced. I grasp her feet in either hand and head down the path beneath the gentle light of the moon.

CHAPTER 2

The psychiatrist works out of an unmarked office on the second floor of an old house turned into boutiques. Down the hall is a wedding photographer, and the main floor is occupied by a graphic design firm. Supposedly it's all about confidentiality and protecting the FBI from potential embarrassment, but Percy feels distinctly awkward sitting on the floral print couch, the plastic cup with his mandatory urine sample resting on one knee.

The door opens and the receptionist smiles at him. She's a younger woman with the charm and inflection of a kindergarten teacher, dipped in flour and Southern fried. "You can come on back, honey."

He follows her down the narrow hallway, deposits his cup of urine on the tray next to the office door, and steps inside.

It's warm today, and he takes off his jacket, tosses it over the back of the chair before he sits down. It took a couple of weeks before he figured out that Ms. Carver was deliberately tweaking the temperature in the room. Now he comes prepared with a jacket and short sleeves underneath every time. He's irritable enough over the continuing sessions, and there's a sense of satisfaction in thwarting Ms. Carver's attempts to manipulate the environment.

She picks up her notepad from the glass table beside her chair. Clicks her pen and looks at him. Calculating. Searching for signs of instability. Makes a note on the lined yellow paper. "Shall we begin?"

He settles himself more securely in the chair. "Why not?"

"You're still taking your meds?"

A sigh. "Yes."

"Both the aripiprazole and the... booster?"

The muscle in his jaw trembles, but he nods. "Yes." The so-called booster is Magiprex. He took it for three days before he got so wooly-headed he woke up not remembering his name.

She pauses, makes a point to look him in the eye. "We do check those samples you give us."

"That's why I'm still taking them." In reality, Percy's only been taking the anti-psychotic to dull the teeth of the depression following him around like a lost dog. He still collects the refills for both. On the days he has an appointment with Ms. Carver, he crushes one of the Magiprex tablets and dumps the powder into his pants pocket. Then dabs his finger in the drug residue and mixes it into the pee cup. He'd not been certain at first that it would work, but they haven't ordered him into an institution or started monitoring his dosing, so it must work well enough.

She presses her lips together, trying to stare him down, but he doesn't look away. Finally, she makes another note, clicks her pen a few times. "How are you sleeping?"

"Like a baby." Another lie. But insomnia would be enough of a flag to put him under more intense supervision.

"No dreams?"

"Maybe. If I am, I don't remember."

Carver stares at him long and intent. Finally makes another note on the notepad. "Let's talk about Delaney Green."

"Okay." He waits.

"The other members of your team reported you seemed to have developed a close emotional bond with this young woman."

Percy nods. "Yes."

"Yes?" She waits for a qualification. Steady. Sharp as a razor.

He drums his fingers on the arms of his chair, mimicking agitation. "Yes, I had a close relationship with Delaney."

"Relationship." She leans forward. "You considered her to be a friend?"

"Friend. Partner. Lover." He shrugs. "We were close."

Carver blinks, scribbles a note, and clears her throat. "You knew her for barely more than a day."

"She had known me for much longer."

"What do you mean?"

"I mean she had known me for years, although I knew her only a short time. I loved her."

"That is a strong word, Mr. Cox."

"And strong feelings, too."

"You did not think perhaps she was using her influence on you? To create a sense of bonding that was not grounded in reality?"

"I considered it." He rubs his fingers through his hair. It's not the first time he's thought about it. Every night since he met Delaney with her green-brown eyes and mud-colored hair spilling down over her shoulders. Every hour since he first felt the electricity and ice in her skin.

"There was a synchronicity to our experience," he says after a pause. "Even if we had met under less... intense circumstances, we would have been friends. I understood her."

Ms. Carver is scribbling furiously. "How exactly does one understand a Power?"

Percy shrugs. "Perhaps understand is an overstatement. But I understood her more than others had. I stood in her shoes when I was younger. The fear and loneliness… there was a connection there. Something other than magic or her influence on the future."

"So you felt sorry for her because of everything that happened to her."

"No."

"You didn't sympathize with the loss of her family? Or the way she had been shut away from society?" There's a triumphant quirk to her lips. "This young woman who had lost everyone she loved, been abused, and nearly murdered as a child, and you felt no sympathy for her."

"I did not say I felt no sympathy. But Delaney... it's hard to explain if you have not met her. But she is not damaged by the terrible things in her life." He pauses. "She is transformed."

Ms. Carver pauses. "Don't you mean she was transformed?"

He leans back in his chair. "She was transformed, yes. But..." This is a game, played fiercely and in an attempt to keep her away from the questions that might bring him to actual harm.

"You think her presence still lingers?"

Percy raises an eyebrow. "You think it doesn't? A woman who pulled and twisted the future like a spider in a web. Who was committed enough to her purpose to embrace death by fire. A Power for certain. And you think that her skin and bones turning to dust is the end of her?"

Carver licks her lips, her face the same grey-white as a t-shirt that's been washed too many times. "Have you seen her, Mr. Cox? Since that night?"

"No." He shakes his head with certainty. He's dreamed of her, but those are just memories. Like Del's house, with her desperate mother filling every space. He sees her in his dreams, but he can't hold her or feel her fingers in his hair or change what happens. No matter how many tears he cries.

"No. I've not seen her since that night she burned. But when I do, it'll come as no surprise."

She isn't expecting that. Her usual mask is gone. Too frightened to maintain an emotional distance. Because she's read all the reports and the thought that Delaney, a Power who could manipulate the future, might come back leaves her cold. "Are you certain she wasn't taking advantage of her pre-cognizance? Maybe that supposed convergence of events was just coincidence." She licks her lips. "Isn't it possible her Power was embellished with imagination and spite? Small town folk who couldn't comprehend what had happened to a child that young and invented an elaborate story to justify the horror of it?"

Percy knows better. He remembers Del's woods, as real as the actual thing. He remembers that it took the full fear and anger of another Power and an old man with a shotgun to put an end to her. *She don't just burn.* But he nods. "Maybe."

She fidgets in her chair and writes another page of notes. The pen scratches loudly on the pad, the tension in her body driving the tip deep into the paper. Finally, she glances up. "I think we're done for today."

He stretches to diffuse the smile threatening to break loose, reaches for his jacket on the back of the chair. "It doesn't feel like it's been an hour."

"There is not much point in continuing further today." The drawer in the table beside her chair squeaks when she opens it, but she is the one who flinches. "Here's this week's supply of medication. Continue to take them until our session next week."

He stuffs the pill bottles into his jacket pocket. "How much longer do you think these will be necessary?"

"Until I say they are not." Ms. Carver glares at him, lips pale under the worn layer of lipstick.

For the first time, he realizes he is not here because they are afraid he might be insane— anxious, depressed, or suicidal. It's not just departmental procedures to mediate PTSD that have put him here week after week. The real fear is that somehow Delaney will have rubbed off on him. Maybe even woken a Power in him.

He considers telling her that he is still only mortal. He gets headaches in the presence of other magic, and his guts hurt when he crosses paths with a murderer, but his Sensitivity is not a Power. It touches no one but himself.

He wishes for a moment that he was changed, that he had the ability to reach into that shadowed world Delaney had traversed so easily and draw her to him.

But he is still only mortal.

He tosses his hair out of his eyes. "Next week, then."

She nods, forcing herself back into her normal cool mask. "I look forward to it."

He slips out the back door of the office, squeezing past a family dressed all in pinstriped blue and white standing in the main hall outside the portrait photographer's space.

Martinez is waiting in the parking lot, windows rolled down and sleeves rolled up. "How'd it go?"

Percy shrugs. "She's still looking for deeper meaning."

"In your relationship with Green?"

"That too." Percy tosses his jacket into the back seat and buckles his seatbelt. "She can't understand why a Power would embrace death like that."

Martinez pauses, one hand on the ignition. "It wasn't accidental?" There's a reason they let him do so many suspect interviews and interrogations; he has a bland quality that makes it hard to read what sort of answer he's looking for. At first Percy had suspected Martinez was reporting to Ms. Carver, but none of their conversations ever seemed to have a bearing on Carver's questions. He can't be sure who Martinez talks to after driving him to the psych appointments, but it isn't her.

"It didn't look accidental," Percy says thoughtfully.

"No." Martinez chews that over for a moment. "But what could she want from that?"

Percy looks at him, sly and amused. "Even you can see the answer there."

"She wanted to be normal."

"Wants," Percy says. "She wants to be normal."

"Wants?" Martinez's eyes are like glass under his lowered brows. "She's not done yet?"

"Do you think she's done?"

He lets his breath out in a hard rush. "No. No, I don't expect she's done."

Percy smiles. "Good."

Martinez shakes his head. "I doubt that." But he starts the car and backs out of the parking space. "Better get back to the office."

CHAPTER 3

The air gets cold as I follow Baby's trail through the woods. Not frosty, like a winter night, but chilly and damp—like the breath of a swamp. Stinks like one, too. The moon pulls a cloud over its face, leaving us in darkness. I take another couple steps before Baby squeaks.

"Ow. Watch where you're going."

I stop, blink hard, and try to see through the dark. Nothing. "I need a light."

She sighs. "Fine."

In the darkness something flickers. Then another. And more. Slowly drifting closer. A pinpoint of light lands on my dress—blinks off, on. Off, on. Joined by more until my skirt is a rippling layer of fireflies, all moving and blinking.

I suppress a shudder at the thought of many legs and wings and start walking again. The light has a liquid quality to it as it reflects off the silver beeches, washing across the dark ground beneath my feet, but it's strong enough to light the way and reveal the lower branches that threaten to scratch Baby's face.

The stink grows stronger. Like a green-choked pond or the rubbery dead smell of rotting mushrooms. Baby's clinging tight. If I didn't have one of her feet in each hand, I think her legs would be caught 'round my neck.

"Is it much farther?"

She shivers. "Just a little ways. Past that thicket."

The path dwindles to the width of my hand, winding through a stand of saplings and honeysuckle. No way through it without getting scratched. I pull Baby down into my arms, tuck the edges of my sweater over her face, and push my way through. It's deeper than it looks—despite the chill in the air, sweat rolls down my back as I trample the brush and wiggle between saplings too thick to bend out of my way.

By the time I reach the other side, I'm breathless, stinging from dozens of scrapes. It's dark for a moment. Then the fireflies regroup on my dress, their flickering light revealing the malignant shape of a lightning-struck oak. The trunk is split open to the ground, each half continuing to grow, the branches twisting at odd angles as they reach skyward again.

I set Baby on the ground and pick at a snarl of hair, trying to remove the spiny twig in the center of it. "What is this?"

She curls one arm around my calf. "This is where Daddy lives."

"But he's… dead." My cheeks flush as soon as I say it. *We're all dead.* I shake my head. "I mean, why isn't he with you and Addie?"

Baby looks up at me. Big eyes shining with the queer yellow-green of the firefly-light. "It's safer this way." She shrugs, an odd gesture on her tiny body. "Besides, he don't like sunlight."

I pace a few steps back and forth, looking. My firefly skirt swings back and forth—heavy under the weight of all them bugs—and the light swings, too. Up to touch the leaves overhead, then down to skitter across the spongy ground. "If he lives here, where is he?"

She points toward the center of the tree. "Down there."

I frown and step up on the bulging roots. In the very center of the split tree is a hole. The splintered wood surrounds it like teeth. Or hair. I'm reminded of a mouth or a woman's privates. "You sure?"

She nods.

"Why can't he just come up here?"

"It's not safe," she says again.

"But me going down into there is?"

"The tree is safe. And the passage below. It's Daddy you need to be worried about." She grins at me, sly-like. "Or maybe you've been listening to those stories you tell for too long."

I close my eyes, thinking. I've always looked fondly on Daddy. The things he taught me helped keep the craziness at bay all those years I was in Greenhaven. But I remember the times he weren't friendly and kind. Times when he and Momma fought, not because she was cracked, but because she put herself between him and us girls.

"He's got a temper when he drinks." The words come out soft, but it seems the woods around us sigh and rustle as though something has let out a breath.

Baby nods, pulls a piece of string from her pocket. "Hold out your hand." When I do, she ties one end of the string around my pinky finger, the other end around her wrist. "When you need to come back up, you tug on that, and I'll pull you back up."

I look at the string, doubtful. "Is it long enough?"

"It will be." She puts one hand on the back of my knee. "Be careful now. Daddy's got a way with words, too."

Before I can say anything else, she shoves me forward into the maw of the tree.

I ain't ashamed to say I squeak with fear, dropping between the splintered edges of the oak, but I'm not falling proper-like. Instead, I drift down like a bit of dandelion fluff, the fireflies swirling around me, and land on my feet. I look up, searching for a glimpse of the sky above or Baby's round face. Nothing.

The fireflies settle again. Not on my dress, but around a small opening that leads away under the ground. I squat down on my heels and take a peek. Smooth packed earth on all sides, the top laced over with furry tree roots. The bugs creep forward, lighting the way.

I don't fancy crawling down there after them, but I figure I don't have much choice, and if I take too much longer, I'll be in the dark.

I tie my hair in a knot on the back of my neck, take a deep breath, and start crawling. I'm not scared of much, but after a few feet, the sweat starts trickling 'cross my back and belly. Partly 'cause it's hard work movin' on hands and knees through this tiny hole in the dirt. Before long, I'm lyin' on my stomach, pulling myself along with my elbows, the roots touchin' my shoulders on either side and brushin' against my cheeks with feathery fingers.

The fireflies crawl on, undaunted by the narrowness of the tunnel. I grit my teeth and claw my way after them, determined not to find myself stuck in darkness.

Finally, they stop at a point where the passage widens out. I creep past them, gingerly so I don't accidentally crush any of them, and stand up in a large room. It's dark, but not pitch black. I blink and squint, thinking I see something on the far side, then stoop and look at the fireflies still huddled inside the mouth of the tunnel. "You coming?"

They retreat with a rustle of wings. Not abandoning me, but not coming any farther neither.

"All right." I brush my hands on my skirt, then put one hand on the wall and begin to feel my way around the edge of the room. Blinking 'til my head aches as I try and see something. Anything.

There's a rustle behind me, and I turn, hoping to see the fireflies have changed their mind. Nothing. I lick my lips and clear my throat, nervous. "Hello? Daddy?"

CHAPTER 4

Percy and Martinez barely get settled at their desks before Elliot comes out of one of the conference rooms along the back of the sprawl of desks and filing cabinets that make up the Special Investigations unit and gestures them over.

"Things go all right?" She looks at Percy intently.

"Yes." Percy nods.

"Good." She flutters her hand to usher them into the conference room where MacKenzie is already waiting. "We've picked up a new case."

Percy looks at the projection screen. Two girls with brown hair and blue-white faces, eyes closed and mouths in the faint smirk the dead have—neither happy nor sad. "Murder?"

"Not exactly." MacKenzie clicks the remote in her hand, and the photo on the left fills the screen. "This is Angela Moore of Savannah, Georgia. She was found six days ago in the parking area outside her apartment. The first responders thought she was unconscious, but after being admitted to the hospital, they discovered she was in a complete vegetative state. Toxicology came back normal, and there were no signs of injury. She did not require ventilation, but she was completely unresponsive to all stimuli. Roughly twenty-four hours later, her heart stopped."

She pushes another button, and the photos make a little do-si-do around each other. "This is Martina Gonzaga. She was found twelve hours after Ms. Moore died. Same condition, breathing without assistance, but otherwise unresponsive. Due to some artifacts found nearby, a specialist was called in." She pauses, eyes flickering toward Percy, then back toward the screen. "He told the hospital staff that Ms. Gonzaga's soul was gone."

Elliot huffs. "Soul?"

"Her conscious self," Percy says. "That unknown quantity that makes us aware, that can contradict our physical selves and allows us to do things instinct would prevent us from doing."

MacKenzie frowns, but continues. "The specialist said he detected traces of a supernatural force that had pulled that... consciousness out of Ms. Gonzaga. Not a physical trauma or accident, but an active ritual of some sort."

Percy rubs his lips. "She died within the next day."

"Yes. And they reached out to us, but..."

"There weren't enough victims to establish a pattern." His words hit the table hard. Not just heavy, but sharp.

"Not 'til a couple of hours ago." Another click of the remote. "This is Emily Grant. She was found just after noon today. The Savannah police contacted us as soon as they got word from the hospital."

Elliot twitches her hair back over her shoulder. "So, if the pattern continues, we've got less than twenty-four hours to try and find her... soul before she winds up dead, too."

"That's right." MacKenzie glances at Percy again. "The question is, are we equipped to handle this?" The downward tilt of her mouth adds a different emphasis. *Are you equipped to handle this?*

He shrugs. "Maybe. The lack of injuries would indicate it's not a creature of some sort. Bad magic is nasty business, but we're probably looking at another person. And he or she will have weaknesses. Leave a trail." Another shrug. "Everything physical can be destroyed."

Elliot leans forward, brown eyes darker than usual. "Do you have any idea why?"

"No." He shakes his head. "But I'll do some reading on the way and once we're there... hopefully we'll pick up something else in person."

MacKenzie nods. "I want to be on the road in an hour."

They all scatter to collect travel bags from the locker room, dig cell phone chargers out of desk drawers, collect laptops and tablets and gear from the tech supply. Percy takes the elevator down to the archive in the basement, narrowly avoiding Martinez, who is not quite talented enough to be in two places at once.

The librarian is an average woman with a taste for black and things that sparkle, and the appropriately vintage name of Connie. She smiles as Percy lets himself into the climate-controlled room that forms the bulk of the archive. "Percival. How goes the quest today?"

"It goes to Savannah." He leans on the edge of her desk. "I need to research the nature and practice of soul-stealing."

Her fingers flutter over the keyboard. "By creature or human?"

"Human, I think. And the bodies survive for a period after the removal."

"Ick." She makes a face. "Nothing worse than limbo." Another rattle of keys. "At least, I'd guess there's not much worse. Maybe if there is a flaming afterlife, limbo would be preferential." She hits a couple of keys decisively. "There's four books in the deep storage, but they've been scanned so you can have them to keep in a handy digital format."

"Just four?"

"In deep storage. But we've got some other volumes over here that are transcriptions from the big collection in DC. You can take copies with you for those." She's marching down the rows, pulling books with plain, grey cardboard covers and black lettering down the spines.

"No digital on them?" He says it teasingly.

"I'm working on it. But the mimeographed Courier is hard enough to read in print form, which means doing text recognition instead of a straight scan and then checking every word to be certain it is correct. And you see how many volumes there are." Connie looks at him indignantly, then pauses. "Oh. A joke."

"Apparently not."

She flushes through her pale makeup. "Sorry. Just been a busy day down here in the crypt. And this thing in Savannah sounds dangerous. Stolen souls?"

"Seems that way." He collects the armful of books from her. "Maybe it's just a deadly disease."

"Boo. Not better." She stomps back to her desk and retrieves a flash drive from one of the ports on her computer. "Here. Your digital copies."

He slips the drive into his pocket. "Thank you."

"It's why I'm here." She smooths her dress. "You'll be careful, right?"

"Always."

"And call me if you need anything."

"You know I will." Percy edges towards the door. "Don't work too hard while I'm gone."

She laughs, awkward, and Percy takes the opportunity to slip out into the hall. Connie has always been friendly toward him, but lately she's been different. Flirting, he thinks. But there's a nervous edge to it, like she's not certain what she's doing.

He pushes the elevator button with his elbow. A year ago he might have been interested, but now he's certain Connie would never be a good fit for him. Not after Delaney.

Ms. Carver has encouraged him to look for a new relationship. *"Maybe something casual. No strings."* But that's never had much appeal to him. It's hard enough to engage with people he spends every day with. Putting that much effort into a few hours of physical contact is not a price he is willing to pay. Even if he wasn't waiting for Del.

When he steps out of the elevator, MacKenzie and the others are gathered near their desks, sorting out the last few cases and packing individual copies of the files they've been sent from Savannah.

Percy slips his books and the flash drive into his shoulder bag and stacks it on top of his suitcase. Martinez has already added the briefcase with laptop, tablet, and the necessary cords to keep both powered up.

"Where've you been?" He looks at Percy, stern.

"Archive." He pats his bag. "Picking up some reading material for the trip."

Martinez rubs his forehead, as though chasing away a headache. "All right. You sure you're ready for this?"

Percy looks at each of them in turn. "I've got to go back in the field at some point. Might as well be today."

Elliot frowns. "This one could get rough."

"True. But you said they already have someone there. A specialist. He can help me with the supernatural stuff."

Mackenzie nods. "Okay. But get this straight. You are not going off on your own. Understand?"

Percy tilts his head in agreement. "Fair enough." He slips his bag over his shoulder, tucks his jacket under one arm, and picks up the briefcase with his other hand. "We don't have much time."

CHAPTER 5

The faint light of the fireflies makes my head ache, each beat of my heart causing the room to pulse as if it is closing around me like a fist. I press my hand against the crumbling dirt. It is as solid as a thing can be this side of death.

I take another step forward. "Hello?"

In the deepest dark part of the room, something moves and sighs.

"Daddy?"

There is a click, as loud and unsettling as the hammer on a gun, and light flares, blinding.

I throw my arm over my eyes, trembling and blinking away tears in the sudden glare. When I lower it, Daddy stands there grinning.

"Mornin', Biscuit."

I swallow hard and knot my fists up tight. I've seen that grin before, and it ain't friendly. But I'm grown now, and Daddy and I stare at each other—eye to eye. *Not like when I was small.* "Hello, Daddy."

He cocks an eyebrow. "Finally decided to come for a visit?"

"Yeah." My eyes are beginning to adjust. I blink at the room—dirt walls and ceiling, bare bulbs hanging at the end of long wires. For a moment I wonder how he got electricity down here, but then I figure if Addie can set the sun and Baby can give me a dress made of fireflies, then surely Daddy can find a way to have light in this muddy hole.

"You and your sisters been all right?"

"I suppose."

He slips one arm around me, tight and sudden-like, the other hand still clutching a can of cheap beer. "I was real surprised to see what happened to you. Not at all what I had planned."

The hair on the back of my neck prickles. "Planned?"

"Here." He pulls me away from the tunnel and the fireflies, waves his hand at the wall.

It's all crisscrossed with lines carved in the dirt, little bits of glass at every point they cross. I frown and squint a little closer. Not just bits of glass. Something moves on each dull surface.

I pull away from Daddy and step closer to the wall, nose almost mashed against the dirt as I look at that flicker of movement. Suck my breath in sharp as I see me and Percy sittin' in the observation room at Greenhaven. Follow one of the lines away from it and see me sitting on the edge of my bed waiting. Another line leads to Percy makin' up his mind he needs to get me out.

But those lines are thin. There are a different set, carved deep and marked all around with chalk. I lick my lips and take a peek at the reflections of what might have been.

Me breakin' a dozen threads so I can walk out the front door of Greenhaven by my lonesome. Me takin' Percy by the hand and leading him into the woods and letting him touch the thing called The Salesman. Letting him suck the fire right out of it. Letting him remember things about himself that are best forgot.

"See?" Daddy jabs a finger against the wall hard enough to knock a clot of dirt loose. "Why ain't you done this?"

"Percy isn't a monster." I stare at him hard with my green eye. "Neither am I."

"Not when you get soft like this." He shakes his head. "I thought I raised you better than that, Biscuit."

"I don't want to hurt no one, Daddy."

He laughs like I done said somethin' funny. Doublin' over and poundin' one fist on his thigh as he splutters for breath. Finally straightens back up, drinks the last of his beer, and rubs his arm across his stubbly chin. "You're a Power, Biscuit. You're gonna hurt folks whether you want to or not."

I look at the wall again, at that deep chalk-rimmed line. Follow it back through a dozen different turning points. Find a piece of glass with the chalk laid thick around it.

The shape that moves on the surface ain't me, but Percy. Mouthin' off to his team in the middle of an investigation. I twitch back, heart bangin' hard against my ribs. I've seen that moment before. It marked the start of his journey to me, the start of his path toward The Salesman. It weren't the first time I seen him, but it were the first I realized what might happen if he went into that clearing and faced poor Jack Green's burning bones.

I force my feet to move again. Follow that line further back, finding more points circled in chalk.

The backroom deal that left me locked in Greenhaven.

The time I saved Nurse Pratt's life and they put electricity in my brain to try and shock the magic out of me.

Momma slamming the door on the tool shed and settin' me and my dead sisters alight.

I turn and glare at Daddy, even though my innards are shiverin' like I'm about to fly into a million pieces. "You been pullin' at my future?"

He grins that grin I seen too many times, like a shark circlin' around and me just a bit of chum about to be et. "Don't look so sour, Biscuit. You didn't think you were the only one layin' hands on what could be, did you?"

"You hurt Percy." I blink away tears. "You hurt me."

"Aw, now." He lays a hand on my shoulder. "I ain't never done what didn't need to be done. But you were meant for something better than growin' old and dyin' quiet."

"No." I shake my head, even though I feel that truth in every inch of me. Brush my hands over that muddy wall, feeling for the way he has turned the future. Feeling for the threads that will change it.

They're still there, quivering with heartache and loss. With my fingers dug into the dirt, I can see a way forward that doesn't end with me or Percy breaking the world to pieces, but it is, by far, the hardest path. I bite my lip, trying to lock away each of the choices so that when the time comes, I can follow this path and not some other.

"I won't become a monster for you, Daddy. Neither will Percy."

"Yes, you will." He leans close and the beer stink on his breath makes my stomach churn. "Once you see the future, you can change it. Your momma may have cut my path short, but I've worked hard to make sure your road is different. You and Percy, see? Powers. Like your mother and I were meant to be."

"Oh, Daddy." My throat hurts, and I swallow hard, tryin' to clear the way for words.

His hand tightens on my shoulder. "But you've gone and changed things, haven't you? All that work I done, and you're here, dead. And Percy still don't remember what he's supposed to be." He reaches down and starts unbucklin' his belt. "I ought whup you good for all the trouble you've caused."

I turn my hand, pullin' Baby's string across my palm and grabbin' hold of it, tight. "I guess Momma did the right thing after all."

His face turns red, and he lets go of my shoulder, haulin' back with that hand ready to belt me. But I'm grown now and, while I might be scared, I sure ain't stupid.

"Baby." I yank at that piece of string as hard as I can.

Daddy grabs at me, but I'm already flyin' back toward the tunnel, which gets momentarily bigger, suckin' me in so that I slide along, one arm stretched out and holdin' onto that string and the other one tucked over my head as I scrape over and under those hairy roots I squeezed past earlier.

The fireflies are comin', too. Their wings crackle and buzz as they try to keep up, their butts blinkin' on and off as they go. And behind them…

"Faster, Baby." My shriek brings dirt showering down.

Or maybe it's Daddy makin' the tunnel crumble around me. He's thicker than I am, so his shoulders stick at all the skinny places, but he keeps comin'. Hands grabbin' hold of the ground and tearin' it away as he roars after me. "Delaney Priscilla Green. You come back here." His hand closes around one ankle, stoppin' me just short of the splintery mouth of the tree.

I look up and see Baby starin' down at me, face as white as a China doll. See her little fingers just about rubbed raw with the strain of tryin' to hold onto that string with both me and Daddy hangin' from it.

"You think you can run away from me, Biscuit?" He digs his fingernails in, clawing his way up my leg.

I pull my free leg up toward my chest, then slam my heel down into his face. Determined to give him at least one good lick for all the times he hit me.

He splutters and lets go.

And Baby, wheezing with the effort, pulls me free so hard I tumble past her and sprawl in the leaf mold.

For a minute we just stay there, me laid out on the ground and her swayin' on the edge of the tree, breathin' hard.

"You've gotten heavy," she says finally.

I smile, weak. "That's what happens when you grow up."

"Hah." She shows off her gums in a toothless grin. "Like I would—" She staggers and slips toward the ragged maw between the two halves of the tree.

Daddy, clingin' to a bit of the string still danglin' from Baby's wrist, starts wigglin' out. Pantin' and cussin' as he works his way through that narrow gap, but the whole time grinnin' that shark-like way.

And Baby just stands there, watchin' him come.

I done the same when I was little. But now I've faced worse and lived to tell about. So to speak.

I grab Baby 'round the waist and tuck her up under one arm. Slap my other hand against that sundered oak and remind it that it once stood tall. These might not be my woods, but they ain't so different than the ones I grew in my head.

The tree groans and shakes its branches, like a dog wakin' up from a nap.

Daddy pauses. He's still half in and half out of the hole in the ground, and all those splinters are startin' to quiver and dig at him. "Biscuit," he says, and his voice is all soft and friendly again. "I didn't mean to yell."

Baby shivers, but I stare at him, first with my brown eye, then with my green one. Overhead, the moon peeks out from behind the clouds, nervous.

"Come on, now. You know I wouldn't really hurt you. I just got mad is all."

The tree groans again, the two halves startin' to sit up.

Daddy's eyes get wide and his mouth opens up real big. "Damn it, Biscuit. I only wanted you to get what I never did. You can still have it. I can fix it. You just have to get back out. Back to the living." The whole time he's wiggling, squirming back down into the ground as the splinters start coming together like two halves of a zipper. "I can fix it. You can still be a Power. If you just let me—"

The last words get cut off as the tree comes back together like a thunderclap.

I pull Baby more comfortably in my arms. "Are you all right?"

"Yes." She sticks her fingers in her mouth and leans her head on my shoulder. A moment later and she's asleep.

The oak moans and sighs, the two halves settling back together. Another moan, so faint I might just be imagining, drifts up from the ground. *Biscuit.*

I swallow hard and march around the tree 'til I find the path running off the other side, walking quick to put some distance between me and the clearing.

I'm grown now, and I ain't scared. But I'm not stupid either.

CHAPTER 6

Elliot drives Percy to the hospital to examine the latest victim. "The SPD specialist is supposed to meet us here."

He nods, flicking through the files on his tablet, pausing to look closely at the photos of the girls before and after they were attacked. And the grimmer autopsy photos. The after photos are strange, almost fuzzy. He squints, tilting the screen back and forth. "That's weird."

"What?" Elliot cranes her neck, trying to get a good look while still keeping one eye on the road.

"It's like there's a double exposure almost. The girls are there, pretty clear. But…" He tilts the tablet again. "Like another image there."

"A glitch in the files, maybe?"

"Don't think so. The rest of it all looks normal." He waves his hand at the pillow and sheets visible around the young woman in the photo.

She nods. "I'll run some analysis on those while you talk to the specialist. What's his name again?"

"Franklin Jones." He flips through to the next file. "Psychic. Tracker. Warlock." He chuckles. "Really?"

"So he's a Sensitive, too?"

"No. Just skilled. Probably a magician who uses objects to help him detect the things I feel in my gut." He clicks the tablet off and folds the cover over it. "Bet he has a bunch of crap hanging from his belt."

Elliot frowns as she pulls into the parking garage next to the hospital. "You are going to play nice, right?"

"Of course. It's just…" He stops, rubs his temple to ease the dull ache that has lingered ever since Delaney passed. Ever since he's been taking the meds.

The ache isn't so bad. A couple of aspirin and a cup of coffee usually chase it away long enough for him to get his work done. But the memories that come with it are less pleasant and harder to shake. Long halls and cold beds. Days and nights of dreamless sleep that isn't sleeping or waking. And the brilliant fire that is the electroshock. Burning and burning 'til the things in his head wither into nothing.

"Hey." Elliot grabs his wrist. "Are you all right?"

He twitches, forces a smile with the next breath. "Yeah. I fell asleep on the plane and it left me a little fuzzy is all." He shakes his head to clear the last of the memories. "I'll be better once I get out and move around some more."

"You sure?"

"Come on. Don't want to keep Mr. Jones waiting." He slides the tablet into his shoulder bag and steps out of the car before she can protest. A part of him thinks he should talk to someone about what he's feeling. But he knows it can't be Elliot or anyone else on his team. *She wouldn't understand.*

The glass doors between the parking deck and hospital lobby slide open as he approaches, cool air wafting out to meet the humid exterior. The hair on the back of his neck prickles, and he rubs it with his hand, irritable as the ache in his head gets sharper. The vague smell of disinfectant is familiar. Frightening.

"Give me a second. I'll ask for Jones at the desk." Elliot brushes past him, threading her way between the neat rows of vinyl chairs and blocky end tables.

Percy adjusts his satchel, smooths his hair across his forehead. Takes a breath, then another. There are whispers in the back of his head, almost as if someone is having a conversation just behind him, just out of earshot. He hears the murmur of voices, but can't understand the words.

"Excuse me?" A lean man with twilight skin approaches. His hair is braided into precise rows along his scalp, the ends falling down past his shoulders. "Are you the folks from Atlanta?"

Percy holds his hand out. "Agent Percival Cox."

"Franklin Jones. I'm the Savannah Police Department consultant." His voice is deep and warm, but there's an echo within it. A whisper of hidden knowledge.

Percy nods. "Not what I was expecting."

Jones raises an eyebrow, and his voice is a degree or two cooler. "Oh?"

"No charms," Percy says mildly. "Last warlock I met jangled and clattered louder than a janitor's keys he had so much stuff hanging from his belt."

"Ah. Right. The charms." Jones relaxes. "The part of town I work, I wouldn't last a day walking around with animal feet or the bones of dead saints hangin' off me." A sly grin. "I keep all that shit back in my basement."

Elliot returns from the desk. "Mr. Jones?"

"Yes."

"Agent Margaret Elliot."

"Pleased to meet you." He shakes her hand, hooks his thumbs into his pockets. "Have you been up to see Miss Grant yet?"

"Not yet. You told the PD you thought there was something… magic involved?" She glances at Percy, seeking confirmation that *magic* is the appropriate term.

Jones crosses his arms over his chest. "There's no *thought* about it. Something is deeply wrong with Miss Grant. Something supernatural, if not something magic. Has been with the other two as well. Even the untrained can feel it." He tilts his head at Elliot. "You'll see."

Elliot frowns. "But how…"

Percy holds his hand up. "I think we should see Miss Grant first. And then we'll try and find answers to our questions."

She purses her lips, but nods, reluctant. "Right. Of course." She flicks her fingers at Jones. "Care to lead the way?"

"Sure." He strides toward the bank of elevators. "This way."

CHAPTER 7

Emily Grant has been placed in a restricted room on a hall that has locked doors at either end. There is an officer seated in a chair by her door. His head is bent over a magazine, but he looks up alertly when the door opens.

"Can I help you?" His words are casual, but his hand drops to his side, to the gun holstered on his belt.

"I'm Agent Elliot with the FBI. This is Agent Cox." Elliot holds out her badge, waits for him to inspect it.

"Officer Sullivan. Savannah PD." He stands up and drops the magazine into his chair. "You're here to see Miss Grant, then?"

"Yes."

He nods, hitches his belt with his fingers, his holster creaking under the weight of his gun. "Go on in. I'll just get someone from the nurses' desk." He strides down the hall.

Elliot frowns and glances at the door, apprehensive.

Jones makes a face. "You'll understand in a minute." He squares his own shoulders, opens the door, and leads the way in.

The curtains are pushed back to let in as much daylight as possible. The fluorescent lights overhead and in the little bathroom are all on. But the room whispers with the impression of something hidden, something watching.

"Jesus." Elliot moves toward the wall opposite the bed.

"Yes." Jones nods. "I don't know if it's some shadow of the magic that was used against her. Or just the unnaturalness of a person without a soul."

Percy edges closer, stooping so that he can look across the figure lying in the bed. Then holds his hand out, slowly moving it back and forth over the still limbs like a diviner search for water.

"Not the shadow of magic, Mr. Jones. This is still active."

"Active how?" Jones leans over Percy's shoulder, as though trying to see what he sees.

Cautiously, Percy lays his hand over Emily's, and the hospital room fades to a pinpoint of light and sound. His heart beats once and a different reality fills his senses.

Crushing pain. She is being twisted and bent into a shape that is both familiar and alien. Screaming. Trying to claw her way free, but the thing that holds her prisoner is the body that is not her own.

"Let me go. Please, let me go. Please. Please."

"Cox." Elliot grabs him by the shoulders and yanks him backward, breaking the connection with Emily's distant consciousness. "Cox."

"Ugh." He staggers, shaking almost uncontrollably.

Elliot gets her arms around his waist, trying to steady him. "What's wrong?"

Percy shakes his head. "Gonna be sick."

"Great." She drags him toward the bathroom.

He shrugs free, doubles over, and pukes into the toilet. It's been a few hours since he ate, so not much comes out but coffee and bile, sour enough to make him shiver. He spits. Pulls a handful of toilet paper from the dispenser and wipes his mouth.

"You all right? Do I need to call the nurse in here?" Elliot rubs his back the way a mother might with a child.

"No. I'm okay." He spits again and flushes the toilet. "Caught me by surprise is all."

Jones is pacing at the foot of the bed. "What caught you by surprise?"

"That. Her." Percy leans against the doorframe, trying to look casual while the wobble in his legs slowly fades. "I guess you can't feel it."

Jones frowns. He edges forward and lays his hand over Emily's the way Percy did. "There's… a buzz. But I can't feel anything specific."

"She's been taken out of this body and… put into another one."

"Another what?"

"Body. Another person. Maybe someone that died. Or was killed." Sweat beads up on his lip, remembering the feeling of being pulled into a different shape. "But she's trapped there. At least for now."

"For now?" Elliot looks at the bed, then at Percy. "You mean until this body dies?"

"Yes." He rubs his forehead. "But I think that is related to what is happening with her soul, not the other way around." He sighs. "I need to do some reading."

Jones scowls. "We don't have much time."

"I know that." Percy pulls his phone from his pocket and moves closer to the bed.

Looking at the body is unnerving. Even squinting, he can't see the shadow image he spotted in the photos because part of him refuses to really look at this empty shell of bones and blood. He takes a picture with his phone.

As with the other photos, there is a second image embedded in it. Still hard to see in that it is a face laid over Emily's own face, but the mouth is different, the eyebrows at a slightly different angle.

"Here." He shows it to Jones. "I wasn't sure what it meant. But now I think that must be the second body. The one she's trapped inside."

Jones crosses his arms over his chest. "So, someone is taking the souls from these girls and putting them in a different body. Why?"

"Maybe the other body is deficient somehow. Someone in a coma."

Elliot raises an eyebrow. "But a coma would be a medical condition. Putting someone else in that body wouldn't fix whatever was physically wrong with them."

Percy nods. "Maybe the person doing this doesn't realize that."

"Nah." Jones shakes his head. "Whoever is doing this is smart enough to know the difference between a physical ailment and a metaphysical one." He touches Emily's hand again. "I'd say it's more like someone is trying to raise the dead."

Percy props his fists on his hips. *Raise the dead.* He closes his eyes, trying to remember what he had felt on the other end of the connection. "Let me go."

Elliot looks at him sharply. "What?"

"He's holding her there. The body is dead, but he… whoever has stolen Miss Grant, is holding her into it."

She touches her gun, holstered on her belt, reflexively. "For how long?"

Jones fidgets. "Not long. Even for a Power, that kind of magic would take a lot of energy. Even more concentration."

Percy nods. "Power or not, he is still a man." He looks at Elliot. "How long can you stay awake before you start to drift off?"

"How much coffee is there?" Her grin fades as she considers the question. "About eighteen hours. Longer if there aren't outside distractions. And I have a lot of coffee. But probably not more than a day." Her eyes get wide. "Oh."

"That's why they keep slipping away." Percy moves closer to the bed, his fingers hovering just above Miss Grant's forehead. "He's losing his grip on them, and once they're free of the other body, they just… cross over."

Jones raises an eyebrow. "Cross over?"

"Dissipate. Ascend. Transcend. Whatever." He waves his free hand. "And the physical dies."

Elliot leans forward. "So we're trying to locate this other body and the kidnapper before he falls asleep?" She glances at her watch. "How many hours have already passed? Six?"

Jones nods. "At least. That's just when she was found. There's a good chance she'd been there since earlier in the day."

"And this creep has already done this twice in how many days? Losing sleep and strength each time?" She looks at Percy again. "Did you see anything when you touched her? A building or anything?"

"No. It was so sudden." Percy takes a deep breath and lets his hand rest against Emily's forehead.

The panic rolls over him in a wave, but this time he is better prepared. Reaching out along the connection, he tries to whisper to the young woman on the other end.

"I need to see where you are."

"Trapped. Please, let me go."

"Open your eyes and tell me where you are. Let me see."

The darkness turns to white. No, it's grey. A ceiling turning murky as the light outside the window fades.

There's a man with dark hair pacing around the edge of the room. Jittery. Frantic. Emily shudders. *"I'm frightened."*

"I know. I'm right here. Just try and see if you can sit up and look out the window."

"I can't. He'll see me."

"It will be all right. I'm right here. Look out the window."

She moves stiffly. Sits up, but there's still nothing but sky visible through the window.

The dark haired man cries out. Comes close and puts his arms around her. "You're awake."

Emily sobs. "No. Please let me go." She tries to pull away from him. "Help me. Help me."

"Who…?" The dark-haired man looks her in the eye, and Percy flinches, feeling the brush of power. The stranger grimaces. "No. Damn it." There's another flare of magic, this one severing the bond that has held spirit and flesh together.

Emily sighs as she drifts free, the room fading away beneath her. *"Thank you."*

"No. Don't. Follow my voice, Emily. Emily. Do you hear me?"

Percy sags against the rails on the bed, both hands pressed against Emily's face. "Follow the sound of my voice. Emily."

The heart monitor beside the bed wails.

"Emily. Emily, come back." He's yelling, shaking the body lying in the bed.

"Percy. Stop." Elliot gets her arms around him again, drags him away from the bed as the door bangs open and the medical staff pour into the room. A couple of nurses usher Elliot and Percy none-too-politely out the door into the hall where Jones is already waiting.

Elliot shoves Percy into the chair where Sullivan had been sitting. "What the hell was that, Cox?"

"He saw me." Percy rakes his fingers through his hair. "He saw me, and he let her go free."

Jones crosses his arms over his chest. "Killed her, you mean."

Percy sags in the chair. "Yes."

Elliot's mouth works for a minute. When she speaks, her voice is cold. "Did you get a chance to see anything?"

"It looked like a house. An old one maybe." He closes his eyes, trying to dredge up the sense of the room. "Wood floors. The plaster on the ceiling was cracked. At least two stories because there was just sky out the window." He shakes his head. "That's all."

"And the creep?"

"Tall. White. Dark hair. She didn't want to look at him."

Elliot leans closer, stopping just short of grabbing Percy by the front of his shirt. "So a tall, white man with dark hair is somewhere in an old, multi-story house with a body."

"Yes."

"If that were any less useful…" She jabs him in the shoulder. "If this is how you're going to behave, you don't need to be back in the field."

"Should I have waited 'til he fell asleep and she died?" Percy squares his shoulders, something small and stubborn waking up inside. "She said *thank you* when he let her go. Leaving her there, trapped and panicked, when there was a chance that I might help her would have been cruel."

Elliot shakes her head. "Maybe. But now we have no lead. Now we will have to wait and see if he snatches another soul."

Percy nods. "Now we have a chance to put the word out before the next one is taken."

The door to the room opens, and the doctor comes out into the hall. "I'm sorry. We did what we could, but there was no response." He rubs his hand across his short cropped hair, and there's a flash of anger in his eyes. "Tell me you're getting close to stopping this guy."

"Yes," Percy says before Elliot can open her mouth. "We're doing everything we can."

"Good." He waves a hand at the door. "I'll get the body transferred to the city morgue as soon as possible."

Elliot nods. "Thank you."

Percy stands and nudges Elliot toward the end of the hall. Jones trails along after, the muscle in his jaw working furiously.

When they reach the main corridor, Percy looks at both of them. "We have more than we did. The shadow in the photos, a basic description of the creep, and the knowledge that he will be looking for another young woman very soon."

Elliot crosses her arms over her chest and glares at him, doubtful. "You think we can get ahead of him this time?"

"I think we have to try. I think we have a chance. But standing around trying to decide whether or not what happened back there was the right thing or not…" Percy shakes his head.

Jones nods. "We don't want there to be a fourth."

Elliot rakes her fingers through her hair, letting her breath out in a noisy sigh. "Fine. We'll start with the image. Get something written up to run on the local news. And maybe this time our guy will make a mistake."

CHAPTER 8

The house, unlike the lightning split tree, is not in the middle of a clearing. There are the woods and the path. And then there is the house, pressed against on all sides by beech saplings and sturdier oaks. Trees and house bound, each to the next, with red stemmed honeysuckle, the white blooms and sweet smell disguising the unyielding embrace.

Despite the vine holding it tight, I recognize it like I know my own hands. And knowing the kind of memories that were stuck inside it when it was in my head, I stop short.

Baby squeezes my neck with her tiny arms. "It's okay. She can't get out."

She?

A thread of song floats out the kitchen window. "Down by the river, mm-nenena."

"Mama." My stomach gets all squirmy. Daddy could be mean, and he left more than one stripe across my legs with his belt, but he never tried to kill me. Not like Mama.

Baby squeezes my neck again. "It's okay. She can't hurt you here."

I work my way around through the brush and climb up on a pile of cement blocks half-buried under drifted leaves. Grab hold of the windowsill with one hand as I look through a gap in the honeysuckle.

Like Daddy, she's just as I remember her. Long brown hair pulled into a messy bun on the back of her neck. A flower-print apron tied over her dress, both of them handmade, but just a little too big. The same wrinkle of frustration in her forehead that preceded an outburst of anger or tears, the same smudge of flour on her temple where she'd pushed her hair back from her face.

I lick my lips and tap on the window frame. "Mama?"

She jumps and squints. Then a big smile spreads across her face. "Delaney. I've been expecting you. You want to come inside?"

I glance at Baby, cradled in my elbow, and she shakes her head. I remember that she is the mistress of these woods and the honeysuckle twined across every opening in the house is her doing. "No, Mama. I think we'll stay out here."

She smooths the hair back from her forehead, leaving fresh streaks of flour, and leans on the edge of the table, heavy-like. But she smiles, even if it's brittle around the edges. "That's okay. I guess you must be on your way somewhere." She scoops two plates off the counter behind her and sets them in the little gap between the window frame and sill. "Have some cake. Green for you, Baby. Yellow for Delaney."

Baby makes a pleased noise and reaches for the green cake with eager hands.

I lift down the plate then return it to the windowsill empty. Look at the yellow one carefully. Despite the chaos in the process, Mama always did have a knack for baking. The petit fours were a specialty. She sold them to the fancy housewives that lived in the middle of downtown, packing great flat boxes of little cakes in every color you could imagine.

This one, topped with a delicate rose made of frosting, looks delicious, but I learned a long time ago to be careful about anything Mama tried to feed me.

She leans on the windowsill, looking out at the two of us. "You've gotten so big, Delaney. Tall and strong." She doesn't say pretty. That's a word saved for Addie with her blonde hair and blue eyes.

I nod though, to be polite. "Yes, Mama. I guess I grew up all right."

Her eyes get sharp. "Have some cake, Delaney."

Baby has finished her own and is eying the yellow one while she licks crumbs and frosting from her tiny hands. She shifts, reaching for it, and Mama snatches it back off the sill.

"No, Baby. You heard me. This one is for Delaney."

My stomach turns over in a cold knot. "Still trying to kill me, Mama?"

She drops the plate on the table behind her, and it breaks as though it is made of sand, little shards of porcelain gusting out to mix with the half-finished petit fours sitting in rows. "Damn it. Look at what you made me do." She turns and glares at the window. "Always were too clever for your own good."

"Maybe if you hadn't been so hellbent on murdering us, things—"

Mama slams her fists on the windowsill. The whole house shakes and creaks. "I never wanted *them* dead. Just *you*, Delaney." She straightens, hands braced against the sides of the window, pushing on it like Samson trying to bring down the temple. "How many times did you tell Addie you were just trying to keep her safe? How many times did you leave her hungry and cold and frightened?"

"I was trying to keep her from getting hurt."

"No." The house rattles, groans, shaking loose a few spiders that dangle from the eaves in surprise. "No, Delaney. You were trying to keep yourself from getting hurt."

I stumble back down off the makeshift step as the paint flakes off the wooden siding. The walls shiver as nails screech loose.

Baby stuffs her fist in her mouth, eyes half-closed as new strands of honeysuckle whip up and around the house. New layers of vine pull it back together, sealing the new gaps.

"You told Addie you would keep her safe, Delaney. But, in the end, who hurt her? I never wanted them dead. Only you." Her voice, wailing like a storm through winter branches, trails off. The house settles again. The only sound is the snakeskin whisper of honeysuckle still creeping around and around 'til only the smallest glimmer of light from the kitchen window is visible.

I cling to Baby, breathing hard as my arms tremble with guilt. "On a hot July day, Mama went cracked, locked my sisters and me in the tool shed, and lit us up like a Christmas tree." Tears burn down my cheeks and I rub them away with the sleeve of my sweater. "It wasn't me that hurt them, Mama. It wasn't me." The last words echo off the house and are swallowed by the trees.

But Mama doesn't answer.

The moon sucks up a deep breath, the shadows getting sharp again as the path glimmers in front of me.

I look at Baby, cuddled up between my breasts. "I never hurt you, did I?"

She looks at me, solemn. Finally, she sighs. "Percy ain't the only one who has forgotten who he was or what he's done," she says. Then she rests her head under my chin and falls fast asleep.

CHAPTER 9

The FBI agents gave Franklin several copies of the face they pulled from the photos of the dead girls. It's not perfect, but for his purpose, it's good enough. And they didn't even blink when he said he needed to go home and do some research, that he would call if he found what he was looking for. That they should call if they learned anything new.

He's doubtful they will bother to keep him in the loop, but the agent who was at the hospital, Elliot, seemed frustrated with the specialist on her team.

Franklin frowns. Something about Percival Cox is gnawing at him. Something he can't quite pin down.

He lays out the last line of salt, carefully connecting each point in the diagram. Stands and inspects his work. The star has four points, each marked with an element—water, air, fire, and metal—with the fifth, earth, in the very center.

He washes his hands in the sink in the corner of the cellar to remove the last traces of salt and ash. Reads through his notes again to make certain he hasn't missed anything. The four-pointed star has less energy, but it shouldn't be able to summon anything that isn't human. If it summons anything at all.

He pulls the elastic off his braids and shakes them loose across his shoulders. It's not like he hasn't done this sort of thing before, but never to this extent. Savannah is full of shades, some of them friendly and some not. Even a few that are just creaking floorboards and a drafty window. But chasing a shade out of its hiding spot and sending it on to whatever lies beyond is not nearly as difficult as trying to call one back from the next realm.

Franklin reads his notes again, but nothing has changed. *Time to work some magic.* He strikes a match and lights the candle on the table. Then uses it to light each of the candles at the points of the star.

A second copy of the photo from the FBI folks sits on the table. He picks it up, lights the corner of it carefully. "Come to me, lost soul. I summon you. Come to me and speak."

The candle flames stretch up tall and thin, and the salt lines glitter.

Franklin drops the burning photograph onto the baking sheet on the table where he had mixed the ash from the first one with the salt. "Come to me, lost soul. Come to me."

CHAPTER 10

The hole opens near my feet. Barely as big around as I am and deep enough the moonlight can't seem to find the bottom, it's more frightening than the passage into the split oak where Daddy lives. Baby wiggles down out of my arms. "That's for you."

I crouch and touch the side. The earth clings to my hand like it will squeeze through my skin. "I don't know." I look at her, hoping to see her pulling the string out of her pocket again. "Are you going to pull me back out?"

She laughs. "No. The string would break when you hit the other side."

"Other side?"

"The living world."

I look at the hole again, narrow and deep and filled with the smell of mud. "This is the way back to Percy?"

"The first of many small steps." Baby puts her hand on my arm. "You'll have to use your voice, Delaney. You won't have any other magic 'til you get your bones back."

"I still see—"

"Yes." She nods. "But you only see what is and you can't do nothing to change it. Not like this. Not 'til you have your bones again."

"Then how can I save Percy?"

She shrugs. "Don't know."

"But it starts down there?"

Baby rubs her nose and yawns. "Yes. I think so."

I look at her, wondering if I need to say goodbye. I've already left one sister behind. *Goodbye is not what needs to be said, even if I never return to this place.* I touch her cheek with my clean hand. "If I've hurt you, Baby, I'm sorry."

She tilts her head, blue eyes dark under the white light of the moon. "Are you sure, Delaney?"

I want to blurt out *yes.* How could I be anything other than sorry? But I know that I have gotten in the habit of saying those words. Sorry I scared you. I didn't mean to. *It was an accident.*

My gut squishes again, the way it did outside the house all swaddled in honeysuckle. Cold and sick feeling. I know, even if I can't remember it, that somewhere I did something terrible to Baby and Addie. "Yes, Baby. I'm sorry."

She touches her fingers to the tears sliding down my cheeks. "Good. Remember that, Delaney." A shift of her weight, slight though it is, knocks me off-balance, and I tumble head first into the hole.

The dirt presses in on me as I fall, my scream lost in the darkness. I try to suck in a breath, tasting dust and salt and the queer buzz of physical magic. The pressure against my skin grows 'til I am not certain if I can bear it any longer. I slither up out of the ground into the middle of a salt ring, still screaming.

Immediately, the weight is gone, and I gulp a breath or two and tuck my hair behind my ears. The man standing on the other side of the salt and candles blinks.

I recognize him, with his dark skin and fine braids falling across his shoulders. At least what I've been seeing hasn't led me wrong yet.

"Hello, Franklin." I smooth the front of my dress, miraculously clean despite having just fallen down a muddy hole between the afterlife and the realm of the living.

"Who the hell are you?" He reaches for the candle on the table beside him, ready to snuff it, and with it, the summons of salt and ash.

"Delaney Green." Uncertain what to do with my hands, I stick them in my sweater pockets. "Were you expecting someone else?"

"Yes." He lifts one of the remaining photos off the table. "I was expecting her."

"I don't think she's coming."

"That seems obvious. But that doesn't explain how you are here instead. The summons was specific."

I laugh, lift a hand apologetically. "Percy took those photos. I mean, not those actual photos, but the ones those are copies of."

Franklin pauses, and his eyes get narrow and hard. "You are connected to Percival Cox."

"In a manner of speaking."

"That still doesn't explain why you are here instead of her."

"You've met Percy? Shaken his hand?"

"Yes. But—"

"What did you feel?"

He tosses the photo to one side, crosses his arms on his chest. "I felt magic. He is a Sensitive."

"Is he?" I edge closer to the salt ring and drag my fingers across the barrier. It ripples like the surface of a pond, feels a bit like one too—cool and liquid. "You know, there is no cure for a man born a Power. There is only draining away his magic or controlling it with drugs or making him forget that he has it."

Franklin is incapable of growing pale, but stillness settles on him. "Cox is a Power?"

"Of a terrible sort. Unintentional and, therefore, nearly uncontrollable."

He rubs his forehead, but it makes sense. The uneasiness that's been tickling away at his insides ever since he first shook Percy's hand takes a specific shape. "Why are you telling me this?"

"Because I have seen what will happen if he is left unchecked. And no one wants that." I remember Daddy, making plans beneath the split tree. "Well, almost no one. And I need your help if I am to keep him from hurting folks."

"What makes you think I can't stop him? Now that you've warned me?"

I look at him solemnly. "There is no doubt you are skilled with this physical magic, Mr. Jones. But you cannot stop Percy. Not by yourself."

Franklin edges forward. "And you can?"

"Not by myself. Not this time."

His eyebrows go up, then down 'til his dark brown eyes are nearly hidden away. He lays his hands against the milky fog of the salt ring's barrier. "Who are you, shade?" And he ain't asking for my name again.

The symbols around the star and the one under my feet flare, and the light pushes through me, stripping away the faded cotton dress and lumpy sweater, the limp fall of my hair and scarred skin. What is underneath is not flesh and blood and bone and guts. Nor am I made of anything whimsical like butterflies or spider-web or even flames.

I hold my hands up, and they are still my hands. Look down and see my breasts and belly are still my own. But I burn.

"Ah." It is not like The Salesman. Not ash and bone crudely formed to resemble something human. This is something… someone human transformed.

Franklin grimaces, trying to hold his fear inside. "What do you want from me, Power?"

"Help," I say. "I will need a body."

"I will not kill for you. No matter what evil you might propose to stop."

"I am not asking you to kill someone. I am asking you to find me a body. One of those girls who have been rendered soulless maybe."

"Why? Why not stay like… this?" He gestures to my transformed self.

I bite my lip to keep my temper in check, remembering Baby's warning. *"You must use your voice, Delaney."*

The candle on the table is burning down. As it flickers, so do I, passing back into the suffocating crush of dirt-that-is-not-dirt before returning to the salt circle. "Listen carefully, Mr. Jones. Percy is beginning to remember that he has magic, and if he is threatened, he will use it. Even if he doesn't mean to. And it will make him stronger. He will use it again, not realizing the fullness of what he does because those he touches with it will be murderers and rapists. At least at first. And his magic will grow and grow until it eats the world."

The candle flickers again, and when I return, I'm gasping for breath. "I need a body so that you may make him forget again. Not with drugs or electricity, but with magic. Make him forget and bind the forgetting into something that he will never try to destroy."

"You."

I nod. "Yes, Mr. Jones."

"And why will he not destroy you? Even if I can find you another… body, you will not look like yourself."

"He will know it is me. And he will love me all the same."

Franklin shakes his head. "Maybe. But even if I want to do this, even if I believe what you say, how am I supposed to call you back?"

"Take my hand."

He hesitates. "Why?"

"So I can find you again." Cautiously, he pushes his hand through the barrier of the salt ring, and I grasp it firm. "When you are ready for my help, spill a drop of blood and call my name. I will come to you."

He pulls his hand back, staring at it as though it might burst into flames at any second. "And if I do not want your help, Delaney Green?"

"Then face him on your own, Mr. Jones."

The candle winks out, and I am caught in the dreadful crush of the passage between the world of the living and the afterlife. Left to scrape and claw my way back through the narrow shaft until I pop out into the woods where I left Baby.

I cough up silt and wipe the mud from my eyes, cold and dirty from head to toe.

Baby stirs, brushing away leaves that have drifted around her like a blanket. "Well?"

"Yes." I wrap my arms across my chest, trying to warm up. Wondering that I can even be cold without proper flesh and bones. "The first step."

"Good." She looks at me, solemn. "Do you want to walk on?"

"In a little while." I huddle down in the leaves. "But let me rest first."

She hums, quiet, and curls up against my belly. The leaves on the ground move, skittering up over my legs and back like so many strange bugs and cover us in a dry, whispering blanket.

I grit my teeth, anticipating the urge to scratch, but the leaves are surprisingly soft and warm. I sigh, eyes fluttering closed as Baby hums. *Maybe just for a little while.*

CHAPTER 11

The hospital room was cold, but Percy couldn't pull the blanket up himself—the padded cuffs on his wrists and ankles kept him from doing much of anything but staring at the ceiling.

He licked his lips. "Mom?" They'd put something in the IV dripping into his arm. It took a few tries before he could get his voice above a whisper. "Mom."

She turned away from the window. "Yes, Percy. Do you need some water?" She reached for the pitcher sitting on the table beside the bed.

He shook his head. "Cold."

"It is chilly in here." She went over to the closet and pulled open each of the drawers in the built in dresser. "Your Aunt Ethel told me they keep it cold in hospitals to keep the germs down. Ah." She pulled a blanket out of the bottom drawer. "Here we go."

Gently, she spread it over him. Her hands shook as she brushed against the leather straps holding his wrists secure, but she folded his fingers into her own just the same. "There. Is that better?"

He nodded, wished his tongue was not so squishy and hard to move so he could tell her the temperature was more to do with vagal response than germs.

The door opened and several men in white coats came in. Percy recognized one of them. *Doctor Whitaker.* Small and crackling with energy, he was the one who changed the bags on the IV and helped him eat dinner one sloppy bite at a time.

"How are you doing today, Mrs. Cox?"

Percy recognized him, too. *Doctor Palmer.* He had threatened to lock Mom up, too, if she didn't calm down and let them strap Percy to the bed.

Mom smoothed her hair, tucking a stray wisp behind her ear, and tried to smile. "Better, thank you."

"I'm glad to hear it," Dr. Palmer said. He flipped through the folder in his hands. "We've been considering how to approach further treatment, and I'm afraid there aren't many options."

"Treatment?" Her voice cracked, and she paused for a moment before continuing. "My son isn't sick, Dr. Palmer."

He looked at her, cool as a winter morning. "Your son killed a man."

"A kidnapper. A murderer. If he hadn't…" Her fingers clutched Percy's hand so tight he whimpered.

"Yes. But this is magic, and there are other concerns. For the future."

Mom shook her head. "I don't understand. Percy is a good boy. Gentle. He would never hurt anyone."

Palmer looked at the notes in the folder again. "But this isn't the first time he's killed something."

She frowned. "He's never—"

"Your neighbors, Jim and Caroline Wallace, filed a report that he had killed their dog."

"Their dog attacked Percy. He still has scars on his arm from it. But it just…" She paused, lips going white. "Oh God."

Dr. Whitaker cleared his throat. "There's no way for you to have known. But it does raise concern about what might happen in the future. If he responds to another threat in the same way…"

Mom smoothed Percy's hair across his forehead. "Of course." She rubbed away tears with her sleeve. "Can you fix him?"

Dr. Palmer slapped the folder with the medical charts closed. "We've had some success in recent years with a combination treatment of Magiprex and electroshock therapy."

Mom trembled. "Electroshock. Won't that hurt him?"

"You will see changes in his behavior. But he will be sedated throughout the treatment, so there shouldn't be much pain." Dr. Palmer smiled as if they were talking about having a tooth pulled.

"And when it's done, he'll be better?" Her hands shook, and she tucked her arms across her chest. "No more magic?"

Dr. Palmer scratched his cheek, absentminded. "We haven't found a cure for this sort of magic, but he won't remember he has it. He will believe he is ordinary." He waved a hand at the third man, who had so far remained silent. "Isn't that right, Dr. Selnik?"

Dr. Selnik nodded. "A crude interpretation, but more or less accurate." He held out a clipboard and a pen. "You will need to approve the treatment."

Mom hesitated.

Dr. Selnik cleared his throat. "You must consider what is best for the boy's well-being. If left untreated…" He glanced at Dr. Palmer.

Dr. Palmer stepped close and laid his hand on Mom's elbow, a gesture that should have been comforting. "I have spoken with someone from Child Services already. They agree that this is in Percival's best interest." He drew himself up so she was forced to tip her head back to look at him. "If you are incapable of making this decision, the state will be forced to intervene and that could lead to… charges. Possible loss of custody."

"Yes." Mom nodded her head. "Of course. You are right."

"Mom." Percy shook his head. "Mom."

"Hush, baby." She pulled away from Dr. Palmer, leaning down to kiss Percy's forehead and squeeze his hand. "We're going to make everything okay."

"Mom."

But she wouldn't look him in the eye. "Give me the forms." She let go of his hand and took the pen to scratch her name, over and over on each page, each stroke loud in the sudden silence of the hospital room. "There." She shoved the clipboard back at Dr. Selnik.

He flipped through the pages, checking to be certain none of them had been missed. "Good. We will see about transferring him to our treatment facility this afternoon."

"I'll be able to come visit him?"

"Of course." Dr. Selnik smiled. "If you will excuse me, I'll get the transportation orders started."

Mom sat back down next to the bed as the doctors filed out. She took Percy's hand again and twitched her mouth into something like a smile, but her eyes were afraid. "It's okay, Percy. Everything is going to be okay. The doctors are going to take you away for a while, but then you'll be all better. I promise."

CHAPTER 12

Percy twitches awake. *Mom.*

Martinez looks up from his laptop with a frown. "You okay?"

"Yeah. Just dozed off. Sorry." Percy reaches for his coffee cup, drinks the last cold swallow with a grimace.

"It's getting pretty late." Martinez squints at the clock on his phone. "There's a couple cots down the hall if you want to try and catch a couple hours sleep."

"Yeah. Maybe." Percy stares at the photos spread out in front of him. MacKenzie did a pretty good job separating the shadow image from the others, better than a lot of security camera stills. But they still haven't gotten any hits from the missing persons' database or DMV records.

In one of them, the angle is slightly different, not a full three-quarter view, but not straight on either. And there's something different about it, an angularity to the jaw that makes him frown.

"Where's MacKenzie?"

"In the other conference room." Martinez sits up straighter. "Have you found something?"

"Maybe." He shoves his chair back and heads toward the conference room.

MacKenzie and Elliot are huddled over a different stack of files, but also surrounded by empty coffee cups and Styrofoam plates filled with pizza crusts.

"What's up, Cox?" MacKenzie looks up as he leans in the doorway.

"That search you're running. On the shadow image. Looking for female only?"

"Yeah. Why?"

He pushes the photo at her. "What if this is a male? See the jaw. And the hairline could be masculine."

"Maybe." She frowns. "Yeah. Okay. I'll run it again. See if we get anything." She pulls one of the laptops closer, typing in the new search with a rattle of keys. "It may take a while. Lot more to search."

"Thanks." His phone beeps, and he pulls it from his pocket and thumbs the alarm off. Time for his nighttime meds.

He's aware of MacKenzie and Elliot watching him, trying so hard to look casual he can almost hear the strain in their muscles.

"I'm going to go get some water. Stretch my legs for a minute."

"Sure," MacKenzie says. "Take your time."

Percy wanders down the hall in search of a water fountain. Most of the offices in this part of the building are empty of people, the lights in the hallway turned down to save energy. Only every other one is on.

His heart is back to its normal rhythm, but he still feels uneasy. He frowns, digging in his pocket for the pill bottle. Nightmares are something he's grown used to, but that one felt more real. More personal. *Like a memory.*

He washes the pill down with a couple swallows of water, then a couple more to get rid of the lingering taste of stale coffee. Wipes his mouth on the back of his hand. He hasn't dreamed about being a kid for years.

He has a few memories of the institution, but before that... Nothing. Except now he has a vague image of a hospital bed and three doctors who jitter and twitch and threaten. *"We haven't found a cure for this sort of magic, but he won't remember he has it."*

Percy looks at the pill bottle, still clutched in one hand. Remembers the Magiprex he's supposed to be taking with the anti-depressant. He pulls his phone off his belt and dials Connie's office. It's late, but she was helping Elliot run down files earlier.

"This is a surprise, Percy," she says by way of hello. "How are those books working out?"

"Impressively dull." He glances down the hall to make sure no one else is around. "Listen, I was wondering if you could do me a favor?"

"Anything to solve this case and get you all back home."

"Well, this is more of a personal favor."

"Oh." Her tone changes from bantering to curious. "And what exactly is this personal favor?"

"I was wondering if you could get me the black files on these meds. Aripiprazole."

There's a long pause. "You know I'm not supposed to give those out without signed clearance. Especially not to... you know."

"Yeah. It's just, I was talking to one of the doctors here, and he noticed

I was taking it and asked if I was aware of the higher risk for early onset dementia." He prefers to tell the truth, but he's good at lying. The back of his neck barely gets hot. "He said the risk varied and that some meds were better than others. I just thought… but it's okay. I'll just wait and ask Dr. Carver when I get back."

There's a faint rattle of computer keys on the other end. "Well. The black file on the aripiprazole won't do you any good without your files to compare." Another rattle of keys. "Not that you'll find much there. Looks like most of it's been redacted."

"Like that's surprising." He waits a beat or two. "I guess I can wait. Not like I can do anything about it now if I'm at risk."

Connie is silent for a moment, breathing heavy on the end of the phone. "I guess it wouldn't hurt for you to look through this. But you can't tell anyone where you got it, understand?"

"Never."

"Okay. I'll send it to your private email."

"You're the best, Connie. I owe you one."

"You be careful down there, all right?"

He nods. "I'm trying my best." Martinez steps out in the hall and waves at him. "Oh. Got to go." He barely hears her saying goodbye, already punching the phone off and sliding it back into the pocket on his belt.

Martinez comes down the hall, quick. "Hey. I've been looking for you."

"Did you find something?" He says it automatic, knowing that crackle of energy from Martinez means a break in the case.

"Yeah. And you'll want to see this."

MacKenzie is bent over the table, trying to get a cable plugged into her laptop. "Come on." The screen on the conference room wall flickers to life. "There." She taps a few keys and the image of a photo ID pops up. "This is Alexander John Michaels. Eighteen years old. There's a missing person's report from a little over three weeks ago."

Percy leans on the back of a chair. "Kidnapped?"

"Maybe, but police suspected he had run away. There's a brief note here about some sort of argument with his parents." Elliot passes out sheets of paper, still warm from the printer. "No specifics. Also an attached file about an assault from two years ago."

Percy flips through the pages, mostly the detailed little boxes indicating the time the report was made and where and by whom. "He got in a fight?"

"No. Looks like he was attacked. There's not much in here, but I've got a call out to the investigating officer, Matt Burns. Going to see if we can get him to come in and share his case notes. But there is a note here that may be important." She taps her finger on the last line on the page.

"Hate crime?" Percy rubs his forehead. "Michaels is not an obvious minority. So… homosexual, maybe?"

Elliot nods. "Queer of some sort, I'd guess. Especially given the circumstances. With the young women. And in that other image, he has long hair."

Martinez leans in the door and tosses Percy his jacket. "Come on."

"Where?"

"We're going to talk to the parents. See if they can give us anything else."

Percy hesitates. "And if Officer Burns comes in while we're gone?"

"He'll stay 'til you get back." Elliot makes a shooing motion. "Now go. We don't have much time left to figure this out."

CHAPTER 13

Franklin is still sitting in the basement, staring at the burned-out salt circle when the phone rings. He gropes around the edge of the table, then taps the button to accept the call. "Hello?"

"Mr. Jones? This is Agent Elliot with the FBI special investigations team."

"Yes, ma'am." He starts getting his feet under him. "Has something happened?"

"We have a new lead. The image that you and Agent Cox uncovered is of Alexander John Michaels."

Franklin blinks. "Alexander?"

"Yes. We were surprised as well, but there's not a lot of ambiguity about the visual match. And he's been missing for close to a month."

"Since before the first girl was attacked."

"That's right."

"Do you need me to come in?"

There's a pause; he can almost see the faint smile she'd given him at the hospital. "Not just yet. We would like you to continue your efforts to see if you can find us any leads within the community."

"Yes. Of course. I'll let you know as soon as I hear anything."

He sits for a moment in silence, wondering if there is something he's missed. Wondering what to do next.

He gets to his feet with an irritable murmur. He's going to need a long night's sleep when all this is over. Most of the salt and ash has burned away, but he gets the push broom and sweeps up the last remnants and dumps them in the garbage can in the corner.

Now that he has a name, it should be easy enough to figure out what sort of role Alexander Michaels has in the attacks. It would be simpler if he were the perpetrator, but somehow Franklin doesn't think that's the case. The shadow on Emily Grant looked asleep. Or dead. Certainly not someone in a position to be stalking the city and taking souls.

And Percy Cox said he saw someone else.

He pours fresh salt into a bowl, crouches on the floor, and, for the second time in nearly as many hours, begins forming a summoning ring.

CHAPTER 14

I can't say Mama ever taught me much.

Maybe she was busy trying to take care of Daddy. Or maybe she just didn't care.

Maybe she meant to and it never happened. But one way or another, she never taught me much.

Not like Daddy, always pulling me into his lap and whispering things in my ear. Not like Addie, showing me how to button my dress up right and brush my teeth so they wouldn't fall out of my head.

Some things though, you learn in between the spaces of what you're taught.

Daddy told me the heart always wins. He told me it was the candle flame in the darkness and a warm embrace on a cold night. Daddy taught me that love was both end and means.

From Mama, I learned sometimes love is not enough, at least not in this world.

Not that it isn't powerful. Not that the pouring out of love like blood or breath or life is ever wasted. But sometimes there are scars that never fade and wounds that never heal.

Maybe it would have been different if she had known Daddy when he was little. Maybe their path could have been different if they had always loved and laughed with each other. But when Mama met Daddy, he already had scars— visible and invisible.

By the time Mama met Daddy, there were some things he couldn't change. Some things he didn't want to change.

There, but for the grace of God, go I.

It was Daddy who taught me the magic of lips and tongue. The way that words and voice give rise to magic big and small. The way a storyteller decides the hero and the villain in the words they speak, making shadows comforting or fearsome as they will.

But it was from watching Mama that I learned the magic of what is said fades unless it is supported by what is done.

I'm not sure I ever remember Mama apologizing for what she tried to do to me and Addie. Maybe because she didn't regret it. Maybe because she knew those actions were deliberate and no matter how soft her voice, she couldn't undo it with words. She couldn't turn it into a story where things were okay.

Not like Daddy. He always said he was sorry, always begged her not to tell anyone, and promised he would be different.

I'm sorry. I didn't mean to hurt you. It won't ever happen again.

Never again, he always said.

It was always a lie.

Maybe if Mama had met Daddy when he was younger, it would have been different. Because she certainly tried hard to save him, even as she got more scars—visible and invisible.

Daddy taught me the heart always wins, but I learned from Mama that sometimes in life, love isn't enough to save those who don't want to be saved.

CHAPTER 15

Percy looks at the house warily. It's a faded little bungalow with a tired porch covering the front. There are screens to keep the bugs away from the yellowed light, but the door sags, letting the moths in to batter against the glass cover anyway. "You sure this is the place?"

Martinez glances at his phone. "This is the address on the license." He looks at Percy intently. "Why?"

Percy shrugs. How does he explain the creeping tension? The coldness drifting like threads of fog from the house. "It doesn't matter." He shoves the door of the car open, trying to smother his irritability. This lead will only end in sadness. He would rather be reading the files Connie has sent, but it would be suspicious if he didn't give Martinez a hand after pointing them all in the right direction.

Martinez leads the way to the door, rings the bell firmly. Almost immediately, a woman answers.

"Yes? Can I help you?" Her eyes are shadowed, face lined with worry.

Martinez glances at the note in his hand. "We're looking for Letitia Michaels."

"That's me." She folds the front of her housecoat in one trembling hand and pats her tousled hair into place with the other. "I'm Letitia. Who are you?"

Martinez shows his badge. "I'm Agent Martinez and this is Agent Cox with the FBI. May we speak with you?"

"Is this about Alex?" Already she is opening the door and ushering them in. "Have you found him? Is he safe?"

"No ma'am. I'm afraid we haven't found him." Martinez steps into the living room smoothly. "But we have some questions. About him. About his disappearance."

"Of course. Would you like something to drink?" She waves a hand at the solid man getting up from the couch. "Jonathan. These men are here about Alex."

"Mr. Michaels." Martinez nods solemnly. "I know it's late. We just have a few questions."

"Sure." He pushes a button on the remote, and the TV falls silent, the image still flickering in the dim room. "Have a seat."

"Can I get you something to drink?" Mrs. Michaels asks again, her hands still fluttering from housecoat to hair, smoothing wrinkles and subduing stray curls.

Martinez shakes his head and settles on the edge of the couch. "No, thank you."

"A glass of water? If it's not too much trouble." Percy sits down in a chair closer to the window.

"Yes. Just a moment." She hurries toward the back of the house.

Mr. Michaels sits back down, a heavy furrow across his broad forehead. "You said this was about Alex?"

"Yes, sir." Percy pulls a copy of the shadow image from his pocket, leans forward to pass it across the narrow room. "Does this look like your son?"

Michaels looks at it. "Yes." He tilts the photo back and forth. "Weird, isn't it? This some kind of double exposure? Or reflection?" A nod at the TV. "We seen a few of those investigation shows. Always finding some little detail that helps them solve the case once they look hard enough."

Martinez pulls his pen and notebook from his pocket. "Those shows are not—"

"Yes," Percy says quickly. "It is a reflection of sorts."

Mrs. Michaels returns from the kitchen and hands Percy a glass of ice water. "Can I get you anything else, Mr. Cox?"

"This is fine. Thank you." He takes a couple of sips while she sits down on the end of the couch next to her husband.

"You said you hadn't found Alex?" She looks back and forth between them.

"No, ma'am." Martinez shakes his head. "But there is a possibility his disappearance is connected to another case we are working, and we were hoping you could tell us a little more about him."

Percy leans forward in his chair. "The missing person's report said that he lived here."

"Yes." Mrs. Michaels nods.

"May I see his room?"

"I'll take him." Mr. Michaels stands up. "This way Agent Cox."

Percy takes another quick sip of water, sets the glass on an end table, and follows Mr. Michaels into a short hallway. "How old is Alex?"

"Just turned eighteen a few months ago." He opens a door, fumbles on the wall for the light switch. "This is his room."

Percy moves into the room, cautious. There's an uncomfortable tickle on the back of his neck, so faint he's certain it's not the presence of magic within this house, but there's something else, too. An echo of grief that he is not eager to step inside.

It's neater than the rest of the house. The books on the shelves beside the closet are arranged in meticulous order—smallest on the top, larger on the bottom. The covers on the bed are completely smooth, the single pillow laid precisely at the headboard.

He opens the closet, pulls the string to turn on the light. It, too, is orderly. Almost clinical. "Is this how he left things?"

"Yes." Michaels shoves his hands in his pockets. "We haven't touched anything."

"There was an attached file on the missing person's report. Of an assault and battery?"

He nods. "That was… a couple years ago."

"One of the notations indicated the police thought it might be a hate crime, but the charges were dropped because you didn't wish to pursue it." Percy turns and looks at Michaels. "Is Alex gay?"

Michaels twitches, glances toward the door. "Yes. But not… not like you're thinking." He moves across the room, pushing the door nearly closed. "Alex is trans. That is… he told us he was a girl."

Percy looks around the stark bedroom. "This doesn't look like a girl's room, Mr. Michaels."

"Jonathan. Please." He flashes a weak smile. "He told us after he was attacked. Before that…" He stares at a worn spot on the carpet for a moment. "He would go out and change into different clothes. Dresses. Or a skirt and blouse. Go to these places where there were other people like him."

"Places. Like a club of some sort?"

"Maybe. I think so."

"Do you remember a name?"

"No." He shakes his head, miserable. "We only found out later and then… then we weren't interested in specifics. We just wanted to fix him."

The hair on Percy's arms stands up, and something hot and sick pinches at his stomach. "Fix him?"

"We didn't know what to do. Alex was our little boy. He played baseball. He liked helping me work on the car. And he was telling us that his body was wrong. That he was supposed to be a woman and wear dresses and date men." He rubs his mouth. "Our pastor said was our fault. My fault. I hadn't taught him the proper way to be a man and that we'd let him come in contact with perverts. But there was a program that we could send him to. That we could fix him. Make him our little boy again."

His eyes are wild as he looks at Percy. "They told us it was therapy. That it would help him. With his confusion. With his depression."

"Conversion therapy." Percy can barely get the words out without growling.

"Yes. That's it." He shuffles to the dresser, staring at the photos laid under the glass top. "But when he came back… Lettie thought he was better at first. They'd cut his hair real short, not long like he used to wear it. And he only wore strong colors, nothing feminine. But he was silent all the time."

"Silent?"

"Alex had always been quiet. Not so much awkward as just a little shy. But this was different. This was… he said almost nothing, and when he did, it was like he was afraid he would say the wrong thing."

Percy swallows hard. Remembering dinners in silence where he didn't dare to say anything, afraid that he would somehow mention something that might be related to magic. Equally afraid to talk about the institution and risk screaming at Mom about what had happened there. Forcing himself into silence because that was safest. "Alex was afraid."

"Yes." Michaels nods. "And I knew something was wrong, so I started reading. About trans. Not the book our pastor gave us. But articles on the actual science of it. I still didn't understand, really, how Alex could look like a boy and not be one, but I realized that Lettie and I had not saved our son. We had only hurt our daughter."

"What did you do?"

"I tried to talk to her. But she thought it was some kind of trick."

"Yes." Percy is familiar with that as well. The suspicion that it is just a test. That Mom is still afraid of him, ready to send him back to the cold lonely room at the institution.

"And then, one day while her mother and I were gone, she just left. Didn't take clothes or money or…" He gestured to the room, everything neat and in its place.

"Alex didn't leave a note? Or give you any sign of where she might have gone? A friend?"

"No." Michaels shook his head. "She was just gone. I did—"

A shriek from the living room interrupts anything else.

Percy follows Michaels back down the hall.

Martinez is on his feet again, one hand patting the air as he tries to calm Mrs. Michaels. "Please sit down, ma'am."

"No. You need to leave." She turns toward Jonathan, and her eyes are wild. "He said Alex was involved with those dead girls. The ones we've seen on TV."

"No, ma'am." Martinez shakes his head. "I asked if there was a chance your son had ever met any of them."

"Alex is a good boy. He would never hurt anyone. Never." Her voice is high and shrill.

"Yes, ma'am we understand. But there is evidence that suggests that your son is connected to these girls somehow, and we—"

"Get out." She lunges for him, hand raised like she will slap him.

Jonathan gets his arms around her, looks at Martinez apologetically. "Perhaps it's best if you leave."

Percy touches Martinez's arm. "Let's go."

Martinez cocks an eyebrow. "Are you sure?"

"Yes." He nods.

"All right." Martinez closes his notebook and slips it into his pocket. "I'm sorry to have disturbed you so late. If you think of anything else." He sets his card on the end table and follows Percy out the door.

CHAPTER 16

Percy takes a deep breath as they step outside, feeling the need for space and quiet.

"You think the parents have anything to do with this?" Martinez steps down off the porch.

Percy shakes his head. "No. Not in the way you mean."

"The mother became very agitated when I started asking about Alex. Like she was trying to hide something." Martinez looks back at the house, a doubtful quirk to his mouth.

"Yes." Percy shoves his hands in pockets. "But not about the disappearance or the girls that have been attacked."

"Agent Cox." Michaels shuts the screen door and hurries down the steps after them. "I'm sorry about my wife. It has been a difficult year."

"Of course."

"There is something else you should know. Something I haven't told the police before because... well, I didn't think it mattered. I thought for certain Alex ran away." He crosses his arms over his chest, squeezing tight as though he is cold. "I saw her once."

Percy frowns. "Her?"

"Alex." He licks his lips and glances over his shoulder. His wife is a pale blotch in the hallway, but he drops his voice lower anyway. "It was downtown. She was walking with a young man. And she was beautiful. But I never told Lettie because I knew if I did then we'd have to tell other people, and I was ashamed." Tears well up, and he rubs them away with blunt fingers. "How stupid was that? Being embarrassed by my smart, beautiful girl."

"This was recently?" Martinez has his notebook out again.

"No. It was before those men attacked her. Before I sent her to that awful place." His lips tremble, and he rushes on. "But she was with a young man. Tall, with dark hair. One of those... like... Goth haircuts. Shaved on the sides and long on the top. But not as pale and he was wearing a t-shirt and jeans."

"Anything else you can remember about him?" Martinez has that bland look on his face—calm and nonjudgmental. "Scars? Or piercings?"

"No. But he had tattoo around his neck. Almost like a collar of some sort."

Martinez makes a note. "Could you see what it was?"

"I wasn't close enough. I didn't want her to see me." His voice drops to a whisper. "I didn't want anyone to see me with her." He starts to shake, tears streaming down his face.

Martinez looks at Percy, questioning. "And you didn't mention this before?"

"I only saw that man the one time. Never since. And… well. If you had seen them together, you would understand." He tucks his arms tighter across his chest. "Alex loved him. And he loved her. There was no way he would have… hurt her. But now I'm thinking he might do something terrible to try and save her."

Martinez nods. "Okay. We'll see what we can find out."

Percy looks at Michaels trying to find some compassion for him. "Thank you for telling us."

Michaels nods, rubs his eyes on the back of his hand. "Alex is dead, isn't she, Agent Cox?"

"We really don't have any information on your child, Mr. Michaels." Martinez closes his notebook, looking more uncomfortable with the half-truth than usual.

Percy puts his hand on Michaels' shoulder awkwardly. "That is very likely, Jonathan. I'm sorry."

Michaels sobs, burying his face in the crook of his arm for a moment. And Percy puts his arms around him. Because no matter what blame lies on him for what he has done, he has lost his son. And his daughter.

After a moment, Michaels steps away, rubbing his cheeks dry again. "I need to get back inside. Thank you."

"Of course." Martinez nods automatically.

Percy gets back into the car. Closes the door, closes his eyes, just trying to breathe.

Martinez slides into the driver's seat, thumps the door shut. "You shouldn't have said that." He leans closer when Percy doesn't say anything. "About his son. We don't know—"

"His daughter," Percy says firmly. "And she's dead."

"We don't—"

"I do." He looks at Martinez. "I do."

Martinez frowns. "I don't doubt your word, Cox. But you can't just go around saying things like that. Not 'til we have something more concrete."

Percy nods reluctantly. "You're right. But he deserved to know."

"Maybe." Martinez starts the car. "Where now?"

"I think I need to talk to the local specialist. Jones."

Martinez frowns. "Why?"

"The man Michaels described might be the one I saw earlier. When I was with Miss Grant."

"And why do you want to talk to Jones about it?"

"He might have a better idea of the locals who have the Touch now that we have a better description."

"Okay." Martinez nods and shuffles through some things on his phone. "We'll try this address and see if he's there. But we're not chasing around the city all night if he isn't."

"Right." Percy props his chin on his fist, watching the streetlights slip by as they drive through the dark city. He's itching to open the files Connie sent him, but Martinez is too sharp for that. He needs Jones to keep Martinez busy, just for a few minutes.

He sighs. *Patience.*

CHAPTER 17

Franklin lights the candles around the ring on the floor and pauses to drink the last couple swallows of coffee from his mug. Takes a deep breath and focuses once more on the circle of salt.

"Alexander John Michaels, I summon you. Come and speak with me."

He doesn't have to wait as long this time. The shade flickers into the center of the ring almost as soon as the last syllable of the name is spoken.

Franklin lets his hands drop back to his sides. "Alexander?"

The shade tilts its head. "Alex."

The voice is lighter than Franklin expected, and he pauses, taking note of the dress and long hair. "You are femme?"

Alex smiles. "Now. But before I was… not as much."

"Ah." Franklin nods. That explains why it is young women who have been taken. "Do you know about the women who have been killed? Souls taken and put into the body you have left behind."

Alex frowns. "I am aware of it. But I cannot stop it."

"Do you know who is doing these things?"

She pushes her hair back from her eyes. "You cannot stop him."

"If he is not—"

"Yes." Her shoulders sag. "He is determined to try and have me back in one way or another. But he will kill you if you try and stop him."

"He will kill others if I don't." Franklin steps closer, taking care not to break the salt ring. "Please. You must help me."

Alex shakes her head. "I can't."

He rubs his lip, thoughtful. "Why hasn't he summoned you back?"

She looks at him, silent, for a long moment. "He did, at first. But every time he went to sleep… I faded away again."

"Your body won't host your soul any longer? Is that why the other girls fade as well?"

"No." She fidgets. "Just like them, I didn't want to stay. He could hold me there for a while, but then… I would leave. I thought after a few times he would give up."

"He no longer summons you."

Alex rubs her hands together as if she is cold. "No. But his purpose remains the same. To bring my body back to life."

"Ah." Franklin nods. "So he has started trying to put someone else in your skin instead."

"Yes." Alex leans close to the shimmering line of salt, and her eyes are wide. "I'm afraid he won't stop."

"That's why I need your help, Alex. These young women don't deserve what he is doing to them."

Alex shakes her head. "I can't stop him."

"Tell me who he is, and I will stop him."

"You can't."

Franklin leans forward, nearly pushing through the salt ring. "I must try."

The door leading in from the backyard shudders. "Franklin Jones. Open up."

He frowns. *Who the hell is that?* But the candle on the table has burned down to a stub and, with it, the magic that has drawn Alex here.

"Tell me his name, Alex. Help me stop him."

She hesitates.

The door shudders again, the frame starting to crack under the strain.

Franklin rests his hands against the magic barrier, as he did with Delaney, teeth aching with exhaustion as he uses up part of himself to bend the energy, and the shade bound inside it, to his will. "Alex. Tell me his name."

Alex shivers, but nods. "Be careful. He will kill you."

"His name."

"Malcolm—"

The door slams open, bits of wood from the splintered edge ricocheting off the shelves that line the walls, and the candle on the table goes out.

"Damn it." Franklin drops to his knees, exhausted.

"Keep your hands where I can see them."

The voice is familiar now that it is no longer filtering through the door, and Franklin blinks against the glare of the flashlight. "Agent Cox?"

Percival bends down to touch the residue of the salt ring. "What were you doing here?" When Franklin hesitates, Percy leans forward and grabs him by the front of his shirt. "What were you doing, Jones?"

Franklin swallows a prickle of fear. He may not be a Sensitive, but he can feel the magic lurking within Cox. Hungry and fearful. "I was attempting to communicate with the shade of Alex Michaels."

The other man, shorter and more solid than Cox, frowns. "Communicate? How?"

Franklin settles back on his heels, keeping his hands on his knees. "I don't think we've met."

"Agent Martinez. Communicate how?"

Franklin touches the salt ring, now little more than a caustic smudge on the old concrete floor, with one hand. "Physical magic."

Martinez looks at the dusty symbols, the melted pools of candle wax. "Were you successful?"

"Somewhat. But I was interrupted." He tilts his head to indicate he is referring to Martinez and Cox.

Cox tightens his grip on Franklin's shirt. "How do we know you are not a part of this? The soul-stealing? If you can summon a shade here…?"

Franklin grits his teeth as magic slithers across his skin. "You told me what you felt in the hospital was a Power, Agent Cox. And I may be skilled, but that is not me."

"You could still be working with him."

"Percy." Martinez edges forward. "Calm down." He settles his gun back into the holster on his belt. "We'll take him back to the office with us. All right?"

Cox lets go of Franklin reluctantly. "All right."

Franklin stands up carefully, doing his best not to look threatening. He's not afraid of Martinez, even with his hand still resting on his gun. But Cox…

Franklin resists the urge to rub the back of his neck, the hair on his arms standing up as though lightning is about to strike. He wonders if Martinez can feel it, too, but doesn't dare ask. "Can I get my jacket?"

Martinez nods. "I'll come with you."

"It's just upstairs. Watch yourself on the steps."

Martinez glances back at Cox. "You coming?"

"I'll meet you back at the car. Just going to look around for a moment." He waves a hand at the basement.

Martinez hesitates for a moment, then nods. "Okay. But don't take too long."

Franklin leads the way up to the first floor, turning on the light in the kitchen when they reach the top of the stairs. "Mind if I get a drink of water?"

Martinez shakes his head. "Go ahead." He paces a few steps, peers into a cabinet. "You're a magician, right?"

Franklin blinks, pulls a clean glass off the drying rack by the sink. "Yes. Why?"

He glances back at the stairs to the basement, then steps in close. "Does he seem all right to you?"

"Agent Cox?"

"Yes."

Franklin gets some water from the tap and takes a quick swallow. "I have only met him once before."

"At the hospital." Martinez nods. "But… there is nothing strange about him? Nothing different about him tonight?"

Franklin drinks more water, searching for words that will not sound like a lie. Words that will not put them both in danger. "I really can't say. But he is tense. I think that is obvious. This case is particularly difficult. Yes?"

Martinez looks at him intently, lips moving silent as though maybe he will argue about it. Then he nods, sharp. "Of course. Are you ready?"

"Almost." Franklin rinses his glass and sets it back on the rack to dry. Then leads the way to the front of the house to collect his keys and jacket from beside the front door. "Will this take long?"

Martinez shrugs. "We've got some questions. About what you were doing. And about the case, that we thought you might be able to help with."

"Right." He shuts the door behind them and follows Martinez down the stairs to the car.

Cox is leaning against the passenger-side door, the shadows on his face stark under the glare of the streetlight. "I was starting to worry."

Martinez shakes his head. "It's fine."

Cox frowns and leans in toward Franklin, pulling open the back door. "All right. Get in."

"Thanks." Franklin climbs into the back seat. He isn't too happy about trusting Delaney Green, but there's no doubt she was right about Percival Cox. *His power is just waking up.*

CHAPTER 18

I wake up after a while, warm and content. Overhead the moon sashays across the velvet sky while stars flutter on the darker fringe just above the tree tops, the fireflies swaying in the shadows below the branches.

For a moment, I have no desire to be anywhere else. For a moment, I think I could just stay here forever.

Baby sighs and nudges me with her little fist. "You awake, Delaney?"

"Yeah."

She sits up, and the leaves scuttle away so that only the soft grass remains beneath us. "I don't think you have much time left. Here."

I cross my legs underneath me and tuck my hair behind my ears. Close my eyes and try to remember the twists of the other threads I saw in the cave under Daddy's tree. "No. It's coming to a close."

Baby smooths the front of her dress. "Are you certain about this, Del? You know it ain't an accident you were drawn to Percy."

That was a thing I had always suspected, but I'd never realized it was not me that had pulled that first thread. Knowing that Daddy has had a hand in it only makes me more determined. "If I leave him by himself… he will do terrible things, Baby."

"He may still do terrible things." She looks at me, big eyes as dark and terrifying as the passage back to the living. "You may do terrible things."

"Yes."

"And you do not fear that?"

"Of course I do. But I am not certain I can walk away from this path I have set."

Her mouth cinches up, and she narrows her eyes. "You can always walk away, Delaney. No matter how many threads you have pulled and chased, there is always a choice."

"I am not certain I want to walk away, Baby. No matter how I was drawn to Percy in the beginning, he and I share something beyond Daddy's purpose. And leaving him alone will not solve anything."

She is silent for a long moment. There is something tired and old resting in the round lines of her face. "No. I suppose you are right."

I rub my eyes, then wipe damp fingers on my dress. "I'll miss you, Baby."

"I will miss you, too, Delaney." She crawls forward into my lap, hugs me as tight as her little arms will allow. "Can I stay with you until you leave?"

"Yes." I cradle her against my chest and blink up at the moon as fresh tears well up.

Baby touches my cheek. "What's wrong?"

"I'm scared, Baby."

"It'll be all right." She snuggles closer, one fist drifting toward her mouth. "You're doing the right thing."

"Are you sure?"

She yawns. "Yes."

Leaves scrabble up into my lap and up to cling to Baby, soft and warm as a bat's wing.

I dry my face on my sleeve and stare up at the moon circling slow overhead. *I will do the right thing. I will.*

CHAPTER 19

hey put Franklin in one of the empty offices with a chair and a cop outside the door.

Martinez looks at Percy, worried. "You sure you want to talk to him? I can do it. See what shakes loose."

"No." Percy smooths his dark hair across his forehead. "I want to talk to him. I'm better now anyway. Coffee helped." He taps the Styrofoam cup with a faint grin.

"All right. Well, I guess we better get to it then."

They bring chairs in, and Martinez waves the officer away from the door with the assurance they will call if they need further assistance.

Percy opens the folder on his knees, plucks a photo of the salt ring, and holds it up. "Tell me about this."

Franklin looks at Martinez warily.

Percy leans forward. "You should be worrying about me."

Franklin tilts his head in acknowledgment. "A summoning ring. I was trying to find the spirit that goes with the body."

"Alexander Michaels, you mean."

"Yes." He nods. "But it did not go as planned the first time."

Percy shifts. "First time?"

"Before you called and gave me the name." He looks back and forth between the two of them. "You understand how it works, right?"

Martinez leans back in his chair. "Enlighten me."

Franklin rubs his fingers through his braids. "In crude terms, it's like making a phone call. You have to have a number. Maybe a name. Or something that belonged to the person. I had not tried it on this case because I had neither." He looks at Percy. "Then you saw the other image. The shadow. I thought I could use it. The image instead of a name."

"But it didn't work." Martinez says it flat. Still a hint of disbelief in the idea of magic the way Franklin does it.

"No." His gaze slides toward Percy, and there is something curious behind his eyes.

Percy shifts forward to the edge of his seat. Something is growling in his chest. Like anger, but with more teeth. "And the magic I felt outside your house? That was you trying a second time to summon Alex Michaels? Not you trying to find another soul to steal?"

Franklin grimaces. "I do not have the skill or the power to pull a soul out of a living being. With preparation and the correct tools, I can summon a shade for a very limited amount of time, but I am incapable of doing what has been done with these young women." The muscle in his jaw twitches. "You know it. You were there in the hospital earlier. You know I am not the one who let Emily Grant slip away."

Martinez clears his throat. "Who then?"

He sits back. "I don't know."

"Another street magician like yourself?"

"No." Percy stands up and paces a few steps around the cramped office. "Jones is right. What I felt was a Power, not a magician."

Martinez sighs. "All right. Let me go see if we can turn up anything useful in the registry." He flips back through his notes. "You think it could be the man Jonathan Michaels saw?"

"Could be." Percy looks at Franklin. "How familiar are you with the Powers in Savannah?"

Franklin shakes his head. "I might know a few, but most you'd never know unless you brushed against their magic."

"This would be a tall man with dark hair and a tattoo of some sort around his neck. Possibly with his head partially shaved."

"Doesn't ring a bell." Franklin says it casual, but Percy's skin tingles with the breath of the lie.

Martinez stands up. "All right. Wait here and I'll see what I can find."

Percy waits until the door closes before he looks at Franklin. "Why are you lying to my friend?" He knots his fingers in the front of Franklin's shirt and pulls him to his feet. "Tell me now or I will hurt you."

"Because the man you are looking for is a necromancer. His power is literally life and death, Percival Cox. Do you really want to take Martinez or MacKenzie with you to face something like that?"

Percy grins, all teeth. "Are you suggesting it should just be the two of us, Mr. Jones?"

"Yes."

"Why?"

Franklin grimaces again, sweat beading on his forehead. "When I made the first attempt to summon Alex Michaels, I was not entirely unsuccessful."

"What do you mean?"

"I didn't reach Michaels, but I did get someone else. Someone who seemed to be very familiar with you."

Percy blinks. "With…" His breath catches. "Delaney."

"Yes."

Some of the anger fades, the sense that something is about to break free diminishes, and Percy loosens his grip on Franklin's shirt.

Delaney. He has been aware that he misses her. But hearing that someone else has seen her, has talked to her, makes him ache, like a bell has been struck within him, sounding and resounding with loss and longing.

He staggers back a step and drops into his chair. "Delaney."

"So she said." Franklin rubs the sweat from his forehead, pulls his shirt straight.

"But you don't know for sure?"

"She was a Power. And she… burned." He sits down and looks at Percy, hard. "She said that you and I must work together or more people will die."

"And you know where to find this man with the tattoo?"

"His name is Malcolm Lance. I don't know where to find him, but I have an idea of how to find him."

Percy chews his lower lip, considering. "And you're certain we should go alone? What if we fail? What will the rest of my team do?"

"We will not fail."

"You think you are strong enough to take on a Power?"

Franklin looks at him steadily. "I think you are."

Percy shakes his head. "I have a sense for magic, but I'm not—"

Franklin raises an eyebrow. "No? Delaney told me there was something powerful in you. Something that had been asleep for a long time, but was finally waking up."

He frowns, the heat in his chest growling worriedly. He remembers the electricity in his head, the drugs melting away years of memory 'til his childhood was nothing but shadows. What if Franklin tells someone else? If Ms. Carver finds out, she will recommend he be put back in an institution for certain. *Maybe I should kill him now.* But the building is too busy, there would be no way to explain what had happened. No good way to get the body out without being noticed. And even if he could, what he doesn't know how to do is find Malcolm Lance.

For that, he needs help.

Percy looks at Franklin and does his best to smile, even though his heart is racing with fear. "You're right. But we'll have to go now."

Franklin nods. "I don't think we have much time anyway. Lance is desperate and the magic protecting Alex's body can only last so long."

"He's going to take another girl."

"Yes, and soon."

Percy pulls the door open and glances out. There is some activity at the end of the hall where they have their command set up, but the rest is quiet and relatively deserted with another hour, at least, before the morning shift starts. He looks at Franklin. "It's clear."

They hurry down the hallway toward the stairs.

"Do you have a car?" Franklin holds the door open, then follows him down the steps. "We won't get very far on foot."

"No. They don't let me drive much." Percy stops at the bottom of the stairs, peers out into the lower hall. "Let's go." He moves toward the doors that lead out to the side street, away from the main desk. "Besides. The departmental cars usually have some sort of tracking in them. If we want the others to stay clear…"

"Good point." Franklin looks up and down the street. "Let's try down here. I think I might know a guy."

"And then?"

"Then we finish this."

Percy hesitates for a moment, wondering how much Franklin knows. If he suspects what will happen after Lance is dead. But if he did, why would he be offering to help? Offering to stay anywhere near Percy? He smiles. "Yes," he says. "Good."

Then we finish this.

CHAPTER 20

"Agent Martinez?" An older man with steel grey hair and eyes to match, stands up as Martinez enters the conference room.

"Yes. That's me." Martinez sets the folder down on the table and holds out his hand.

"Officer Matt Burns." His handshake is solid. "They told me you had some questions about the Michaels case."

"Ah. Yes." Martinez pulls out his notebook, flips to an empty page. "You investigated the attack two years ago, is that correct?"

"Yeah. And the disappearance. Thought at first they might be related."

"They weren't?"

Burns shrugs. "The attack was some idiots beating up a girl because they were too embarrassed to admit all they'd seen was a nice pair of tits."

Martinez frowns. "I'm not sure I follow."

"There were witnesses. And all of them said those men were harassing Michaels, catcalling and shit, before any of them figured out she was trans."

"I was under the impression Alex Michaels was attacked by a group of boys from his school."

Burns grins, dry as dust. "You've been talking to his mama then."

"That's right."

He rubs his hand across short-cropped hair thoughtfully. "It wasn't boys that attacked Alex. They were grown men who intended to hurt her. Maybe even kill her. And when she disappeared, my first thought was they had come after her again."

Martinez glances through his notes. "There were no charges filed the first time."

"Parents didn't want the scandal. And the DA could have filed but didn't. Differences of opinion on who was responsible."

"So you thought maybe those men meant to take another swing at Alex Michaels."

"Yeah. But when I checked them out again, half of them were in jail for a different assault. One was dead. The other two had moved out of state."

"Any of them tall, white, with dark hair and some sort of tattoo around their throat?"

Burns frowns. "No. But that sounds like one of the witnesses." He flicks his fingers reflexively, as though adjusting his grip on a gun. "Malcolm. Malcolm Lance. Always seemed to be something weird about him. When Alex disappeared, I tried to track him down again. Just in case he was involved."

"Tried?"

"Yeah. Couldn't find him though."

Martinez nods. "Okay. You mind staying for a while? I'll see if we can run this name and pull anything up, but I might have more questions."

"Sure. Is there coffee around here?" Burns glances around the conference room.

"Over by the copier. Help yourself." Martinez has his phone out, dialing Connie's office.

"Hello, Luis. What can I do for you?"

"I need you to run a search for me. Look for property, financial records, anything on Malcolm Lance." He flips through the folder with the interviews from the Michaels assault case. "Age 32. Born in Savannah."

"Okay." There's a faint rattle as she types. "Hmm. I'm not finding much recently. There were some bank accounts. A rental agreement, but all that stopped about two years ago."

"So, no idea where he is now?"

"No. Wait a minute." There's a long pause, more typing. "Looks like there was a house that belonged to a great-uncle. Passed into his possession five years ago. It was on the market for a while, but not recently."

"Utility bills?"

"Nope. But there was a complaint filed with city Code Enforcement about the grass on the property. No indication of who they talked to, but it looks like it's been being taken care of because there are no more complaints or fines."

"Okay. Send me that address and we'll check it out."

"Sure." Another flutter of typing and his phone pings, indicating a text message. "Hey. Did Percy get those files I sent?"

Martinez pauses. "Files?"

"On his meds. He was worried about some sort of interaction or complication. He asked to see…" She pauses, a nervous flicker in her breathing. "Well, I sent him the black files on the anti-depressant and the Magiprex."

Martinez swallows hard as a cold knot forms in his stomach. "When?"

"Last night. I mean, I thought it was okay. He was worried about the drugs interacting with his Sensitivity, and I thought he deserved to know if the anti-depressant was going to hurt him…" She trails off. "I shouldn't have done that, should I?"

"Let me call you back in a few." Martinez thumbs the phone off and pulls at his chin. Thinking hard about the change he's felt in Percy. Like standing too close to a storm.

Ever since he met Delaney Green, Percy's been different. Quiet, more intense than before. And sometimes, like at Jones' house, there's a feral glint in his eyes.

Martinez waves a hand at Burns sitting on the edge of the conference table with a Styrofoam cup of coffee in one hand. "You armed?"

Burns raises an eyebrow but twitches the edge of his jacket back to show his pistol holstered on his belt next to his badge. "Sure. Is there a problem?"

"Maybe. Maybe not." He checks his own sidearm. "You got a minute?"

Burns slurps the last of his coffee from the white cup and tosses it in the trash. "Yeah."

"Just keep a few steps back and keep an eye out."

"For what?"

"You'll know when you see it." He can't quite bring himself to make an accusation against Percy. But he can't ignore the possibility that something has changed.

Martinez pauses outside the door to the office where he left Percy and Jones. Glances at Burns, who sidles against the wall, hand resting on his gun, with a nod.

"Hey, Percy?" Martinez knocks on the door, then pushes it open. *Empty.* "Damn." He steps into the room, instinctively checking to make sure no one is hiding. Make certain that Percy hasn't stuffed Franklin Jones' body behind the stack of boxes in the corner.

But the room is deserted.

He steps back out into the hall. "He's not here."

Burns relaxes. "Who?"

"My partner was interviewing a street magician who's been helping with the case."

"Jones?"

"That's the one." Martinez pulls his phone from his belt and thumbs through the directory.

"And you're worried about him?" Burns' eyes narrow. "Or your partner?"

"Both. But it looks like they may have left." Martinez pauses while the phone dials Percy. Trying to organize a reasonable excuse for him to come back in right now.

Burns tilts his head. "Hear that?"

A faint thread of sound, electronic and repeating every few seconds, drifts from down the hall. Martinez sprints toward it, tips the recycling bin on its side. A cascade of crushed water bottles and soda cans spills on the floor. And in the middle is Percy's phone.

The screen blinks. *One Missed Call.*

Martinez's phone is mumbling quietly in his hand. "… is unavailable to take your call. Please leave a message—" He thumbs it off. "Damn it."

Burns picks up Percy's phone slowly. "Why would he leave this behind?"

"Because he doesn't want us following him."

"Following him where?"

"To find Malcolm Lance." Martinez opens the message from Connie. "We're going to need to check out this address immediately. And we're going to need back up."

"You think Jones is that dangerous?" Burns follows him up the hall toward the conference room.

"No, but I'm certain Lance is. And…" He shakes his head, still unwilling to say anything about Percy. "We need to be prepared."

Burns nods. "I'll get things moving. We can roll out in five."

"Make sure everyone understands Malcolm Lance is deadly. Approach him with extreme caution. And my partner and Jones may be there, too."

"You want us to treat them with caution, too?"

Martinez nods, reluctant. "Yes. But avoid the use of force if you can."

Burns looks at him for a moment, then nods. "All right. We'll do our best."

CHAPTER 21

The house sits at the end of the block on the edge of town. There are big plastic sheets covering the downstairs windows and a stack of lumber on the wraparound porch.

"Someone's been renovating." Cox nudges the ironwork gate, and it swings open silently.

"Yeah." Franklin follows him into the yard cautiously. The strap from his satchel digs into his neck, and he pauses to adjust it. Maybe he should have left some of the salt at his house, but he's not certain what will happen here and prefers to be prepared.

Cox is still hot with magic, though he's not looking at Franklin with such deadly intent at the moment. Distracted, maybe, by the prospect of facing Malcolm Lance, of confronting a necromancer.

Franklin rubs sweaty hands on his shirt as they walk up the stairs to the porch. "Do you think he's here?"

Cox looks at him with a scowl. "You're the one who brought us here."

"Yes. I'm certain this is where he's keeping Alex Michaels' body. I meant, is Lance here right now?"

"Oh." Cox frowns, eyes sliding half-closed while he concentrates. "No, I don't think so."

"Okay. So what do you want to do?"

"Look for a way in." Cox squeezes past the stacked lumber and moves toward the back of the house.

Franklin follows more slowly, trying to put together some sort of plan beyond what he has done so far. *Get Cox by himself.* Delaney Green promised to help, but only if she had a body. He combs his braids back from his face, remembering that Alex Michaels' corpse might be lying inside the house. *Maybe...*

"Here." Cox has the back door open. "Come on."

Inside the house is bare, no furniture, the walls torn back to studs or covered in new sheets of drywall. The floor is nothing but plywood tacked down over the joists. Franklin coughs as their feet stir drifts of plaster dust and peers into the other rooms. "Nothing here."

Cox nods. "Second floor, I think."

Before he can say anything else, the back door bangs open, and Malcolm shuffles in, a woman draped over one shoulder like a roll of carpet.

For a moment, no one moves. Cox and Lance stare at each other, predators sizing each other up.

Franklin swallows against a yelp of fear, knowing in every part of his being that he is far more mortal than either of these two. Knowing his best chance to survive is to let the two of them clash. A little voice in the back of his head begins to scream.

Delaney Green. Delaney Green.

Malcolm lets the woman drop to the floor, and magic rolls out to touch the room.

"Aih." Franklin doubles over, his heart laboring in his chest.

Cox staggers as well, but lurches forward to grapple with Lance. They sway back and forth before Malcolm punches Cox, knocking him back a few steps, before he snatches up a dusty baluster from the deconstructed staircase and clobbers Percy in the side of the head.

Franklin curls up on the floor, trying to force air into his lungs even as the magic nearly crushes him. *Breathe. Breathe, damn it.* Just as the room begins to turn dark at the corners, the pressure eases.

He's aware of Malcolm moving around the room. The stairs creak. Then he's being lifted and carried up to the second story of the house.

Lance drops him roughly to the floor, pauses to pull a plastic zip tie tight around his wrists. He groans and Malcolm touches his chest, magic coiling out lazily. "Be still and you might survive this."

Franklin lets his eyes drift closed, waits for the footsteps to fade, the distant creak of the stairs. *Not much time.* He rolls over and gets his feet under him. His heart struggling in his chest. He almost falls when he stands, head swimming. But adrenaline kicks in, forcing him back into something closer to a normal rhythm as he tries to get his bearings.

Alex Michaels' body is laid out in the middle of a salt ring. There are stitches down each arm where her wounds have been closed; her skin is greyish, but the eyes are still clear. Held from decay and rigor by the magic writ into the ring.

Franklin stumbles forward. If Delaney Green is to help him, she will need a body. He doesn't figure she'll be too keen on this one, but it's the only one he's got.

There's a little table with various tools laid out. Preparation for the next attempt to transfer a soul. A bowl of salt, one of sulfur. Candles. Several charms. And a sharp knife.

Franklin doesn't have time to try and cut himself loose. He grabs the blade and squeezes. "Son of a bitch." Blood flows freely from the cuts in his fingers, and he steps into the salt ring and drops to his knees beside the vacant body. Presses his bleeding hand against the cold face.

"Delaney Green. Come to my blood. Come to my blood. Hear my summons, Delaney Green, and follow my voice."

There's a scuff of footsteps at the far end of the room, slow and heavy.

Franklin risks a glance and sees Malcolm shuffling through the doorway. Percy is laid across his shoulders, still unconscious.

He leans closer to the body and spreads his fingers wide, letting the blood drip freely. "Delaney Green. Come to my blood. Come to my blood. Hear my summons, Delaney Green, and follow my voice."

"Hey. What are you doing?" Malcolm drops Percy to the floor and strides toward Franklin. "Get your hands away from her."

Franklin groans as the air gets thick around him a second time. "Delaney Green. Delaney Green." He struggles against the magic crushing his chest, the edges of his vision turning dark and bloody. "Delaney Green. Delaney. Green."

CHAPTER 22

This time there is nothing to think about when it comes to passing through into the realm of the living. The ground pulls me down before I can think.

And this time it hurts.

No longer just pressing in on me, but crushing me.

Bones force themselves into place while flesh and skin wrap around me, merciless as a strangling creeper around a sapling. I try to suck in a breath, nearly folding myself outside-in with the effort, and sit up with a screech.

Despite his hemmin' and hawin' when I spoke with Franklin from the midst of the salt ring, he has managed to find me a body and put me into it. Not that it seems to do me much good. I can barely stay sitting up, much less stand. And when I try to speak, all that comes out is an uneven croak.

Malcolm lets go of Franklin and drops to his knees beside me. "Alex?"

My throat is too dry to make much sound, which is just as well because I'm not sure what to say. Baby told me I wouldn't get my magic back unless I found my bones again. Not these that my soul is currently wrapped around, but my own. But I don't know if that will fool Malcolm.

I cough and rub my face. My fingers come away sticky with drying blood. It's not like I haven't touched worse, but I make a face anyway.

"Let me clean that off. Wait a minute." Malcolm stands up and goes into another room for a moment.

To my right is the girl Malcolm meant to steal his next soul from, but she's unconscious and tied up real thoroughly anyway.

I look at Franklin. He's still curled up on the floor, conscious, but wheezing for breath like he's been running for days. I'm certain he'll try to help, but he's close to dead.

Percy stirs, flopping over on his back with a groan.

Franklin turns his head and looks at him. "Hey. Cox. Wake up." He keeps his voice low because Malcolm is still close.

Percy mumbles but doesn't open his eyes, blood trickling down his cheek from the gash on his head.

There are footsteps at the door, and Malcolm returns, fumbling a glass, a ratty cloth, and a pitcher of water. He glares at Franklin. "Are you talking?"

Franklin shakes his head.

"You open that mouth again, and I'll stop your heart for good."

I shudder. If he follows through on that threat, I won't be able to shut Percy's magic back up. Not on my own. Not yet.

But he turns away from Franklin and crouches beside me. Pours water into the glass and holds it up for me to drink.

"Just little swallows."

I nod and sip obediently. Trying to take my time and give Percy a chance to regain consciousness. And trying to get used to being back in flesh, never mind that it is not my own.

Malcolm sets the glass to one side and pours water over the washcloth. "This might be cold." He wipes the cloth over my face, removing the film of blood Franklin left there.

Out of the corner of my eye, I see Percy's breathing change—more rapid, then deliberately slow.

Malcolm sets the cloth down and brushes the hair back from my face. Looks at me closely. The momentary affection he had fades, and his fingers slide around my throat. "You're not Alex."

"No." My voice is still rough, and deeper than I am used to. I blink, startled at the sound of it. "She is not coming back."

"I will find a way to—"

"How? By putting another woman's soul into this body? As I am now?" I wave a hand at the kidnapped young woman. "She will not be Alex either, no matter how hard you try to tie her soul to these bones."

"I will teach her. How to talk like Alex did. The things she loved. I will show her how to be Alex."

"But she will not be." I lay one hand on his shoulder. The cloth he used to wash Franklin's blood away is still on the floor, and I wind it around my other hand slowly before taking hold of the empty water glass carefully. "I am sorry, Malcolm, but Alex is gone. And she is not coming back."

He shudders, but leans close. "You don't know that."

"Oh, I know a thing or two about coming back from the dead, Malcolm. And Alex isn't going to make that journey."

His fingers get tighter around my throat. "Who are you?"

"My name is Delaney Green. And you should let go of me now."

"Or what?"

"He's going to kill you."

"The street magician? Or the other one?"

"Percy," I say. "He's going to kill you."

Malcolm glares at me, fighting the urge to turn and look.

Percy rolls over onto his hands and knees, then stands up. He's swaying, disoriented maybe. But even from here, even with my own sense of magic dulled, I can feel energy rolling off him, dark and hungry.

Malcolm turns and looks at him, frowns. His own magic curls across my skin, my breath clotting in my throat.

I get hold of the glass real tight and smash it into the side of his head. It isn't enough to knock him out, but he reels back, blood dripping down his scalp where the glass cut him.

I scramble back, awkward in this long-legged body, hands and feet skidding in the salt that now covers the floor. Malcolm raises his hand, and for a moment, my heart slows down.

Percy rushes forward, catching Malcolm with his shoulder and knocking them both sprawling.

The pressure in my chest fades, and I crawl toward Franklin. There's still a shard of glass clutched in the rag I wrapped my hand with, and I set the edge of it against the plastic cable tie around Franklin's wrists and saw through.

The air is painful, full of magic that prickles like an electric shock and smothers like tar.

Franklin coughs and wipes his mouth on the back of his hand. "I hope you know what you're doing."

Me too. I nod and try to smile reassuring-like. "Let me do the talking. All right?"

He nods. "Okay."

CHAPTER 23

Malcolm's voice, a desperate growl, trails off, and the magic fades, too.

Franklin looks at me, wide-eyed, but says nothing.

I smooth the front of my dress and try and look calm and non-threatening. Malcolm could see that I was not Alex, but will Percy be able to see that I am Delaney? Or will he just see these scarred wrists and short hair and a jaw that is too strong?

Percy stands up and his eyes are wild, mumbling to himself as he stares down at Malcolm's crumpled body. "They'll try and put me back. They'll try and silence me again." He turns and glares at Franklin, and the air crackles with energy. "You mustn't tell them."

Franklin shakes his head. "I don't intend to."

Percy tilts his head, considering. "Don't intend to. But what if they ask questions? Or threaten you? You might tell them anyway."

"No, Percival. I'm not going to tell anyone." Franklin's voice is steady, if pitched a little higher than normal, but he takes a half-step, putting me more squarely between him and Percy.

Percy takes a step forward himself. "Perhaps I should make certain you don't tell anyone."

"Percy." This voice still sounds strange, and I rub my arm out of habit, but the scars are different.

He pauses, looking at me as if noticing me for the first time. "Who are you? I thought you would be…" His mouth knots up with confusion.

"Percy," I say again. "Look closely. It's me."

He blinks, some of the tension leaving his shoulders as he tries to figure it out. Finally, "Delaney?"

"Yes." I move toward him slowly. "Yes, Percy. Oh, I have missed you."

He raises his hands, wrists still bound, and touches my cheek with trembling fingers. "I have missed you, too." His eyes narrow. "How do I know that it's you? That it's not a trick?"

I take his hands and press them against my flat chest. "This may not be my flesh, and these are not my bones, but I know you can still feel the warmth of my fire-kissed soul."

Percy frowns. "Maybe."

I slip my arms around his neck. "Do you know what I have been doing while we have been separated, Percy?"

He shakes his head.

"I have been searching for a way back to you. Searching for a way to keep you safe like I have always done."

"Always?"

"I didn't face The Salesman because I was afraid you would burn, Percy. I held that fire close and anger close because I knew you wouldn't be consumed." I lay one hand over his heart, feeling the tremble of energy even with this dull flesh. "I knew this would wake and even I might not be able to keep you safe."

Percy clutches at me, fingers knotted in the front of my dress. "But now? What can we do now?"

"Now we must be clever and patient." I lean close, looking him square in the eye. "Do you trust me, Percy?"

The magic boiling in his chest rumbles, but he nods. "Yes."

"They cannot use the drugs or the electricity to make you forget if you have already forgotten."

"Already forgotten?"

"Franklin is going to help us. He will take away the memory of this." I wave a hand at the room. "And this." I tap my fingers against his chest. "It will not be easy for you. They will ask a lot of questions you will not be able to answer, but they will not put the electricity in your head again."

Percy frowns. "If I forget this, won't I forget you?"

"Yes." I pull him closer. "But I will not forget you, Percy. And I will find a way to bring you back to me."

"Are you certain?"

"Yes."

But the magic growling in his chest, and the fear that feeds it, blossom again in his eyes. "No." He shakes his head and pushes me to one side. "I will not hide. I will not wait to be hurt again."

Franklin backs away from him, hands empty and held out in an attempt to ward him off. "Percival. I am not going to hurt you. No one is going to hurt you."

Percy growls. "I will make sure of it."

I snatch a length of wood out of the pieces stacked against the wall. It is heavier than I expected and my arms are still wobbly, but I swing it hard, catching Percy in the side of the head with it.

He groans and tumbles to the floor.

I look at Franklin. "Quickly."

He rummages through his bag and produces what looks like a large medical syringe. "You are lucky I had this. Hopefully it will work as you intend."

"You did not tell me there would be needles involved."

"You didn't tell me he would be all homicidal."

"I did say magic that will eat the world. I thought the murdering was implied."

"Eh." He rolls Percy onto his back. "I need you to put your hands under his chin and hold his head very still."

I kneel, one leg on either side of Percy's head and lock my fingers under his chin. "This isn't just a cheap lobotomy?"

"Not if you hold his head still."

"And you're certain it will work?"

Franklin looks at me, brown eyes intent under the tired slope of his brow. "Do you have a better idea?"

I close my eyes for a moment, feeling Daddy pulling on these threads. "No," I say. "This is the only way."

"Then hold him still." He pulls Percy's eyelid down and sets the needle against the wet, soft membrane in the corner of his eye. Slowly, and with such care it almost seems the needle is shrinking, he pushes it in toward Percy's brain. He's muttering softly. Latin maybe, but I've never been good with other languages—it could be just about anything.

As he whispers, I feel the faintest trickle of energy flowing from him. Not magic, that's centered in the arcane syringe, but energy. Just like the salt ring, he only produces the current for the elements that possess the magic, blessed salt or raw silver or lightning-forged glass.

I catch my lower lip between my teeth, expecting to see blood bubble into the syringe, but there is surprisingly little. A single crimson thread shivers up the glass tube, like a rain drop chased across a windowpane. And after it comes something dark and muddy, but insubstantial.

Franklin's whisper fades, and he pulls the needle free and holds up the syringe. "That should be it. What do you want to do with it?"

"Do with it?"

He shrugs. "When I've done this before, I've destroyed the memories. But… this is different. You said you should hold it."

"Yes. In case he needs to remember. Later." I rub my sweaty palms on my dress. "When have you done this before?"

He frowns. "My sister. She… some memories do more harm than good."

"Oh." I eye the needle, seemingly longer now that I'm realizing I'm about to get stuck with it. "Is this going to hurt?"

"I think so." He moves, no longer crouched over Percy, and pulls the edge of the dress up 'til his fingers brush the skin just below my ribs. "But the needle will be the least of it."

I nod. "Go ahead."

Tears well up as the needle pierces the skin, but it is little more than a pinch. What follows is far worse. I clap my hands over my mouth to stifle a wail of fear, sweat slicking down my back in the space of a couple rapid heartbeats. Fear, and the knowledge of magic that consumes, that takes a part of that which it kills and keeps it. Ever changing, ever growing.

It is not Percy's magic, just the sense of it, but it takes every ounce of control I have to not snatch up the piece of lumber I used as a club before and bludgeon Franklin with it until he is still and bloody. But neither the fear nor the anger are mine, and after a few terrifying moments, they recede, creeping into a dark little space next to my heart where they mutter indistinctly.

Franklin pulls the needle free of my belly and sets the syringe back in the wooden box. Looks at me warily. "Well?"

"He is very afraid." I brush my fingers across Percy's forehead, smoothing the dark curls of hair back from his eyes. "The kind of fear that you cannot hide, cannot take away. Not forever."

Franklin frowns, props his arm on his knee. "But for today?"

"Yes. For now, he will not remember the fear or the magic. For now, he is still safe."

"And when he starts to remember again?"

"I will do something about it. Then. Not now."

Franklin sighs and nods. "All right." He looks tired, a tremble to his hands that makes me glad any business with needles is over. "I don't know how we're going to explain this."

He stands up and stretches. Glares at the cuts on his hand. The bleeding has slowed, but his hand is still sticky. "I guess we'll... ugh." He doubles over clutching at his chest.

Percy, still unconscious, trembles—his breathing labored and his heartbeat slowing to almost nothing.

The hair on my arms stands up, skin crawling with the touch of magic. I let my hand drop to my side and grab the piece of wood still lying on the floor. "Stop this, Malcolm."

CHAPTER 24

Malcolm looks at me, and his eyes are bloody, his skin almost translucent so the veins in his neck and arms lay dark and unsettling across muscle and bone. "I will get to you in a minute."

I am not afraid of the afterlife. *Been there, done that.* But I know that if this body is emptied out again, Percy's memory, hidden under my skin, will no longer be contained. If it were just lost, that would be one thing, but I'm afraid it will find a way back to him, and that would be a bad thing.

I stand up and grip the piece of wood, tight. "No," I say. "No more."

In the distance, sirens howl. No doubt Martinez and the others following up on the address Connie gave them. Which is good, because Percy and Franklin both will need to be checked over. But it doesn't leave me much time.

It ain't like I've never killed no one. For sure there was Ms. Drowner, though that was an act of mercy despite all the unkindness she visited on me. And the Trainer boys, with all their possible futures burned to nothing in a single moment.

Some might even say I killed Sheriff Mains, setting him on that road to the storm-crushed clearing with the weight of eight extra years dragging at his conscience. Some might say I had a hand in the loss of my sisters, keeping them too close while Mama tried to stop me from turning into someone too much like Daddy.

But my fault or not, all of those deaths were the pulling of threads and changing futures.

Malcolm is violent. Visceral. The old wood snap of bone as I strike his head, the corners of the piece of lumber driving splinters deep into my hands, and the splatter of blood on bare skin, thick and warm as spit.

Maybe it's the knot of anger and fear I stole from Percy, maybe it's the last threads of Malcolm's magic trying to catch hold of me, but my heart burns as I hit him over and over 'til it seems all his blood is poured out on the worn floorboards.

Footsteps echo on the stairs, and Martinez and Elliot come through the door, guns out. "Let me see your hands. No sudden moves."

Elliot's voice is muddy under the rush of my own heartbeat. I let the piece of wood drop from my hands and shuffle back a few steps before my legs give out entirely.

There are more voices. The floor shakes as more police officers enter the room, some of them moving to check on Percy and Franklin, some moving to check on the kidnapped woman, all of them skirting the pile of flesh and bone that used to be Malcolm.

I close my eyes and try to slow the hammering pace of my heart. Swallow against the bubble of nausea and taste blood.

Someone grips my shoulder, shakes me to get my attention. "Alex."

I open my eyes and look at Martinez. "Who?"

He frowns. "Alex Michaels. We've been looking for you."

"I'm sorry." I shake my head. "I don't know... is that my name?" I blink and look around the room slow. "Can you tell me how I got here? I don't remember."

CHAPTER 25

They put me in a little room with a table and a couple of chairs. The fluorescent lights overhead buzz against the back of my neck, a mosquito whisper that never stops. It matches the faint buzz in my hands, the wounds left where the paramedics pulled the splinters out of my hands, slathering them with lidocaine and covering it all with gauze to keep me from picking at the torn skin.

There's a mirror on the wall opposite the table. Two way, of course. I don't need to be able to feel the threads running from the other side to know that I'm being watched, but it's a little boring not being able to close my eyes and watch them back.

The door opens, and Martinez enters with a folder tucked under his arm. He shuts the door gently and takes the seat opposite my own. "Sorry about the clothes."

I touch the sleeve on the bright orange jacket. "Am I going to jail?"

"That remains to be seen."

"Oh." I raise my hand to tuck my hair behind my ear, but Alex's hair had been short. Shaggy, but not long like mine. I comb the bangs smooth across my forehead and set my hand back down on the table. "I didn't mean to kill that man."

Martinez opens the folder on the table and spreads a few photos out. "This looks pretty determined."

I stare at my hands, ignoring the peculiar appeal of the Rorschach-like pattern of white flesh in the midst of the dark blood. "I wanted him to stop hurting those other people. And he said… he said I was next." I cup my hands together and make my thumbs do a little do-si-do around each other to try and keep them from trembling. Thinking. Remembering well enough the fear that made me hit Malcolm so hard and so many times.

"I was afraid," I say.

"Because you'd been attacked before?"

"Before?" It's hard to meet his gaze. He and I never really spent time together, but I know he watched the interview at Greenhaven. Probably watched me everywhere else we crossed paths in the few hours I was with Percy. And Martinez is sharp and looking for anything out of the ordinary. "I'm afraid I—"

"Don't remember." He ruffles through the papers in his file folder. "Two years ago, a group of men attacked and beat you. Badly. They left you unconscious in an alley."

"No. I don't remember." But I feel those scars in this skin, the ache in these bones from those injuries, and it makes me shiver. "I'm sorry. I didn't know what else to do. He said he was going to kill me next and I just… I was so frightened." I slide my hand across the table instinctively and clutch his fingers. "I didn't mean to do this, but I didn't want to die."

"No? But you'd tried to kill yourself." He doesn't pull his hand away, but pushes another photo forward. This one the paramedics took of the uneven slashes down both arms, each stitched closed with dozens of tiny knots.

"I don't remember that." Tears spill over as I look at him. "Please. I don't remember anything except him." I brush my fingers across the pictures of Malcolm's dead body. "I just wanted to get away, but he wouldn't… so I hit him 'til I couldn't feel him anymore. Couldn't feel that… that fist around my heart anymore. And I'm sorry for it, but he said he was going to kill me."

Martinez looks at me for a long minute. Finally, he sighs and pulls his hand away from mine. "Okay." He begins collecting the photos and putting them back into the file folder. "Seems a lot of memories got lost in that room."

I do my best to look puzzled. "What?"

"One of our agents, one of the men you saw being attacked, doesn't have any memory of what happened either." He says it casual, but his eyes are fixed on mine. "Funny, right?"

I shrug. "I guess." I pull the cuff of the jacket down over my hand. It's an instinctive gesture—I used to do it to hide the scars on my arm.

Martinez gets real still and, for a moment, I'm not sure either of us breathe. He slips the last photo back into place and looks up at me. Slow. Cautious. *Sharp indeed.*

The divot at the bridge of his nose tells me he doesn't know for certain, but he suspects it's me. I lick my lips and smooth my hair across my forehead again. "Are you okay?"

He twitches in spite of himself and slaps the folder closed. "Tell me your name again."

"Alex Michaels. Alexander, I guess." I hesitate. "That's what… that's what they told me. The paramedics."

"And your middle name?"

I shake my head. "I don't know."

Martinez sighs. "All right." He stands up. "For a moment there you reminded me of someone."

"Oh?"

He shakes his head. "It doesn't matter. Wait here. I'll be back."

I sit back in my chair as he closes the door behind him. I'm tired and, despite the jacket on the prison uniform, cold. Slowly, I tuck my hands against my chest. The cuts from the wood splinters are beginning to sting again, and I bite my lip against the urge to scratch at them.

Instead, I stare at the two-way mirror, blue eyes staring back at me. And how many others on the opposite side of the glass? Is Percy watching me? Like Martinez, he won't know it's me sheltering inside the skin of Alexander John Michaels. And with Martinez watching me…

I sigh and drop my gaze to the table. It will not be safe to approach Percy for a while. Not until the uncertainty about what happened in that house has faded. Not until I have some idea of what to do next.

I curl my hands tighter over my heart. *I will not forget you Percival Cox.*

CHAPTER 26

After a while, a woman comes in with an armful of clothes. "If you'll follow me," she says, "I'll take you to a room where you can get changed."

In spite of myself, my hands tremble. "Changed?"

"Yes. You're being released into the custody of your family. They brought some clothes for you to put on."

I stand up obediently. It's a relief to not be going to jail, but I'm almost as nervous about going home with the Michaels. Although I look like their daughter, I am not her. Even with the pretense of amnesia, they will anticipate something I cannot give them.

But the other options are worse. Telling the truth about my secondary existence would land me back in an institution. And no doubt Percy as well. Not to mention poor Franklin, who would likely just wind up in prison.

This road is lonely and difficult, but it is still my best way forward.

I follow the officer down the hall to a bathroom, the clothes clutched tight against my chest.

"I'll wait out here," she says. "If you need anything, just let me know."

"Thank you." I try to smile, still feeling like I am inhabiting this body at a distance. The smaller movements in particular are hard, like trying to pick up marbles with my toes.

There is no table or shelf in the bathroom, so I balance the clothes on the edge of the sink. The tile is cold against my feet, and I work the prison clothes off as fast as I can, trying to avoid looking at myself in the mirror stuck to the wall.

This is only temporary.

I don't know how I'm going to get my own self back, to rid myself of this skin, these parts that are not my own, but I will do it. I have to do it.

For a moment, I lean on the edge of the sink, gasping for breath and trying to keep my heart beating as I force my soul to stay put.

These bones are mine. To break, to love.

They serve me well. I move and speak and hold. My bones, but they are not *mine*.

I could write my name a thousand times with a razor blade, but this skin is not my own.

Bones, skin, and scars. Intimate. Strange.

My soul remains.

To break, to love. Unburning and immortal.

This is not my final form.

There is a knock on the door. "Excuse me? Are you okay in there?"

"Yes, ma'am. Just a minute." I smooth the shirt across my tall and lanky body, comb shaggy hair back from my face. Collect the bright orange and white prison uniform from the floor and balance the sandals on top.

The officer produces a plastic bag when I emerge. "Just put those in here."

I don't know if they're going to the lab for further processing or to the laundry. Maybe even to the trash. At this point, I don't care. I just want to go somewhere safe and lie down. The twist in my gut says it may be some time before I can find a safe place.

Martinez comes down the hall. "If you're ready, I'll take you downstairs now." He looks about as uncomfortable as I feel, and I have a sudden urge to put my arms around him and tell him everything will be okay. Even if it's not today.

But I just nod. "Okay." My chest aches, desperate to see Percy again, and I fix my eyes on Martinez's shoes leading me away. Down the hall to the elevator. Another hall. And finally to a lobby with neat rows of chairs.

Letitia and Jonathan Michaels stand up and hurry toward us. Then stop a few feet away, clinging to each other.

I slide my hands into my pockets. "Hello."

Letitia is the first to move, rushing forward to put her arms around me. "Alex. Oh, my darling."

I tremble. Should I put my arms around her? Ignore her? Martinez is still watching me. Still searching for a glimpse of the person he saw earlier. So I clear my throat and say the hard thing.

"I'm sorry. I don't... do I know you?"

She shudders, but doesn't let go. "It's me. Mom. And your dad." A frantic waggle of her hand and Jonathan steps forward, too.

"Hello, Alex."

I nod, awkward. "Hello."

Martinez frowns and props his hands on his hips. "The police may have some follow up questions for you, but for now, you're free to go."

Jonathan extends his hand. "Thank you, Agent Martinez. And when you see Agent Cox…"

"I will give him your thanks." Martinez claps me on the shoulder. "Be careful, Alex." Then he's striding away, and I am left alone with the Michaels.

For a moment we just stand there, nervous and staring at each other. Finally, Jonathan pulls his keys from his pocket. "You ready to go home, Alex?"

"Yes." The smile still feels weird, but they don't seem to notice.

Letitia doesn't let go as we walk out to the car. "I've made all your favorites for dinner. I hope you still… well, I'm sure you'll like them. And then you can go to bed or watch TV or whatever you want."

Jonathan circles the car, unlocking the doors with the key. "Alex isn't a child, Lettie."

"No. No. Of course, not." She smiles up at me, apologetic. "I just meant. We're happy you have come home. And whatever you want…" Tears spill over, and she brushes them away. "We want you to be happy, too."

"Okay." I nod. "I'll try."

"Good." Jonathan nods and pulls the driver's door open. "Then let's go home."

I climb into the back seat, pulling my knees in close as I fill more space than I am used to. Stare at my hands, knotted in my lap, because if I don't, I will stare at the building in a desperate attempt to catch a glimpse of Percy.

I cannot see the road ahead of me. Cannot see anything outside my own flesh and bones, and that scares me. How will I find my way forward? Find my way back to Percy?

My hands are cold, and I tuck them against my chest and the flicker of warmth hiding there inside this nearly-dead flesh. My soul, still burning even while all my other magic has left me.

I take a breath and then another. Painful, but still breathing. Still living. Still holding tight to the one thing I know for sure.

This is not my final form.

OF FLESH AND BONE

PROLOGUE

The summer that Baby came it fell to me and Addie to make the weekly trip to pick up our box of food.

With Daddy gone and Mama laid up on the couch, her feet so swelled up she couldn't get her shoes on, there was barely any money coming in, and that meant visiting the food bank every Friday to get a loaf of bread, a stack of those slices they call cheese but really aren't, plus some canned things that might or might not be enough to feed the three of us 'til the next weekend.

There was no proper building for the food distribution, so the folks that ran it would be at a different church each week. They said it meant they didn't have to waste money on rent, and it gave the do-gooders a chance to volunteer and actually do some good.

So Addie and me would get the wagon out of the tool shed and take turns pulling it to the church, then pull it home together.

Sometimes we went to the Pentecostal Church across the railroad tracks and got in line with a bunch of folks who were smooth and brown, not all freckled and blotchy with the heat like us girls were. It was a longer walk, but the ladies who put the food into our box were always nice, sometimes slipping a couple extra cans into our share and asking after Mama.

But most the time we wound up at the Greater Third Baptist Church that was in the middle of town.

There weren't no First or Second Baptist anymore. Whatever disagreement made folks split off to make their own building and baptize how they saw fit had been reconciled or forgotten. But one thing they seemed to agree on was the character of poor folks.

Ms. Skinner, a tall woman who always looked like her bones were a size or two too big and drew blood-red lipstick over her lips to try and make her look more feminine, stood at the beginning of the row of folding tables—clipboard in one hand and a ballpoint pen in the other. "Green, yes?"

"Yes, ma'am." Addie bobbed politely, one hand plucking at the hem of her shorts as if she would make a proper curtsy.

Ms. Skinner rattled her pen against the clipboard. "Where is your mother? An adult is supposed to be present to receive food."

"She's at home, ma'am. Restin' like the doctor told her to."

Ms. Skinner shook her head. "She should be working. Keep you girls fed."

Addie was pinker than usual, her blue eyes pale and icy, but she nodded. "Yes, ma'am."

"God helps those that help themselves," Ms. Skinner said.

Addie tilted her head back and stared up at the steeple with its freshly painted cross at the top—all neat and white. Not like the Catholics who like to remind you it was a weapon and keep Jesus pinned there, forever sacrificing himself.

"Well..." Addie paused, tossed her hair back over her shoulder. "I reckon if we could help ourselves, we wouldn't need God's help."

Ms. Skinner squeaked, and her mouth drew up so tight, I thought she might turn her head inside out. I ran my fingers over the threads runnin' left and right and straight ahead just in case there were one where that happened. There weren't.

Ms. Skinner scribbled something on her list, the tip of her pen tearin' a hole right through the paper. "Sign." The curl in her lip said, *If you can.* But just 'cause we were poor didn't make us stupid.

Addie signed her name and handed pen and clipboard back. "Thank you, Ms. Skinner. You have a good weekend." She didn't wait for a response. Marched down the row of tables collecting our loaf of bread and stack of cheese slices wrapped in paper, three cans of soup and three of vegetables.

And I stacked all of them in the box in the middle of the wagon, neat-like so the bread didn't get crushed.

At the very end was Mrs. Fuller, who didn't attend any of the churches but still showed up every week to help sort and pass out the food. She had a few boxes of her own, with dozens of little paper bags lined up neat inside. "Morning, Addie. Morning, Del." She took two bags and handed them to us. "Chocolate chip this week." She smiled.

"Thank you, ma'am," Addie said dutifully.

I was already unfolding my bag and pulling a cookie out. The chocolate chips were soft with the heat of the day and made sticky marks on my hand, but they tasted almost like they'd just come out of the oven. "Thak uu," I said.

"Of course, Delaney." She beamed and leaned close. "Everyone deserves something nice. Right?" She dropped three more paper bags into our box. "One for your mother. And some for later." She hugged me, then Addie. "Go on now. It's getting hot, and y'all don't need to be walking in the sun."

"Yes, ma'am." Addie nodded, pulled the wagon around, and we started back the way we'd come.

Ms. Skinner waved her hand to get our attention as we passed. "Tell your mother the carpet plant is hiring."

It's funny how the same words can mean different things comin' from different folks. Just a trick of the tongue that turns a phrase so the words come down like a judge's gavel.

Ms. Skinner said, *The carpet plant is hiring*, but she meant something else. Despite the warmth of Mrs. Fuller's hug still restin' on my shoulders, all I could see was how short my dress was, the sleeves dug into my armpits and the fabric across the front stretched tight because I'd been growin' but my clothes hadn't. Despite tasting compassion, all sugar and butter and chocolate in my mouth, I felt the uneven weight of my hair—crooked 'cause Addie never could get it quite straight across the back or the front.

I didn't need to think about it; my hand found those threads runnin' off in every direction, automatic. Looked for one that would put Ms. Skinner in her place. Pulled at one that had her tumblin' face first into the table of canned goods and spendin' the next few months with a broke jaw wired shut.

Addie caught me in the ribs with her elbow. "Stop it, Del."

"Ow." I glared at her. "I'm not..."

She fixed me with that cool blue stare, dizzying as a cloudless sky. "Stop."

I licked a smudge of chocolate off my fingers. "You know she deserves it."

Behind us Ms. Skinner caught her foot on a crack in the pavement and stumbled into the table with the canned goods, knocking a stack of pork n' beans off onto the ground—*plonk, plonk, plonk*. But she straightened back up, unhurt and bossy as ever. "Pick those up. Next time maybe you should set the tables up where it's flat."

I scowled and kicked a piece of gravel up the sidewalk.

Addie grabbed me by the elbow. "We all deserve somethin' terrible, Del. But if we all got what we deserved..." She shrugged. "Most of us would never get the chance to do somethin' good."

I pulled at my dress, still wishin' it were long enough to cover my knees. "We ain't done anythin' to deserve somethin' terrible, Addie."

She looked at me for a long moment.

I tucked my hand behind my back, guilty, even though all those threads still trembled around us.

Ms. Skinner leaned on the edge of one of the tables, red-faced as she pointed her finger at Mrs. Fuller. "Coddling them. Cookies. They need to get to work." Her voice rose higher and higher.

Addie shook her head. "Come on, Del. Mama'll be waitin' for us."

We trudged up the street, pulling the wagon behind us. At the corner I glanced back.

Ms. Skinner staggered around, one hand pressed against her chest, as the other women all fluttered around her. Her knees gave out, and she dropped to the pavement.

Mrs. Fuller bent over her, the abandoned clipboard in her hands, and fanned Ms. Skinner's face. "Go call an ambulance. Quick."

I caught my sneaker on a crack in the sidewalk and nearly pitched headlong myself. "Addie..."

There was a hint of teeth in her grin. "We all deserve what we get, Del." She tossed her hair over her shoulder. "Some of us more than others."

CHAPTER 1

Living with these borrowed bones is hard.

Perhaps because they were dead when I tried to make them mine. Perhaps because, try as I might, they are not mine. *They never will be.*

It has been weeks, months even, since I first saw this face in the mirror. Every day it is still a stranger who stares back at me. Every day it becomes harder and harder not to peel back this skin to try and see myself. Harder and harder not to cut off these parts that are different so I can feel more like myself.

But I know that the thing that is me is invisible. I could cut all the way to this borrowed heart and still not glimpse my own face.

I know the thing that is me is invisible.

And every day it fades a little more.

CHAPTER 2

Mama Lettie still forgets sometimes about using *she* or *her*, but Alex disappearing seems to have changed her. She forgets sometimes, but she tries.

This morning she fixes my hair so that it softens the strong jawline and helps me dress. Long sleeves, of course, because—though the long wounds on my arms have slowly healed—the scars remain. Likewise, the skirt falls to mid-calf to hide Alex's bony knees. To hide my knees.

I duck my head to hide a flicker of guilt. It should be Alex who smiles at her mother, Alex who can finally sit and talk about girlish things. I know that she is happier elsewhere, in the life beyond this one, but I can't help but hurt over the fact that this love is not meant for me. Hurt for Alex who must only feel it from a distance, and hurt for myself, selfishly, that I must wear this skin to have a mother love me like a daughter.

Mama Lettie returns with two cups of tea, sweet with sugar and sharp with lemon. "Are you hungry? I can make a sandwich."

"No. Thank you." I take a sip of tea. "Maybe later."

She fiddles with her own cup. "You have gotten so thin." A smile, thin and cracking as onionskin. "It worries me, is all."

"I'll eat when I get home."

Mama Lettie's eyes flicker. "You're going out?"

"For a little while."

"Will you be back for lunch?"

"I don't think so. But I'll be here for dinner."

She nods. "All right. I'm making that chicken poppy seed casserole."

"My favorite." I smile to reassure her. For a while the Michaels didn't let me out without one of them with me. Afraid I would be attacked again. Afraid I might disappear again.

The counselor we see every other Tuesday has persuaded them that I should have time to myself. She says it's part of the process of "Letting Alex be Alex." Now I go for walks every couple of days, sometimes down to the library to do research. Sometimes just wandering around parts of the city as I try to unravel the path that lies ahead.

These bones don't see the future like my own.

Mama Lettie sips her tea. "I was thinking maybe we could go to that little art shop downtown. They have classes. Well, not classes exactly. Groups, I think they call them. You go and they show you how to do a painting. It could be fun. I stopped in to see what they offer the other day. There's a nice one with sea shells that we could do, and they have an afternoon group coming up for it in a week or so."

"Sure." I drink my own tea slowly, appreciative of the warmth. I love Mama Lettie, but she is never comfortable with silence. Her voice fills every room like water pouring into a bucket—steady, persistent, smothering.

"They have others. I got a card if you want to look at their website. There's a Van Gogh one. Not really *Starry Night*, but styled after it. Or a winter scene. I thought maybe the shells would look nice in the bathroom, but whatever you want."

I set my empty teacup on the bedside table. "Maybe we can look at it this evening. After dinner."

"Yes. Good. We'll look at it this evening." She collects my cup and moves toward the door, apparently satisfied that I will be coming home. "Are you sure I can't make you a sandwich? To take with you?"

"I'm all right."

"Okay." She disappears down the hall to the kitchen.

I collect my bag, a big thing made out of canvas that holds a handful of pens and some tape, a pair of scissors, and composition book. My real journal is hidden elsewhere, but it would look funny if I went out with all those pens and no notebook. I make little entries in this one about day-to-day stuff. The things I don't care if anyone reads.

I haven't caught Mama Lettie or Papa Michaels trying to go through any of my things, but I can't risk it.

Mama Lettie comes out of the kitchen as I go down the hall and follows me to the front door. "You be careful, okay?"

"Of course." I hug her, awkward. Most things I've learned how to do with these longer legs and arms, but affection is not something that has ever come easy. "I'll be back for dinner."

She smiles and nods and stands behind the screen door, watching me walk out to the street. I know she'll stand there for a while after I'm out of sight. The first few times I went out on my own, I came back to find her still there with the same cup of coffee or dishtowel or half-finished crossword in her hands.

I have done my best to reassure her each time I leave that I will be back. It is harder every time, knowing that someday I will say those words and they will be a lie. *Soon.* But not today.

Two blocks down and one block over is a small house that has been empty ever since I came to stay with the Michaels. There is a fence around the front and sides, but in the back, it's all weeds and a little plastic garden shed. I pull the door open just far enough to get my arm inside and grab my real journals, slip them into my bag, and head back out to the street.

I've got a ways to go today.

Growing up there was always talk about folks with the Touch and rumors about who might have the Gift. But it was never out in the open, not officially. Folks knew that Neeny Johnson had a way with the cards, and old Granny Nichols could give you a little sack full of god-knew-what and money would flow your way.

Folks knew, and sometimes you would hear those whispers behind hands or closed doors, but if you wanted something magic, you couldn't go to a store and ask for it.

Savannah is different. Folks like Franklin Jones can be found in the weekly Nickel Saver. There are little shops wedged in next to the Asian grocery or the Vintage Vinyl Emporium that sell charms and totems and most of the bits and pieces you would need to make your own.

What they don't have are books about or histories of the Touch. I have checked with the library and found a few, but they are mostly silly. Speculations on whether the Fey were real and if the Vikings brought secret knowledge to the Americas or if the First Nations already possessed it—if in different tongues.

I know the things I'm looking for exist. I have seen the archive in Atlanta, hidden in the basement of the government building. I suspect there may be a collection here in Savannah, but when I ask the tiny Mrs. Dihn, she just smiles and says, *No books here.*

I stop for a moment to get my bearings. I've been to this part of the city before, but only once.

A young man lounging on the steps of an ancient apartment building nods his head. "You lookin' for something?"

"Fisher Street."

His eyes get narrow, but he sits up and points. "Almost there. Two more blocks."

"Thank you." I walk on, feeling the weight of his gaze on my shoulders—not hateful so much as curious, but it still makes my shoulders tense and my heart gallops along faster than before.

It is a relief when I reach Fisher Street and a few minutes after that, the little old house with the name *Jones* on the mailbox.

There isn't a button for a doorbell, so I ball up my fist and knock. Try not to fidget while I wait. There's a creak and shuffle inside and the door opens.

"Hello, Franklin." I smile and do my best to ignore the oh-shit look on his face.

He licks his lips. "Delaney Green."

"Oh, you can call me Alex."

Franklin leans out of the doorway, looks up and down the street for a moment. "You by yourself?"

"Of course."

He pushes the door open a little more, but leans against the threshold, arms crossed. "What do you want?"

"I need your help. May I come inside?"

Franklin hesitates, then nods. "Yeah. All right." He pushes the door all the way open and steps back. "Come on in."

CHAPTER 3

Franklin leads the way back to the kitchen, drops into a chair beside a tiny table wedged in one corner, and motions to the other chair. "Have a seat."

There's a cutting board on the counter behind him, with a couple slices of tomato and paring knife. A piece of bread and cheese and a little pile of shaved ham sit on a plate next to it. "Didn't mean to interrupt," I say with nod to the half-prepared sandwich.

He shrugs. "It can wait." He doesn't offer to make me one.

I sit, tug my bag around into my lap. "Still summoning shades in the basement?"

He frowns. "What do you want, Delaney?"

Right to the point then. Fine by me. "I need your help, Franklin."

He narrows his eyes. "Help with what?"

"Magic books. I need to know how to do a thing, and there must be books about it, but no one will show them to me." I smile as sweetly as I can. "I thought you might have a foot in the door, so to speak."

Franklin rubs his forehead. "Books."

"Yes. About magic."

"And what thing is it you need to know how to do?"

I press my hands against my bag, the notebooks inside full of the bits and pieces I can still remember of the future, all the research I have done on the past. All of it dependent on trusting Franklin now, in this moment. "This body will not last."

He chuckles. "None of them do."

"No. I mean, it will die soon. Not in years as yours will, but in months. Weeks even."

"Ah." Franklin leans back in his chair, studying me. "Maybe that is for the best."

"You would rather Percy goes unchecked?"

"Egh." He pulls at his lower lip, remembering maybe the terrible magic that nearly killed him after we faced the necromancer. "Yes. He is a problem."

He leans forward, brown eyes intent. "I know you said you loved him. But are you certain it would not be better to...end him?"

"Kill him, you mean." I resist the urge to smile. In this moment, it would be a threat.

"Yes."

I rub my thumb against the scar on the inside of my wrist. I've seen that ending, too—Romeo and Juliet with more blood and fewer tears. "That future is messy."

"So you say."

"Here." I pull the notebooks out and slide them across the table toward him. "See for yourself."

Franklin shakes his head. "I'm not helping you find another body, Delaney. Once was enough."

"I don't need another body, Mr. Jones. I need mine."

He tilts his head, eyes narrowed. "Your body was destroyed."

I brush that aside with a flick of my fingers. "Flesh maybe, but my bones... they buried those on the spot." I touch my face, a little self-conscious. "And this stuff can be remade. Around my bones. Because they are...well, powerful."

Franklin presses back in his chair 'til it digs a hole in the plaster wall. "That's the thing you want to do." He's nearly breathless, sweat slicking down his temples. "Even you must know that's forbidden."

"Because it requires the sacrifice of one body to complete a second. But this one has already been abandoned. No soul will be cut free. No innocent will die."

"It's not just..." He pauses, swallows a couple of times. "The book you are talking about is hard to find. And the thing you mean to do requires a pentagram. You will need help from others. You will need someone with Power."

"Percy is a Power. And for the others, I'm certain your sister can help us find those who are familiar with this thing."

He reaches back and snatches the knife off the cutting board on the counter, leans forward 'til the tip prickles against my cheek. "You stay away from my sister."

I do my best to look calm and kind. "I am not the one who is going to hurt her. But I may be the only one who can save her."

"No." He shakes his head. "You stay away from her."

The tip of the knife stutters across my skin, leaving a trail of hot pinpricks, blood welling up, slow. More scars, but I'm not worried about those. *This is not my final form.* "How many times have they come after her? How many times have you taken those memories from her so she would not live in fear of the next?"

Franklin's lips pull back from his teeth. "There is no stopping them. No matter how far she runs—"

"I can stop them." I shift in my chair so I can lean forward to take his other hand—pressed flat against the table—without further cutting myself. "For good. But I will need your help."

His hand trembles, and I do my best not to, even as the hair on the back of my neck stands up at attention. "Why should I believe you?" His voice is rough.

"Have I lied to you before?"

"Not that I know of."

"Ah." I squeeze his fingers gently. "Help me, and I will help your sister."

He is silent, the fear of me and love for his sister flickering in the depths of his eyes. Finally, he lets the knife drop to the table where it turns a lazy circle and stops—the blade pointing at me again. I nudge it to one side with my free hand, push the notebooks toward him again. "You will need to read these before we begin. So you can understand how strange our path will be."

Franklin opens the first journal and looks at the drawings, the notes scrawled every which way. "This may take a while."

I push my chair back and stand up. "I'll come back tomorrow."

He frowns, but nods. "Okay."

For once my smile does not feel as awkward. "Good. I should go. Mama Lettie will be waiting for me."

"Yeah." He follows me to the door. Leaning out to peer up and down the street again. "Tomorrow then."

"Yes."

"Come around the back." And he closes the door sharp.

I smooth the front of my blouse and turn out toward the street. I am nervous about leaving my books with him, but he must know that I trust him or we will not succeed.

The young man who gave me directions is still sitting on the steps when I pass back by. I wave and he nods in acknowledgment, but I don't stop to talk. The sun is beginning to drop in the west, and I have a ways to go if I want to get home by dinnertime.

CHAPTER 4

The streetlights are beginning to flicker on by the time I get back to the Michaels' house, but the porchlight is off.

For a moment I wonder if something has happened to Mama Lettie. The breeze shifts, bringing with it the smell of burning tobacco and the sickly-sweet stink of artificial strawberry.

I hitch the satchel around behind me and slip through the gate into the backyard. The trees are unkempt, and the light spilling from the kitchen door doesn't reach more than a few feet. There is a steady orange pinprick in the deepest shadows at the far corner of the yard.

"Mama Lettie?"

The orange blob shudders and disappears. "Alex. I wasn't expecting you to…" She shuffles forward, the hand clutching the cigarette hidden behind her back even as the smoke drifts over her shoulder.

"It's time for dinner, isn't it?"

For a moment, we just look at each other. Finally, she grins, lifts the cigarette to her lips, and takes a long drag. "Don't tell Jonathan."

"I never do."

"Ah." She nods and stubs the last of it out, then flicks it over the back fence into the pass-through.

It is an odd secret that I share with both of them. Papa Michaels smokes in his truck. Mama Lettie has a pack hidden back here in the trunk of the scraggly dogwood tree, a plastic baggy providing protection from rain and ants. They both pretend they don't know about the other, and I don't say anything about it.

Papa Michaels has told me how he used to smoke, but quit a few years back to please Lettie. Until Alex went missing, he says. But he hasn't had the heart to tell her how he's picked it up again.

For her part, Mama Lettie has never offered a reason for the cigarettes smoked in the dusk. I suspect she's had this secret habit for many years. Not that it matters. *Everyone has secrets.*

She tugs the front of her shirt a couple of times to try and fluff away the lingering smell of burnt tobacco. Then slips her arm through mine and walks me toward the house. "Best get inside before your father comes home. He might wonder why we're standing out here in the dark."

I nod and follow her up the steps into the kitchen. It's warm and smells of cornbread and green beans. There's also a tray of fried chicken with molting breading. "I thought you were going to make casserole?"

"Oh." Her lips tremble. "I forgot."

"I like fried chicken," I say quick, trying to ignore the fact that it is one of the sorriest batches of fried chicken I've ever seen. "Still can't get the breading to stick?"

Lettie flushes. "I don't know. Maybe the oil wasn't hot enough."

I pinch a bite off the nearest piece, blow on it when I realize how hot it still is, and pop it into my mouth where I can hold it with my teeth instead of my fingers. "Tastes good. That's what's important."

For a moment, she stares at me, eyes wide and hands knotted under her chin. Not the first time, but there is something keener this time. I stand straighter, wary. Wondering if I have done something wrong. "Mama Lettie?"

She waves her hand as if shooing away a fly. "It's nothing. Go and put your things away, and then you can help me set the table."

"You sure?"

"Yes." She turns away, surreptitiously flicking away tears. "Make sure you wash your hands, too. I don't need any germs from the bus at the table."

"Yes, ma'am." I walk through the living room to the hall and glance back over my shoulder.

Lettie stands at the stove, adding a little more salt to the green beans. But she pauses, bending over almost as though she is in pain, and I hear a sob, quickly muffled in a dish towel.

I duck out into the hall, quick, before she can turn to look at me, and tiptoe up to my room. Maybe she's sick. But Papa Michaels hasn't said anything, and neither has been to the doctor lately. *Have I done something wrong?*

I hang my jacket and satchel in the closet. Stand for a moment in the dark room. Waiting. The face in the mirror stares back at me, barely more than a pale blur.

Finally, she hollers from the kitchen. "Alex? Are you coming? Table won't set itself."

"Coming." I take a breath, still uneasy, and hurry to wash my hands. Whatever is wrong, I don't have time to fix it.

CHAPTER 5

After dinner Papa Michaels claims a spot on the couch in front of the TV, a glass tumbler with a couple fingers of whiskey balanced on his knee. He's not like Daddy. He doesn't get mean when he drinks; he just sits and breathes heavily when the commercials get all feel-good or the characters in the show start crying.

I help Mama Lettie with the dishes and putting away the leftovers while the TV chatters and giggles through the eight o'clock sitcom.

Mama Lettie hangs the dish towel up to dry as I put the last of the plates back in the cabinet. "You want to watch TV with us for a while?"

"Maybe in a few minutes."

"Okay." She nods and smiles. "Okay. I'll save a spot on the couch for you."

Papa Michaels barely looks at me as I cross the living room and into the hall. The tumbler resting on his knee is already empty, and he's sinking into the cushions with a slow deliberation.

I worry about leaving them, Mama Lettie and Papa Michaels, but I know that staying here is not helping them. Although they have come to a certain acceptance of Alex, there is a hole here I will never be able to fill. I hope that once I am gone they will heal from all these wounds—visible and invisible.

I sit down on the edge of the bed and pull out one of the blank books. Draw a line and number it like I am doing math in elementary school, but this one goes to thirty and then begins to repeat. I am counting out days. A couple of hatch marks at the bottom of the page keep a tally on the weeks.

Some things are going to happen whether I am there or not. And others only begin when I start them. Making it match up, especially now that I can't see anything beyond this minute, requires some careful counting.

There is a knock at the door, and Mama Lettie peeps into the room, hesitant. "Alex?"

"Yes, Mama Lettie." I close my book, but let it sit in my lap.

"Here." She holds out a little book with a lavender cover. "I was going through some things in my dresser and I found this. My mother gave it to me when I was a girl and...well, I thought you might like it."

I take it, run my fingers over the floral pattern on the cover, all embossed with gold leaf. "Sonnets from the Portuguese."

She sits down beside me on the bed. "It's a little over the top, I guess you'd say. But some of it is nice." She touches the ribbon threaded between the pages. "This one in particular reminded me of you."

I open to the page she's marked. The sonnet is numbered ten with a Roman numeral. On the facing page is a delicate geometric design with a quotation inside it. *And while the wheel of birth and death turns round that which hath been must be between us two.*

"That's Edwin Arnold," Mama Lettie says quick. "I meant the sonnet."

I smooth the pages carefully.

Yet, love, mere love, is beautiful indeed
And worthy of acceptation. Fire is bright,
Let temple burn, or flax; an equal light
Leaps in the flame from cedar-plank or weed:
And love is fire. And when I say at need
I love thee—mark!—I love thee—in thy sight
I stand transfigured, glorified aright,
With conscience of the new rays that proceed
Out of my face toward thine. There's nothing low
In love, when love the lowest: meanest creatures
Who love God, God accepts while loving so.
And what I feel, across the inferior features
Of what I am, doth flash itself, and show
How that great work of Love enhances Nature's.

I lick my lips and stare at the page as if still reading, but my heart is pounding. The verse, despite its overly romantic language, does speak to me, but nothing I have seen or learned about Alex makes me think she would have felt the same.

Mama Lettie watches me, an uncertain tremble around her lips. Her hand drifts in the air between us, a gesture I have seen her use when trying to coax the feral neighborhood cat from under the back steps.

"It's pretty," I say finally. I close the book and start to hand it back to her, but she shakes her head.

"No. I want you to have it."

"But your mother gave it to you."

"Yes. And now I'm giving it to you." She puts her hands over mine, still with that searching look. "Because I want you to have it."

"Thank you." I smile, a little stiff, but everything is a little stiff these days.

Mama Lettie nods and stands up. "Jonathan and I are going to have some ice cream. If you want to come and have some...or I can bring you a bowl."

"No. I'll come out. Just let me finish this." I shift the notebook in my lap.

If she's curious about it, she doesn't let it show, just nods again. "Okay. Don't take too long or it will melt."

I put the book of poetry on the table beside the bed and open my notebook again. I was just about finished anyway. I know what it will say even without writing out all the gaps and days.

Time is running out.

I scribble the last few notes, then put the notebook on the bedside table with the book of Barrett Browning sonnets. I am confident Franklin will help me, because he wants to help his sister again. But the others...

Martinez will be tricky. Although he understands the risk more than most, he will be less willing to help me fix this mess. Not the way it needs to be fixed.

I stand up and smooth my skirt. Time for ice cream and sitting with Mama Lettie and Papa Michaels one last time. The rest can wait until the morning.

CHAPTER 6

The dreams began when these second-hand bones started to cool. They were fragments at first—flashes of people and places I know. As this skin grows looser and my time in this flesh shorter, the dreams have gotten longer and more detailed.

I think they are like the unending visions I used to have of the future, or the dreams of the present I had while I was in the afterlife with Baby and Addie. But there is an oddness to them I never experienced before.

They only happen when I am asleep.

I guess that is the point where my soul is closest to being separated from this tired body. Or maybe they are just dreams, churned up by the near-constant recitation of the contents of my notebooks—my brain refusing to let go of the problem before me.

How do I save Percy? How do I save myself?

I recognize the FBI office in Atlanta. Desks clustered in various groups of four or six. The little conference rooms along the back wall with sliding glass doors that provide silence but not privacy. There's a part of it on the end of the room where I never followed Percy or any of his team. I think it is another hallway and individual offices, but it jitters and glitches when I look at it. First I see a doorway and a corridor beyond, then only a blank wall.

The rest of the floor of desks and windows and not-so-closed conference rooms does the same out of the corner of my eye. It settles down if I look at it straight on, but stammers and trembles around me as I focus on the subject of this dream.

Martinez.

The other desks are empty, the windows at the other end of the room dark, save for the glitter of other skyscrapers and dull glow of a nighttime sky that never grows completely dark. Martinez rattles off the last few sentences of a report and hits the save button. Leans back in his chair to stretch, turning casually to see if he is alone.

He leans down and pulls open the bottom drawer of his desk and reaches all the way to the back. A grimace and he pulls out a battered file folder nearly three inches thick. Another glance around to make certain no one else is around, and he pushes his keyboard out of the way and flips the file open.

At the very top of the stack of reports and clippings is a photo of five young girls in front of a Dust Bowl era house, with *The Mulvaheney Sisters* printed neatly along the bottom edge of the print. They are not smiling for whatever photographer decided to preserve their childhood for posterity. I see a reflection of myself in their blank stares and dirty knees, the hint of a sixth pale face in the window that might be their mother—too sick to stand in the sun and have her picture taken.

But even in the old photograph, even with the youngest one still sucking her thumb, there is an echo of the Power that lies within them. Not like mine, and not so much like Percy's either, though I know they put it to destructive ends. But these girls cannot hide the magic in their bones the way Neeny Johnson did and channel their energy into reading cards or tea leaves or poorly formed glass.

Martinez frowns and sets the photo to one side. He shuffles through the photocopies of scrawled police reports, faded newspaper clippings, and blocky faxed sheets detailing a string of murders that stretches across decades. His hands move out of habit, the same way I thumb through my notebooks— already knowing what they say, but reading them again anyway.

I don't know if it's a glitch in the dream or if Martinez and I are just so focused on the photos and clinical phrases of death, but when Percy drops into the chair at his own desk, we both jump.

"Cox." Martinez flushes, slowly collecting the contents of the file folder and putting them back in order. "I thought you'd left for the day."

"In a few minutes." Percy points his chin at the stack of paper resting under Luis's hand. "Your cold case?"

"Everyone needs a hobby." Martinez folds his arms over his chest and leans back in his chair. "You want to take a look?"

Percy shakes his head. "Thanks, but I'd rather leave that behind at the end of the day."

"Right." Martinez picks up the photo of the five little girls again. "Does it ever scare you? Knowing that there are folks out there who can suck the life right out of you? Knowing that they could look just like me? Or you?"

Percy picks up a stray pen off his desk and drops it into the canister sitting beside the stapler. "I guess most the folks we deal with look like you or me whether they have the Touch or not."

"Maybe." Martinez tucks the photo away and puts the whole file back in the bottom drawer of his desk. Pauses, looking at Percy with a worried crinkle between his eyebrows. "You all right?"

Percy is silent for a moment. Finally, he digs in his jacket pocket and pulls out a folded piece of paper, tosses it onto Luis's desk. "You know about that?"

Martinez unfolds it carefully. It's a lot cleaner that most the photocopies in his file, though the toner is flaking along the creases from having been repeatedly folded and unfolded.

Local Boy Escapes Killer

The headline at the top of the page seems extra-large. Below is a grainy photo of eleven-year-old Percy, and an even blotchier driver's license photo of the creep that tried to murder him.

Martinez blinks a couple times, then folds it up and hands it back. "Yeah." He looks hard at Percy. "Did you?"

Percy rubs his fingers through his hair. "I dunno. I mean, I guess so. But I don't have many memories from...then."

"Because of the Magiprex." The change in Martinez's voice is slight, but my heart aches with it.

"That's right." Percy straightens the phone on his desk, moves the stapler a half-inch to the right. "It doesn't say outright, but...I think I used magic to kill that man."

"That criminal," Luis says.

"Yeah. But if that were true, if I used magic against another human being like that, it would make me a Power."

Martinez pushes his face into an expression that looks thoughtful and leans back in his chair again. His right hand slides down to rest on the sidearm holstered on his belt. "Could be. You know the classifications are—"

"Complicated and arbitrary." Percy glares at him. "I know. I've read the handbooks. And the papers. And the old texts. All of it putting folks like me into little boxes and categories based on what we could do and what we might do and whether our parents drowned or burned or turned to dust when someone stabbed them with a silver knife. And meanwhile I've walked free, helping find the folk we think are monsters, and folk like Delaney are locked away forever 'cause she survived something she shouldn't have."

Martinez frowns and swivels his chair so that his right side is farther away from Percy and unsnaps the holster. "Delaney was in Greenhaven for her own good."

Percy slams his fist on the desk. "Del was in Greenhaven because they were scared of her. And they drew lines and ticked boxes and said, '*She's a Power,*' so they didn't have to feel guilty about locking up a child."

"Okay. Okay." Luis nods. "You're right. But what does that have to do with you?"

"So I killed someone with magic before. A criminal, sure. But I killed him. And everything I've read says that's a place I can't come back from. Everything I've read says it's only a matter of time before it happens again." Percy's anger fades, giving way to resignation. "You know it, too."

Martinez uncurls his fingers from the butt of his gun and secures the holster again, deliberate. He leans forward, both hands on the desk. "You ever shoot someone, Cox?"

Percy nods. "A couple times."

"Ever kill someone with your gun?"

"No."

Martinez rolls his shoulders, as if easing a crick in his neck. "I have."

"Gil Mains," Percy says, automatic.

"That's right. And a few others before." Martinez stares at his hands for a moment. "It's not any different. I have a gun. You have magic. We can both kill if we want to."

"And if we don't want to?" It's a whisper, Percy staring at him wide-eyed.

"Then we don't."

"What if I can't help it? What if I can't control it?" Percy touches the folded piece of paper on the desk.

Martinez sighs. "You can't control everything, Cox. Sometimes...sometimes you only have a lot of bad choices in front of you. But when it comes to taking a life, there's always a choice."

For a moment they are silent, staring at each other. The far wall shimmers— hallway, then wall, then something that looks like a pinball arcade.

I focus all my attention on Martinez and Percy as the dream starts to break up around us.

Percy stands up. "I'm sorry."

Martinez shrugs. "We all make choices."

"Want to walk down with me? Grab a beer maybe?" Percy's already fading.

Martinez sits as his desk for a moment. Pulls his phone out of his pocket and clicks through the phonebook to a name I recognize. *Ms. Carver – Department Psych.*

He sits for a moment, thumb poised over the button to dial. Finally, he taps back to the main menu and tosses the phone onto the desk. He stares up at the ceiling as the conference rooms are swallowed up in a swirl of light and sound. "Damn it, Cox. Don't make me choose with you."

CHAPTER 7

I put on jeans and a t-shirt, pull my hair back neatly on the back of my neck. Trying to present as male is difficult—it makes me want to pull off all my skin and cut away these unfamiliar parts—but I will be away from all my normal places soon. The places I have found where I can pee in relative safety or order a coffee without someone hassling me about my height or how my face ain't pretty enough to be wearing a skirt.

It's a painful thing to do, but it will mean less difficulty as I travel back home to find my bones. *It's only temporary.*

The house is quiet. It's Wednesday morning. Papa Michaels will have left for work before dawn, and Mama Lettie has a Bible study down at the church.

I shrug into a hoodie and stuff a clean pair of underwear and socks into the bottom of my satchel. Then tuck the new notebook in on top, and the lavender and gold book of sonnets Mama Lettie gave me the night before.

There's about three hundred dollars in the top drawer of my dresser—carefully collected over the past few months doing odd jobs for the Michaels or the old lady down the street. It's not much, but it should help Franklin pay for gas and food while we travel. I tuck a couple twenties in my pocket and put the rest inside the pair of extra socks in the bottom of my bag.

I pause to smooth the blankets on the bed and turn the light out in the closet, making sure everything is in its place. I've written a letter. It's taken me weeks, writing and rewriting the same few sentences over and over again as I tried to find the right words to tell Papa Michaels and Mama Lettie how much their kindness has meant to me. Tried to explain that I cannot stay with them because all that kindness still can't make this my home.

I pull the envelope out of its hiding place and write *Mom and Dad* on the outside. Add a little heart and prop it up on the dresser next to the hairbrush. Now that I'm getting ready to leave, it feels like a hollow, almost cruel, gesture, but it's all I have. I can only hope they will find some comfort in having something to hold onto after I've gone.

The house is supposed to be empty, but when I reach the kitchen, I find Mama Lettie sitting at the table with a cup of coffee and half a pack of cigarettes. The windows and the back door are open, so the smoke drifts mostly out to the yard. It's hard to say how long she's been sitting there waiting, but there are three or four butts already stubbed out in the ashtray next to her coffee cup.

For a moment, everything remains still. Me standing in the kitchen doorway, my satchel clutched against my chest, and Mama Lettie sitting at the table, smoke curling from the cigarette pinched between her fingers.

Finally, she takes a drag and reaches for her coffee. "So you're leaving, then."

Something in her eyes tells me she don't just mean for the day. Something in the way her lips tremble, smoke curling in and out like river weed drifting with the flow, tells me she knows I am not Alex.

"Yes," I say.

She sighs and takes another drag on her cigarette, the end glowing bright as she sucks on the filter. "Well," she says after a minute. "I made you some food." She stubs out the cigarette and goes over to the fridge. "Some sandwiches. And cookies. There's a couple fruit cups in here. And plastic stuff to eat it with." She holds out a paper grocery bag, the top rolled up neatly so it's easy to carry.

"Thank you." I take it and fit it down into my bag. It's bulky, but it ain't too heavy.

"You're welcome." Mama Lettie nods and reaches for the pack of cigarettes again.

"How did you know?" I ask it as gently as I can, but she still flinches. Fumbles with the lighter, the striker rasping over and over again as she tries to get a flame. "Here." I take it, light it, and hold it steady while she pulls on the cigarette 'til the end is burning red hot.

"Thanks, honey," she says, less awkward than I have ever seen her, despite the shake in her hands. She plops down in her chair and picks up her coffee cup, scowling when she realizes it's empty.

"I got it." I take the mug, fill it up, stir in the sugar, and hand it back. Then settle in the chair across from her. "How did you know?"

"That you were leaving?" She shrugs, sips her coffee. "Found that letter under your mattress last week. I didn't mean to. Just was changing the sheets and thought I'd flip the mattress..." She leans back in her chair, looking at me. "But I've known you weren't Alex for a while now."

I raise an eyebrow. "Really?"

Mama Lettie grins. "Oh, sweetie. You've done a good job pretending you don't remember, but...you're still not her. There's little things. The way you sit. The way you're glaring at me now." She takes a puff off her cigarette. "I wasn't sure at first, but a mother knows her child." Her grin softens. "You're not Alex."

"I'm sorry." My chest aches, and I rub it, trying to soothe away the hurt. "I didn't mean to hurt you."

"No, honey. You gave me a chance to love my daughter. Not just inside, but where the world could see." She slurps her coffee, nervous. "I hope that she knows that."

"She does." And that may be a lie, but it sounds true.

Mama Lettie nods and brushes away tears. "She's happy where she's at? Not hurting anymore? Not sad?"

"Not hurting. Not sad."

She covers her eyes with her hand, sucking in a few hard breaths. Then smiles at me, lips trembling with the effort. "And you? Are you going to be okay?"

"Yes, ma'am."

"You're certain? Alex or not, you are always welcome here."

"I know." I stretch across the table and take her hand. "Thank you."

She grips my fingers tight. "Will I see you again?"

My heart aches so I can barely breathe. "No," I say, gently. "I don't think so."

She cries. One hand clutching mine, the other covering her eyes as she sobs.

"Mama Lettie." I stop, not knowing what else to say. "I'm sorry," I mumble finally.

She waves her hand and rubs her cheeks dry on her sleeve. "Don't be sorry, honey." She lets go of my hand and plucks a napkin out of the needlepoint box in the center of the table. Blows her nose. "Don't be sorry." She stands up. "I shouldn't keep you."

I stand up more slowly, wondering if I should leave her alone. "I could stay a little while longer if—"

"No, no. You have some place to be and I'm just going to sit here and smoke the rest of that pack." She rummages through her purse, then holds a handful of money out to me. "Here. Take this."

"I can't."

"Yes, you can." She presses it into my hand and folds my fingers around it. "It's not much, but it should be enough to get a place to sleep for a week or so. Okay?" And there's a steely edge to her voice that says she won't be refused.

"Yes, ma'am." I tuck the money down into my bag. "Thank you."

"Ah." She smiles and slides her arms around me. "You be careful, all right?"

"Yes, Mama Lettie." I look down at her, doing my best to look stern and not broken. "You too."

She gives me a squeeze, then steps back and leans against the counter. "I'll be all right."

I nod, unable to trust my voice, and walk out the kitchen door. Then around the corner of the house and past the kitchen window, trampling heavily down the driveway. When I reach the front corner of the house, I pause and tiptoe back to peer in through the kitchen window.

Mama Lettie has her face in her hands, shoulders shaking. But then she straightens up and marches to the table and lights another cigarette. One hand on her hip as she blows a mouthful of smoke toward the ceiling.

I swallow against the lump in my throat and tiptoe back toward the sidewalk. She'll be all right, I think. Maybe not at first, but she'll be all right.

The air shimmers with heat as the sun climbs toward zenith. I tuck my hands in my pockets and start walking. Franklin will be waiting.

CHAPTER 8

Franklin doesn't answer the door at first. For a moment, I wonder if he has left already. Maybe he took my warning that his sister was in danger seriously, but preferred not to take me along. I knock harder, prepared to slip around the back and break in if I have to, but the lock *snicks* open and Franklin stares out at me, bleary-eyed. "I thought I told you to come around back."

"I forgot." Which is true. "Long night."

"Yeah." He steps to one side. "Come on in."

"Thank you." I step inside, and he shoves the door shut, already turning down the hall toward the kitchen.

"You want a cup of coffee?" He gestures to the pot on the counter, the last few drops just trickling out of the basket.

"I guess." My notebooks are spread out on the table, a plate with half a sandwich sitting forgotten in the middle. Franklin, I realize, is still dressed in the same clothes he had on yesterday. "You didn't sleep?"

He pours coffee into two mugs. "Not in a bed." He nudges the books aside to set the cups down. "Sugar?"

I shake my head and take a mug, sip from it politely. The coffee is hot and bitter, but I'm not here for the food. "Well?"

He drops into the chair on the other side of the table. "You've done a lot of work over these past few months." He smooths the pages of the nearest book, takes a gulp of coffee. "You certain it all adds up like this?"

"Yes." I take another sip from the mug, shudder at the taste, and set it down.

He frowns, rubs his braids back from his face, and slurps down more coffee, apparently oblivious to the heat of it. "And you're going to keep my sister safe, right?"

"In exchange for your help, yes."

"And if I don't want to help you?" He rubs his chest. "Last time almost killed me."

"I remember." I turn my cup on the table, watching the dark brown liquid tremble and shimmer with the reflection of the yellowed light overhead.

"Why should I risk that again?"

"Because I can help you stop the threat to your sister for good." I shrug. "Or, you can run off to Atlanta and try and move her someplace else. Again. Try and hide her from the Sisters. Again. And hope that maybe this time they won't find her. Again."

"Egh." Franklin tosses back the last of his coffee, then reaches for the pot to refill his mug. "And you're certain..." He pauses, staring at the confusion of pages laid open on the table.

I spread my hands across the books. "This road, as hard as it is, will mean your sister will be safe. Not just for a year or two. For good."

"There is a lot of risk written here."

"Yes. But how much have you already done to save her?" I reach across the table and take his hand, impulsive. "I want to help you, Franklin. Not just because you can help me, but because you already have. And I want to help you."

He shakes his head. "Shit, Delaney." He stands up and stomps out of the kitchen. Muffled swearing echoes down the hall.

I collect my notebooks, organizing them back into sequence. Wondering if I should leave and come back later, once he's had time to think about it some more.

"Hey." Franklin hangs against the doorframe. "You coming?" He's wearing a different shirt, and his hair is pulled back.

"Coming?" I blink at him, even though this is the thing I hoped would happen.

"You said you wanted to see the magic books. If we hurry, we can get there before Mrs. Dihn closes for lunch."

"Ah." I pick up my journals and clutch them against my chest. "I'm ready."

Franklin ushers me back down the hall to the front door. "I'll meet you out by the street." He locks the door behind me, and I go down the steps to the sidewalk to wait.

There's a rumble of an engine behind the house, and Franklin pulls down the weed-smothered driveway in an old Chevy Nova. "You want to put those in the trunk?"

I shake my head and climb into the passenger seat. "That's okay. I need to look through them again."

CHAPTER 9

Mrs. Dihn's store is in an older brick building—part grocery store, part herbal supply, part charm warehouse. Unlike a few tourist boutiques in the more popular sections of town, there are no complete charms here. But the glassed-in shelves behind the cash register are crammed full of rock and bone and feathers and roots, all the bits and pieces necessary for folks like Franklin to build the most common charms.

Mrs. Dihn herself is small and flawless. Shiny dark hair drawn back modestly, golden skin, and dark brown eyes that burn when she sees me. But Franklin steps past me and leans on the edge of the counter, friendly-like.

"We need to see the books."

Dihn's lips thin. "So you are helping this one?"

"More or less."

She glances at me, and I square my shoulders against the urge to take a step back. "Good morning, Mrs. Dihn."

"Egh." She leans across the counter toward Franklin. "You know what she is?"

"Yes."

"If she has promised you something..."

Now Franklin looks at me, but there is no doubt in his eyes. Just resignation. "You know there is only one thing that I would make this sort of deal for."

Dihn's eyes narrow. "Laurel?"

"Yes. And the Sisters."

"Ptah." She mimics spitting before bustling around the end of the counter to look up at me. Her eyes glitter like glass, and are as sharp, too. "You will take care of the Sisters?"

I nod. "Yes."

She reaches up to grab my face, fingers pinching my jaw as she pulls me down so we look in each other's eyes. I have not told Franklin what I actually intend to happen to the Sisters. Maybe I don't have to. Maybe he is more concerned with his sister's safety.

But Mrs. Dihn seems to see.

She flinches. A sly grin pulls at her rose petal lips, reminding me that Franklin and his sister are not the only ones the Sisters have hurt. She leans so close I feel her breath against my skin. "You swear to me that you will do this thing, Power?"

"I swear it."

"Ah." Her smile grows. "All right. You may read the books." She bangs her hand on the bell sitting on the counter. When there is not an immediate response, she rings it again, turning to yell at the back of the store. "Mark."

A large young man with the same golden skin and dark hair emerges from a half-concealed hallway. "Yes, Mom?"

"Watch the store."

Mark looks at Franklin and me, face impassive, but his blue eyes are just as sharp as his mother's. "Yes, Mom," he says. He pulls his smartphone from his pocket and settles on the stool behind the counter.

Mrs. Dihn gestures for us to follow her. "This way. Quick."

She leads us back through the curtained doorway, down a narrow hall to a battered wooden door. There is a faint jingle as she pulls a ring of keys from her pocket and unlocks it. The stairs on the other side are caked with dust and fall steeply into darkness. I glance at Franklin, who nods and steps past me.

"Watch your step, Delaney," he says.

I lick my lips and follow him down the stairs. As I reach the floor, dirt and brick by the feel under my sneakers, the little bit of light from the top of the stairs is snuffed as Mrs. Dihn pulls the door shut and locks it again. A switch clicks.

Bare bulbs dangle from the arch of a tunnel. I shiver, remembering Daddy's muddy hole in the afterlife, but the air is musty, not rotten. Mrs. Dihn marches ahead of us without hesitation. She unlocks another door at the end of the tunnel, and we move into a large, low-ceilinged room cluttered with stacks of books.

Dihn locks the door behind us, flips a few more switches on the wall to turn the rest of the lights on. "Which books?"

"Just one. The Book of the Dead."

"Sit there." She gestures to a little table and chair directly beneath one of the hanging lights. She disappears back into the shelves.

I sit down, looking at Franklin. He leans back against the wall beside the door, arms folded across his chest. If he is uneasy, it doesn't show.

Mrs. Dihn returns with a leather-bound book under one arm and a roll of duct tape in the other hand. She sets the book down on the table with a thump, the metal locks on the cover chiming like bells. She peels a length of tape off the roll, bites down on the edge to tear it loose. "Mouth," she says.

"What?" I look at her uneasily.

"The things in this book cannot be read aloud. Not here. Not even a whisper. You tape your mouth or you don't read."

"Oh." I pull my notebook and pen out of my satchel. "I need to—"

"Copy, yes." She nods impatiently. "That is fine. But not speak out loud."

"Okay."

"Bite your lips." She demonstrates, and I imitate and let her tape my mouth shut.

It's not very comfortable, but I don't intend to be here long. I open my notebook to a fresh page as Dihn unlatches the book and pushes it across the table toward me. She retreats to stand next to Franklin. I pull the book closer and lift the cover.

It's no wonder she took precautions. I don't read any language other than English, but the letters on the page prickle against my fingertips—sharp enough that I look to make certain I am not bleeding.

I turn the pages carefully. And quickly. Ancient language or not, every page makes promises to me. Some whisper, seductive—a crone seeing a beautiful reflection in the mirror or a queen surrounding by fawning suitors. Some shout—a black-clad knight clutching a bloody sword, a king seated on a throne that covers the world.

My head aches with it, sweat dripping from the end of my nose, cold and hot, as I struggle to turn each page. Mere sheets of vellum, but they grow successively heavier 'til it is like lifting gravestones.

I reach the center of the book, and this is the most seductive whisper of all—the promise of life unending. It spreads across two pages, words and image woven together so neatly it is hard to distinguish one from the next. Beautiful for all that it is drawn entirely in shades of blood and ash.

Franklin straightens and takes a half-step toward the table. "Delaney."

Mrs. Dihn grabs his arm, tight. "No."

I grab the edge of the page with both hands and pull. It resists at first, but I ain't interested in eternal anything, and after a long moment, the book concedes, and the page drifts over light as a dandelion seed.

The next few are quieter, and I turn past them as fast as I can. I may not know these old tongues, but I know what I'm looking for. I've seen that future, down in Daddy's dirty cave, and though I don't know the magic to make it happen, I know what it will look like.

The illustration is horrific. Flames everywhere and two bodies—the bones tearing out of one, the flesh melting off the other like wax. I swallow hard and remind myself that I won't feel any of it, pull my notebook close, and begin to copy the words and diagram off the facing page.

The duct tape pulls against my skin as I instinctively try to sound out the unfamiliar words. I bite my lips harder and focus on the letters, writing them out as neat and quick as I can. The diagram is the trickiest part. The symbols are not in a familiar alphabet, but each curl and slash must be accurately recorded or the magic will not work as it is meant.

The effort of it makes me sweat, and the tip of the pen digs deep into the paper. But, finally I finish. Compare my page with the one in the book one last time, then close both notebook and the Book of the Dead.

Mrs. Dihn steps forward and closes and locks each latch, each chiming a different sour note as they snap together. She disappears back among the shelves, and I tuck my notebook into my satchel before peeling the tape off my mouth. The inside of my mouth tastes vaguely metallic, deep valleys left in the skin from my teeth.

Dihn returns. "Are you done?"

"Yes, ma'am."

"Good." She leads the way back up to the store, unlocking and locking the doors as we go.

Mark is still sitting behind the counter, poking at something on his phone. He glances toward us as we push through the curtain, but says nothing.

Mrs. Dihn turns and grasps my wrist hard. "Remember what you promised me, Power."

"I will."

She squints at me suspiciously. "Don't come back."

I smile. "I don't intend to. Thank you for your help."

She pulls the front door open, shooing me and Franklin out into the heat. The door shuts behind us with a jingle of the bell over the door, immediately followed by the click of the deadbolt. Dihn turns the sign around so that it reads *Closed* and pulls the blinds down.

I look at Franklin.

He shrugs. "She is not fond of Powers."

"Because of the Sisters."

"Among others." He tugs his keys from his pocket. "I guess we're headed to Atlanta next."

"Yep." I follow him to the car.

"I need to stop back by the house and pick up a few things."

I slide into the passenger seat, wincing as the heat from the vinyl soaks through my jeans. "We don't have a lot of time."

"I know. But I'm not facing the Sisters unprepared." He starts the engine. "It'll only take a few minutes."

There isn't much point in arguing—he's the one driving the car. "Okay." I press my hands against my satchel, wanting to take my notebook out and look at the copied page again. But, although my copy lacks some of the dark magic possessed by the blood and skin pages of the real Book of the Dead, it's not a good idea to risk saying any of it aloud.

I slouch further down in the seat, trying to soak up the warmth.

Franklin glances at me. "Are you okay?"

"Just trying to get warm." I tuck cold hands against my chest with a smile that feels colorless.

He pauses, sweat beaded on his own earthy skin. "Are you okay, Delaney?" he asks again, deliberate.

"This flesh is failing." I lick my lips, still tasting blood. "But it's got a few days left in it."

Franklin reaches behind the seat, rummaging around for a moment before tugging a towel out from under a pile of empty water bottles and a pair of muddy shoes. "Here. It's a little sandy, but better than nothing."

"Thanks." I wrap it across my chest and tuck my knees up. So tired. My eyes slip closed, the sun shining red and gold through my eyelids as Franklin drives back to his house. My hands still tremble, anxious to be doing something. But there will be time enough for that soon. For now, I should rest.

CHAPTER 10

The sun is sinking in the west as we get close to Atlanta, the traffic creeping in and out of the city as folks head home after work.

Franklin has thumbed through the radio dial a few times, but it's mostly commercials and pop artists who sing about love like it can be quantified. He switches the radio back off, and we sit in awkward silence as we slowly move toward the city.

I pull the little book of poetry out of my bag and turn through the pages slowly. Stopping to examine the artwork or read a line or two. Anything to keep busy so I do not have to worry too much about what is coming.

"What are you reading?"

"Sonnets from the Portuguese." I hold it up with a sheepish grin. "Mama Lettie gave it to me last night. Kind of sappy poetry, but I like it, I guess."

He nods. "Straightway I was 'ware, so weeping, how a mystic Shape did move behind me, and drew me backward by the hair; and a voice said in mastery while I strove.—"Guess now who holds thee?"—"Death," I said. But, there, the silver answer rang,—"Not Death, but Love.""

I blink at him, surprised. "Yes."

Franklin chuckles. "I studied that in college."

"Oh." I stare at the page, an odd mix of irritation and jealousy rolling around in my stomach. I have always loved poetry, but I've never had the chance to study it. Just read the books in the psychiatrist's office, and even that was difficult with the Magiprex scrambling my brain.

"You don't have many black folks go to college where you're from?"

My cheeks get hot. "Not many folks period." I look at him. "But maybe especially not black folks." I trace the edge of the illustration on the facing page, bleeding hearts in a style that is both realistic and intricately stylized. "But that's not..." I shake my head. "What did you study? Besides these."

"They called it Classical Studies. Greek and Latin. Literature. Some music and art."

I tuck my knees up against my chest, watching him curiously. "How did that lead you to magic?"

"It didn't. That came later. After Laurel was...attacked. I meant to be a teacher." There's a wistful note in his voice, but whatever regrets he has, he shrugs away. "Came in handy though once I started learning magic. Lots of Latin and Greek involved."

"I guess." Powers don't need all the tools and materials that street magicians do. Our magic comes from our flesh and blood.

"What about you? Before you were...separated from your bones."

I shake my head. "I was in an institution. I read books the psychiatrist gave me, but no one tried to teach me anything. Probably wouldn't have stuck anyway. I was on meds."

"Ah." He is silent for a moment. "I'm sorry."

I turn the page, staring blankly at the printed words.

The first time that the sun rose on thine oath
To love me, I looked forward to the moon
To slacken all those bonds which seemed too soon
And quickly tied to make a lasting troth.

The lines ripple, and I slap the book shut and stare out the window as tears threaten to spill over. "I would have liked to study poetry. It always had a magic that I couldn't touch—words and rhyme and meter."

Franklin laughs, dry. "There's plenty of magic in your words, Delaney."

"It's not the same." I say it sharp and bitter. Too many things I should have had that I didn't. Not things, like clothes or jewelry or a TV, but opportunities. *The chance to live.* Poetry is just the obvious metaphor.

I rub away tears with the back of my hand. Take a deep breath. "I'm sorry. I didn't mean to snap."

"Nah. It's okay." Franklin looks at me, and for the first time, there's sympathy in the lines around his eyes. "Maybe once you have your bones back, yeah?"

"Maybe." I know that my future doesn't lead that direction, but there's nothing to be gained in dwelling on it now. "Maybe."

CHAPTER 11

y the time we get into Atlanta, the sun is down—the sky overhead a murky grey as the light from the city washes out the color of night and hides all but the brightest stars. We wind along smaller roads, passing signs that offer new housing starting at half a million dollars. I wonder if maybe I have misread Franklin once again, but he turns down a series of side roads 'til we reach a neighborhood that looks a lot like Crossing does.

Old trees and a mix of houses built after the World Wars. A few garbage cans sit at the curb, white or black garbage bags peeking out from under the lids.

Franklin flashes a tired smile. "Almost there."

The ornament hanging from his rearview mirror—a piece of quartz and copper wire, with hammered metal feathers on either side—turns in a slow circle, then spins faster 'til the feathers whistle.

"Damn it." Franklin steps on the gas. "They're already here."

I clutch at the door handle as he turns into a driveway in front of a faded blue ranch house, tires squeaking as he slams on the brakes. "The Sisters?"

"Yes." He's already out of the car, opening the trunk and grabbing vials and charms. "Here." He tosses me an aluminum baseball bat. "Don't hesitate to hit any of them that get close."

I nod and follow him toward the house. He doesn't head for the front door, slipping instead around the side of the garage to open a door with a key on his key ring. It's dim inside, the glow from the streetlight filtering through the narrow windows in the garage door. But the garage itself is nearly empty, except for a small car parked in the middle. The driver's side door is open, keys in the ignition and radio still mumbling softly.

The muscles in Franklin's jaw harden. "This way," he says quietly.

The door into the kitchen opens without a sound. There is a murmur of voices from down the hall, and Franklin moves forward—quiet, but quick.

I wrap my hands tight around the bat and follow behind.

The living room is a mess. All the furniture has been shoved back against the edges of the room, the carpet torn up, and a five-pointed star drawn on the floor and lined with salt. Franklin's sister, Laurel, lies in the middle, leather straps around her wrists and ankles screwed straight into the floorboards to hold her fast.

The Sisters each stand at one point of the star, singing the words that will drain Laurel's magic out of her and into them. The melody is instantly familiar—the Book of the Dead sang the same thing to me when it promised eternal life. The salt-lines glitter, energy creeping along them as the various points connect.

Franklin doesn't hesitate. He pulls a vial from his pocket and throws it against the diagram on the floor. The glass breaks and dirt spills out, crossing the salt-line but not breaking it completely.

The Sisters sing one final note, triumphant, and Laurel arches off the ground with a moan.

Franklin pulls another vial from his pocket, but the Sisters are moving now—eyes bright with the magic siphoning from Laurel. One of them strikes him in the chest with her palm, and he staggers back, wheezing for breath.

A Sister steps toward me, and I hit her in the shoulder with the bat. It shivers, and my hands and arms burn like I've stuck my fingers in an electrical socket, but she shuffles, momentarily off balance. Gritting my teeth against the coming shock, I hit her again, this time putting my weight into it and aiming for her head.

She reels back, shuffling through the edge of the diagram. Salt scatters across the floor and the magic breaks—the explosion of air and energy knocking me back into the hallway. I'm aware of another one of the Sisters coming toward me, something glinting in her hand.

The bat slips from my hand when I swing it, but not before it connects with her knee.

In the living room, Franklin is yelling old words, and the air turns bitter with the scent of burning herbs.

I push up onto my hands and knees, then to my feet. The Sister with the knife comes at me again, and I ball up my fists and hit her. A little blindly. Reminded that this body, although it is failing, is still far stronger than my own ever was. The difference between living and spending years locked up inside.

When my knuckles hit her cheek, it's like punching a cinderblock, but she still stumbles back, then turns and follows the others who are making a fast retreat out the front door. I snatch up the baseball bat and start after them.

"Delaney." Franklin shakes his head. "Let them go."

For a moment, I consider following them anyway, but he's right. The Sisters won't be in a mood to talk now. I shut the door and lock it.

Franklin drops to his knees beside Laurel, fumbling with the leather straps around her wrists. He's shaking, gasping for breath, with deep lines around his eyes that I don't remember being there an hour ago.

The drill the Sisters used is lying on the floor. I get it switched to reverse and start backing out the screws holding Laurel's restraints in place. As the last one comes free, she curls up against Franklin, sobbing.

"It's okay. Shhhhh." He wraps his arms around her, even though he's shaking like a dry leaf in autumn.

It doesn't seem like a good idea to stay here, but neither of them seem capable of walking on their own. My own body is aching, but, for once, the distance between this flesh and myself is useful.

I go back down the hall to the kitchen and get a glass of water, take it to Franklin. "Here."

"Thanks." He gulps a few swallows, then touches the glass to Laurel's lips. "Have a drink of water."

She sits up and takes the glass in both hands, taking quick and nervous sips. Staring at me. Not like Franklin does, straight on and fierce. This is more like when folks see someone in a wheelchair. Glancing at me sideways while pretending not to look.

"Can you get a blanket?" Franklin jerks his head toward the other hallway. "Bedroom is at the end. Whatever you can find."

"Sure." I turn the lights on as I go, grab the blankets off the bed, and start back to the living room. As I pass by one of the other rooms, I catch a glimpse of my own face staring at me. I nudge the door open further.

The room is empty except for a stool and a wooden box full of charcoal and pastel sticks. But every inch of the walls is covered in drawings. Some of them blend together to form other images, some are distinct. The largest and darkest is me. Not this borrowed face, but my own.

My arms ache with the weight of the blankets bundled against my chest. I tug the door back closed and return to the living room. Hand one blanket to Franklin, the other to his sister, then settle on my heels, arms resting on my knees, chin resting on my arms. Look at Laurel in what I hope is a friendly way. "I knew you had the Touch. I didn't realize you could see the future."

Laurel takes another sip of water, looking at me more directly. "Isn't that why you're helping me? So that I can guide your way forward?"

CHAPTER 12

Franklin shakes his head. "Delaney's deal is with me, Laurel."

She looks at me, sharp, and I nod. "Franklin and I are helping each other."

"Helping you do what?" She grabs my wrist when I do not immediately answer. "Helping you do what, Delaney Green?"

"To get my bones back."

Laurel turns to Franklin. "Is this true?"

"Yes." He takes her hand, reassuring.

"And you know what it is she intends?"

Franklin's gaze slides to me, a heaviness settling around his eyes. "Enough of it, yes."

"But the other Power she means to wake—"

"I have faced him before." He touches his chest instinctively. "And this time will be different."

"Franklin."

"Nah." He leans his forehead against hers. "It's all right."

Laurel clings to him, fresh tears cutting glittering tracks across her oaken skin. But she doesn't argue.

Franklin looks at me while his sister cries on his shoulder. For a moment, I see his past laid out as clearly as I used to see the future—all the sacrifices made to try and protect her. I see how desperately he wants it to be over. How, even now, he would drain his life away to keep her safe.

"Do you think they'll come back?" I ask in an attempt to change the subject.

"Not tonight." Franklin looks around the ruined living room. "And I don't think we should stay here."

Laurel nods in agreement. "We should go somewhere else."

He squeezes her hand reassuringly. "Why don't you go get some clothes? Put some shoes on. And we'll go."

"Okay. I'll just be a few minutes." She heads down the hall toward the bedroom.

I rest my chin on my knees, exhausted. The rush of adrenaline that came with facing the Sisters is fading, the familiar chill and fatigue settling back in.

"You should probably clean that," Franklin says.

"What?"

He nods at my hand, the knuckles torn and bleeding from punching the Sister. "You should wash that. There's probably some bandages in the bathroom."

"Right." But when I try to stand, I plop back down, shaking with the effort.

Franklin's eyes narrow, and he stands up, not too steady himself. "Wait here."

I wait, trying to breathe, wishing I could curl up on the floor and go to sleep right there. Franklin returns in a moment with a plastic first aid box tucked under his arm. "Come on." He pulls me upright and guides me into the kitchen.

I lean on the counter with one hand and stick my bloodied fingers under the faucet. The cold water stings, but I grit my teeth and let it run 'til the torn skin is clean.

Franklin has the first aid kit open, antibiotic cream and a roll of gauze sitting on the counter. He squeezes a dollop of ointment on each wounded knuckle, then begins winding the gauze over it—putting loops between each finger like I'm prepping for a boxing match.

"Lucky you didn't break your hand," he says.

"They are stronger than I expected." I look at him, realizing the kind of courage it must take to face that kind of magic knowingly. I had always assumed he didn't fully understand what he was facing with Percy. Now I am not so certain.

He knots the gauze on the back of my hand and trims the ends up neatly. "There. If you have to hit someone again, you should have a little protection." He pauses, looking at me. "What?"

"I think I may have underestimated you."

"Egh." He tucks the remainder of the gauze back into the box.

"You know that I won't hold you to this deal if you don't—"

"No." He shakes his head. "I'll help you. And you'll take care of the Sisters."

I nod. "Yes."

Franklin licks his lips, rearranging the things in the first aid kit until the lid closes properly. When he looks up, his gaze is intent. "You have to understand, Delaney. I would make a deal with the devil himself to keep Laurel from having to face this again." A flick of his fingers indicates the trashed living room down the hall, the situation in general.

"Ah." I grin, exhausted, and tired of being so serious. "Then it's a good thing you met me first, isn't it?"

He raises an eyebrow. "Is it?"

I could reassure him that I don't mean to hurt him, but I know that sometimes not meaning to hurt someone isn't enough. "Tell me something, Franklin Jones. I understand why you would deal with me now, but what about before? The first time with Percy?"

He shrugs. "I've seen what happens when Powers are left unchecked." There's a sense of wariness to him. Wondering perhaps what will keep me in check once I'm back in my bones. Besides my good nature, I mean.

"I'm ready." Laurel stands at the door of the kitchen. She's changed clothes and pulled her hair back with a scarf. A backpack hangs over one shoulder, and she holds a small duffel bag in her other hand.

"All right. Let's go." Franklin takes the duffel bag from her, and we go back out of the house through the garage. The air is soft and smells of earth and pine needles. Overhead, the sky is the color of a bruise, all purple and blotchy with clouds.

Franklin locks the door behind us, and we move to the car, quick. Down the street is the hollow rumble of plastic wheels on pavement—a neighbor dragging their trash can down to the curb. Laurel shudders and clutches at Franklin's arm, watching the shadows under the trees in an undeveloped lot across the street.

But it remains quiet.

Franklin opens the trunk and tosses the bag in while Laurel climbs into the back seat. He shuts the trunk, takes a final look around. "Come on."

I collapse into the passenger seat, barely getting the door closed before he puts the car into gear. The streetlights blur overhead, and my eyes slide closed as we head back into the rush and swirl of the city traffic.

CHAPTER 13

The motel is a kitschy sprawl of one-story brick around a faded blue swimming pool. There were a handful of cars parked outside the row of paint-blistered doors when we signed in—the noise that's come through the wall, mostly couples paying $30 for a couple hours away from prying eyes.

As the windows grow light with the approaching dawn, the whine and groan of enthusiastic lovers fades, replaced by the rumble and sigh of traffic filtering under the motel room's door to tease me awake. My hand aches. All of me aches, but my hand is more distinct.

I wiggle my fingers and immediately regret it, knuckles throbbing as if I have just rubbed them against the dirty sidewalk outside. There's a bottle of acetaminophen on the table beside the bed. I dump a couple tablets into my hand and shuffle into the bathroom to get a glass of water.

Alex's face stares back at me in the mirror, pale and gaunt. I resist the urge to smash it, and swallow the pills, washing them down with a glassful of lukewarm water from the faucet.

The door between my room and the one Franklin and Laurel opted to share is open. I peek in and see they are both still asleep. Laurel curled up under the covers like a baby—knees to chin—while Franklin sprawls in the other bed as though he fell asleep when he touched the blankets. For all I know, he did.

I'm still trembling with fatigue. Mortal bodies do not handle conflict with Powers well. Maybe Franklin has a bit of the Touch without knowing it. Maybe he'll die before he turns forty. But it doesn't surprise me he's spent.

My satchel is on the floor between the beds in my room, and I pull my notebooks out and spread them across the covers, turn on the light, and settle down to read. It is habit more than anything else; I know what is in between the scuffed covers. I know what I need to do next. But it is comforting to read the words again, since I can't feel the threads around me.

I rummage in the paper bag Mama Lettie gave me, then unwrap a peanut butter and jelly sandwich. My stomach churns at the thought of eating, but I know it's necessary. There are only a few days left, but I won't make it to the end of them if I don't eat.

There's a whisper of movement in the doorway.

"You want a sandwich?" I hold the bag up, gaze fixed on my notebooks, but I know that it's Laurel standing there in the shadows.

She shuffles forward, wary. Arms wrapped across her chest as she settles on the far edge of the other bed. "What are those?"

"Research." I flatten out the corner of a curling bit of paper—printed copies of various news articles I found at the library. "Leverage."

Her brows draw down in a scowl. "Franklin would have helped you without me involved. Probably."

"Yes." I had been uncertain about Franklin at first, but he is proving to be more of a paladin than a street magician. "But Martinez is tricky."

Laurel tilts her head, her fingers ticking against her knee. "The FBI agent," she says after a moment. "Doesn't he want revenge?"

"Ah." I had avoided Martinez before. He was smart and, despite his blank exterior, good at reading people. It had made sense to keep my distance because the things I needed Percy to see were things that would have prompted Martinez to make sure I was put back in Greenhaven.

It wasn't until I started trying to track down the Sisters that I realized Martinez was connected in much the same way as Franklin. That his partnership with Percy was not coincidental, but deliberate.

I'd had to dig deep to find the original articles, morbid pieces of journalism that focused less on the loss of Francesca Martinez and more on the peculiarity of her murder. Headlines full of *Satanists* and *Devil Worshiping Cult*. Columns full of concern about what it meant for the young women of the community and the bluster and fear of a dozen preachers. At the end of the first story was a single line: *Martinez is survived by her young son.*

Connected in the same way as Franklin, but with greater loss and deeper anger. The rest of the clippings, awkwardly following his career with the FBI through brief mentions of his name, didn't say he had pursued that path because he wanted the women who stole his mother's magic to die. None of them indicated he had transferred from team to team, always chasing the Sisters, always a few steps behind.

But I knew there was a reason I had never been able to separate him from Percy. Not without later disaster. Because Martinez chose to stay with Percy, not just as his handler—keeping tabs on a hidden Power for the department— but as a friend. Forcing them apart, fracturing that bond, meant Martinez always came back later, cold and clinical, to put an end to a couple of monsters.

Laurel fidgets, pulls her knees up against her chest. "I suppose we all want revenge."

"Oh?" I don't mean to seem doubtful, but I suppose she hears it in my voice.

She licks her lips. "Maybe not Franklin. He just wants things to be normal. Not dangerous."

"But you want revenge."

"Yes." A glance toward the door to the other room, but it remains empty. She leans toward me. "You saw what they did to me. You know what they have done to others. Franklin stopped them last time, too, but..." She touches her face—the deep lines around her eyes and mouth, the gray hair at her temples. "You'd never guess I was younger than he is."

"I'm sorry." I reach for her instinctively, but she flinches, turns her head to stare at the growing sliver of light between the curtains. I tuck my hand back in my lap, reminding myself that she has reason to distrust anyone who is a Power. "Have you seen them come after you again?"

She stares at her toes. "No," she says finally. "I've only seen you stop them."

There's an edge to her voice I can't quite figure out. "Somehow you don't seem too thrilled about that."

"Because I've seen what happens afterward." She glares at me. "I've seen the cost of you getting your bones back. I know what follows you."

I blink at her, confused. "What?"

Her lip curls back from her teeth. "Don't tell me you haven't seen it. Other Powers crawling back from the dead to seize a place in this world. It starts with you."

"Oh." I do remember the thing she's talking about. A thing so far distant that even when I could see my threads clearly, it was still mostly shadows and whispers. "You mean Daddy. He's been trying to get back here for a while."

"And he will succeed because of you."

I understand her fear now. Ain't nobody wants to see Daddy come back. And the twinge of guilt because—even more than Franklin—she wants to be free of the Sisters, no matter what the cost down the road.

I try to smile, harder every hour in this dead form. "I won't let that happen."

Laurel balls up her fists, but doesn't hit anything. "I have seen it."

"Once you see the future, you can change it."

"You can change it." Her shoulders droop, hands falling back into her lap. "The rest of us must suffer what is coming."

I think about Martinez, choosing friendship with Percy, choosing that friendship over his other loyalties, and binding himself to Percy's future whether he realized it or not. Everyone has the ability to change the road ahead, my gift lies in seeing how many roads there are, in changing the future of others every time I change my own.

"There is always a choice, Laurel." My smile feels thin as a sheet of toilet paper, and as worthless.

Laurel nods, more a gesture of habit than of agreement. "Make certain they cannot hurt anyone else." It's a whisper, but my skin crawls with the edge in her voice. She doesn't wait for a response, already slipping back into the other room.

I glance down at the notebook in my lap.

The photo at the top of the article is grainy, but Martinez—standing in the midst of the team he worked with in Texas—stares up at me. Solemn. Determined.

He wants revenge.

CHAPTER 14

There's a Waffle House across the parking lot from the motel. Once the sun is fully up above the horizon, I put my shoes on and walk over to buy pancakes, eggs, and bacon for the three of us.

The lady behind the counter looks at the gauze wrapped around my knuckles. "Rough night, honey?"

I shrug. "I've had worse."

She grins, dry, and tucks a yellowy strand of hair behind her ear. "Haven't we all?" She pulls her pencil and receipt book out of her apron pocket. "What can I get you?"

Going back across the parking lot, three Styrofoam boxes in a plastic bag in one hand, a pressed paper tray with three cups of coffee in the other, the city hums around me. The hiss and growl of traffic, the invisible prickle of electricity flowing through a million wires—for a moment this flesh trembles with it as though body and soul will shake apart.

I gulp a breath and bite the inside of my cheek. *Not yet. Not yet.*

The sensation passes, leaving me cold and numb. But still breathing. I fumble the door to my room open and set the coffee and food on top of the dresser next to the TV.

Franklin leans through the doorway from the other room. "Where were you?"

"Breakfast." I hand him a takeout container and a cup of coffee. "There's cream and sugar here, too." I dig the handful of sugar packets out of my pocket, then the tiny thimbles of cream. The other pocket is full of little tubs of syrup.

Franklin shakes his head. "That's okay." He takes a quick sip from the cup. "Are there forks?"

"In the bag."

He grabs a set of plastic ware and settles on the edge of the bed. "How's your hand?"

"Sore." I peel the lid off a cup of coffee, tear open a handful of sugar packets and stir them in with a few splashes of cream. It still tastes mostly brown and hot, but it helps to chase away the clinging chill.

Laurel stands in the doorway, wary. "Franklin?"

"There's food." He swallows a mouthful of pancake and points to the boxes on the dresser. "You should eat. It's good."

She makes a face. "Are there hash browns?"

"Pancakes," he says. "Just eat."

"Fine." Laurel collects her breakfast and plops down at the head of the bed.

I take the remaining container, a couple of syrup tubs, and sit down on the other bed. My stomach churns. I taste coffee and acid on the back of my tongue. The food does little to settle the nausea, but it covers the sting of the reflux and fills the cold hollow under my ribs.

Franklin washes down the last few bites of egg with his coffee, wipes his mouth on the back of his hand. "Now what?"

"Now we talk to the Sisters."

He frowns, but nods reluctantly. "I suppose you know where to find them."

"Yes." I rummage through my notes, find the book with the address written in it.

Laurel peers over his shoulder. "That's a dangerous part of town. Lots of folks with the Touch. Magicians." Her gaze slides over to me. "Powers, even."

"We won't be there long." I lick the last smudge of syrup from my fingers. "We shouldn't be there long. Best if you stay here though."

Laurel looks at Franklin, worried. "I don't know."

He touches her knee, reassuring. "It'll be all right. And we'll be back soon."

"But—"

"You've seen it. We'll be back."

Laurel shudders, but nods. "Be careful."

"Of course." He tosses his empty container into the trash, tips the last of his coffee out of the cup. "Let me get my keys and jacket and we can go."

"Sure." I open the book of sonnets where I have hidden the page copied out of the Book of the Dead. The piece of paper, torn out of the notebook, is folded up so there is less temptation to read those forbidden words out loud. I still have to resist the urge to look at it, and, instead, tuck it into my jeans pocket.

Laurel watches me from the bed, sullen. "You take care of him."

"Yes." I can't help but grin. "I'm not done with him yet."

She scowls, unamused. "If you hurt him..."

"No one's getting hurt," Franklin says from the doorway. "Not today, anyway." He shrugs into his jacket. "You ready, Delaney?"

I nod.

He points at Laurel sternly. "Lock the door behind us. Stay inside. We'll be back soon."

CHAPTER 15

A handful of soup can lights in the ceiling provide just enough light in the bar to make out the little tables with wobbly chairs scattered across the sticky concrete floor. This time of day it's also deserted. A couple of women sit in a booth in the farthest corner. There's a flash of silver jewelry and pale faces and then they draw back into the shadows.

The barkeep is busy pulling mugs from a plastic dishwasher rack, drying the edges with towel before stacking them behind the counter with a precision that speaks of years of practice.

Franklin takes a deep breath. "Stay close," he says, and leads the way toward the bar.

"What can I get you?" The barkeep looks up, sees me, and the muscle in his jaw twitches. "Uh-uh. We don't serve underage in here."

"I'm not here to drink." I slide onto the nearest bar stool. "I'm here to speak with the Sisters."

"I don't know—"

I rest my bandaged hand on the bar. "I think they'll want to talk to me, too."

He pauses, eyes flicking back and forth in his head as he glances between me and Franklin.

Franklin twitches his jacket open, rests his hands on his hips. The charms on his belt jingle softly.

The barkeep's lip shivers back from his teeth. "I expect they will." He touches the stack of glasses behind the counter. "You'll keep it civil, right?"

"If they do."

He hesitates. "All right. Back this way." He tosses his towel onto the half-empty rack of mugs and leads the way toward a doorway in the corner. A few strands of ugly beads dangle from the door frame, too far apart to make a sound even as we shoulder through them.

The barkeep leads the way past a pair of scuffed doors that say "Men" and "Women," pauses almost imperceptibly outside one marked "Office," then knocks on the last door in the narrow hall. "Sarah?"

The floor creaks, but the door doesn't open. A woman's voice filters through the paint-caked wood. "Yeah?"

"It's Alvin. You've got some visitors."

The door opens an inch to reveal a wedge of pale face with a purple bruise blossoming on her cheek. Green eyes narrow as she looks past the barkeep and sees me and Franklin.

Alvin wipes his hands on the front of his shirt, nervous. "They said they want to talk."

"Hold on." The door slams shut, and there's a muffled flutter of voices on the other side. The words are indistinct, but the feeling is clear—arguing about whether or not to let us in. Finally, the door opens again, wider this time, and Sarah motions us inside.

I go in first, letting Franklin stay back and guard the exit. If things go as I expect, it will be an unnecessary precaution, but between the two of us, he still poses a bigger threat to the Sisters. Better to give him some distance and let him watch our way out.

The five Sisters settle around the edge of the room, each keeping enough distance between them that it would be difficult to attack them. One of them keeps glancing out the window next to her, peering up and down the street before looking back at us.

Sarah crosses her arms on her chest and glares at us. "What do you want?"

"To make a deal."

"A deal." She looks back at the others. "For what?"

"I need help with this." I pull the folded page that I copied out of the Book of the Dead from my pocket and hold it out.

Sarah takes it, unfolds it with her fingertips as if she is handling something unpleasant. For a moment she is quiet, studying the diagram and the archaic language surrounding it. Her eyes narrow, and she looks at me suspiciously. "This is forbidden."

"The taking of life to perform it is forbidden." I spread my hands. "But this body has already died once. There will be no...censure for putting it to this use."

The woman by the window shuffles her feet, uneasy. "What is she talking about Sarah?"

Sarah hands her the paper silently, never taking her eyes off me. "I'm still not sure I understand. If you have the use of this body..."

"It is failing." I take a half-step closer. "I have been separated from my own bones, and I need them back. To do that, I need your help." A twirl of my fingers to indicate the five of them.

The woman by the window shakes her head. "We are not strong enough. If we were, we would not—" She breaks off, eyeing Franklin lurking by the door. "We are not strong enough," she says again.

"I can provide a source of Power."

Sarah tilts her head. Glances back over her shoulder at the others. "You said you wanted to make a deal. What are you offering us in exchange for our assistance?"

"I am offering what you have been trying to steal." I grin as they all look at Franklin. "No. Not from Laurel." I straighten my shirt, suddenly self-conscious. "But once my flesh and bones are remade, I will let you take a portion of my Power."

The woman by the window shakes her head. "How do we know it is not a trick? How do we know you can do what you're promising?"

"How do you know I'm not?"

Sarah steps in close, catching me under the chin as she looks deep in my eyes. Her fingers hurt, but I don't flinch away, just wait for her to find the truth hiding under this borrowed skin. It takes her longer than it took the necromancer. I guess maybe because she isn't as strong. But when she sees it, she flinches as if burned—shaking her hand like she can feel the heat of my soul.

For a moment, she looks like she will run—past Franklin at the door or even out the window behind her. Then the greed that has driven her all these years kicks in. She smiles. "All right. How do we make this happen?"

"Crossing, Georgia. Two days. There's a ruined house in the woods outside town where my bones lie. You'll be able to feel it."

Sarah nods. "All right. In two days then."

"Good." I look at Franklin.

He reaches back to open the door wide, then steps into the hall—not turning his back on the Sisters. "Come on, Delaney."

The barkeep is sweeping up as we head toward the door. He pauses to lean on his broom for a moment as we pick our way between the tables. "Y'all good?"

Franklin grunts as he holds the door for me.

Alvin scowls. "Have a blessed day," he calls after us.

"Asshole." Franklin drops into the driver's seat of the car and starts the engine.

I scramble into the car and shut the door hurriedly. "Are you okay?"

"Yeah." He rolls his shoulders and waves his hand, as if throwing something away. "Some devils are harder to deal with than others."

CHAPTER 16

When we get back to the motel, we find Laurel sitting on the curb outside the rooms, a cigarette clutched in one trembling hand.

Franklin eases the car into an empty spot and leans his head out the window. "What's wrong?"

She shakes her head, takes a long drag.

I step out of the car, tired already. "Laurel?"

She glares at me. "Take a look inside."

The TV is on, the voice of a news commentator droning like a lone fly against a window pane. "The FBI has not issued an official statement yet, but our reporter has uncovered a string of similar cases stretching across decades and several states. Previous investigations have not resulted in any arrests."

The woman on the TV shuffles her papers. "Which leads us to this hour's Hot Topic: are the restrictions on the use of magic enough? Joining me are Dr. Lucas Tan and Dr. Amelia Esperanza."

Franklin punches the mute button on the remote as the experts say *Hello* and *Thanks for having me*. Video rolls in the background, police tape and flashing lights. A sheet-draped figure and the rough lines of a five-pointed star scratched in a dirty alley.

Laurel props herself against the doorframe, cigarette held out to one side so the smoke won't drift into the room. "They killed someone else."

"Ah." My legs are too tired to have this conversation standing up, so I plop onto the edge of the bed.

She glares at me. "Did you know? That they would find someone else?"

"No. But it was a possibility. It's what they did last time."

"Last time?" She sucks on the end of the cigarette, blows the smoke into the hot summer air. "Last time Franklin kept them from sucking me dry and they ran before they could be caught."

"Not before..." I pause, remembering the arcane syringe Franklin used to steal part of Percy's memory. "Oh."

"What do you mean, oh?" She takes a final drag on the cigarette, smashes it out against the stucco outside the door. "This is your fault, isn't it?"

I look at Franklin, uncertain what to say. Villain is not a role I am accustomed to playing, and no matter what I do next, Laurel will only look at me with deeper disgust.

She stomps her foot, petulant in her anger. "Why are you looking at him?"

Franklin sighs. "Because it's not her fault. The Sisters were desperate. Especially after having used so much energy trying to steal your magic." He squares his shoulders as though bracing for a blow. "They had to find someone else."

"But last time..." She trails off, eyes going wide. "No."

"Yes. Last time they found someone else, too. Not as strong perhaps. Not the one they wanted to begin with. But they had no choice." He licks his lips. "And then, when you heard it on the radio, you were so upset. So guilt-ridden." A shrug. "It seemed better that you not remember."

Laurel rolls her fingers into fists. "You took part of my memory?"

"To keep you safe. To keep you from hurting."

She punches him—hard enough to cut his lip on the edge of his teeth.

"Laurel." He tries to catch her by the arm, but she slaps his hands away.

"Don't touch me." She pushes past him to the other room and slams the door behind her.

I clear my throat. "I'm sorry."

"Nah." He wipes the trickle of blood off his chin with the back of his hand. "I knew she might find out someday. That's on me." He turns the TV off and drops the remote onto the dresser. "I hope your lover is more understanding."

My cheeks turn hot. "Me too."

"Are you okay?"

"Yes." I press my cold fingers against my face to try and soothe the flush of embarrassment. "Just not used to thinking about Percy in that way."

Franklin tilts his head, amused. "No? I saw the way you looked at him. The way he looked at you."

"I mean. Just not that word, I guess." I pull my books closer, searching for Martinez's phone number.

He touches his lip again. "Ouch."

"You need some ice for that?"

"It's not that bad."

"And Laurel?"

He glances toward the closed door. "She'll be okay. Just give her some time."

I find the page I'm looking for. "You want me to call Martinez? Or should you do it?"

"I'll do it." He takes the notebook from me. "You want to meet him somewhere, right?"

"There's a walking trail not too far from here. Has a big parking lot, not too public, not too isolated."

"Okay." Franklin pulls his cell phone out of his pocket. "Give me a minute."

I curl up on the bed while he steps outside. Wish there was more coffee. Or I'd worn a different shirt under my jacket. Something to help keep the last spark of warmth in this cold body.

"You ready to go?"

"What?" I twitch awake and upright.

Franklin has that furrow across his forehead again, worried. "I said, are you ready to go?"

"Yes. Sorry. I must have fallen asleep." I grit my teeth and stand up. "Let's go."

"Maybe we should grab something to eat on the way."

"Coffee," I say, pointing myself at the door and willing my feet to move. "I could use some coffee."

"Okay." He pulls the door shut behind us. "There's a burger place on the corner."

"Great." I drop into the passenger seat, trying to maintain control over clumsy arms and legs.

Franklin pauses, looking at me hard. "You sure you're okay?"

I grin. "As okay as a ghost in a dead body can be."

He frowns but starts the car. "Right." Backs around and pulls out into the street. "Let's get you some coffee then."

CHAPTER 17

Franklin leans against the side of the car, arms crossed over his chest. He watches the parking lot. "You sure he'll come?"

"Yes." I'm sitting on the edge of the back seat. The door is open to let the warm summer air circulate, but I struggle not to shiver. Even with my jacket on and the warmth of the late afternoon sun touching the side of my face, I'm still cold.

"What if he brings the cops with him?" Franklin shifts, the muscle in his jaw fluttering.

"He won't."

He looks at me doubtful, and I comb my hair back from my face. "He won't. He wants to see the Sisters done away with, too."

Franklin nods reluctantly. "I hope you're right. Otherwise we're both about to land in an interrogation room."

A car pulls into the other side of the parking lot. Not one of the big black SUVs the Special Investigations team drives, but small and practical. After a moment, Martinez gets out. He turns, looks around. Touches the holster on his belt and then walks over, slow and deliberate.

Franklin steps away from the car, hands hanging loose at his sides. "Agent Martinez. Thank you for coming."

"Mr. Jones." Martinez pauses as I slide out of the backseat. "Alex Michaels. What are you doing here?"

I smile and wrap my arms across my chest. "I need your help with Percy."

"With Percy?" His eyes narrow, and he steps close and looks at me intently, as if he will pull this flesh right off of me and reveal what is underneath. "Delaney," he says finally.

"Yes." The hair on the back of my neck prickles.

Martinez shudders and, with visible effort, pulls his hand away from his gun. "I thought you were gone."

"Not yet. And I need help with Percy." I look at him sternly. "You need help with Percy."

He's silent for a long moment. "Maybe." He looks at Franklin. "What about you? What are you doing here?"

"The Sisters are after my...sister. Delaney has proposed a way to solve my problem, and hers, at the same time."

Martinez scowls, a predatory hunch to his shoulders. "So it is the Sisters that have been working in Atlanta."

Franklin nods. "Yes. Doing what they always do."

"Stealing power from others." Martinez touches his gun again, then crosses his arms on his chest. "Tell me how you intend to stop them."

Franklin combs his braids back from his face. "It's complicated."

"An exchange," I say. "They will help me regain my bones, and once I am me again, I will let them take a portion of my magic."

"And Percy?" Martinez looks at me sharp.

"He will help put me back in my bones. He will use up that lingering power in a way that will not hurt anyone." I spread my fingers like a magician revealing a hidden card. "Everyone gets what they want and no one else gets hurt."

Martinez paces a slow circle, staring at the pavement. Props his hands on his hips. "Why are you telling me this? Why not just go to Percy?"

"Because he doesn't remember I've returned. Because I need you to do something he won't."

His frown deepens as he considers what exactly Percy wouldn't do. Finally, "Like Gil Mains, you mean."

"Yes."

"And what's to keep Percy from coming after me when I separate this body from your soul?"

"He'll be too busy trying to bring me back to think about you. And afterwards..." I shrug. "His magic will be diminished. And changed."

"And the Sisters?" He leans in close. "How do you plan to handle them?"

"They'll get what they want," I say, firm. "And so will both of you."

"I want them dead." His voice is low, but the look in his eyes makes my heart lurch. He may not have the Touch, but the anger lurking within him is eerily similar to the thing that hides inside Percy.

"And what would you do to make that happen?"

"Anything." There is no hesitation, no tremor of doubt.

I put my hand on his shoulder. "Help me, and I will see that you get what you want."

Martinez grips my elbow, hard enough it makes my fingers tingle. "Promise me."

"They will die."

He glances at Franklin, who nods. "So she has promised me."

Martinez lets go of me, reluctant. "All right. When?"

"Day after tomorrow."

"In Crossing?"

I nod. "Yes."

He rubs his forehead. "It may be difficult getting away. Bringing Percy with me."

"You'll figure it out." I cross my arms over my chest, trying to hide another wave of shivers.

Martinez looks at me—weighing what he wants, calculating what he will do to get it. "And Percy? You'll not hurt him?" He says it reluctantly.

"It is not an easy road." I resist the urge to put my arms around him. "But keeping him separated from his past… This is better."

He nods. "Maybe." Again his fingers brush against his gun. A reassurance maybe. Or a warning to me. "If anything happens to him…"

This time I am not able to refuse the instinct. I lay my hand against his cheek. "I know." I lean closer. "Do not let go of your friendship, Luis."

He steps back and glares at me. Angry maybe because I have seen the weakness in him. A weakness we both share. *Percy.*

My legs tremble, vision blurring. Even the heat rolling off the blacktop is not enough to chase the chill away. I hold my hands out and try to find my balance as ground swings underneath me.

Franklin puts his arms around me, quick, gently guiding me the few steps back to the car. "You need to rest."

I fold up in the back seat, too tired to do anything other than mumble *thank you.*

Martinez says something. The words are muddy.

Franklin is less garbled. "She doesn't have much time left."

"And you're certain... promised? That she... once she's... she wants?" His words drift in and out, drowning under the noise of the blood in these ears.

"She hasn't lied to me yet." There's a stubborn note in Franklin's voice.

"That you know of." Martinez must have moved closer.

I struggle to try and open my eyes, to sit up and tell them that they do not need to be afraid of me. *Not this time.* But this body refuses. Clinging to the semblance of life is hard—cold sweat prickling in my hair, the old penny taste of blood on the back of my tongue—and there isn't energy for anything else. It doesn't matter. The car shifts as Franklin climbs back in, and the engine purrs, soothing.

For a moment, I feel a twinge of guilt. This will not save everyone—the Sisters have already taken lives. It may not satisfy Martinez's anger either. But it will keep others from being hurt in the future. Not just safe from the Sisters, but safe from Percy. *Safe from me.*

I drift more deeply into sleep as the car sways around me. I cannot save everyone, but I can save some.

CHAPTER 18

Franklin leans back in his chair, feet propped on the edge of the bed. "Shit, Delaney. Are you sure?"

"Yes."

We reached Crossing in the early evening and checked into the old motel on the edge of town. Now, Laurel sleeps in the other room while I have sat Franklin down and explained to him, in detail, what I expect to happen tomorrow.

He's already looked through my books—all the notes on past and future—but this is more precise. More concrete. More terrifying.

Franklin takes a swallow from the beer he picked up at the gas station on the corner and stares at the ceiling. He is silent for a while, finishing off the last of his drink methodically.

I curl up against the headboard and wait.

Addie always said you can't depend on other folks. They promise things they can't do. Or they break the promises they've made. The only thing you can count on is yourself. Other folks just let you down, she used to say. Even if they don't mean to.

I have found that generally not to be true. Not with folks who care for those around them. In a general sense. In a specific sense. And there ain't much love in this world that is more specific than Franklin's love for his sister.

He swings his feet down off the bed and leans forward, dark brown eyes fixed on me, intent. "And you are certain you will keep us safe? Even when they break their deal with you?" His hands shake.

I lean over and take his hand in mine. "Not everything I say is true, Franklin. But this is not a lie. I will keep you and Laurel safe."

He sighs. "Right." He lets go of my hand and stands up, slow. "You should get some sleep. Tomorrow will be hard."

CHAPTER 19

ercy sits at his desk. Overhead the lights flicker and buzz, but he doesn't seem to notice. I guess since I am the one dreaming about him, there is nothing abnormal about the guttering light.

He tucks his tablet into his shoulder bag, stands up, and slides his phone into his jacket pocket. Straightens the cup of pencils and double checks to be certain he has logged out of his computer. Satisfied that everything is as it should be, he slings his bag over his shoulder and heads for the elevators.

I follow behind.

The descent to the lobby is slow. I press back into one corner. I don't know if it will make a difference if I try to touch anyone within these dreams, but I'm not certain I want to risk it. If they aren't just the generation of my obsessive subconscious, I don't want to risk the barely controlled application of my Touch.

Percy stands in the middle of the elevator, staring at his reflection in the polished stainless steel doors. Every so often there is a beep as we pass another floor. Slowly dropping down through the building, the shadows grow thicker with each passing moment as if we are descending not just to the lobby but into the ground itself.

As the darkness grows, my grip on this moment loosens. I hear screams in the distance. Nightmares breathing down the back of my neck eager to disrupt. Without meaning to, I take a step toward Percy.

He turns and looks at me. Not just in my direction, but at me. The lines around his mouth fade, replaced by a wistfulness I have only seen when he held me in his arms. "Delaney?"

The elevator *dings*, and the doors slide open. In an instant, the shadows are gone. Percy blinks and shakes his head. Adjusts his bag hanging from his shoulder and steps out into the lobby.

The night security nod as he passes. To me they are faceless, but not frightening.

Percy steps out the doors and heads down the sidewalk toward the edge of the block that makes up the FBI offices. Tugs his phone from his pocket and glances at it. It's late, but there should still be a bus running. If not, he'll catch a taxi closer to downtown.

He waits for a moment at the corner for the lights to change even though the street is wide and empty. In the distance the interstates hum with traffic.

The light changes, and he crosses the street, hands in his pockets, and a knot at the bridge of his nose—thinking.

I follow a step or two behind. The buildings on either side of us jump and glitch. I've never been here before, and it's hard to imagine the location without waking myself up.

Halfway down the block, Martinez is waiting, leaned back against his car, arms crossed on his chest.

Percy stops. "Martinez."

"Cox." He is in his shirt sleeves, collar undone. Always with the gun holstered on his belt.

Percy looks up and down the block. There are a few other cars parked against the curb, but the buildings on either side of the street are mostly dark, and the street is empty. "What's going on?"

Martinez chews the inside of his lip for a moment. "I need your help."

Percy nods, automatic. "Sure."

"You won't be able to talk to anyone else on the team about it. Not yet, anyway."

"Okay." Percy looks at him expectantly.

Martinez raises an eyebrow. "Just like that? No questions, just…okay."

"Did you want to have to talk me into it?"

Martinez grins, sheepish. "Well. I might have had a whole speech prepared. Answering all the questions you have about your abilities, returning to your roots, and finding those things you want most." He shrugs. "Probably sounds better in my head anyway."

Percy has gotten so still that for a moment my dream-addled brain presents him as a cardboard cutout. "Answers," he says finally. His voice is papery, too.

"That's right."

Percy runs his fingers through his hair. "And Delaney?"

Martinez nods solemnly. "Yes."

Percy sighs, glances back down the street. I am glad I have taken momentary shelter in the dark wedge of an emergency exit. If I were not drenched in shadow, I am certain he would see me this time. "Are we leaving now?"

"No. Tomorrow. A little before lunch. Meet me in the parking garage down the block."

"Okay." Percy nods. The knot in his forehead eases. "Okay. Tomorrow."

Martinez pushes himself away from the car, already fishing his keys back out of his pocket. "See you in the morning."

CHAPTER 20

The clearing in the woods is much the same as it was the last time I was here. The ruined house has collapsed further in the intervening months, kudzu and honeysuckle covering the exposed wood in a layer of rippling green. But in the middle of the clearing, where The Salesman's box disintegrated and Gil Mains broke my burning flesh from my bones, there is a mound of dirt that even the stubborn chickweed won't dare to grow on.

Franklin opens the trunk and pulls out a shovel. "Guess I'd better get to work."

I swing my feet out of the car. "I'll help."

He shakes his head. "You sit tight. Last thing I want is you passing out of that body before the others get here and leavin' me to try and talk everyone into carrying on with this little deal."

Even if I didn't feel two breaths away from dead, I don't have much desire to dig, so I nod. "Okay."

Laurel makes a face, but she pulls a second shovel out of the trunk and follows Franklin across the clearing toward the barren patch of red clay.

I huddle in the back seat of the car. Waiting. Hoping I haven't waited too long. Hoping the others show up. It is so much harder trying to shape the future when all I have is my words, but even without magic behind it, the tongue is a powerful thing.

The sun is warm, and I doze off. When I wake up, Franklin and Laurel have abandoned their shovels, using their hands and pieces of wood scavenged from the collapsed house to clear the last of the dirt away from the sprawled bones. *My sprawled bones.*

I stagger out of the car and shuffle across the clearing. Drop awkwardly to my knees.

"Careful," Laurel says as I reach out to touch the smooth white skull. "They're hot."

Franklin wipes his face on his shirt sleeve. "Come on. We'll need wood for the fire."

They head into the woods, looking for fallen limbs. Arguing with each other. I don't have the energy to try and figure out the gist of their conversation, though I still catch individual words bouncing through the trees. Not that I need to know; it's easy enough to guess. Still arguing over whether they should go through with this. I wonder if Laurel is telling her brother about the monster that follows me in the afterlife. He already knows about Percy.

I hold my hands over my hot bones, willing this dead heart to beat just a little longer.

A car engine rumbles nearby. Martinez's car edges slowly into the clearing. He pulls around to park next to Franklin's Chevy Nova. When he turns the car off, the silence is almost deafening.

Percy gets out and slams the door behind him. "What are we doing here, Martinez? You said there'd be answers."

Martinez gets out more slowly, rolling his shirt sleeves up. "You'll see."

"I'll see what?" Percy pauses, looking at me. "Who's this?"

I reach under my jacket and lift the edge of my shirt. Find the soft bruised spot just under my ribs where Franklin hid Percy's stolen memories—the truth about what happened with the necromancer in Savannah. The skin tears open easily under the pressure of my fingers, blood trickling down my belly as the memory drifts out like a dark thread.

Percy staggers and digs his knuckle into his temple. "Ugh." When he looks up, there's a darkness around his eyes that makes me shiver. The air around him ripples, the magic that was forgotten coming to the surface in a single breath. He holds up his hands, and his shoulders hunch up as though he is expecting a blow. "No." He turns and glares at Martinez. "What is this? What have you let me do?"

Martinez backs up a few steps, keeping the car between the two of them. "Go talk to her," he says firmly. "She will explain."

"She will hate me." He tries to pitch his voice low, but the words hiss in the muggy air.

I stand up, unsteady. "Percy."

Percy twitches and changes direction to circle around me.

I tuck my hair behind my ear. I never forget that this is not my flesh and bones, but looking at him—for the first time in months—I am more aware than ever of this flat chest and lanky arms and legs.

"Delaney." He touches my cheek with trembling fingers. "Oh, Del. I'm so sorry."

"Sorry?"

"I would have saved you if I could. Even if it meant…" He shakes his head. "It doesn't matter. I'm still a monster."

"Ah. No." His body is warm under my hands, and I cling to him, tears flowing as I realized how much I have wanted to hold him again. "You aren't a monster."

His hands tighten on my shoulders, and magic flushes against my skin as his anger and fear struggle behind his eyes. "You know what I've done, Delaney. In Savannah. Before that."

"Percy. If you knew the things I've done, the hurt I have caused." I rest my forehead against his. "We will do better in the future."

He shudders and that deadly, childish growl of magic in his chest subsides. "Are you certain, Del?"

"Yes." I smooth the hair back from his eyes. "You are here now. And soon I will have my bones back, and we will never be separated again." It feels strange, touching him with these hands, but they are all I have for now.

And, despite the unfamiliarity of this form, he holds me close. "That is all I have wanted, Del."

"I know." I lean my forehead against his. "I know."

There's a murmur of voices, and the Sisters emerge from the edge of the woods. They pause when they see Martinez and Percy. Lean their heads together to whisper to each other.

Finally, Sarah steps forward. "Who is this? I thought this deal was made between you and us."

"It is." I reach down to grasp Percy's hand, tight and reassuring. "But I promised you a source of Power. Percy will provide you with what you need to reunite me with my bones."

She eyes me, suspicious, but edges closer. "And him?" A nod to Martinez.

I shrug. "He will separate body and soul when the time comes."

Martinez, to his credit, remains quiet, arms crossed over his chest. Drawing on that blank disposition he uses in the interrogation room to hide his true intent.

Sarah nods. "All right." She twitches her head at the other four Sisters— carrying a couple plastic milk crates between them, jars and uncomfortably sharp tools chiming gently inside. "Let's get this over with."

CHAPTER 21

Franklin and Laurel return, arms full of fallen branches. They pause when they see the Sisters, but Franklin murmurs to her—reassuring—and they walk forward, drop the firewood on the ground.

"Here." Franklin nudges it with his foot. "Will you need more?"

Sarah considers the pile of wood, the space where my bones lie. "Maybe," she says.

"All right."

Laurel is already trotting back into the woods, eager to put some distance between herself and the Sisters. Franklin follows more slowly, waiting until he has passed between the first of the trees before turning his back to the clearing.

Percy pulls me closer, watching uneasily as the Sisters begin marking a five-pointed star with salt on the ground around my exposed bones. "Delaney. What is going on?"

"They are going to help us get my body back. Not this." I hold up one cold hand. "But my real body."

He frowns. "That sounds dangerous."

"Yes. But not impossible. Not if you let them draw on your magic, Percy. Not if you call my soul back from the afterlife."

"Afterlife?" Now he looks truly alarmed. "What if I can't?" His arms tighten around me, painful. "There must be another way."

"There isn't."

He shakes his head. "Why can't you just stay as you are?" He presses his forehead to mine. "It doesn't change my love for you."

I pull away from him. I know he means to comfort me, expressing that he can love me in any form. But it hurts that he doesn't understand how hard it been staying in this body that is wrong, that is not me. "Even if this form were not mostly dead, Percy, I couldn't stay in it."

"It doesn't matter to me," he says. To prove his point, he leans forward and kisses me. Clumsy at first in his eagerness, but sincere.

Tears slick down my cheeks, and I tangle my fingers in his hair, even as I draw back. "It matters to me, Percy. I cannot stay like this."

The lines in his face deepen, anger struggling with grief. "I could find another way." His gaze slides past me to the Sisters, busy carving lines in the red clay. "You know I have the necromancer's magic now." He says it quiet, but his magic rises in response. "This body may not be right, but I could get you another one."

"No." I say it sharp. "Percy."

He looks at me, and I see the marks left on him, left on his magic from every time he has used it. The snarling aggression of the neighbor's dog, the fear and callousness of the creep that tried to steal his life, and the desperate obsession of the necromancer. "Why won't you let me save you, Delaney?"

"Because that will not help me." I knot my fingers in the front of his shirt. "I need my bones. Not these. Not theirs. Mine."

Percy's weight shifts, and I move with him, keeping this body between him and the Sisters. "Besides, we said we'd do better in the future." It's harder than ever to smile, but I do my best.

Percy frowns, but he nods, reluctantly. "You are right. I'm sorry." He smooths the cold tear tracks from my face with his fingertips. "I just... I don't want to lose you. Not again."

"Put me back in my bones and, I promise, we will never be separated again."

"Yes." Percy nods. "I will do whatever it takes."

Thunder whispers in the distance, the hot summer sky overhead slowly turning grey and dark. A cold breeze curls through the muggy afternoon, teasing sweaty skin.

Laurel and Franklin bring more wood, then retreat to stand with Martinez. The Sisters finish their salt diagram and lay out the wood, start the fire with a word and a flash of energy.

Sarah looks at me. "We're ready."

I clasp Percy's hand tight and wobble forward. The fire stretches up and out, sucking greedily along every dry branch and twig piled over my bones. "You will let them use your magic?"

"Yes." Percy touches my face again, tender. "And I will draw you back."

"Don't hurt anyone while I'm gone," I say sternly.

The thing in his chest snarls, but he nods, focused on me and not on his fear. "May we only be parted a moment."

Martinez moves closer, looking at Percy warily. "You ready, Delaney?"

"Yes." I step back across the salt lines, and the fire reaches out to caress my shoulders.

The Sisters begin to sing, the arcane words turning like smoke beneath the storm-dark sky, and Percy drops to his knees with a groan as they draw his magic out of him.

Martinez pulls his gun from his holster. The muzzle flashes once, and I fall back and down into heat and darkness.

CHAPTER 22

Grass presses against my cheek, vaguely sticky. I lift my head and see that, once more, I have returned to my sisters.

Addie stands on one side in her brilliant, always-summer, always-daylight field. The grass ripples—green, then gold—as the breeze moves one direction and then the other.

Baby's woods, silver beeches and dark oaks tied up with the green and white and blood of honeysuckle, lie on the other side. The moon and clouds send shadows chasing each other across the pale leaves on the ground.

And me, sprawled in the middle, dusky sky overhead, thick grass and weeds under my hands. I sit up, pull my sweater close across my chest.

"Delaney." Addie strides toward me, no bigger than she was last time—still a lanky fourteen—but somehow, she towers over me. "What are you doing?"

I lick my lips and squint up at her. "What I want."

She tilts her head, blue eyes sharp and cold. "What you want don't tend to end well for the rest of us."

"I'm older now."

"And wiser?" Addie's lips curl in a bitter grin.

"Maybe." I stand up, brush the broken blades of grass from my knees. "But what happened to you and Baby, that wasn't all on me."

"Some of it—"

"Yes. But not all." I touch her shoulder, hesitant. "And no matter what I do, I can't change the past, Addie."

She scowls, stuffs her hands in the pockets of her blue jeans. "You could bring him here, you know. Build a house. Live with us." She nods her head toward Baby, sitting in the roots of a massive oak.

I saw that future in Daddy's cave. Where I go back and the Sisters are destroyed, but Percy and I are, too. A future of sunny days and moonlit walks under the silver beeches. But that future leaves a hole in that distant conflict that has frightened Laurel so deeply.

That future ain't the one I want.

I shake my head. "Sorry, Addie. But I'm not done with the world yet."

Addie hisses, sun-kissed cheeks turning red. "You are playing with fire, Delaney. How many years will you have before your Power comes back? Before his does? And then what? You think you'll just keep on living like you don't have it?" She leans up into my face. "No matter what good thing you mean to do, you'll hurt folks."

"I won't."

"You will." She puts one hand on the back of my neck, pulling me down—eye to eye. "You think Mama ever wanted to hurt folks? But look what she did to us, bringing us into the world and then trying to take us back out of it with her next breath. To Daddy. Look what Daddy did. Remember the scars he left? That's what folks with Power do, Delaney." A breath, lips trembling. "That's what I did. What you've done. What you'll do again."

"I'm going to be different."

"How?"

I put my arms around her, trying to remember that even my words aren't worth anything if I don't mean them. "I am sorry for what I did to you, Addie. All the times I hurt you." My throat aches, and I force the next words out stubbornly. "And I forgive you for the times you hurt me."

Addie stares at me, wide-eyed. "Not enough," she says finally.

I shudder. Anger blooming in an instant, whispering about all the times I suffered because Mama thought I looked too much like Daddy, all the things Addie did unnoticed because she was so much like Mama. *Unfair, unfair.* But I know where that road leads, and I have promised—never again.

The ground under my feet shimmers, and I feel Percy calling to me. "I have to go." I start to fall, but Addie grabs my wrist, tight.

"No." She braces her feet on the ground, holding me fast. "No. I won't let you."

"Addie." I kick my feet and pry at her fingers with my other hand, trying to break her grip.

Beads of sweat glitter on her forehead, but she clings tight. "I can't let you. This is for the best."

I look over my shoulder at Baby curled up in the roots of her oak tree. "Baby."

Baby scowls and sighs. "Let her go, Addie."

Addie shakes her head again. "No. It is not safe for her to be in the world."

Baby toddles forward, stares down at me with big blue eyes. "No. But that's where she belongs. For now."

"Baby." Addie is pleading.

"Let her go." Baby's voice is small and light, but the ground ripples with the force of it.

Addie bites her lip. "Fine." She glares down at me. "Don't come crying to me when it all goes wrong, Del." Then she lets go, and I drop into the crush between this world and the last.

CHAPTER 23

When Franklin called my soul into the body of Alex Michaels, it was terrifying, like being shoved into a trunk or stabbed or filled up with mud 'til I nearly drowned in flesh that was not my own.

This time is different. My bones call to me.

I wrap myself around them like greeting a lover, settling into my own familiar shape and pulling new skin into place like smoothing the wrinkles out of a favorite shirt. It is weird, still, but the panic is absent. This is coming home in the truest sense.

All that remains from the fire is the ash, drifting like feathers as I sit up and stare at my right hand. My hand. My legs. My belly and breasts. Even the old scars left by the iron chain have returned—no longer lumpy, but bright as silver against my skin still glowing white hot.

Percy is on his hands and knees, groaning with every breath, but, despite the hurt, there is no trace of regret in his eyes. The faint whisper of what is left of his magic has changed, too—no longer hungry and afraid. Restoring flesh to my bones has altered the tenor of his power so that it is no longer bent for destruction.

Franklin moves forward, almost on tiptoe, to slip his arms around Percy and pull him back toward the relative safety of the cars as the Sisters begin to sing again. This time it is the old forbidden melody that has allowed them to walk this earth for years, undying.

"Aih." I shudder as they tear magic out of me. Trying to remember to breathe, to let go of what I mean for them to have. It still hurts, and I curl up, whimpering with pain as they fill themselves up with fire and heat, my own body slowly cooling. By the time they finish, I no longer smoke in the dark and humid air, and the ground doesn't crack beneath my touch.

The Sisters look at each other, bright and rippling with the Power they have taken from me. Frightening. Not just because of the raw energy sitting in their skin and bones, but because it is still not enough. They look at each other, and there is no glory in the Power they hold, only bitter and terrible greed.

I push up to my feet, trembling as I grow accustomed to my own self.

Sarah saunters toward me, the ash billowing and curling around her feet. The other four Sisters spread out, moving toward the cars with a lazy stride.

"Did you expect us to just walk away?" Sarah grins at me. Her teeth are nearly transparent. The veins under her skin are dark threads beneath her shell-like flesh. "Leave that one to chase after us again? Leave anyone to remember what happened here?"

"Delaney." Franklin's voice cracks, bordering on the edge of panic. He and Laurel have Percy propped up between them, backing slowly toward the edge of the woods as three of the Sisters prowl toward them.

Martinez is drifting a different direction, the fourth woman following him like a cat stalking a bird.

Sarah wraps her hand around my throat, fingers hot and stinging. "Did you really think this little deal would save them?" A twitch of her head toward Franklin and Laurel. "You've fucked this up."

I sigh. "So greedy."

"What?" Her hand tightens on my throat.

Her thread is easy to find—bright and thick and trembling with stolen Power. I run my hand across it. Across the threads of the other four. Not snapping them or pulling them onto a different road. Just... touching them.

"I promised Martinez you would die here." I look her straight in those fire-kissed eyes. "I was willing to break that promise if you walked away." A shrug. "But maybe that was because I knew you wouldn't."

They have all paused, feeling my touch on their futures.

Martinez eases his gun free of its holster.

Sarah hisses at me. "Don't be stupid. You're not strong enough for that."

She has a point. They have drained away so much of my magic I can barely see the various futures flashing across the clearing—just glimmers of light and whispers of movement caught out of the corner of my eye. Not that it matters. I have promised Addie and Baby to do my best not to hurt folks.

I lift my hands away from those swollen threads. "I don't have to be."

Lightning sears overhead and strikes the ruins of the house—the resulting crack of thunder knocking all of us back a step and tearing the clouds open overhead. Rain splats down. Slow at first, with single heavy drops that break through the leaves of the surrounding trees like stones on glass.

I take a breath and a half-step away from Sarah.

More thunder growls in the distance, and the rain pours down—cold as ice. There is a noise, like a bottle breaking on pavement, and one of the Sisters closest to Franklin disintegrates.

Sarah lifts her hand, watching in horror as her white-hot skin cracks, little red lines spreading from her fingertips across her palm and up her arm.

The other Sisters crumble into gory bits. Their mortal flesh too fragile to tolerate the fire of magic and the quenching wet and cold of the pouring rain.

Sarah screams in fury and snatches the knife from her belt. Lunges toward me with the blade. Her ankle shatters underneath her, and she staggers and drops to her knees. She glares at me even as little pieces of skin fall away like bits of stone. "You'll pay for this."

The magic setting her on fire, my magic, flares brighter and collects around her bloody hand still clutching the knife.

I frown. She must know she cannot hurt me with what is my own.

She smiles, part of her chin sliding off and shattering against the wet red clay. Turns and points the knife and the rising magic at Percy. She might not be able to hurt me, but she can hurt him.

For a moment, everything seems to slow down.

Laurel lets go of Percy and starts to back away. My heartbeat crashes in my ears as I try to move my feet, to reach for Sarah. Franklin fumbles at his belt, grasping for a charm to ward against the coming magic.

Sarah opens her mouth, triumphant. "D—"

The gunshot is a faint imitation of the thunder rolling overhead, but the bullet catches her in the side of the head, and she shatters into pieces.

The rain spears down in glittering threads. Franklin moves like a man wading through deep water, putting himself between Martinez and Laurel.

And Martinez creeps toward me, the muzzle of his gun staring at me like a third eye.

I wait.

I know there are some futures in which he kills me here. Kills all of us. But my Power is faint; I cannot see what will happen next.

The storm boils overhead, clouds thinning as the rain and lightning tear away to the east, and the crush of water and noise fades 'til there is only the erratic *drip-drip-drip* of the trees surrounding the clearing.

"Martinez." Percy steps forward, hands empty. "Luis," he says after a moment. "It's done."

Martinez twitches. Adjusts his fingers on his gun.

"Luis. Enough." Percy takes another step forward.

Martinez glances at him. Shuffles his feet. Finally, he lowers the gun and puts it back into its holster. He picks up a stick off the ground and pokes at Sarah's messy remains. Stands up and looks at me, wary. "Okay," he says. "It's done."

CHAPTER 24

Percy hurries across the clearing and folds me in his arms. "Delaney."

"Percival." I lean up on tiptoe and kiss him again, lingering this time. Feeling his heart beat against my hands—a homecoming of a different sort.

He covers my hands with his and pauses. "What's this?"

I hold up my left hand and see that the pinky finger is short—the last two bones missing, though the skin has closed over the stubby end, smooth and clean.

"Are you all right?" Percy steps back and looks at me, anxious. Worried perhaps that I have other missing pieces.

"Yes." I wiggle my finger, thoughtful. "Maybe a bird stole them." I smile at him. "It's all right. I have nine others."

The clouds break apart and sunlight streams through, making me squint against the glare. I cover my eyes with my hands and lean against him again. "I'm tired."

He sighs, breath touching my ear. "Me too."

Martinez clears his throat. "Miss Green?"

I open my eyes reluctantly.

He holds out a blanket, more awkward than I have ever seen him. "I thought you might... 'til you can find some clothes."

"Thank you." The wool is scratchy against my skin, but I pull the blanket around my shoulders, welcoming the protection from the sun on my tender flesh.

Franklin wrings the rain from the edge of his shirt. "We should go back to town. Put some dry clothes on, get something to eat."

Percy nods in agreement, but I hesitate. It may have been years since I had been outside of Greenhaven, but some folks will know my face.

"What's wrong?" Percy slides an arm around me, protective.

"What if someone recognizes me?"

He frowns. "Recognizes you?"

"I'm not a complete stranger here, Percy."

"Yes, but..." He stops, suddenly nervous.

"What?"

Martinez puts his hand on my shoulder and pulls me toward the cars, points to my reflection in the window. "You have changed," he says simply.

I blink at myself in the makeshift mirror. Although my body is mine again, my face is different. The eyes—one muddy brown, the other green as spring—are the same. But my face is rounder, the features stronger. I think perhaps I see a hint of Alex in the slant of my jaw. It isn't the face I had in Greenhaven, but, somehow, it isn't not my face.

I take a breath, considering my bones and the flesh covering them. There is no doubt they are mine, but they are thicker, stronger than before. I am thicker and stronger than before.

I look at Percy, wondering if this is his doing. There is a momentary glint in his eyes that tells me it is not an accident. He wraps his arms around me with no hesitation, no sense of strangeness. "Delaney." He murmurs it against the short fuzz of hair that covers my head.

I realize that he cares less about what my outside looks like, preferring to have me strong and solid than have me just as I was before.

"You understand?" Martinez looks wary.

"Yes." I squint at my reflection again. "Just as well. I'm not certain I'm ready to tell this story about coming back from the dead yet."

Franklin leans his elbow on the roof of the car across from me. "Folks still might wonder what happened. Seeing that tall young man leave and...you come back."

Martinez frowns. "He has a point."

"Then we should stay somewhere else."

Franklin pushes his braids back from his face. "Where? Crossing is small."

I slip my hand into Percy's. "I know a place."

CHAPTER 25

The house is much the same as it was when I last saw it fifteen years ago. Dustier, but not so much as you might expect. Spider webs dwell in the corners of the front room where the sun don't touch them, the glass in the windows blurry from years of rain and pollen and no one to clean them.

The siding on the front porch is still pockmarked where Sheriff Mains and his deputies put Mama down. The bullets themselves is long gone—pried out and counted and stored somewhere down at the Sheriff's office.

Inside has the mark of violence, too. Patched plaster on the walls where Daddy's fists left holes, the rip in the couch cushion where Mama got too close with the butcher knife—scars left on the house itself, though I expect no one except me really sees them or hears the whisper of old arguments in each creak of the floorboards.

After some discussion, Franklin and Martinez go back into town to get me something to wear and food for everyone.

Percy plops down on the sofa, ignoring the dust that breathes out of the fabric and folds over him like welcoming arms. The Sisters have pulled his magic out by the roots. I know there's still a little piece down in there, like crabgrass waiting to grow back twice as big now that it's been broken off. But for now, he is just spent.

The last few motes of dust are still settling in his hair when his eyes close and he falls asleep.

I tiptoe upstairs, breath held as I listen for every familiar squeak of the stair treads, the blanket slipping off my shoulders so one corner trails behind me. There are only two rooms tucked up here beneath the hot slope of the roof—the one Addie and I shared on the left, and Mama and Daddy's room on the right.

I know there's nothing left in my room but dust and bedsprings and the shadows of those years before I understood why Mama and Daddy fought with each other. The door to the other room groans like an old man as I push it open, sunlight peeping through the peeling newspaper over the window.

Even when the social workers had come and packed up my clothes to go to Greenhaven, no one had dared to touch Mama's things. The room sits exactly as she left it, plus a few spiders living above the headboard.

There are a couple of dresses hanging from the clothesline that serves as a closet. The right shoulder is more faded than the left, but it doesn't fall apart when I pull it off the hanger. Faded is still more comfortable than the emergency blanket.

I slip the dress over my head. It's a little long, the hem nearly brushing my ankles. Mama always was tall.

There's a whisper of voices, and I turn toward the bed.

Mama and Daddy lay next to each other, bare skin showing every place the sheet don't cover, heads leant together and hands clasped.

"I love you," Daddy says.

And Mama flushes and smiles, shy. "Me too."

He touches her cheek, tender. "I'm going to take good care of you, and you and me will live here and have babies and be happy forever."

For a moment, her lips tremble and a shadow creeps in around her eyes. "We will?"

He props himself up on one elbow. "Sure, darling." He takes her hand again. "Forever and ever."

The floorboards creak. Laurel stands in the doorway, staring at me—wide-eyed and nervous. "This house is haunted."

I shrug. "I guess most places are. If you know where to look."

She rubs her arms, as though brushing away a chill, though it's hardly cold up here under the sunbaked roof. "You grew up here?"

"Yes."

Laurel glances over her shoulder toward the empty room I used to sleep in. "Was it... when you lived here, too?"

I guess maybe she can't see my Great Granny Jean knotting the rope around the banister, the other end around her own neck. "Yes." I watch Granny Jean swing her legs over the railing and drop toward the hallway below. "But those ghosts aren't as loud."

I remember being scared a few times when I was little, going up or down the stairs and seeing my great-granny come hurtling out of the darkness toward me. But she never hurt anyone 'cept herself. And sometimes, in the dusky hours when the sun had dropped into the woods and the moon hadn't crept up out of the trees yet, she would sit on the front porch and sing old gospel songs.

She shakes her head. "You mean to stay here?"

"Maybe."

"I don't see how you can stand it."

I rub those silver scars on my arm, thoughtful. "Some ghosts come with us. No matter where we go."

Laurel shudders, one hand drifting up to touch the grey patches in her hair. "Yes," she whispers. She licks her lips, sidles closer. "You ever wish you weren't like this?"

"No."

"But you've been hurt so much because of it." She bites her lip, shoulders hunched.

"Ah." I reach out and take her hand, remembering Alex and her scars. "The world hurts everybody. Touch or no."

Her fingers tighten around mine, but she says nothing.

"Franklin will be back soon," I say. "Why don't we go wait on the porch?"

CHAPTER 26

Percy and Martinez are pacing back and forth at the end of the driveway, taking turns on the phone. Trying to present something sensible to the government powers-that-be in Atlanta.

Laurel is curled up on the swing at the end of the porch, head resting on her arm and sound asleep.

Franklin nudges the door open with his foot and comes out to sit beside me on the steps. "Beer?"

"Sure." I pop the can open and take a curious sip. "Jesus. That's awful."

"You drink the whole thing and it will be less awful." He takes a hefty swallow by way of demonstration.

I take another swallow, wince. "You sure?"

"When have I lied to you, Delaney Green?"

"Ah." I hold my breath and drink a little more. "What are you going to do with them?"

"What?"

I hold up my left hand and wiggle the pinky stub. "My bones. What do you plan to do with them?"

He sits very still for a long moment, the edge of his beer can just touching his lip. "Hah," he says finally. He tips his head back and finishes the rest in a few noisy swallows. "Not sure."

I nod. Sip at my own beer, which still tastes mostly of piss, and stare out across the weedy yard.

The sun has dropped in the west, long shadows creeping out of the woods to touch the house and driveway. Soon it will be dusk and the fireflies will come out to look for love in the unkempt grass.

Franklin looks at me, brows drawn in and lines around his mouth like he's chewin' something over. "Are you mad?"

"About my bones?" I shake my head. "Nah. I suppose everyone needs a weakness."

He chuckles. "Your pinky ain't your weakness, Delaney." And his gaze slides away from me to rest on Percy—still pacing back and forth at the end of the driveway.

"This is true." I take a few gulps from my beer. A lightness settles in my feet and hands. I tip my head back, gaze rolling across the ragged treetops, wondering if I will float away. But I know it's just the beer.

I turn my head over to one shoulder and look at Franklin, trying to keep my voice serious. "You hold onto those though. Someday they might be important."

He raises an eyebrow. "Might be?"

I giggle. "Might be. Will be. The future's always changing, Franklin."

"Not your future." He says it thoughtful. I know Laurel has been talking to him. Talking to Martinez, too. Warning them, maybe. Or trying to convince them to do the thing she can't.

I drain the last few swallows from my beer can, trying to reclaim the fading buzz and failing. I set the empty can aside and wish the sun would hurry up and set so the heat would let up. "You hang onto those bones," I say again.

Franklin looks at me, solemn. "Yes, ma'am." He stands up before I can say anything else. "I gotta piss."

"Bathroom's in there. Should flush, we got the pump on the well going a little while ago."

He disappears into the house, and I stretch and shuffle my feet.

Martinez has left Percy to his phone conversation, wandering across the yard as if by accident, but drifting steadily toward the burned-out carcass of the tool shed.

I sigh and stand up, picking my way across the yard to stand beside him. "You get things worked out?" I ask after a moment of silence.

"For now. Percy's going to take an extended leave while you figure out what you want to do."

"You told them his magic is gone?"

Martinez looks at me, and his eyes are dark and unreadable. "For now." He glances over his shoulder, but Percy is still on the phone, and turns to face me square. "How long?"

"Maybe never."

He shakes his head. "Don't lie to me, Delaney."

I shrug. "Years, I think."

"How many?"

"Fifteen. Ish. I think."

Martinez nods. "I expect so, too. And it's changed, too, hasn't it?"

I blink at him. "Yes. But how…"

"I always wondered why you would come down this road. And don't tell me it was just because you couldn't leave The Salesman unchecked." He raises an eyebrow, but I say nothing. "It wasn't until I saw him today, turning that rage into something else so he could bring you back, that I figured it out. This road was not about saving yourself. You were saving him."

I look at him for a long moment. "Could be I can't do one without the other."

He nods, unsurprised. "Laurel says you are still going to doom us all. Some other darkness following you. Or returning despite your best efforts."

"That is still some years off. And you know how the future is."

His eyes narrow. "And your magic?"

"It will take less years." I reach out and touch his shoulder, impulsive. "I don't mean to hurt anybody though."

His mouth twists in a wry grin. "You never do." He raises his hand before I can respond. "Nevermind. Just… don't make me regret seeing you again." His gaze slides toward the charred ribs of the collapsed tool shed.

I lean close, looking at him kindly with my brown eye. "I promise. I'll be good."

Martinez sighs. "Right. I should get on the road. I've got meetings out the ass in the morning."

"You be careful," I say, automatic. And for sure, I don't mean anything by it, but his hand drops down to touch his gun, and I remember how he didn't hesitate to put a bullet in my head in the middle of that cursed clearing.

The screen door on the porch bangs—Franklin returning from the bathroom.

The noise breaks the tension, and Martinez takes a step back, lets his hands rest at his sides. "I'll be seeing you, Miss Green."

I wait until he starts toward his car to let out the breath I've been holding. Our next meeting won't come for years. *It won't be long enough.*

CHAPTER 27

s night settles around the house, Franklin and Laurel leave for the motel in Crossing. Franklin promises to return in the morning with more food and clean sheets for the bed upstairs. Laurel promises nothing, climbing into the car without a word.

As the rumble of Franklin's car fades—a space quickly filled with the peep of tree frogs, the creak of cicadas under the dark-columned trees, and the rustle of leaves in the soft breeze—Percy leans down to kiss me. His fingers catch the fabric of my dress, drawing it slowly upward, my skin revealed to the velvet dark night one inch at a time, until I lift it over my head and stand naked in front of him.

Then it is my turn to untuck and unbutton and peel away his shirt and trousers so that we lean together—skin to skin.

We lay down on the porch, which is hard against elbows and knees, but take turns resting on each other. It is no less awkward than our first night—*our only night*—together, but there is more laughter. This time will not be our last.

After a while, we are both spent and Percy lays his head between my breasts, content. The moon has crested the tops of the trees, and the yard is full of silver, but here, on the dusty boards of the porch, it remains soft and shadowed.

"Will you stay here?" I ask, once my breath has returned.

"Huu." He sighs, settling more comfortably on top of me. "It seems that way."

"What about your work? With Martinez?"

"They are talking about letting me take more of a support role. Research and history."

I run my fingers through his hair. "You'll be happy with that?"

"I'll be happy with you." He tilts his head, looking up at me. "I'll always be happy with you."

I am silent for a moment, considering that. For sure this house has baggage, but every other place will too for folks like me and Percy. Still... "You don't mind staying here?"

"No. Why?"

I stare up at the flaking blue paint on the porch ceiling. "Laurel says this house is haunted."

At the other end of the porch, Great Granny Jean starts to sing. *Coome on dow-own to the river. Coome down to the water, child.*

"Ah." Percy yawns and curls around me tighter. "There aren't any ghosts here, Delaney. Just family."

EPILOGUE

On a hot July day, Mama tried to kill me for the last time.

Addie and I had taken the baby down to the church to see if we could get some formula. She hadn't taken to nursing like she should, and Mama had been distracted and irritable—going back to work making fancy cakes as if she hadn't just given birth a few days before.

By the time we got back to the house, me carrying the baby and Addie pulling the wagon with the half a case of formula tins, plus our normal loaf of bread and stack of cheese, we were all red-faced and sweating.

Addie scooped up the box with the formula and stomped up the stairs to the porch. "Bring the rest inside, Del."

I juggled the baby back and forth from one arm to the other, trying to get the other box tucked up against my chest. Finally just laid the baby in the box next to the bread and cheese and cans of soup and picked it all up. Shuffled up the steps and kicked the screened door to get Addie's attention.

"Hold on." She pushed the door open with a scowl. "You don't have to be so loud."

"Sorry. I'm hot. So is the baby." I trudged into the kitchen and put the box down on the floor. Wet my hands in the sink and rubbed them on the baby's face to try and cool her off. She fussed, but not with any strength.

Addie stood, one hand on her hip, as she squinted at the directions on the cans of formula. She punched a hole in the top of the can and poured some into the bottle, then screwed the rubbery nipple on the top and held it out to me. "See if she'll drink this."

I settled on the floor cross-legged and cradled the baby in my arms, rubbed the nipple against her mouth. She latched on, but after just a minute, she turned her head away, fussing. "She doesn't want it." I looked up at Addie, worried.

"She's probably just hot and tired. Try a little more in a few minutes." Addie put the rest of the cans of formula up in the cupboard. Took the loaf of bread and stack of cheese and put them in the fridge. "Oh. Looks like Mama left us a snack." She pulled out two little plates, each with a single fancy cake in the center and a strip of masking tape on the edge with our names written on them.

I put the baby down on the floor and stood up eagerly. Mama didn't normally let us have any of the cakes she made, and we knew better than to try and sneak one. I reached for the yellow one and paused, head aching with knowledge that there was something wrong with it. It was hard to tell what, exactly. I saw Mama putting ground glass in it, and also something powdered that came out of a pharmacy bottle.

I let my hand drop to my side. "I can't eat that."

Addie paused, looking at the cakes carefully. "They look all right to me."

I touched the edge of the plate with her name on it and nothing happened. No flash of the past, no headache. For the first time, I realized that Mama wasn't trying to kill us. Just me.

I shook my head. "She's fixed mine. I can't eat it."

Addie frowned, her hands fidgeting on the edge of the table. "But mine's all right."

"Well, yeah. But..." I paused, a hot flush creeping up the back of my neck. She meant to eat hers even if I couldn't eat mine. And the unfairness of it, not just that she was going to get cake and I was not, but that Mama's fear and obsession would be focused just on me, was too much.

I smashed my fist onto the plate and splattered gooey crumbs across the table. Then scraped the mush off my hand and tossed it into the trash can.

Addie's cheeks bloomed red, and she stretched up to her full height, thin and lanky after a hot summer of growing. "Delaney."

And I felt bad, but I didn't see why she should get cake if I didn't. "You know you can't trust Mama's food."

"You keep sayin' that, Delaney, but I ain't never got sick." Her lips stretched out in a humorless grin. "Maybe Mama is right about you after all."

I shook my head. "You take that back."

"Or what?" She took a step toward me. "You think you can pull on my future, Delaney?"

The baby fussed, high and thin. I wet my hands at the sink again and picked her up, smoothing cool fingers across her hot little head. "Shhhh. It's all right."

Addie shook her head. "Telling her stories already."

"Stop." I turned on the faucet and wetted one of the dish towels. "She's really hot, Addie."

Addie shrugged. "We're all hot." She looked at the plates on the table, and her grin got sly-like. Quick, before I could try and stop her, she snatched the fancy cake off my plate and shoved it in her mouth.

"Addie, no. Spit it out." I tried to grab hold of her, but with the baby in one arm, I couldn't move very fast.

She swallowed the cake with a grimace, then poked her tongue out at me—all green and sticky with icing. "See? It's fine."

"It's not." I stared down at the baby, afraid and uncertain what to do next. The baby seemed really heavy, little arms and legs twitching like she was trying to shiver, but so hot she wasn't sweating. "Addie, please. I think something's wrong."

"Put her in the sink, then."

I turned the cold water on, not really cold because it was the middle of summer and the pipes got hot even running under the ground, and rested the baby in the sink. Splashed water over her tiny chest and arms and legs. The shivering stopped, but she wouldn't open her eyes or fuss—just lay there, breathing fast and light. "Addie."

I looked at my sister, but she was leaning hard on the edge of the table, her face gone white as bone. She coughed and rubbed her hand across her mouth—blood smearing across her chin.

"Delaney." Her voice shook, and she coughed again, another thread of blood trickling from the corner of her mouth. "I don't feel good."

Outside there was the noise of an engine, and the gravel in the driveway crunched and popped. Mama was home.

I tucked the baby up against my chest, ignoring the water soaking through my dress, and grabbed Addie by the arm. "Come on. Quick."

She stumbled after me, out the kitchen door and down the steps. There wasn't time to run into the woods, and I didn't think Addie would make it very far anyway, so I turned toward the tool shed.

Addie tripped and fell. "Ow."

"Come on." I pulled the door to the shed open. She pushed back up onto her feet unsteadily—blood running from cuts in her hands and knees. Staggered into the shed and collapsed against the wall, coughing and gasping for breath.

I tugged the door shut behind us and crouched in the darkness with the baby in my lap. Threads of light crept in under the door and between some of the boards so it wasn't pitch black. I could see Addie huddled across from me, spitting blood into her hands and tryin' not to cough.

"Delaney. Addie. Where you girls at?" That was Mama, yelling from the porch. I wiped the baby's face with the edge of my dress and held my breath.

Most times, if Mama couldn't find us in the house, she would just sit down to wait. There'd been too many conversations with the social worker when we'd hid before for her to start stomping through the woods tryin' to find us.

Addie coughed. I couldn't blame her. Whatever Mama had put in that cake, it had cut her up good. But once she started, she couldn't stop—shaking and wheezing as bright red ribbons of blood poured out of her.

"Addie?" Mama's voice came closer. "Delaney. Where are you?"

Addie looked at me, pale and helpless. "Sorry, Del." Then she sagged against the ground and didn't move.

The baby sighed, too. She turned her cheek against my chest and got real heavy in my arms. She wasn't my fault. But I cried and kissed her head and waited for Mama to find me.

She pulled the door open, and sunlight fell on me like the church folks' judgment. "Delaney. Where..." She stopped, seeing the baby lying white and still in my arms. And Addie sprawled on the ground in a smear of blood.

For a moment, her face turned white and stiff. She knew the hand she'd had—sending us out in the heat so she could make that terrible cake meant to take me out of the world for good. She knew. And she turned all that guilt and anger on me.

"Just like your father. Hurting everyone who gets close to you."

I clutched the baby against my chest. "This is not my fault."

"Nobody will believe that." She raised her fist like she was going to strike me, but couldn't bring herself to step through the door. "You and your lying tongue. Anyone that believes your stories is a damn fool." The guilt faded, replaced by rage. "I'll make sure no one has to listen to you ever again."

She slammed the door shut, and I sat in the dark and sobbed, breathless in the heat. "No, Mama. Please. I promise I'll be good."

After a few minutes, something slapped against the walls, and I smelled gasoline. The muffled *whump* when it ignited pushed the flames around the edges of the boards—fire licking hungrily at the dry wood.

And, with both my sisters dead and no way out, I lay down on the floor and waited to die.

The heat grew nearly unbearable, and my dress smoldered and broke apart. But something else happened.

I'd seen the future before, little bits and pieces. Mostly terrible things that Mama had planned. But that was always fragmented. Never more than a few heartbeats of what might be.

As the heat sank into my bones, I saw all of it. So many threads. So many choices. So many futures in which I became every terrible thing Mama had told me I would be.

For a moment, I wondered if maybe she was right.

Maybe I was always destined to be a monster.

The tin roof overhead screamed as it peeled back off the nails holding it to the rafters. Or maybe that was Mama outside using her tongue the best way she knew how.

I closed my eyes and laid my hands on those threads. So many choices. But every one was a choice, every one had a chance to go a different way. *I might be a monster, but I don't have to be a villain.*

I took that heat and magic shimmering along my bones and pulled those threads. The chain Daddy used sometimes to pull Cousin Larry's car out of the ditch tumbled off a collapsing rafter and landed on my arm—red hot iron laying imperfect circles across my skin. I screamed and the door shuddered, like someone was throwing themselves against it.

Having made my first choice—to live and not to die—I let go of those threads.

The door busted in, and a burlap-covered shape snatched me up off the ground and threw me over their shoulder. Out into the sunlight and across the yard. And with every step, I whispered to myself.

I promise. I'll be good.

ACKNOWLEDGEMENTS

Stories never happen in a vacuum. Many thanks to the strong, brave, loving people in my life who have showed me how to persevere even when things look grim – you all inspire me in every way.

In particular, many thanks to Marian, who read the first drafts and encouraged me to take more risks. And my second readers Adelle, Evelyn, Joy and Robby. Thanks to Jay, for his encouragement and insight, for helping me put the last touches on these stories and for clearly loving my characters as much as I do.

Thank you to Bob Mecoy, my ever-patient agent, for his enthusiasm and encouragement.

And thank you to the readers who keep coming back. Your enthusiasm and support is priceless.

ABOUT THE AUTHOR

A.G. CARPENTER writes fiction of (and for) all sorts, with a focus on the speculative. With over a dozen published short stories, her work has appeared in Twitter-zines such as One Forty Fiction and Trapeze Magazine, online publications Daily Science Fiction, Goldfish Grimm's Spicy Fiction Sushi, and Abyss & Apex.

The Weather's Always Fine in Paradise - a collection of short stories and novelettes, Mothers Last Child – a bio-punk novelette, Jacquelyn and the Sparkly Emo Vampire Goat – a humorous fantasy novelette, and Brass Stars – an SF Western novella are available now.

Carpenter graduated from The College of Santa Fe with a degree in Moving Image Arts (B.A, 2004) and is still an avid fan of film making, with a preference for movies in which things explode. She lives in the southern United States with her husband, their lively son and a herd of cats.

ALSO FROM FALSTAFF BOOKS

Want to know what's new
And coming soon from
Falstaff Books?

Try This Free Ebook Sampler
http://bit.ly/falstaffsampler

Follow the link.
Download the file.
Transfer to your e-reader, phone, tablet, watch, computer, whatever.
Enjoy.

www.ingramcontent.com/pod-product-compliance
Lightning Source LLC
Chambersburg PA
CBHW050547190726
48283CB00007B/2046